MW00448676

A WITCH CALLED RED

BOOK ONE OF THE RED WITCH CHRONICLES

SAMI VALENTINE

A Witch Called Red is the first book of The Red Witch Chronicles, an urban fantasy series containing magic, paranormal adventure, and vampire mayhem along with swearing, violence, and adult situations.

Reading Order:

- Down & Out Witch (Prequel Novella)
- *Terror in Tahoe* (Newsletter exclusive prequel short story)
- A Witch Called Red – Book 1
- *Oracle in the City* (Newsletter exclusive short story)
- Long Witch Night – Book 2
- Witch Gone Viral – Book 3
- Witch on the Run – Book 4
- Small Town Witch – Book 5
- The Hired Witch – Book 6 (Coming Summer 2021)

Get exclusive reads, updates on my new books, and the skinny on the latest hot Urban Fantasy/Paranormal titles by subscribing to my newsletter at SamiValentine.com. Go there to sign up!

Dedicated to the people who helped encourage and inspire me to write and publish my debut novel: Jamie, Derek, Alex, and the fabulous ladies of the Get Shit Done Club.

All rights reserved. No portion of this book may be reproduced in any form without permission from the publisher, except as permitted by U.S. copyright law.

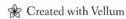 Created with Vellum

PROLOGUE

Consciousness hit her like a wave of anxiety. She didn't know what was going on, but she needed to get out of this hospital bed now.

Pushing the thin blue blanket down, she winced at a sudden pain in her wrist. She studied the unconnected IV ducts on her bruised wrist. Why did her patient bracelet read *Jane Doe*? That wasn't right. None of this was right. Why didn't the hospital know her name?

"What the fuck?" She didn't recognize her own raspy voice. It sounded like she hadn't spoken in over a hundred years.

A sleepy snore interrupted her meltdown. Head tilted back, the snoring man sprawled out in a chair at the foot of her bed. He couldn't have been a well-wisher for another patient. A white curtain clearly divided the shared hospital room.

She squinted to study his shoulder-length mullet and East Asian features. A faded Metallica logo on his denim vest peeked out from under his folded arms. The left arm was tanner than the right. He looked like a roadie for a metal tribute band. Nothing about him sparked a memory. Who was he?

"Hey, Mister," she croaked out, throat too dry for more than a whisper. Spying a small pink plastic mug on the bed stand, she drank and tried again. "Hey!"

"I wasn't there—" The man jumped in his chair as his dark eyes flipped open. "Oh, shit, you're awake."

"Unless this is one of those weird dreams where you only think you wake up," she said. The pain in her wrist and the general ache all over her body were evidence of reality. She remembered the blue sky, the plane overhead, and the grass underneath her. Then a shadow loomed over her, features slowly becoming clear. It had been him. The man in the chair. He carried her to his van, then the rest was a blur until they reached the bright lights of the hospital. "You brought me here. Um, where is here? Actually, let's start with who are you?"

"Vic Park Constantine. I found you off the 126 near Coyote Creek. You're at the Sacred Heart in Eugene."

She said the city name slowly, reading the patient bracelet again, but nothing stirred beyond a punchline from an old Simpsons episode. "Why am I here?"

"You tell me. I'm just a guy who thought he was going to take a nap in his van after a long drive. Then I found you. Your neck is all marked up, bruises and fang bites... What happened to you?"

She recoiled from him. *Fang bites on the neck?* Like a peek behind a dark veil came the chilling awareness that humans were far from the apex predator. It wasn't a montage of memories; more like his words shook supernatural trivia into her mind. She might not have known where she was, but she knew what bumped in the night.

Fire and stakes killed vampires. Blessed silver wounded and repelled them. Crosses were a toss-up. They had supernatural speed and strength with fangs equipped with venom to put their victims in thrall. She couldn't remember a single one, but she knew them better than herself.

"A bite? Like a dog or a, um, vam—. Nevermind." She stopped herself before she sounded insane.

Vic cracked the privacy curtain to glance at the other sleeping patient in the shared room. He looked back at her, an eyebrow raised. "You were going to say vampire."

"Would that be crazy if I did?" She held her breath.

"Not to me." He grinned, brows lifting. "Who are you? The police couldn't find anything when they ran your prints."

She opened her mouth, but the words died. It wasn't as if her name was on the tip of her tongue. The answer was a big blank just like where she came from. She knew concretely that she was a white woman, who had watched the Simpsons at least once, and knew that monsters existed. Everything else was fuzzy. "I don't know."

"How'd you get out there?"

"I don't know, I can't remember anything."

Vic leaned forward, elbow on his knee, and cocked his head. "How do you know you were attacked by a vampire then?"

She shrugged. That was a question she could answer. *Finally.* "I assumed because you said fang bites. Oh, God, what if it was a were-wolf?" She examined her fingers as if claws would sprout at any moment.

"No, it looks like a vampire's handiwork. You have some old bite scars too." He slumped back in his chair and rubbed his chin, curiosity twinkling in his gaze. "What color are your eyes?"

"Um, brown?" She guessed, frowning as she realized she didn't know. She reached up to find her hair in a bun, held back with two ties, and let it down. Looking at the long red waves, the sight didn't jog her memory; it just made her realize she would have to use a lot of conditioner until she got it cut.

"No, green." Shaking his head, he stood and walked closer. He put his hands on his hips, staring at her like she was a two-headed calf. "So, you don't remember anything?"

"Not about me. I think I have some general stuff." She pursed her lips, the question kickstarting her brain synapses like slapping an old TV on the fritz. "I remember silly things like rhymes—Columbus sailed the ocean blue in 1492. Which I have some negative opinions about, apparently. I know what a molecule is, and that Brad Pitt and

Jennifer Aniston broke up. Which I also have some negative opinions about." She frowned. "Nothing about me."

"What day is it?" Vic tossed out the question like it was a pop quiz.

She shrugged.

"Okay, that isn't fair. You've been unconscious for a while." He crossed his arms. "Who is the President?"

"Barack Obama." She said slowly, surprised at the random civics question.

Brow furrowing, he tilted his head. "No."

She laughed. This guy was funny. "Okay, I know that I'm amnesia girl, but don't mess with me like that. It's not even two years into Obama's presidency."

Holding his hands up, mouth hanging open, it took Vic a few tries to spit the words out. "You think its 2010?"

Her ears buzzed at the date. She pinched herself. "I'm ready to appear naked in English class reading a book report now."

"Tough titties on that kitty. You're awake, alive, and missing the last eight years. And you don't know where you've been, Red?"

Eight years... If she was in her twenties, that was nearly a third of her life. She pinched herself again. It still wasn't a dream. She frowned at him. "Red?"

"I gotta call you something."

"So, what's your deal?" She swallowed back her growing alarm. He knew about the supernatural, maybe he could help her. At least she had a nickname now. Red... It was better than Jane Doe. "Hunter? Vigilante? Trucker? Kind of the same thing, I guess, but probably not a Bard."

"What? Why not?" Huffing, he looked down at himself. "I am, for your information. From a long line of them."

"You just look so business in the front and party in the back." Red grinned. She might not have memories, but her sense of humor still worked.

In addition to Jennifer Aniston's love life, she knew enough about the supernatural world to remember the players. Hunters were scattered vigilantes, bounty hunters, and people who couldn't resist the call to fight the darkness. The Brotherhood of Bards and Heroes was an ancient order of scholars who acted as mentors to the supernatural champions who kept demons, vampires, and more dark beings at bay. Vic looked more like a drunk guy at a honky-tonk yelling for the band to play "Freebird" than a Bard.

"I know my badass style makes me stand out from the stuffed shirts, but I have my credentials. I had a few years at UCLA too before I dropped out." He lifted two fingers for emphasis before crossing his arms. "I'd ask you how you know about the Brotherhood, but I reckon you'd say you don't know."

Red nodded. Her brain was too busy remembering the entire lyrics to the *Fresh Prince of Bel-Air* theme song to provide any useful information. "You said my prints didn't come up in the check?"

"Nope. You were in a bloody white dress, roughed up, without any ID. No phone. Nothing."

Dipping her head, she felt suddenly shy. She had no idea what she looked like. "Can you bring me a mirror? Anything to look at myself in."

Vic nodded, looking around to grab a spoon off the rolling tray beside the bed. He handed it to her.

Red looked at herself, distorted in the spoon's curve, and pulled away the bandage on her neck. The mass of purple bruises stood out first, the puncture wounds nearly lost in the color. Her skin was chalky pale, and dark circles lay under her bright green eyes. She had only woken up but looked and felt like she could sleep for another week. "It's weird. I'm familiar, but I wouldn't…" How could she explain the feeling of seeing a face that she barely recognized, yet instinctively knew, reflected at her? "What happened to me?"

"I'd hoped you'd tell me." He shrugged, gesturing to her. "My simplest theory is that you're a hunter who crossed the wrong vamps. Some can mesmerize their victims to forget, but I've never seen anyone with their brain scrubbed so hard. You looked thrashed."

"Yeah, maybe the other guy looks worse." Swallowing thickly, she felt her chin wobble as she stared at the reflected neck wound. She put the spoon down on the bed.

"Whatever it was, it wasn't good. Maybe that's why you can't remember. The vampire opened the amnesia door, and your brain said, 'don't mind if I do.'"

Red frowned at the Jane Doe ID bracelet, wondering what could be so bad that she forgot not just eight years, but her whole life.

"Or maybe it was dark fairies." He raised his hands, shoulders lifting. His voice pitching higher as he tried, and failed, to sound comforting. "And you escaped from their realm, and this is just inter-dimensional jet lag?"

Her lips twisted in a gallows' smile. Red wanted to laugh as much as she wanted to cry. It felt ridiculous to even think she had amnesia even as she experienced it. "Is that supposed to be the bright side? Because that's not any better."

A male nurse wearing blue scrubs and a bright white smile on his dark face came into the room. "Hey, hey, you're awake!"

Vic slipped out while the nurse fussed over her.

Red let herself sink into the pillows. Sleep claimed her in a fitful wave as she visualized her face and found a stranger staring back. She woke to a parade of baffled social workers, curious doctors, and finally a detective.

In a suit rumpled from too much sitting with a mustard stain on the lapel, the bald detective took quick notes in his notepad between brisk questions. The pen stopped moving while he studied the bite marks on her neck. His beady blue eyes blinked in recognition behind his glasses.

Familiar like a sunset, Red recognized this old pattern from law enforcement. Strange crimes ended up as cold cases when the witnesses spouted fantastic tales. The supernatural might have been a secret to most humans, but she guessed this cop had seen his fair share of the weird. He was just too close to retirement to chase shadows.

"Before you go, could you give me Vic's number? The man who helped me. I'd like to thank him."

He looked through his notes before jotting down a number and handing it to her. "Thank you for your cooperation, ma'am."

Later, the nurse tried to convince her to stay in bed, but Red felt a weight pressing on her chest the longer she stayed in the hospital. Something about them gave her the creeps. In donated baggy jeans and a T-shirt that read *North Dakota: Best for Last Club*, she tied up the laces on her leather boots. She had been found wearing them. They were the only thing she could claim. Her bloody dress and underwear had been taken somewhere as evidence long before she woke up. She had to wonder what dress went with vintage black boots.

Walking to the nurses' station, she dialed the number, scanning the detective's even scrawl. What was she even doing? Vic was a stranger. Even when she asked for the number, she knew she was going to say more than a thank you.

He picked up after two rings. "Vic. Talk."

"Hey, it's me. Red." She sighed, realizing she hadn't exactly practiced what she was going to say beyond that she was going nuts in this hospital. "I know this is weird, but I can tell you're more useful than the cops. Can you come get me?"

"I'm always more useful than the fuzz," Vic said dryly then sighed. "Okay, Red, let's be real. You've got no name and nothing more than the knowledge that something supernatural hurt you. I know how this ends. I've been there, just with more memories attached. You gotta choose. Those social workers at the hospital can get you into housing, maybe work, something. I'm running after jobs from the Brotherhood like a hired hunter. I'm not the kind of Bard you're thinking of. I don't have a library or a hero. You roll with me, you'll find yourself living out of motels, hanging out in a van, always on the highway. You'll earn a cut of whatever bounties we can claim until you're ready to run loose. In the meantime, I control the radio."

Red looked around the nurses' station. She knew what he was saying was true. No specific memories came to mind, but her left hand curled as if around an invisible stake. "That works for me. I'll meet you out front."

"Alright, kid. Keep in mind that this is temporary. I'm a loner. You can stick around, but you'll need to be useful. You'll be my..." He snapped his fingers. "Intern. Prepare for danger, research, and beer runs."

"I'm in."

1

OCTOBER 24ᵀᴴ, Past Sunset, a gas station on the edge of San Bernardino, California, USA – Over A Year Later

The call about the murdered woman found on the beach came in after breakfast. Red was behind the wheel before noon. Eight long hours later, they were in LA County.

Her boot crushed broken glass as she walked across the parking lot of what looked like the loneliest gas station in the inland empire. Heat radiated from the ground. Dead scrub brush surrounded the lot. The old light pole painted an orange circle on the pavement. Coyotes howled in the distance. She didn't need the reminder that predators stalked the night.

Red hiked up the reusable shopping bag on her jean-covered hip, rattling the six pack inside. *Vic should be grateful for this,* she grumbled to herself, after she drove most of the way from Reno. Even after a year as his intern, she was still doing his beer runs.

A convenience store door dinged behind her. The clerk almost hadn't accepted the twenty she had laid on the counter. A bloody thumbprint on the bill had made the Latino man cross himself and say a small prayer. Somehow she understood despite the language barrier. That was a new one to tell Vic. She didn't know her own name, who she was, or where she came from, but apparently, she could understand Spanish. Another quirk of her supernatural amnesia.

Stopping by the black van, she paused to look at the balding right front tire and put the beer on the stubby hood. Car maintenance wasn't one of her lost skills, but she was quick with the simple mechanics that Vic showed her. It was what he appreciated the most about her, but they couldn't keep patching the tire. The Millennium Falcon, the van also affectionately known as the Falcon, needed a new one soon.

She noticed movement out of the corner of her eye and pulled a stake out of her pocket. "I see you. Neon isn't that stealthy."

The youth, skateboard under his arm, stopped short from a run that would have put an Olympic athlete to shame. His sun-streaked mop of blond hair would be the envy of any surfer. Unnaturally white fangs poked from underneath his top lip. Dropping the board, he crossed his arms over a orange tank top. "No ragging on the duds."

She summoned magic from the well of energy centered over her navel. At least she assumed it was there. Vic had taught her a lot, but she was on her own when it came to magic. Reliable as an old beater car, prone to stalling, but her power could still throw a baddie off-guard. It had taken months for her to even float a pencil. She wouldn't call herself a witch just yet. She had been practicing with all four elements, but only Air ever answered her call.

Heartbeat picking up, Red lifted her eyebrows and squeezed the stake. "Do you have a soul?"

"Fuck no," the skateboarder snorted. "Do I look like a loser?"

Red wrinkled her nose. "You look like an undead Backstreet Boys reject."

He charged.

She tossed the stake and forced her will onto the air, harnessing it to propel the stake toward the vampire. She couldn't reliably make things fly, but she had almost mastered gliding. Her focus scattered as the urban coyotes yipped closer.

The stake embedded deep in the wrong side of the vampire's chest.

"Effing A, lady!" The skateboarder stopped and hunched over, grabbing at the stake in his shoulder. "Who are you?"

"That's what I keep asking." Red shrugged. She tried to pull the stake back with her mind, but her energy fizzled and popped. The air molecules fled from her control. She dodged the rocketing stake, and it hit the side of the Falcon. Jogging backwards, she glanced around in search of it, brushing her hair over her shoulder and out of her face.

"Whose fang marks are those?" The vampire turned paler, clashing more with his orange neon. "Are you claimed? I don't need the heat, man, not with another vamp and not with the Blood Alliance."

Red bent to retrieve the fallen stake. He wasn't the first vampire to notice the old scars on her neck. Most vampires gave them a second glance, even though they were indistinct after laser scar treatment. Heart thumping, she banged on the van door, wondering where the hell Vic was. Did he decide to take a piss or something? She shook her hand, willing magic out of it, but couldn't produce a spark. Her energy was exhausted after making the stake fly.

"Since you're not squawking a name, I figure you're fair game. Cool beans." The skateboarder hissed and revealed his fangs. "Let's see what you taste like, weirdo."

Red raised the stake, but it was too late.

The vampire slammed her against the van. "I don't think the catch and release rule from the supreme bitch applies to whatever the hell you are."

She kneed him between the legs.

The skateboarder stumbled back with a yell and grabbed his crotch. A ding from the convenience store door drew his attention. "Shit, now I have to take him out too. Fuck, my sire is going to be pissed. Gonna yell at me in European."

He rushed her.

Red had the stake ready to jam it through his heart as he collided with her. The breath knocked from her, she managed to huff out a quip. "Daddy issues?"

The skateboarder stilled and staggered to the side. His pale face decayed rapidly, blond hair falling to dust, leaving greasy bones to fall in a heap. The skateboarder couldn't have been too old in death.

When a vampire was staked, the magic preserving them seemed to snap, leaving the body decaying rapidly as if to make up for lost time. The oldest ones barely left dust. Sunrise would take care of whatever was left, leaving burning bones to greet the new day.

A figure at the convenience store's door drew her eye. He turned the sign over from open to closed. She could imagine that a night clerk saw enough weirdness to teach him to mind his business. Most humans didn't know what bumped in the night, but some people couldn't avoid it. Red was one of them.

The van's side door slid open. Under the hanging Tibetan prayer flags and Christmas lights in the blanket-strewn back of the van, Vic popped his head out. Giant headphones hung on his neck. His laptop blared behind him on a bean bag. The supernatural world knew him as a hunter, one of the few who were brave enough to go after were-wolves. He had a badass reputation, but she was one of the few who knew he was a TV junkie.

"What did I miss?"

"Oh, you know, nothing much, just fighting for my life against an undead Tony Hawk wannabe. Discovered I know basic Spanish." Red rolled her eyes. "Standard beer run."

"*Español*, eh?" Vic asked, then quickly added, "*Hangug-eseo malhal su issni?*"

"Um..." Red cocked her head.

"Well, now we know you know Spanish but not Korean."

They had made a game out of trying to jog her memory. They'd learned that she knew how to stake a vampire, was good at math, and had enough magic to occasionally get her out of a pinch. Not her real name. Even after she read through a baby name book.

She brushed her wild red hair off her shoulder. For a guy who believed in nearly every conspiracy theory, he hadn't been very imaginative with her nickname. It stuck anyway. "Still, I bagged a vampire by myself. Not bad for an intern."

"I know what you're angling for and we'll talk about you taking the hunter's challenge after this job." Vic stepped out of the van and studied the vampire's bones. The six-pack of beer on the hood of the Falcon soon distracted him. Brushing his black mullet back, he nodded to Red. "IPA? Nice." He cracked open a beer and slurped it down before crushing the can against his head. "Thirsty Thursday, am I right?"

"It's Wednesday." Red pulled the stake from the vampire's empty rib cage before she walked around to the driver's side of the van. "Come on, didn't you say your buddy was in Culver City? We still have an hour left on the road."

"Don't worry. Quinn's a PI and a vampire—he'll still be awake." Vic grabbed the beer. Sliding the side door closed on his TV watching nest, he climbed into the passenger seat beside her. "All we have to worry about is if he got called to his other job."

"Other job?" Red asked. Vic's stories made it sound more like Quinn skulked in alleys saving maidens rather than sat on a payroll.

"I never said he was a successful gumshoe." Vic shrugged. "He moonlights as a sketch artist for the LAPD sometimes. Does a bit of this and that for the Supreme Master of the City when she calls on him, too."

"Sounds like a character." Red shrugged, it was his choice on their cases. Besides, she was curious to learn more about her mentor. She knew a little bit about Vic's years at UCLA, where he ran from being a Bard and ended up spending more time with a souled vampire detective than in his computer science classes. He made it sound like he spent most of his time stoned and doing surveillance.

She backed the van up, then gunned it, running over the skeleton on the way out of the parking lot to make it unrecognizable. The vampire's brittle remains shattered under the Falcon's tires. Sunrise would burn the bone fragments, but a complete skeleton didn't take long to raise questions. From the back, the laptop's volume distracted her from her brewing question about Quinn. "What were you watching?"

"Period piece."

Red looked over at Vic in his sleeveless denim vest and Lynyrd Skynyrd shirt. "Like Jane Austen?"

"No, it is about Victorian hookers, but tasteful. It's a BBC show." Vic folded his arms, glaring at her out of the corner of his eye. "What? I don't just watch 9/11 documentaries or YouTube videos about the FBI. I have layers."

"Uh huh." Red smirked, pressing her lips together to keep from commenting on his eclectic tastes. She refocused on the puttering LA traffic. She navigated through the light traffic on the wide boulevard, following the signs for the 66 to get to the 10 based on her memory of the map she had read earlier. Vic was paranoid about Google and banished any GPS from the car. "Can you turn it off since you're not watching it?"

The van jerked, tire popping loudly. A tardy warning icon blazed to life on the dashboard. Turning into the vehicle's slide, she put on her hazard lights.

"You okay?" Vic asked.

"Yeah, I bet it's the front tire." She steered the Millennium Falcon over to the shoulder and turned right into a darkened strip mall, parking in front of a closed nail salon.

"We have a donut in the back." Vic sighed and opened the door.

Unbuckling herself, Red rubbed her temples. She had driven most of the eight hours from Reno, each mile tempting herself with Vic's promises of the amazing shower at his friend Quinn's place. Culver City was still an hour away, and with a flat tire... That shower felt so out of reach.

Clever English banter boomed behind her from tinny laptop speakers.

Twisting in the van's high seat, she climbed into the back to turn off the show that Vic had left on. On her knees, she turned the laptop around to look for the off button when she noticed the screen.

Lounging in a boudoir, the woman lay in stockings and corset, her English accent coy as she flirted with a dark-haired man in a tuxedo.

Slapping the laptop closed, her heart raced. The adrenaline flat-lined in her system. Dragging air through her lungs, she slumped on a bean bag chair and put her head in her hands. She leaned her head between her knees, trying to catch her breath. What was it was about the scene? Trying to calm her breathing, she didn't look up when the side door slid open.

"Hey, easy, Red," He said, low and gentle, crouching in front of her. "Keep your breathing steady. Through your nose. That's it." He didn't ask what she had seen or what it meant. It would have been like asking how she understood Spanish. She wouldn't have an answer.

"I hate this. I can't avoid triggers if I don't know what they are." Red choked the words out as she tried to calm her ragged breathing. She told herself that the anxiety was just a side effect of another failed potion to unlock her memory. "I can't trust myself if any random thing could set me off."

"Sure, you can trust yourself. You know who you are."

She glowered at him.

"You don't have the bio, but you know the essence. That's enough. The rest is baggage." Vic shrugged. He gestured to the makeshift bed of bean bag chairs in the back of the van. "Take a nap. I'll get us back on the road."

Red rubbed her neck, feeling the nearly invisible fang marks, then laid down on the bean bag in the nest of blankets. She might know that she hated cobb salad or loved Harry Potter, but it wasn't the same as knowing what formed her.

After over a year, she still knew as much as she did when she woke up in that hospital in Eugene. They had crisscrossed the West and met half the active hunters and a few retired ones. None had recognized her. Even talking to a spirit or two hadn't brought more than obscure riddles about her mother. A long-dead pilgrim told her she came from a long line of witches, but they hadn't found a coven missing a member. Desperate, she had even let a vampire try to mesmerize the truth out of her. It failed. Every clue was a dead end.

Her hands shook.

Red had long ago accepted that Vic was probably right. She was an inexperienced hunter that tangoed with the wrong vampire who mesmerized her so forcefully that her mind had deleted her memories. What she might have suffered didn't keep her up at night. It was the question around what she loved. Who were her parents, who were her high school friends, what was the story behind the black lyre tattooed on her left shoulder? Those were the questions that haunted her.

She needed something to take her mind off the anxiety washing over her and grabbed a citronella candle from a plastic milk crate filled with supplies. Staring at it, she tried to visualize a blue flame erupting from the wick.

Magic came in many forms, from the ceremonial magic of exorcisms and blessings that even muggles could do, to harnessing the power of the elements. She had been trying to make a spark for months. If she thought air was difficult, fire was beyond her even more. Yet, Red still squinted at the squat white candle in the tin.

Light, damn you, light!

The scent of citronella made her nose twitch, and she couldn't concentrate. Why wasn't magic as simple as killing a vampire?

"Fuck." She tossed the candle back into the box. Who was she fooling? She was as good at magic as she was at remembering.

Red might have been an intern, but she had been hunting long enough to know that you rested when you could. She curled up on the multicolored bean bag, trying to breathe deep and push past the faceless ghosts to steal some sleep.

The night was still young, and they had a murder to solve.

2

Wind howled as snow sleeted against the window. Red shivered before she buried deeper into the blankets. Smiling, she leaned against a firm, bare chest and looked up.

The dim light cast shadows over the face, always obscuring him from view except for the storm gray eyes staring back at her.

She ran her fingers over his high cheekbones, chilled as if carved from marble, to comb through his mussed hair. "Do you at least have a secret handshake?"

"Afraid not, kitten. We have a lot of inane rituals, but handshakes are not one of them."

Red pouted. "Not going to lie, I'm a little disappointed."

Chuckling, he rolled her under him, faster than she could process. Rising on his palms, lean biceps tensed, he stared down at her.

Red ran her hand down his defined abs to the ridged V-shape of his hip. "What about—"

He kissed her, lips brushing softly as he ran his fingers through her hair. His hand cupped her breast, thumb circling her nipple. He pulled back, grinning, before peppering kisses down her neck. Cold lips started a fire on her skin.

Breathless, she forgot all about what she was going to ask.

Red arched her back. She fell off the bean bag onto the floor of the Millennium Falcon, foot kicking the tackle box tied to the van wall. Panting, she pushed herself up. Her body seemed to want to fall back into sleep to carry on where she had left off. This wasn't the first time she'd had a vivid dream of the mystery man.

In Nevada, Red had tried a shamanic ritual to help remember past lives and repressed memories. It only gave her disjointed, shadowy dreams. The details faded by dawn, leaving only impressions behind. It was the first time she'd heard his voice.

Sex dreams—amazing sex dreams, if she were honest—weren't the only time that the mystery man made a cameo in her subconscious. She had dreams of watching him prowling behind upright stone stabs, ashes under his boots, yet she knew he would protect her. His face had always been obscured. She tried to hold on to image of his chiseled features, his soft black hair, and the look in those gray eyes... The face faded, and she couldn't keep it. It dissolved as her eyes opened.

Red could only capture flickers. Not of memories, but images that rarely made sense in her dreams. Surreal times and places that she couldn't have been—moonlit pyramids, crumbling towers, locomotives puffing dense black smoke. Also, places so mundane she could have seen them anywhere—a classroom, a cemetery, and a red diner booth. Her dreams were like a will o' the wisp in a bog.

After a gas wasting trek around Lake Tahoe, she left without real answers. Again. And she was $200 in the hole with Vic. She trusted her subconscious as much as her memory. She got up, adjusting her jeans and black tank top before opening the Falcon and stepping outside.

"I almost have it," Vic said, hunched over the van's front tire. "I texted Quinn, so he knows we're running late. He's not much of a talker, but he gets livelier after dark."

She leaned against the open van. "Most vampires do."

"Can you be cool around him? It can't be easy to be around vamps, even knowing that he has a soul." He shrugged, refocusing on fixing the flat. "Considering."

"I'll be cool." Red shifted on her feet, embarrassed about her freak out. She'd been trying to prove to him that she could be more than an intern, that she was ready to take the challenge to officially join the Brotherhood of Bards and Heroes. That meant acting like a hunter. It didn't matter if his friend looked like Dracula, she was going to be a professional.

"You weren't cool with them in OKC." He stilled his hands on the socket wrench.

Red sighed and sat down in the open side door of the van. "You know I chilled out after working with Souled Sal in Oklahoma. I don't have the best history with vampires, but I know the difference between the good guys and the bad ones."

"You sure?" Vic raised his eyebrow. "A vampire might have been the one to erase your memories, and it's chill to be around them?" He shook his head, chin jutting out. "I don't buy it. Were-wolves killed my family, and it doesn't matter who they are, even the good ones. I can't not think about it. You've had some rough weeks. How are you gonna react when you're sitting across from a vampire?"

Chin resting on her palm, she met his gaze. "If you tell me they're hunters, that's enough. We all come to this life differently. I'm not going to get all PTSD on your friend. You know I don't crack in a fight. It's just when it gets quiet."

Vic wagged a grease-darkened finger at her. "All I'm saying is don't stake Quinn. I was once his intern."

The chop of a motorcycle sounded in front of them, getting closer. A headlamp blinded her before the bike came to a stop. Red looked away, leaning into the open van to avoid the high beam.

"Thanks for the blinding light. I didn't need to see what I'm doing," Vic muttered.

The rider popped out his kickstand and killed his engine. "You should be thanking me, mate," he said sardonically. He sounded English even muffled through the helmet.

Red covered a small gasp as her ears perked up at his voice. She peeked out at him from the open van door.

The stranger swaggered toward them, cutting a lean figure in dark denim and leather. Streetlight reflected off the safety pins and patches of old punk bands on his jacket. "Quinn owes me for driving to the far side of Rancho Cucamonga."

"Oh, boohoo, we've been on the road all day." Vic sneered, tightening the final lug nut on the tire and pulled the socket wrench away. "I didn't tell him to send the welcome wagon."

"LA is crawling with vampires. Not everyone plays nice like we do."

Vic waved his hand as he stood. "Yeah, yeah, we already staked a douchebag in board shorts on our way into town. What's your name again? Lucas, Ice Pick, maybe Greg?"

"Greg? Really?" The biker took off his helmet to revealed black hair and high cheekbones that models would die for. Skin untouched by the California sun, he had been plucked from the mortal coil in his twenties. His lips were full and looked mischievous, but sorrow lingered in his pale gray eyes. The shadows only added more mystery to his handsome features.

Red furrowed her brow, straining to catch his voice, forcing her jaw not to drop. He sounded so familiar. She stood and stepped beside her boss. "Who is he, Vic? Another friend?"

The biker scanned her from head to toe, eyes widening. Lips gaping open for a moment, he clenched his jaw and looked away.

"No, Sid Vicious here is one of Quinn's." Vic shrugged as if there was no accounting for taste then grinned. "I'm giving him shit. He's cool. His real name isn't Greg."

The biker barked out, "Who's the bird?"

"Red?" Vic jerked his thumb at her. "My intern."

"We don't need your help. Get her out of the city tonight." The biker put his helmet back on and hopped on his bike. He kicked back the stand with a final look at them. The motorcycle spun around and sped out of the parking lot.

"Whiskey tango foxtrot!" Vic waved his hands over his head trying to flag the biker down. "What about all the sensitive Blood Alliance bullshit? Vampires not playing by the rules. Quinn called in one hell of a favor on this."

"Are we being punk'd?" Red rubbed her chilled arms. "I need to know who that is."

"That was Lucas Crawford—proof that a soul doesn't stop you from being a dick. He's the annoying vampire cousin that Quinn can't shake off. Works for him sometimes."

"What's his deal?" She tried to ask casually.

"He's a souled vampire. Enough said." Vic shrugged and knelt to put away his tools after tightening one last lug on the wheel.

"His voice sounded familiar. At least, I think it was." Red admitted before describing the flashes and snippets of the dreams she could remember of the granite stone circle. She kept the sexy bits to herself. "Hard to explain since it's a lot of flashes of images. I think he was trying to help me. I can't remember more."

"You've had spooky dreams and mistaken identity before. We chased the leads all around Nevada desert, but didn't get to go to Vegas once," Vic lamented, toolbox under his arm. His fatigued eyes narrowed to slits before he shook his head. "This is some *Memento* shit. Lucas has been hunting the west for decades. He might have saved you once upon a time. Maybe you're remembering something, but maybe not."

"Well, he was acting all weird." Red didn't know what worried her more—learning that a mystery man from her dreams was dead or the possibility that her mind was playing tricks on her.

Could it be a souled vampire thing? She'd only met a few on her journey. Traveling the byways on demon hunts, she had found more of the original unrepentant kind. All vampires were animated by a demonic instinct, but for the last hundred years, more and more had been bewitched to feel their human conscience. Poetically speaking, they had their souls returned. Technically speaking, they were cursed to feel remorse and empathy. All the facets of the human emotional condition that the demon essence possessing their bodies suppressed. It might not sound like much to a human, but after countless nights of murder, that guilt was a karmic bitch. It was meant to be.

Gaze distant and uncertain, Vic hoisted his toolbox into the van. "He usually sticks around to make with the banter, but it's probably just the hundred vampires descending on the city for the Blood Summit. We need to get to Quinn. He said something about this case being different."

Red hopped into the driver's seat. She put her hand over her heart, trying to calm it, before she stuck the key into the ignition. The pale gray eyes of a demon flashed in her mind as she drove through the City of Angels.

3

Red stepped through the broken glass of the building's entrance, following Vic into the first-floor hallway. Curry lingered in the air from the Indian restaurant next door in the rundown strip mall. After business hours, all the offices were dark except for the first on the right. She rested her hand on the leather hunter's kit strapped to her waist. It might have looked like a medieval fanny pack, but it held her snub nosed revolver loaded with wooden bullets.

A small plaque on the cracked open door read *Quinn Investigations*. Red peeked inside, alarm drying her mouth. Loose papers and toppled file cabinets covered the floor of the small front room. Two men bent over the secretary's desk. She took a picture with her cellphone quickly.

Skinny and hunched over in a *Rick and Morty* shirt, the shorter one typed into the desktop computer, his tongue stuck out between white fangs in concentration. He looked as if he hadn't gotten much sun even when he was alive.

His associate was dressed like a bank supervisor. The bald Black man glared at the files as if they were stocks going belly up. He looked up, brown eyes glowing amber, and hissed.

Pushing the door open, Vic hit the lights and raised his shotgun. "Wooden tips, cucks."

"I'll rip that out of your hands and shove it up your mullet-wearing ass," the bald vampire said.

"I guess we won't be appealing to your souls. Let's try your brains." She stepped in front of Vic as she put her phone away. "Bad time to make trouble, what with that fancy vampire summit and all. Quinn has enough connections to make a stink."

"Come on." The shorter vampire pushed his glasses up the bridge of his nose and sprinted out the door fast enough to stir Vic's mullet as he passed.

Left behind, the black vampire adjusted his suit jacket lapels and stepped away from the desk. "Hunters, eh? Is that how far the mighty Quinn Byrnes has fallen?"

Vic blew a raspberry.

"I'm a witch, so watch it, pal." Red lifted her hand, trying to look more confident than she felt, summoning her magic, pleading with the little bit left to listen.

He widened his stance and raised his fists. "I don't scare easy."

She slammed her palm forward, drawing upon the well of energy within as she called to the element of air.

The vampire flew back and hit the window, taking the cheap Venetian blinds with him as he fell through the breaking glass. An alarm sounded, and a floodlight came on outside the building. His bald head reflected the light. Grimacing, the vampire brushed off his suit and fled in a blur.

"I wanted to shoot that one," Vic whined.

"Yeah, somehow I don't think your friend wants either dead vampires or gunshots in his office." Red bent over at the waist and controlled the urge to dry heave.

Sweat beaded on the back of her neck. Chills rolled down her spine. That spell looked cool, but now she felt like she was getting the flu. Too much magic took a toll. She would need to remember to eat or meditate to center her energies. Sex, massage, ecstatic dance worked too according to the grimoires that she had read. She hoped that half-melted candy bar in the van would do the trick.

"If he's still alive." Vic gritted his teeth, looking around. Fear glimmered in his brown eyes. He stomped past her to open the door on the left. "He has an apartment in the basement."

Red nodded before she turned in a circle, surveying the trashed office. The vampires certainly made themselves at home. She stepped over to a fallen filling cabinet and pushed it upright. Trying to keep the files together, she gathered up the loose papers and folders and placed them by the cabinet they had spewed out from. She found an open safe, ripped from a wall somewhere else, on the floor by the desk.

The safe had been cracked, its metal front hanging open as files, boxes, and books spilled out of it. She pushed the items back into the safe, trying not to look at them. No cash or jewels, just the ephemera of a very old life. A photo album lay open to reveal a sepia portrait of a light-haired woman in a crown and medieval garb, lounging in a Victorian parlor. She closed the album quickly, feeling like she was spying, and shoved it into the safe.

A torn piece of paper fluttered out. She picked it up. The sketch paper had gone soft with age. She set it on the pile with the others, face up. It was a sketched figure of a blindfolded woman in repose on it. The paper had been ripped at the bust line, leaving only the face, tensed bare shoulders, and an arm raised over the head. She picked it up again to study the anticipation in the woman's mouth and jaw.

The aged pencil marks had faded, but the lines came together in a forehead, mouth, and chin that resembled the one she saw every day in the mirror.

Unsettled, Red pulled out her phone and took a quick picture of the sketch before shoving it back into the photo album and pushing both back into the safe. She stood, thoroughly creeped out. That had to be a weird coincidence. Besides the sketch didn't look like her that much! She was imagining things, just like with Lucas. Had she been looking so hard for clues about herself that she saw them everywhere? Hadn't she learned anything from that wild goose chase last month?

Relieved grin stretched across his face, Vic stepped into the office and opened the door wider, showing a smaller private room behind him.

A tall, broad-shouldered man walked out, rubbing a hand over spikey blond hair down to a growing bump on his temple. He had a rugged masculine look with a strong jaw and brow. A dark V-neck shirt clung to his defined chest in wet patches. His pale skin and unnaturally white teeth pegged him as a vampire, but the brooding glint to his brown eyes marked his soul.

"They caught the old man in the shower!" Vic said, chuckling even as he gazed at Quinn like a comic fanboy meeting Stan Lee. "Didn't even see them."

Red raised her eyebrows. She could call the vampire a lot of things, but old wasn't one of them. Whoever had turned him had caught him on the cusp of thirty.

"You don't need to sound so happy about it." Quinn glared at Vic without bite in his eyes, his tone droll and quiet.

Vic snorted, lips perking up in a repressed grin. "You're the one who was always going on about vigilance when I was at UCLA."

"You used to hunt high and end up at In-N-Out Burger," Quinn said dryly. He looked over at Red, and his stone expression grew stonier. "Who's this?"

"My intern." Vic gestured with a deadpan expression. "She keeps up my Twitter."

Red stepped forward and held out her hand. Vic had told her so much about his adventures with Quinn that she felt like she knew him. She could recite the story of when they fought zombies at In-N-Out, at least. "Pleased to meet you, Quinn. He's told me more about his college years than you might have wanted him to."

"Vic likes to talk." Quinn shook her hand, releasing it quickly as if burned. He stepped away from her and looked around at his office before his eyes landed on the safe. "They were thorough."

"I tried to pick up a bit, but you'll have to see if they stole anything." Red studied him, wondering if they were thinking about the same sketch and the spooky resemblance. She tried to tell herself that she was being paranoid. Quinn had been an artist for centuries; it wasn't strange for him to have drawings. Vic had warned her to be cool and she was already looking for reasons to be suspicious about his dead friends.

"You said this vamp case was delicate." Vic gestured to the room wryly. "It looks like the Watergate burglary up in here."

Red stepped up to the men and held out her phone after swiping to the next-to-last picture. The sideways shot of the burglars wouldn't win awards, but it wasn't too blurry. She held out her phone. "Do you recognize these vampires?"

Quinn stared down at it, no sign of even repressed recognition in his gaze, before shaking his head. "No."

"Alrighty." Red quirked an eyebrow at her boss as she tucked away the phone. He'd said his friend wasn't a talker, but monosyllabic would've been a better description.

"Tell us what you have on this case," Vic said, punching the other man on the shoulder playfully. "We popped a tire, staked a vampire, and crossed states to get here, Q. All you said was a model was found drained on the beach."

"Staked a vampire? Describe them." Wariness straightening his posture, Quinn crossed his arms. "Master or minion?"

Red considered her answer. The Blood Alliance had changed a lot of traditions, but like sire and childe, there were some hierarchies that couldn't disappear. She remembered reading that the old vampire bloodlines each had their own unique definitions of what made a master vampire. The way she saw it, the difference between a master and minion was the power—who took orders and who followed. "Definitely a minion. Tallish, blond, skateboarder. He couldn't have been more than a year or two dead. Attacked me in San Bernardino. Ring any bells?"

Quinn frowned. "He's not from LA. Or if he is, he's not on the city list of vampires."

"If he was here for the Summit..." She began, stroking her chin. "He drove a long way for a meal when the supreme might be offering willing bleeders to her guests. What sire would let that young a vampire head that far afield to make mischief? Too many old, canny ones around for that."

"True." Quinn lifted his eyebrows at the observation. "He might have been passing through."

"Great, then let's assume we don't have to worry about the Supreme Master or the Blood Alliance coming for us," Vic said, flapping his hand before turning to the vampire. "What about the reason you made us drive here from Reno?"

"Olivia Greene. A jogger found her on Tuesday morning, washed up on a beach."

"We read the paper." He rolled his wrist, motioning for the vamp to continue. "Give us some new details."

"The name is new." She pulled up the browser on her phone and plugged the name in. She glanced up from the typical social media influencer posts to address Quinn. "I found her Instagram. She was represented by DB Models. Have you heard of them?"

"DB Models?" He tilted his head at Quinn, mouth curled up like he'd sniffed bad milk. "So, that's why Lucas told me to beat feet. It's a family affair."

"What?" Her gaze darted between him and the PI. She had heard a lot about their adventures, but she wasn't seeing the connection.

"Quinn's ex-wife runs the modeling agency," Vic commented, his expression freezing. "Delilah Byrnes is the Notorious DB."

Quinn flicked an annoyed glance at him. "It's more complicated."

"Yeah, it usually is." Red said quickly to head off whatever was brewing between the two men. She might have gotten some wacky stories, but she could tell that this vampire drama ran deep. It wouldn't be the first time a hunter gave up a case that hit too close to home. "Do you need help because you'll be recognized investigating, or because you don't know how deep you'll dig?" She lifted her hands, palms out, with a sympathetic head shake. "I'm not judging you either way."

"Both." Quinn looked away.

Vic frowned. "Ease up on my bro. It's complicated."

"No problem. I don't know either Quinn or Delilah from Adam. It makes sense to bring some new faces around. Give us what you have on the case, and we can start digging into it tomorrow." Red shrugged. She'd follow Vic's lead, since she owed him. It was his bromance that led them here. This wasn't your usual souled vampire, or at least Vic thought he was more. Quinn asked for help. That was all the information her boss needed to get them on the road. Red tried to slap on a friendly smile for his sake.

Vic stretched. "Yup. I've got you covered, brother."

"I need to be kept in the loop," Quinn said, making eye contact with them before hunching his shoulders.

"Your office is headquarters, man." He repressed a yawn.

Red covered her own, eyeing the vampire curiously when she realized that he seemed immune to returning their yawn. That was a funny quirk in biology she filed away to ponder later. How much more would she learn about his kind before this was over? She didn't say that she trusted him, but she had worked cases with hunters she had trusted less. "If you need help, let me know. I get the feeling that the break in made your folders more organized."

"Lucas does the filing." Quinn straightened with a small twitch of his lips that Red interpreted as a smile. He rubbed his fingernails on his chest before looking down. "Sometimes."

"So, he's like your secretary? Does he answer your phone?" She laughed at the mental image of the surly immortal doing customer service. "Sorry, I met him tonight, and I can't imagine him in a headset."

Quinn's smile disappeared. "He saw you?"

"Yeah, I forgot to mention what a dick he was tonight," Vic said, forehead crinkling. "I thought we were mates or chaps or whatever is British for friend."

"Lucas checked in, said I should leave town, then bailed," Red said. She had recognized him tonight, and a part of her could have sworn that he had done the same.

Quinn's expression didn't change but he tensed her words. "I told him to check on Vic. The Supreme Master has declared that LA will be a model city, but we have new vampires in town for the Summit. I thought you'd be alone. Better to send her on a Grayhound to Flagstaff."

"You need a little faith in my mentoring abilities. She's not a body builder, but she's field tested."

"Lucas was rude, you know." She looked at the safe, concealing the mysterious sketch. He wasn't the only one that was cryptic either. Why did every souled vampire want her out of the city?

Vic laughed, shaking a warning finger. "That's what you get for hiring relatives."

"It's been said." Quinn rubbed the healing bump on his head, self-consciously. "I need to board up the window and call the security company. I'll email the background check that I got on the victim. You'll have it before you get to your hotel."

Shrugging, Vic narrowed his eyes and slowly turned. His tone came out cool. "See you at sunset then."

Red followed her boss out of the office, feeling eyes on her as she closed the door. Quinn turned away when she caught him staring. She caught up with Vic in the parking lot. "I don't know him, but was that weird?"

"Damn right it was! He has an extra bedroom and a couch. A nice couch." Vic shook his head. "Sending us to a hotel. Cold. Ice cold. Damn, after eight hours in the van, too."

"You spent most of it sleeping or watching TV in the back," Red pointed out without sass. She owed him after he had spent half of a month on a dead-end lead on her origins. One more on a long list. At this point, she was ready to believe his crazier theory about dark fairies kidnapping her.

"Still. He could have given me some warning that Delilah—his sire, ex-wife, and professional ice queen—was connected to the victim." He shook his head as he got into the driver's side of the van. "I still haven't decided if she asked him to investigate or he's doing it out of guilt. He doesn't make small talk, but the brood-meister at least gives me the heads up."

"Does his ex-wife have a soul too?"

"Not just that, but they're the original gangsters."

"Oh, that's right... He just looks so normal, I wouldn't have..." She licked her lips, trying to reconcile the stoic vampire in the center of Vic's wacky college shenanigans

and the Quinn Byrnes from the Brotherhood's legends.

"You just met two of the four vampires so bad that the soul special was invented just for them." He started the Falcon. "Delilah turned Quinn, and they rampaged around Europe for a century before turning Selene, who I hope you never meet because she is nuttier than a peanut farm. Lucas found his way into the crew after the nut job made him, then he never left. Blood, bodies, and mayhem piled up before they crossed the wrong dude. August first, 1900, the day everything changed." Vic snapped his fingers.

Red whistled, impressed. "The spell heard around the world."

"Exactly. They didn't just piss off the wrong dude, they pissed off a magical librarian—which you never want to do. Killed his family or something. The guy, Father Matthew, doesn't just shove empathy back into them, he writes a little guide to exactly how he did it with vague suggestions on how someone without soulmancy skills could do it. You know librarians, always trying to get people to read. Add a printing press and you get..."

"The August Harvest."

"Yup. Thirty odd years of mages and more slinging souls at vampires. Breaking down the old bloodline system into a chaos of purges, revolts, and suicides. Vampire World War until the Blood Alliance brought order to the undead. It's essentially modern feudalism, but it's something." He shook his head. "It all started with that guy."

"Really that's Quinn Byrnes?" Red furrowed her brow. She would have expected a Dracula type in a cape with old world charm, not a stone-faced guy in a V-neck, hunching his shoulders and awkwardly deadpanning his way through small talk. "The Black Libertine, himself."

"Yeah, might as well be called the Stingy Libertine, now," Vic said as he turned onto the highway. The lights of Los Angeles spread out before them.

"I saw something weird in his office." She described the sketch. "It looked like me, I swear."

Lifting his eyebrow, he puffed out a long breath. "You told me after Nevada to call you out on chasing non-clues. When I found you, I called Quinn to ask about mystery redheads. If he had drawn a picture of you, he'd tell me. Think about it—the sketch was ripped up and faded. Maybe you're seeing yourself because you want to."

Rubbing her forehead to soothe the growing headache, she nodded. "You're right. I just... I want to know who I am."

"I haven't given up on that. We'll get there. First, we need to solve a murder."

After pulling into a no-tell motel advertising both daily and hourly rates and checking in using a fake ID and credit card, the two hunters entered the dingy room. Vic immediately started channel surfing cross-legged on the bed closest to the door.

Bushed from using so much magic, she brushed her teeth. She changed into her knockoff House Ravenclaw pajama bottoms and baggy North Dakota tourist T-shirt in the tiny motel bathroom. Yawning goodnight, she slipped between the surprisingly clean sheets and fell into a dreamless sleep on the lumpy mattress.

Metallica blared as a low vibration skittered on metal.

Red jumped awake, blinking at the ringing cell phone on the stand between the beds. She yawned; half tempted to pick it up just to make the old rock song stop. Vic didn't listen to anything from this century. He had gotten her hooked on classic rock, but it wasn't the time for a vintage Metallica wake up.

"Your phone." She propped herself up on an elbow and squinted at the screen, surprised at the familiar name—Fat Jake Crispin—that she only saw on emails with their bounty orders from the Brotherhood of Bards and Heroes.

He coughed and rolled over, grabbing the phone. "Vic. Talk." His eyes snapped open, and he bolted upright, looking over at her and gesturing for something to write with.

She walked over to the empty rickety desk and tossed him a pen before looking for paper. The motel was too cheap to provide swag beyond brittle soap bars, but she did find a small notepad under a Gideon bible in the bottom drawer. It was monogramed with 'Smith and Reaper, Financial and Legal Services.' She tossed over, thankful for whichever ambulance chaser had left it.

From Vic's lack of sarcasm, the call must have been serious. She waited until he hung up. "Must be a red-letter day to get a call from headquarters."

"He'll never forget it, either." Cheek twitching, Vic ran a hand through his hair. "He lost his only daughter. Found drained. She was signed with DB Models. Crispin already talked to the LAPD. There's another connection between the two vics. Both had a snake eating its tail carved on them."

"Quinn left that detail out." Red kept the emotion out of her tone as she got back into the other bed. After enough road trips, she'd heard all of Vic's stories twice, and the best ones even more. She felt like she knew Quinn already. It didn't stop her doubts about him.

Vic knew her well enough to read the skepticism of his friend. His nostrils flared as he huffed and lay back on his flat pillow.

She couldn't stop herself from grumbling. "So much for keeping each other in the loop."

He gritted his teeth and pinched the bridge of his nose. "Hey, he might not have known."

She tiptoed the sore subject, wanting rest more than an argument. "What now?"

"Sleep. After that we do what you do in LA, some yoga, hit the beach, then check out the nightlife."

Red had a sinking feeling about this case. Suspicious master vampires, uncertain allies, and now a Bard's murdered daughter? This case was supposed to be business. It was turning personal. Like a wooly mammoth trapped in the La Brea tar pits, she felt herself being drawn in deeper.

4

OCTOBER 25TH, Before Dawn, The Pump House Bar in Downey, Los Angeles, California, USA

"I really don't like this." Red pushed open the battered door of the Pump House.

The hole-in-the-wall bar was sandwiched between an unopened taco shop and a nail salon in the southern part of Downey, known to the world for the oldest McDonald's, and known to a smaller number for having the oldest hunter bar in Los Angeles. In the pre-dawn hours, the city buzzed with cars making their 6 a.m. commutes, yet a hush lingered over the strip mall.

Small mirrors, iron horseshoes, and silver crosses lined the entry-way. She avoided her reflection and the on-edge squint that announced that she wasn't caffeinated. The decorations might have looked like rustic flair to a civilian, but they were like a security system. It would be hard for anything but a human to come through without detection.

The rest of the place was trapped in the middle of last century down to the portraits of John F. Kennedy and Buzz Aldrin. An old timer in a cowboy hat at the bar stared ahead, cupping a mug of steaming coffee in his hands.

"I thought you wanted to try yoga." Vic followed behind her, pushing his sunglasses down to take in the wood-paneled room decorated in NASA memorabilia.

"Not with a vamp teaching it." She muttered under her breath so the lone bartender couldn't hear. Vic had woken her only an hour after Fat Crispin's call with the order that they needed to see the Supreme Master of LA at a pre-sunrise yoga class. Fuck that.

Vic gasped dramatically, miming clutching fake pearls. "Racist."

"Cautious." Red rolled her eyes. She'd had her fill last night of cryptic vampires, their secrets, and being kept in the dark. Maybe she wasn't as experienced as him, but this whole case set her on edge.

Vic might have looked at Quinn with puppy worship in his eyes, but she couldn't shake the fact that the blond souled vampire hadn't told them about what was carved on the victim, or that his ex-wife Delilah Byrnes had a direct connection with her. Then adding the Bard's daughter to the body count... Fat Jake Crispin might have written their bounty checks, but she needed more than an order from the home office before she walked into a vampire's nest. She almost hadn't walked out of the last one.

A hunter's bar could give them the earful of gossip they needed to stay one step ahead of their enemies and allies. You could find crews coming in for a drink after a night's hunt at the same time others were getting cheap coffee and settling any bounties before hitting the road out of town. That was the theory, at least.

In a place like LA, this cramped bar should have been full. It was empty except for the bartender and the cowboy. Vic made it sound like he could get home fries here any time of day. It didn't smell like home fries had been made here for a long time.

He took his sunglasses off and met her eyes. "The place has changed. I think they dusted."

Red leaned against the counter and held up two fingers. "Coffee, please. Black. To go."

"I'm Vic. It's been a spell since I blew into town, where's Murphy or Derek?"

The bartender, sallow-faced and sleepy, shrugged before turning to the coffee pot. "Vacation to Palm Springs. They won't be back until the first week of November."

"Can I still get home fries?"

"No kitchen, Vic. I only know how to make coffee and pour the beer. It's just me and Chuck here, keeping the fires running." He nodded at the old-timer.

She shifted to face Chuck. "We saw a lot of California hunters passing through Reno when we left."

He blew on his coffee, puffing his white mustache up, before sipping. "No one will return until after All Souls' Day at least. You should get back on the road. Might make it to someplace sunny like Arizona."

"What makes you so certain?" Vic asked.

The older hunter's steely gaze pierced them. "The Blood Alliance's powwow. There are enough souled vampires to keep the peace in town, the supreme made it clear. Most hunters decided there are other monsters in the west."

"Y'all take orders from the head vampire?" She tried to keep surprise and disdain out of her voice. There were a lot of under-ground powers jockeying for position in the supernatural world. Vampires were just the tip of the iceberg, even if their society was more organized. Most hunters stayed neutral or actively resisted which ever supe claimed their city.

"Does it look like it?" Chuck tipped his hat back, his voice low but the threat coiling like a rattlesnake ready to strike.

Vic looked between them and tilted his head at the bartender, motioning for her to pay. He adjusted his jaw, eyes narrowing at her.

Oops, talking too much again. Red had gotten the hang of hunting demons, but keeping her mouth shut was still a work in progress. She slapped down a few bills and gestured for the man behind the counter to keep the change.

"We're here on a Brotherhood case. Julia Crispin was found drained last night," Vic confided to the other hunter.

Chuck's shoulders sank and he pulled off his hat. He sighed, placing it over his heart. "That pretty English gal had some stones on her. Maybe too many, getting so close to the vampers like that. I don't know much. I retired once the Brotherhood made that truce with the damn undead. I refused to be put on her list." He shook his head, slamming the weathered cowboy hat back on.

"Who, Cora Moon?" Vic asked.

"She has lists of vampires, lists of hunters, lists of lists." He slurped his coffee with a grimace. "Best be off now, don't want to be late for yoga."

Red raised her eyebrows and grabbed the to-go cups. Now, she really didn't like this.

"We'll be around if you hear anything." Vic nodded to him, then led the way out the door to the Millennium Falcon.

Rush hour started early and ended late in LA, but the sun still hadn't risen when they finally reached their next destination. It lay in the weird middle ground between the hard scrabble neighborhoods on the edge of Inglewood and the UCLA campus. You wouldn't have thought that the historical skyscraper was the vampire headquarters in LA by looking at it.

Moon Enterprises was a social good startup listed in Essence Magazine as one of the top ten black businesses on the rise in 1992. Beyond the article and a local business registry, the internet couldn't produce any more about the company. The shadowy CEO was known to the neighborhood but kept a low profile without giving a single quote to the press.

"Are you sure this is place?" Red asked as she eyed the crowd of smokers in the corner of the parking lot kitty-corner to the tall building.

Vic walked through the haze of smoke, hands in his pocket. "This used to be my hood. Or at least near it."

"Hey, how many people do I gotta tell?" A Hispanic man in a

plaid shirt mumbled as he flicked his cigarette. "No yoga, no hot meals, no nothing."

"We have an appointment." Vic jerked his thumb over to Moon Enterprises.

"That's what they all say, *hombre*." The guy shook his head. "Better not try that door until after sunrise."

An unmarked car that screamed law enforcement pulled up, and a too-pale blond uniformed officer opened the passenger's side door and half stepped out. Vampire? It wouldn't be the first time one had worn a badge. He slapped the top of the car. "Hey, I thought I told you punks to move along!"

His Asian partner muttered something to him before waving at the crowd from the open driver's side window. "The center is closed for the next two weeks, folks. Have a good morning!"

The crowd wandered away, muttering, as the car drove off.

Vic kept walking towards the building. "The Brotherhood is sending us in here, but they can't do squat if it goes south. No hunters to call in for backup, either. That's why there is a bonus in the bounty in case we get maimed."

She glared at him but followed across the street. "I really don't like this."

"You keep saying that..." Vic shrugged. "Red, I'll do the talking. I mean it." He pushed the intercom button next to the darkened door. "Cora Moon is expecting us. Two Bards come to pay our respects."

"I'm a Bard now?"

"Congrats on the promotion." He pushed his sunglasses up atop his head.

She tensed, wishing for a stake. Fat Crispin had sent them instructions to come unarmed as official representatives of the Brotherhood. It was at the supreme's insistence. The move had a pure political meaning—the Bards came when summoned. It was clear who ruled in LA. Her hunter's instinct still screamed at her to arm herself. She knew a stake wouldn't be nearly enough to protect them from the vampires inside, but it still felt like she was walking in naked.

Red pushed away the flashbacks from Oklahoma City and tried

to center her breathing. This was the land of the teddy bear souled vampires, or so she tried to tell herself.

The door opened automatically into a small tinted-glass entryway. They walked inside. Her heartbeat jumped as the door behind them closed, sealing out the early dawn, and the one before them opened. A supernatural ward suppressed her magic. This lair might have been open to the public, but it had unseen defenses. Her adjusting eyes only made out the silhouette of a gloriously full afro and a white smile.

"Welcome, my Bard brothers."

Vic stepped forward. "Howdy. Miss Cora Moon, I presume."

The vampire wore a white bodysuit, hemp necklaces, and a pink tie-dye scarf around her head. She beckoned them forward. The faint smell of patchouli and lavender lingered around her. She looked like a hippie, yet that aura was pure master vampire. Her smile was wide and dazed, but her brown eyes took them in with laser focus. She walked like she owned the city. In a very real way, Cora Moon did.

Five vampires in black suits flanked them like secret service. Their jackets concealed the bulges of filled shoulder holsters.

Red kept at Vic's heels as they moved into the dimly lit lobby painted with murals of proud brown skinned people in African garb in 70s hues. The place had the look of a well-funded community center, but the energy was of a business hotel filled with conventioneers.

Two clerks wearing headsets typed at inhuman speeds in between answering questions at the circular front desk. Milling pairs and trios walked to the elevator and into the swinging doors of darkened hallways. Their eyes shone with amber light as they looked up at Red and Vic. They were all vampires.

"I heard you offer a hungry man a hot meal here." Vic looked around; his hands balled into fists in his pockets as he tried to make small talk.

"I can hear that belly growl, son, but with the Blood Summit, I had to close the first-floor drop-in center to the public." Cora gestured them forward past an open door where a PowerPoint presentation glowed over a crowd settled in a large room. It had been transformed from a cafeteria into a conference space. A projected slide read *Tips to Avoid Trending on Twitter. 1. Smash the phone or camera first.*

"Usually we have vegan breakfast cooking in there. Tonight was our first round of knowledge-sharing workshops before the official committees. Some go longer than others. We only get together every two years, and some vampires have more to say than others." Cora rolled her eyes. "*Prétentieux, je sais, mais que pouvez-vous faire?*"

"Conferences really are all the same." Vic chuckled, but his laugh was thin.

"I am lucky that my homegirl Delilah is happy to hostess."

Red glanced at Vic to see if he picked up on the name. Did Cora mean Delilah Byrnes?

Cora pushed open a door into a brightly lit room painted with Sanskrit characters and lined with shelves of yoga mats. One teal and gold tie-dye mat remained in the middle of the room. "You two are a excuse to chill out for a bit."

"Crispin said you were a friend to the Bards," he said.

"Our truce was the capstone of my work in the last century." Cora smiled proudly. "I want peace. I've tried to create it here as the Supreme Master."

"Crispin's daughter was killed," Red said, then wished she hadn't. Vic had told her to keep quiet, but following the rules wasn't her strong suit.

"And I want her killer brought to justice. Trust me, chica, I am making this a true City of Angels." Cora wore a reassuring smile on her pretty face. How much of it was genuine?

Vic glared at Red and coughed. "Miss, can we trust in your protection while we investigate? I know this is a sensitive time."

"Let's drop the tension. You missed the class, but we can still relax a bit." Cora strode over to a high shelf. Her hands and feet pressed flat to the wall beside it, rising like a spider to grab two yoga mats at the top.

Red took a half step back, watching the supreme was the exact opposite of relaxing. She had seen wall crawlers before. Usually, she had a gun with wooden bullets to take them down. All vampires came with super speed, senses, and strength...some came with extras. They called them the Gifted. She called it creepy.

Standing on two feet, Cora climbed up the wall and strode across the ceiling. Gravity pulled at her brown afro, but her poise was as graceful upside down as it was on the ground. Flipping like a gymnast, she jumped to the middle of the room and unrolled both mats out flat. She dropped into a lotus pose on the tie-dyed mat. "Sit. Your auras are as tense as your shoulders."

Vic and Red looked at each other before walking closer and sitting cross-legged.

"Um, yeah. This is cozy." He drummed his fingers on his bent knee. "You know that Crispin doesn't just want answers, he wants..."

"He wants to see the vampire who killed his daughter staked. Preferably by his own hand." Cora shrugged, heaving out a saddened breath as if grieved by the cycle of violence. "It's an eye for an eye, but that happens when a man loses his baby girl. Any vamp in my city who is stupid enough to break my rules and go for a Bard's kid is fair game."

"You really mean that." Red tilted her head. She had met supreme masters before, but they were usually less like an earnest vegan social worker. Then again, she'd never met a souled vampire who managed to run a city.

"Yeah, I just run a soup kitchen, an after-school program, and job development training for single moms for the diabolical glee of it." Cora shook her head before stretching her arms over crossed legs and posing her fingers in a complex yogic gesture. "You haven't met many like me, hunter chick; I can see. Let me educate you. Running around trying to end the world is for crusty old-world vamps. I created a sustainable community in LA. That means all of us, even the unsouled vamps, have a social contract. This Summit is my chance to school these immortal fools that it's not optional to give peace a chance. Obviously, you will both have my protection during your investigation."

"Kick ass." Vic bobbed his head like a hummingbird after

drinking a can of Mountain Dew. "The Brotherhood will keep you informed."

"You'll be safe here, sugar," Cora said to Red, then put her hands into a praying position and addressed them both. "Now, let's take a deep breath before I have to run to my next meeting."

They breathed until a bodyguard in a black suit came to the door. Cora departed, giving a cheerful farewell of *Namaste* with four bodyguards trailing behind her. Another escorted them through the now crowded lobby of vampires complaining about social media. Red glanced around at the assembled horde and tried to keep her breathing normal, even as she wanted to run.

A vampire in a yarmulke sighed and slapped his hand on the shoulder of a black man in a red suit. His New York accent cut through the crowd. "And I thought the printing press was bad for business!"

"I'm ready to sleep." The vamp wrinkled his nose. "I hope our rooms smell less like the homeless than the seminars did."

Primal instinct told her to run. Her brain agreed, but she kept close to Vic's side, hoping that she looked as unaffected as he did. Head down and a calm pace to her feet, she felt like a lamb among wolves. The smoggy LA air had never felt fresher than when they stepped outside Moon Enterprises. Brows knitting together, she glared at Vic.

"I already know what you are going to say. None of us like this," he said. "Come on, let's get some home fries and a nap in before we hit the beach."

"You know how to treat a girl. Diner food and crime scenes." Red put on sunglasses, already feeling the heat of the day bouncing off the concrete buildings. The sun had risen, but she felt the shadows closing in.

5

OCTOBER 25TH, Night, Club Vltava off Sunset Strip in Los Angeles, California, USA

Sunset followed them as they returned to the motel to clean off the sand from the beach. The last lights of the California sun turned the city to gold, the mythical El Dorado, making Red understand for a moment why so many young creatives were drawn here like gold miners of the past. Beyond a pretty sunset, the day was a bust.

They had found nothing new and no witnesses at Olivia Greene's murder site.

Quinn emailed the background check and the pictures he had taken of the police report, but they hadn't gleaned anything close to a lead beyond DB Models. Unlike Julia Crispin, Olivia Greene was exactly as she appeared at first glance: a normal girl who'd stumbled onto the supernatural. Fate would push her murder into that percentage of cold cases too weird to investigate. If it hadn't been for

Vic needing to take a piss and a nap by Coyote Creek after a long drive, Red could have been the same statistic.

Vic always prayed for the victims, but she swore justice. She figured between the two of them some power out there would take pity.

Hours after sunset, the two hunters dressed to hobnob with aspiring celebrities and current has-beens. The city blazed with lit up billboards, neon signs, and streetlights. No star could be seen through the smog reflecting the light, leaving the night sky a dark burnt orange.

He cursed, navigating through the stop-and-go traffic on Sunset Strip to the next crime scene.

Red frowned as the last download from Fat Crispin's email attachment stalled on the laptop. "Damn, out of data until we get that bounty." She transferred a few photos to her phone.

"Fantastic," Vic grumbled.

"The Brotherhood must have some clout to get the LAPD to pony up so much info about the case." Red sighed as she closed the small laptop and untethered the cell phone before pushing it underneath the seat and covering it with a layer of washed energy drink cans. Vic called it urban camouflage.

"The Brotherhood has people in more places than you'd think, but this wasn't them." He kept his eyes on the road, avoiding her gaze. "I bet the deal with the Supreme Master of LA got us the files. The protection is the cherry on top. Can't say that it'll stop anyone from killing us if they really wanted to, though."

"Cheerful," she said. "Crispin was detailed, as usual. I can't imagine writing a crime report like that for my kid. He even estimated to the minute how long it would take him to analyze the surveillance camera footage."

"Duty is mother's milk to the Brotherhood. We vowed to be a shield to humanity. That doesn't stop in grief," He said, jaw tightening.

Red studied him, letting the silence grow as she hoped he'd

continue. He'd told her everything about his time at UCLA, but he never gave details of his time training in London with the Bards.

Vic grunted, changing subjects as quickly as he turned right. "I'm going to violate one of my sacred beliefs."

"Parking garage?"

"Parking garage." He began ranting about pay parking, late-stage capitalism, and civil liberties as he turned into the three-story garage. Then, as always, he quoted the Constitution as if the founding fathers could have foreseen the automobile.

Red let his grumbles and confusing blend of political ideologies roll over her. After a year riding shotgun with him, she had heard all his gripes about federal, state, and municipality overreach. She rolled down the window to let in the night air, hot and dry even in October. They were going to check out the ritzy club and the alley where the second victim, Julia Crispin, had been found.

Her family wasn't just a venerable clan of supernatural scholars. The bounty on staking the vampire who killed Julia would keep Red and Vic afloat for months. He made it sound like the Crispins were an oversized old money family with more arms than an octopus and at least five named Jacob, which led to the Fat Crispin nickname. Ironic, given that he was a skeletal beanpole of a man.

Vic said he kept his distance from the Brotherhood, but he still seemed to know everyone. She envied that. He had strong history on both sides of his family, from Henry Constantine who adopted him, to the Parks—his biological family he had lost to a werewolf attack. He even had an adopted brother named Lashawn out there. He had collected people in his life.

Red had a big blank when it came to friends and family. She had Vic and the scattered people she had met on the road, but everything before August of last year might as well have been a question mark. She might never find the answers she wanted, but they could find some for Julia Crispin.

Getting out of the van, she adjusted the drape of her slinky green dress. The asymmetrical skirt covered her to the knee in the front while exposing her lower thigh at the side. The back was high, but the neckline plunged low. Not her usual look, but it was trendy and distracting enough to stupid dudes in case she needed to chat one up for information.

Vic had tried to convince her that everyone in LA wore heels, but Red wasn't sure. She put foldable black leather flats in her black purse as backup. 5'7 might have been short in the land of models, but heels were a recipe for a sprained ankle if they got in a fight. He could fight in the heels for all she cared.

Walking together to the sprawling line at the half-open, rounded, red-varnished double doors, she looked up at the black letters above. Club Vltava. She had already looked up the club, operated by Novak and Novak Company, distinguished by a rare drink selection comprised of European vintages like Vinho Verde from Portugal and Slivovice from the Czech Republic. Two of the Kardashian sisters came to the opening last week. Besides being owned by vampires, it was like every other hot spot hyped up on social media.

"Ugh, a line." Vic scowled. He had forgone his denim vest and donned a dark blazer over his jeans and a Boba Fett T-shirt. His mullet lay slicked back. He looked like a tech startup founder ready to burn investor cash. "I don't understand waiting to buy a twenty-dollar cocktail at a place with a drink minimum."

She smirked. "Blend in. Pretend you have money."

"I wouldn't spend it on this." He listed better things, in his opinion, to spend twenty dollars on, from a plate of chicken and waffles to new windshield wipers, as they waited in line.

A beefy bouncer in a black suit glared down at them from nearly seven feet. He was human, but judging by the jagged scar cut down his dark-skinned cheek, he wasn't someone to strong arm or flirt with for an invite inside. "Not feeling you two tonight. What is that, bro, a mullet?"

"Hey, this hairstyle is big in Korea, pal."

Red fluffed out her loose red hair, forcing a smile as Vic argued with the bouncer. She looked over his bulky shoulder.

The open door led a black painted hallway. A pale, brown-haired man in a pinstriped suit with a white Bluetooth device in his ear walked down the hall, chatting as he swiped through his phone. His thumb was a supernatural blur. His teeth were the tell-tale brilliant white of a vampire. He looked up when he reached the bouncer. His eyes flicked over her, head to toe, but without any heat in his gaze.

"Let them in without cover." The vampire chuckled. "My brother likes gingers."

"Free? Thanks!" Resisting the urge to cringe, Red knew the charge could come later in blood instead of cash. She curled a lock of hair around her finger, pretending to flirt, even as her stomach sank. Oh great, there was a dead guy in there with a redhead fetish.

"Even with this dork, Arno?" The bouncer asked, glancing askance at them.

"Hey!" Vic huffed.

"She's hot enough." Arno shrugged.

Vic glared at the bouncer as he took her arm and led them away. "Dork? I don't know what he's seeing. I look badass."

"That's right, honey."

They disengaged in the short hallway, passing the people taking the cover charge, into the elevator. She and Vic had pretended to be a couple on jobs before, but it always felt like taking her cousin to the prom. They ended up having to stop themselves from making each other laugh and breaking cover. Tonight, they had to play it cool. This wasn't just any nightclub.

The elevator filled up with the other clubbers, then rose to the second to the top floor. It opened to a dark, fog filled, strobe-lit dance floor playing electronica. Vic stepped out with a sigh. "Great, Euro-trash music."

"Come on, let's do a lap, then see if they have an IPA for you." She motioned with her head, and they walked around the large chamber.

Along the wall, alcoves and niches were filled with white pillows that glowed in the strobing black lights. Two bouncers stood in front of a wide staircase and a sign on a pedestal read *PRIVATE PARTY*. They turned some tanned blondes in tiny black dresses away.

A pale man, bald and blinking behind round glasses like a worn-down accountant in a wrinkled brown suit, stepped in front of the bouncers. The velvet rope lifted. He looked over his shoulders, fangs just barely visible on his lip, before disappearing up the stairs.

Red stopped Vic and nodded towards the frumpy vampire. "It looks like that is where the real action is."

"No, it just walked through the door."

She frowned. There was entirely too much delight in his voice. He had an idea. These usually ended in a fight. She turned to see who Vic was waving at—Lucas. She brushed an errant lock behind her ear and shifted on her heeled feet, feeling unsteady all of a sudden.

Lucas tightened his jaw and glared at Vic before his eyes widened. He glanced at her up and down, and a dumbstruck expression flashed across his face before he collected himself and stomped forward. "What are you two doing here?"

She smiled to spite his grumpiness. "Oh, you know. When in LA, go where the beautiful people are."

Vic jerked his thumb at the staircase. "Get us into the vamp party upstairs, Greg."

"Oi, enough with the Greg business," Lucas scoffed with a small resigned smile.

Red looked away to hide her smirk. After he'd left them at the strip mall, Vic had declared him Greg forevermore.

"Whatever, Greg. We're working for your boss and with the local vampire fuzz. What's the deal with upstairs?"

"It's a big to-do for the Blood Alliance, speeches and kumbayas between vampires—souled and unsouled. Quinn sent me to be bored to tears up there and report back."

Red put her hands on her hips. "It can't be a coincidence that a girl was found drained and dumped here right before the big pep rally. That's a message. We just need to know who it's for." She glared when Lucas opened his mouth to argue. "Come on, this is a PR event with enough souled vampires that we know it'll be tame.

We're not going to start a fight. We just want a look around while we have most of the town up there."

Lucas crossed his arms. "Then they can get a look at you." His eyes flicked to Vic. "Both of you. You shouldn't be in this club."

"It's hard to investigate a murder if you don't see the full crime scene. I doubt Julia spent the whole night in the alley." She folded her arms and composed her most determined face. Vampires, souled or not, only respected confidence. No one wanted strangers taking over a case, but Quinn had given this to them. Lucas would have to respect that.

"Come on," Vic said. "We'll hang out in the background."

As if unsettled by an unseen wind, the human throng parted— the Supreme Master Vampire of the City had arrived. The tall dark-skinned woman stepped onto the dance floor. Strobe lights caught the yellow of her patterned caftan as Cora Moon raised her arms and moved her hips, dancing through the crowd. Her large brown afro framed her thick brows and soft hazel eyes. She wasn't alone.

A pale man stepped behind her, cellphone at his ear. His white eyepatch added intrigue to his princely features. In dark slacks and a light jacket, black hair pulled back in a low ponytail. he strode with the impatience of a rush hour commuter in Manhattan. A blonde woman was at his far side.

"Is that...?" Vic said.

Lucas stepped closer and gestured for them to turn around for privacy. He huddled closer. "Brilliant detection. Yes, the flower child is here and that's her second-in-command and public relations prick, Michel de Grammont. You've stepped into the viper's den and found the head vipers."

"Awesome, let's rock and roll. Get us up there." Vic rubbed his hands.

The vampire looked between them. His eyes lingered on her. "Okay, Vic. You're my date."

"What?" Red huffed. She had been handed this case too.

"Hell yeah! I won this round of dream date." Vic pumped his fist up. "You can scope out this level and the alley. I'll let you know what the stiffs are doing upstairs."

"You're so lucky I brought flats with me. I knew I'd end up doing the dirty work." Shaking her head, she folded her arms. "I can't wait to get out of these heels and into cozy socks."

Lucas's face gained a brooding edge as he stared at her with a sad smile.

"What?" Red frowned and tilted her head at him. It was hard to focus on the case when he looked at her like that.

"Nothing. You reminded me of someone." He gestured Vic forward. "Away we go to be bored by speeches. Rah rah, unity between vampires." He walked away but glanced over his shoulder at her as if she were a mirage about to disappear.

Watching them go, she pushed her loosely curled hair out of her face to drape over the covered back of her dress. Questions about Lucas bubbled up like a witch's brew. She couldn't stop staring, but neither could he.

Who was he really? No, that was the easier question to answer. This was the doozy—why did she remember him from a dream that had already crumbled into scattered sounds and flickering visuals? For an amnesiac, she had a good memory. She remembered what she ate for lunch last Tuesday, but these dreams didn't belong to that tidy, conscious side of her brain. The dreams came from the unhelpful part of her brain that brought on panic attacks and spontaneous language fluency.

Red turned away as the two men reached the top of the stairs. she strode between the dance floor and the low padded white benches and chairs clustered to the side. Stepping to the corner of the metallic topped bar, she pulled out her phone and waited in the line. It took forever for her turn. Once at the counter, she flipped to the picture of Julia Crispin, wearing her Oxford University shirt, and held it out. "Did you see this girl?"

The Hispanic bartender in a black dress shirt and white bowtie put her hand on her hip. "Are you going to order or what? I got customers."

"I get it." Red looked for the cheapest drink she could get on the menu then ordered a glass of Portuguese wine. "I just need to know what happened to Julia."

"I already told the cops what I know. What's it to you?"

"I'm a friend. Her dad wanted me to ask around. He hasn't been able to book a flight yet from London." Red pretended to look mournful. Lying to strangers had gotten easier over the last year. Now, questioning witnesses was second nature.

"Shit, sorry." The bartender ducked her head, showing the bright green streaks in her short pixie cut. "She's been here every night since we opened last week, but outside tipping like a stingy Brit, I didn't see any more than that. She usually walked out with a daddy type. Rich white guys. But I wasn't doing more than making drinks." Eyes darting around, she said with urgent emphasis. "They were really *really* white guys."

"Say no more. Thanks." Red nodded, understanding immediately. She pulled out cash, wincing at dipping into her skinny wallet, and put the bills on the bar. The other woman hurried to help the growing line.

Alone again, she sipped the Portuguese Vino Verde. It was more than she wanted to spend, but the light bubbles made her smile, summoning up the feeling of sunshine and beaches. The mini mental vacation was quickly over as she refocused on the job at hand. She had gone over the case files. The Los Angeles Police Department had done a thorough job with questioning Julia Crispin's grad school friends, roommate, and even Delilah Byrnes at work. They had covered her days, but what about her nights?

She scanned the nightclub, trying to imagine the mindset of the vampire who bit Julia Crispin. It was a good hunting ground, but it was a terrible place to dump a body even in the alley behind it. Too many witnesses, too much political scrutiny. It was a move that only the clueless would make. Unless it was an intentional statement. An accidental meeting with an random vampire in an alley would have been quite the coincidence anyway. She walked around the perimeter of the dancefloor, trying to answer the question: who killed Julia Crispin?

Olivia Greene, the first victim, was just a regular blonde sorority girl from Orange County who had become a model. Julia, however, was raised in a Brotherhood family. She knew what bumped in the night. Fat Jake Crispin wrote in his report that his daughter went to school, modeled on weekends, and was at home by a sensible bedtime. Father might have known best, but he didn't know it all. He certainly didn't know that she had been signed specifically to DB Models.

With two floors, plenty of seating space, and a rooftop, Red couldn't imagine what could have led Julia out to the alley. She had seen smokers out on the front sidewalk, so she doubted there was a smoking area out back. It had to have been one of those 'really really white guys.'

Fat Crispin had noted that his daughter didn't do drugs, but he didn't mention that she regularly hung out in vampire clubs. The other patrons in their mix of hipster and designer fashions were rich enough to have a dealer on speed dial. Why skulk in an alley to find your brand of high when you had a trust fund?

Finding herself back at the large bar, close to a door marked employees only, Red set her wine glass on the bar.

An overly tanned man with a manbun leaned close and smiled. "A pretty lady shouldn't have an empty glass."

"I'm good." She nodded and stepped away from the bar. Goose-bumps rose on her arms when she looked over Man Bun's shoulder to the figure standing in a dark corner.

A flash of green and white strobe lights briefly illuminated a high forehead, dimpled chin, and chiseled jaw. Masculine lips curved over fine white teeth. The lights reflected off dark blonde hair.

Déjà vu hit her like an ice cube down the back of her dress. Red stepped around Man Bun, ignoring him as he opened his mouth to speak to her again. She waited for the lights in the club to shift again to reveal the man in the corner.

A stylish suit covered his broad shoulders, and—well-tailored as it was—it couldn't hide his strong-arm muscles. He held a blonde glamazon loosely, one hand on her lower back and the other brushing her hair off her shoulders before running up her neck. His fingers looked too pale against her tanned cheek.

Vampire. Red knew she should step away, but something about him... It didn't jolt a memory, but it jolted her. What was it about this town? Why did she feel like she was seeing ghosts around every corner? He was a stranger. Wasn't he? She pushed her chain purse strap higher on her shoulder, telling herself to move.

He turned his head, the easy flirtatious grin softening before his mouth gaped open. His blue eyes widened on her like a poor kid seeing unexpected presents.

She took a step back, breath catching, then disappeared into the crowd. The shiver going down her spine wasn't fear, but something about him compelled her. Was he one of those vampires with the gift to mesmerize?

"Juniper!"

She didn't turn at the shout and instead slipped behind a grinding couple on the dance floor. The club went dark as the music dropped. Lights came on in a cascade of beats.

The blond vampire appeared in front of her, hands clasped behind his back. "Miss Juniper St. James."

Biting back the startled squeak at his sudden presence, Red weighed her options. She could pretend to be a clueless human and scurry away to save her cover. That had cons too. If he thought she would be easy pickings, she didn't want to have to stake a vampire under the nose of the Supreme Master of the City. She didn't care how handsome this wannabe playboy was, she wasn't going to be intimidated. She told Vic that she was ready for the hunter's challenge. She had to prove it.

"Not cool," she said. "First off, I don't know who you are, but it's rude to pop out all vampire-like. and second, even if that was my name, I'm not a dog to be called after."

"What game are you playing?" He stepped closer, brow

furrowed, a smile quirking at the corner of his lips. His eyes darted over her face as if expecting her to evaporate.

She folded her arms. "I could ask you the same thing. Far be it from me to give you advice, but sprinting across a dance floor full of humans isn't really keeping a low profile, Mister."

"Juniper..." Blue eyes concerned, he frowned and put his cold hands on her upper arms. He stared down at his hands as if in shock to discover she was solid. "It's me, Kristoff. Kristoff Novak."

Her heart began to race. She stepped back. Why did he act like he knew her? She might have forgotten her enemies, but they could remember her. Was he one of them? He stared at her like a long-lost girlfriend. Fear tightened her stomach.

Kristoff let her retreat.

She told herself to run. Curiosity made her stay. He recognized her, but the name was all wrong. Juniper St. James... the name sounded like it belonged to a romance author. Whoever he thought she was, he needed to know who she worked for now and that she wasn't a snack. She lifted her chin. "I don't know who you think I am, but if you're Kristoff Novak, then you're one of the owners of this club, right?"

He nodded, putting his hands behind his back, lips curling into a smirk. "This is one of mine."

Red pursed her lips at the brag. He stared at her with too much interest. This was what passed for friendly banter among the undead and she wasn't here for it. Bringing more chilly professionalism into her tone, she said, "I'm here on an official joint investigation with Cora Moon and the Brotherhood of Bards and Heroes. I will need you to cooperate, Mr. Novak." She held her breath, waiting for the reaction. Powerful vampires didn't like to cooperate with hunters.

"Mr. Novak, is it?" His smirk grew wider, accentuating the dimples in his chin and left cheek. "You have my full cooperation. Ms...?"

Covering her surprise, she ignored the question and held out her phone, showing him Julia's picture. "Did you see this woman here last night?"

He raised an eyebrow. "Sure, she was here. But she left alive, as I would be happy to show you if the cops hadn't taken our security footage. My brother and I run a tight operation. None of ours would be so stupid to break Cora's laws, especially not when they'd have to answer to me first."

She returned her phone to her purse. "You don't have a soul, do you?"

"No, but I have a brain." He shrugged. "Arno and I have opened a new club. We don't need the heat."

Red snorted. "Oh, so you're the brother who likes gingers?"

His grin turned flirtatious. "You would know, Juniper."

She didn't like the familiarity in his voice. She had intended to ask him more about Julia, but curiosity gnawed at her. "Why are you calling me that? My name's Red."

"It's impossible, but you look..." Kristoff leaned forward to sniff at her neck. His lips hovered over her skin. "You even smell..."

Instinctive fear bolted up. Red jumped back from him. "Hey! Personal space, dude." She pulled a blessed silver cross out of her purse to shake it at him. Crosses might have been hit or miss for her faith level, but blessed silver made any vampire think twice. "Ugh, I'm not a cupcake to nibble on."

"No, you're more like a macaron." Kristoff smirked and snapped his head to the side, looking across the dance floor. The flirty manner popped like a bubble. His irises flashed amber. The tips of his fangs poked out under his upper lip.

Lucas stomped through the dancers toward them. The strobe lights reflected off his patched leather jacket and ripped jeans. The dark hair dipping over his gray eyes didn't hide the demonic yellow flicking in the depths.

"Has he claimed you?" Kristoff asked, his voice raw with urgency.

"What is it with vamps?" She snorted and shook her head. "I'm under the protection of the Supreme Master. No one is claiming me."

"Red, you need to step away from this soulless tosser." Lucas glared at the other vampire, his gritted jaw highlighting his high cheekbones. He jammed his hands in his pockets as if to stop himself from throwing a punch.

"How long were you going to keep her a secret?" Kristoff's tone turned to a growl.

"So, not friends?" She sighed and glanced around. Instinctively, the other humans had given them a wide berth even on the packed dancefloor. People were good at hand waving away the supernatural but there were limits. How big a scene were the two going to make? She didn't need a rescue, especially not from a vamp that already thought she couldn't handle herself. Lucas was supposed to be minding Vic at the private party upstairs, not agitating her witness. If expressions could talk, Kristoff's would be cursing. She rubbed her left temple. "I'm in the middle of questioning him."

"Novak thinks you're someone you're not," Lucas said. Worry battled with anger in his gray eyes. "You're in danger, even if he seems...domesticated. He will play the friend before he stabs you in the back. It's what he does."

"Your soul doesn't change what you've done." Kristoff sneered. "Don't act like you're better than me."

"I don't need to act." Lips pursed in grim amusement, Lucas held his hand out to her.

The club went dark again as the music rose to a frantic beat.

Red found herself pulled against a hard chest. Her head tilted to the side as fangs dug into her neck. She gasped, but she couldn't scream, and her arms went limp. She had fought vampires before, even had one or two dig their fangs into her, sending enough venom into her system to bring her into a numbed thrall. Nothing felt like the wave of pleasure that radiated from this bite. She panted, trying to tell herself that her trembles were struggles against the firm arms. It happened in seconds, even if time felt slower in his arms.

The lights came on.

She snapped her gaze to the vampire's head buried in her neck. Her eyes widened as her skipping heartbeat dropped. It was Kristoff.

Fangs retracting, the vampire licked at the bite, his arm around her waist. His biceps tensed as if ready to pull her away from the crowd for round two. Kristoff turned her chin to meet her gaze, smirking. He knew exactly how his bite felt. "Mmmmm, Red, you're delicious... *and mine.*"

Cringing, Red pulled away from the bloody tongue on her neck as reality set in. The ecstasy in the thrall ebbed away like low tide. "Wait a second!"

His chilly fingers brushed her cheek as he grinned, a mix of relief and elation in his blue eyes contrasting with the blood on his lips. "I claim you with this bite."

"Bastard!" She jerked away. After Oklahoma, she'd thought she'd learned to never trust a vampire without a soul. It only ended with fangs in your neck. Her head spun as the eerie pleasure fully evaporated.

Red winced at the pain in her neck. It didn't hurt as much as the anger and humiliation of being so stupid, caught by a vamp on a hunt. She wanted to be taken seriously by the others and now she was the damsel in distress. Stomping on Kristoff's foot, she angled an elbow to slam into his nose and stumbled away on her stupid heels.

"You can thank me later," Kristoff said.

"Doubt it." Pressing on her wound and backing up to Lucas, she flipped the other vamp off. "The Supreme will hear about this."

Amber in his eyes, Kristoff wiped off his chin with his thumb like an animal in a tailored suit. He brought the digit to his mouth, staring at her. "Tastes like strawberries."

"Bugger the Black Veil." Lucas rushed forward. He grabbed the other vampire by the collar and clocked him across the face. "You won't get this close again."

Kristoff headbutted him before raising his fist. "Give me time. She'll want me close. Juniper did."

Lucas growled before tackling the taller blond vampire around the middle and bringing him down to the floor.

The club went dark again, and the frantic techno music grew louder.

The loud, dark chamber was too big and loud for even a vampire fight to draw much attention from the rest of the humans. Red could still hear the growls, hisses, and thump of fist on flesh. Warm blood dripped under her hand from her neck, she fished out some tissues to press on the bite with the other. She stepped away from the fighting vampires, to blend into the few startled, tipsy club-goers gawking at the fight.

She thumbed out a quick text to Vic. The dim light of her phone screen caught Kristoff and Lucas rolling on the ground in the curling smoke of the club's fog machines. Pain made tears come to her eyes. She gritted her teeth. Fucking vampires...Fat Crispin was going to get an earful about this deal with Cora. She wanted to investigate a crime scene, not start a fight at an undead UN party.

Arno Novak ran from the front of the club, yelling into his Bluetooth earpiece before pulling it out to throw at his large bouncer. The vampire in the white eyepatch and black ponytail came down the stairs from the VIP party. He got there first.

Shit. Red ducked behind a chick in a big black hat when the strobe lights came back on. She tried to stay out of view of the vampires as she eavesdropped.

"Boys, boys..." Michel de Grammont, the Supreme Master's right hand, stood with his arms spread between Lucas on one side and Kristoff and Arno on the other. His white eyepatch was purple in the blacklights. "Such behavior at this historic event. Miss Cora has brought the cream of the Alliance to our fair city to marvel on how we've managed to integrate between souled and not—dove and bloodliner, all while maintaining the Dark Veil. We are on the world stage, and you fucking monkeys are taking a shit on it."

The brothers exchanged a glance. Kristoff dipped his head. "He challenged my claim on a human. I reacted. Apologies."

Lucas gritted his teeth and cracked his neck, rolling his eyes.

"*Je m'en fous!*" Michel spat out, clearly not giving a shit as he straightened his lapels. "I expect more from the Novaks, since the Master of Portland speaks so highly of you two. You're a diplomat, Kristoff, act like it." He turned his glare to Lucas. "And you. Get the fuck out before you draw any more attention. If Cora hears that you were challenging a claim...you know the rules. You're lucky Delilah has me wrapped around her finger, or I'd bring you to the supreme myself. Test me, and I will."

Lucas glared at Kristoff and turned away. "Already gone, mate."

Hiding behind some clubbers, Red walked to the elevator, clutching the bleeding mark on her neck. She grimaced at each bump of an elbow or a shaking booty.

Lucas caught up and reached out to stop her before he stilled himself. He handed her a black bandana instead. "How's the bite, kitten?"

"Doesn't feel great. Let's get out of here." She took the cloth and pressed it over the tissues on her wound before walking into the open elevator and hitting the button for the ground floor.

The marks hurt but they weren't deep. Kristoff Novak had fucking nibbled on her. If he wanted, he could've ripped her throat out while Lucas watched. She recognized the name from her research on the club, but she hadn't planned on questioning him. Even when she imagined the scenario, she hadn't expected anything more than the usual vampire deflecting banter. Maybe some threats. Not whatever the hell that was.

Curiosity had had her chatting with him like a teeny bopper expecting sparkles instead of fangs. After a year of hunting, she should've known better. She was pissed at Kristoff but also herself. She had stuck her hand in the lion cage and was surprised she got bit. How could she be so stupid? These were the kind of mistakes that would keep her out of the Brotherhood. Vic taught her that you kept out of a vampire's sight until you were fixing to kill them.

Now, she had new marks on her neck. And a question that wouldn't go away. Who was Juniper St. James?

"Your chest is covered in it, kit—er, Red." Lucas distracted her as he pulled off his jacket and put it around her.

"Thanks. I definitely can't return this dress now." The smell of leather and sandalwood enveloping her, Red tipped her head down as they approach the front entrance. The bouncer came into view. She glared at him as she stomped forward. The feel of eyes on her back made her look over her shoulder as she walked onto the sidewalk.

"Red." Kristoff called out from behind her. His voice said her name slowly, as if to roll the word over his tongue to taste it. "Lucas was the one who was kicked out. You should stay."

"Fat chance." She glared at him.

"Doesn't matter. I can always find what I claim." Kristoff smirked. His suit jacket had disappeared in the scuffle, leaving only his slacks and gray shirt, ripped at the neck, revealing some of his toned chest. Blue eyes raked over her body before softening on her face.

"That's a myth." She stormed past Lucas down the sidewalk.

Kristoff Novak wasn't the first to have tried that on her. If they could always find their claimed humans, then wouldn't the mysterious vampire who had roughed her up outside Eugene have found her already? She might not remember what had been done to her, but she didn't need to be claimed again and find out what she had missed.

Lucas smirked and held up his hands. "Lady made her choice, Novak."

The vampire crossed his arms, his keen gaze following her. "She doesn't know what she's choosing."

6

**OCTOBER 25TH, Night, Alley behind Club Vltava off
Sunset Strip in Los Angeles, California, USA**

Red held her tongue until they had some distance from Club Vltava.
She was trying to solve a murder, not become a victim herself.

Lucas had behaved like the real action was up in the Blood
Alliance mixer held on the second level of the club. Did he suspect
who would be there? He should have warned her that a vampire, who
he obviously knew, could be gunning for her.

"What was that back there?" she asked. "Who the hell is Kristoff
Novak?"

"A damn twat who thought diplomatic immunity would stop me
from kicking his ass."

"Turn down the testosterone, Lucas." Red winced at her still
throbbing bite mark. Novak played host to the Summit party, owned
a building on Sunset Strip, and could bite her then get a slap on the
wrist for it. It was enough to calculate how far she had swum down
shit's creek. "Who does he think I am?"

"You live long enough, you see some faces again. Never thought

I'd see hers. Not when she died over a hundred years ago." Lucas looked away as if the sight of her hurt him.

"Juniper St. James." Red furrowed her brow, and the realization hit her like a shovel to the face. She didn't know how she felt about being a doppelgänger. Or the fact that more and more vampires seemed to recognize her in Los Angeles. It's not like she hadn't noticed. Now, she knew why. "Is that why you and Quinn have been acting weird? I look like someone you two knew back in the day?" She shook her head. "Why didn't you tell me? Or at least tell Vic? He's sensitive and took all the cold shoulder personally."

"Because that sounds insane. 'Hey stranger, you look like my dead girlfriend. Kristoff always had a thing for her so stay out of LA until he leaves.'" He chuckled, then grew serious. "Seeing your face... It brought up a lot of memories."

"Bad ending?" She looked down, wanting to wince at her words. Of course, it was. Two feuding men and one dead woman wasn't the sign of a happy ending. How could something between a vampire and a human end well?

"Something like that."

"I'm sorry. You cared for her. That was callous to say."

"I loved her as much as I could without a soul. Not nearly enough. Fair warning, I'm the original bad boyfriend." Lucas put his hands in his pockets. "She was nice like you are."

"I'm not fucking nice." Red crossed her arms before looking down and stepping aside to avoid stomping on a praying mantis strolling down the sidewalk.

"You're a little Billy Badass." He shook his head to hide a smile, then his face fell. "Let me see that bite."

"I think I have had enough vampires in my face." Sassing through the pain, she pressed harder on her neck wound.

Lucas arched an eyebrow. "I have good eyesight. I don't need to loom over you."

Red pulled back the jacket and the black bandana to reveal the two fang marks on her neck. The bleeding seemed to have mostly stopped. Weird. The bite must have been super shallow. She mopped up the drying blood. "Hurts, but I'll live. As a claimed human. It's a territory thing, I know. I'm like a hydrant that he only peed on so you couldn't."

"That's one way of describing it." He shrugged. "Might not be far off. The bastard didn't waste any time, that's for sure."

"What does that even mean in a city like this?" She wasn't a scholar of vampire society, but she knew enough of the rules, and when vampires set rules, they could always break them.

The Blood Alliance was the ultimate vampire authority, but each supreme master ran their city differently and interpreted the Dark Veil policy in their own special way. Older than the Blood Alliance, it was the agreement made by the entire supernatural community to stay hidden from humans. Each supernatural community enforced in it even in towns not ruled by vampires. In Oklahoma City, the Dark Veil was upheld by leaving no witnesses.

Vic and Red had barely gotten out of OKC alive.

Los Angeles had the most souled vampires in the West. A catch and release rule would have gotten supremes ripped off their thrones in other cities. Where did that leave claimed humans in this land of the cuddly vampires? She had already learned that Cora didn't have the out-of-towners under the same control as her own people.

Red hugged an arm to herself. "You know him. How fast should I be running?"

"He can't turn you in LA county. Even if you didn't have Vic and the Brotherhood behind you, Cora keeps tight control on our numbers." He said the last sentence as if to remind himself.

"No, but he can put me in a car and take me up to Portland. I'm not so naïve to think that the supreme wouldn't let him if it helped her agenda." She tied the bandana tight to her neck and shivered before giving him back his coat. "I got blood on your coat. I made it more punk. You're welcome." She sighed and started walking down the sidewalk to the opening of the alley behind Club Vltava.

"Where are you going?"

Red didn't look back. "I might as well do my job. Between all the macho brawling, I didn't get to do much sleuthing. Give Vic a text and tell him to bring the van around."

Fighting monsters, solving crimes, that was something she could focus on. This doppelgänger business only made her head hurt, while thinking of Kristoff's claim chilled her. She was still annoyed with herself. Why had she let down her guard?

She pulled off her heels one at a time as she walked, putting them in her purse before jamming the flats on her feet, mentally cursing herself for listening to Vic. Her ankle tendons stretched in painful relief to be on flat feet. As she walked down the alley, lights came on from hidden sensors. Club Vltava took up the corner of the block with three back exits and a closed garage door to the alley. She was impressed by how clean and well-lit it was. Kristoff might not have been able to keep the dead bodies off his doorstep, but he certainly took out the trash.

Red pointed at the cracked surveillance cameras above the doors. "Someone's taken out the cameras." She squinted. Had the murderer taken notes at the Blood Summit workshop? "Looks like they threw a rock at the lens of each one. That wasn't in the police report."

She stepped under the police tape and looked for where Julia had been found. In the crime scene photos, the woman huddled in a corner made by the fence and dumpster. One arm stretched out towards the bottom of the dumpster as if she had died trying to lift herself up.

Red crouched by the spot. Partly to see better, and partly to stretch her hamstrings. Julia had been found with her face looking toward the club. Tilting her head, she tried to focus on what Julia had seen.

"You should be getting a plaster on that wound," Lucas murmured behind her.

"If you had finished draining someone, would you just drop them?" She asked over her shoulder.

"Not my game anymore." Lowered face in shadow, he put his hands in his pockets.

"Hmmm, but if you did now..."

"I wouldn't leave them near the rubbish." He said, his voice low.

"I'm doing a bit of pop psychology to guess if it was a souled vampire or not." Red looked over at the dumpster and the alley floor. The crime photos Fat Crispin had sent rose in her mind. Julia had been bruised on her face and hands, but her wounds were defensive, not from extended torment. The Bard's Daughter had fought to the end. Red flipped to the crime photos on her phone gallery, stood, and handed him the phone. "What do you think?"

Lucas took it, fingers avoiding hers, and looked down. He tapped to the next. "A rush job. Looks like a quick feed and dash."

"Except they had enough time to take the cameras out." She looked at him with her phone. Her eyes bludged out as his thumb swiped further back in the gallery. She lifted frantic hands, waving them in warning. "Hey, no more peeping."

"How'd you find this? It was lost." Lucas gulped, staring down at her phone. The torn sketch of the blindfolded woman that she had found in Quinn's safe stared back. He handed it to her.

"Then I guess I found it. It was on the floor when those guys did the smash and grab at the office. I noticed the creepy weird resemblance. It's her, isn't it?" Red filed away his shocked expression. Vic had thought she was losing it when she brought up the sketch. Hell, she thought she was losing it. The weird glances, the sketch, the odd familiarity in Lucas' aura—it was all becoming clear.

"It's Juniper." He turned away to hide eyes troubled with memories. He put a hand in his pocket, rocking back on his heels, before he turned around. Steadying himself on the dumpster with a thud, his fingers dented the metal. "That should have stayed lost."

"You might want to ask Quinn how it ended up in his safe." She mentally added *and then tell me*.

His head perked up. "Do you have it? The full sketch?"

"No, I just saw that one piece and put it back in the album it fell out of."

Headlights flooded the alley. A breeze pushed an old Styrofoam cup out from under the dumpster.

Red put her phone in her purse and looked over her

shoulder to see the Millennium Falcon before she looked back to Lucas. They were strangers who had met before. She had met him in barely remembered dreams, and he had loved a woman with her face. What did that leave them? She shifted her feet. "I'm guessing that this sketch is from your bad no-soul days."

"I wasn't just bad; I was the worst. And I taught Kristoff everything I knew."

"I'll keep that in mind about the both of you." She put her hand on her hip, trying to strike a pose that was something other than creeped out. A claim mark on her neck felt as terrifying as the idea that she was a double for a dead woman. "Let's do what we came here for."

She refocused on the alley. The crime scene techs had picked it clean, but the breeze and Lucas's bear grip on the dumpster had freed trapped trash from underneath it. A glimmer reflected in the dirt and wrappers on the ground. "Hey, can you move that?"

He nodded and pushed the large container aside like a human man would move a cardboard box.

Vic hopped out of the van. "Come on, idjits. Stop playing with trash."

Lucas stepped toward him. "Took you long enough."

"I had to get out of a paid parking garage."

Red let the bickering roll over her as she walked over to the dumpster and pushed her foot around to move the few pieces of litter. She bent over and picked up a small circle of old gold—half of a locket. She turned it over to see a small sepia portrait of a petite blonde with wide-set eyes and a coy smile.

"Vic, get the first aid kit ready. I'll join you in the van in a second," she said slowly, studying the pretty face captured in the faded daguerreotype.

Vic gave her a look that said they were talking later.

Red walked over to Lucas. "Do you only see her when you look at me?"

"I'm trying not to." He cocked his head. His brows drew together, his mouth soft as his gaze seemed to memorize her. As if she would fade like a ghost.

"What happened to her, to you?" The question burst out before she could stop herself.

His face darkened, old fury held tight even after lifetimes. "Hunters were after us. I got a soul then Kristoff left her to die to save his own ass."

Red blinked, and the vampire was gone, leaving her alone with her long shadow cast in the van's headlights. She looked down at the locket half and brought it close to her chest. She wasn't thinking about the woman in the locket, she was thinking of another woman from the past.

Juniper. Her doppelgänger.

Who was this woman who had captured the hearts of two master vampires and held them even a century after she died?

7

Vic drove, his fingers clenched on the wheel, listening to her story in silence as they breezed through the night traffic. Pulling into the motel parking lot, he glanced at Red. "We can't stay here tonight."

She wasn't surprised. They traveled light in case they needed to make a quick getaway. The Bards could do a lot, but they couldn't force Cora to go against an ally like the Prince of Portland over an unofficial intern who hadn't taken the hunter's challenge yet to join the Brotherhood. She got out of the van. "We can't keep driving on the donut."

They moved quickly into their motel room. Red changed out of her club clothes in the bathroom, wiping the blood off her skin, surprised to see the fang marks already scabbing up. She tossed the bloody green cocktail dress into the lined waste bin and stepped out of the bathroom to find him stripping the linens off the beds.

Vic poured some beer onto the blankets and sheets on the floor to ensure they were laundered. They worked together to make sure to clean all the trash and stray hair, and wipe down their fingerprints before they carried the small plastic waste bag into the van to burn the contents later. Scents, prints, blood, all could be used to track them either magically or the old-fashioned human way. These were the first things he had taught her: fake names, no traces, keep moving.

"You're freaking me out, Vic. You're not talking."

"I'm thinking." He put the van in gear and sped out of the parking lot, turning right. "We can't stay in LA. Quinn pulled us into some deep shit and didn't give me any warning."

"Agreed," she said, trying to find the balance between sensitivity and 'I told you so.'

Vic shook his head and pounded the steering wheel. "He could have mentioned you're a dead ringer for a long dead girl. I would've never taken you to that club if I knew. This is fucked up. Vampires don't just claim humans and defy a supreme master for kicks. If there's bad blood between Novak and Lucas, you're right in the middle of it now."

He had no idea. Red had been stuck between the bad vibes. "You didn't see the fight. It isn't just bad blood. It's some serious hate. I stumbled into old love triangle drama."

"You don't want to be the chew toy stuck between those dogs. Lucas can be a dick, but he has a soul. I don't know Novak, but he's got you in his sights."

She glanced around the nondescript boulevard of billboards and one-story shops. Everywhere in LA still looked the same to her. Even the neighborhoods where they warned you not to have a flat tire looked similar, just with more graffiti and pawn shops. "Where are we going?"

"To get some answers. I've lost one partner on a hunt. I'm not losing another." Vic gritted his teeth as he took the off-ramp toward Culver City. The van skittered across the lanes of traffic. He put "All Along the Watchtower" by Jimi Hendrix on the stereo.

She held on to the 'oh shit' handle above the passenger side door. She knew better than to argue with Vic Park Constantine when he was on a mission. After a barely legal race to through the LA streets and parking crookedly across two spaces, he stomped into Quinn Investigations.

She followed him into the office. It looked mostly clean after the robbery beyond the stacks of files on the small couch and coffee table. The large window had been repaired. Blue painter's tape still clung to the frame.

Quinn sat behind the large desk with two stacks of files in front of him and a filing cabinet pulled close to his rolling chair. Fluorescent lights washed out his blond hair. He stood, pushing the folders aside, his handsome face nearly blank except for a nervous furrow to his brow. "Hey."

"Hey...? That's all I get, after tonight?" Vic snorted, tossing his hands up before tucking them peevishly under his armpits. "Come on, Q."

"Who do I look like to you?" Red put her hands on her hips. She tilted her head to better show the white bandage on her neck next to the strap of her black tank top. "Because to Kristoff Novak, I look like a long-dead Victorian snack. Guess who got claimed tonight? Hint: it wasn't Vic."

Quinn's eyes widened.

"I didn't even get anyone's phone number." Vic groused, but then his lips thinned, and he shook his head. "Dude, you could have given us a heads up! Lucas fought Novak off, but I could have been down an intern tonight."

"Where did he find you? At the beach working the Greene case?" Quinn asked, confusion pressing his eyebrows together.

"No," Red said, lifting a correcting finger and jutting her hip out. "We got word of another victim from the Brotherhood—a Bard's daughter who was dumped behind Club Vltava. Looked like the same MO, from the bite marks to the ouroboros carved into them."

Quinn crossed his arms. "What happened with keeping me in the loop?"

"Don't play that card, hombre," Vic said, tersely setting his chin. "We'll ignore the red-haired mystery in the room for a moment." He counted off the points with his fingers. "One, did you know that Olivia Greene had a snake eating its tail scratched on her? Because you didn't tell us. That's the Alaric Order symbol—of which, you may recall, Delilah was once a member. You too. Does a scary vampire society ring any bells?"

Quinn nodded, shoulders drooping and arms dropping to his sides.

"Two, you would have known if you just let us crash in your pad. How many times have I passed out on your couch? Which I guess leads me to my last damn point: you didn't tell me about this doppelgänger bullshit! I get not telling her because it's freaky, but me?" Vic pointed at himself. "I was the Robin to your Batman."

"He's really the one who's suffered the most." She rolled her eyes.

Quinn sighed and sat on the corner of his desk. He rubbed his knuckles absently on his white V-neck shirt. "You're right. Not about Vic." He furrowed his brow. "But the other points."

She stepped forward, not ready to ease up on the vampire. "Lucas was less cryptic than before, but I only got that I look like his dead ex-girlfriend, and Kristoff is bad news. I don't know what the hell is going on. It feels like I'm being dumped blindly into some Downton Abbey drama."

"I thought I was imagining it when you walked in. I haven't seen a picture of her in a lifetime. The resemblance is uncanny." Quinn shook his head. "I was going to find an excuse to send you away before anyone else could see you."

"Well, I've been seen, but I don't know what they see." Red gestured to her face. Being a woman of mystery had been an asset before on jobs, no one could blow your cover if no one knew you. Now, she had to worry about mistaken identity. Would it end with Kristoff Novak biting her again?

Quinn sighed. "They see a vampire's courtesan."

"What is this, Undead Pretty Woman?" Vic quipped.

She rolled her eyes at him, then glowered at Quinn. "Who is Juniper St. James? Because that name came up a lot tonight."

"That wasn't her real name. Just what we gave her." He rubbed his knuckles on his chest like a nervous tick. "I never learned her real one." The sentence came out like a guilty confession.

"Go on." Red rolled her fingers for him to continue. She tried to hide her disquiet under the veil of professionalism, feeling Vic watching her.

"It's an old story. I'm a villain in it, don't mistake me." Quinn furrowed his brow. "She was part of the family, but we were more like the Manson Family than the Brady Bunch." He looked Red in the eye, his brown eyes filled with guilt, self-loathing, and sorrow. Enough to make her want to take a step back. "Juniper St. James was an accomplished woman despite everything."

"Everything?" Red crossed her arms. Were vampires incapable of spitting out a story? "Which means?"

"Everything we did to her," Quinn said. "Juniper was Lucas's paramour, but she essentially functioned as the human servant to the four of us. My filing didn't look like this when she was my secretary." He looked around the office before his brown eyes flicked back to Red. "She played nursemaid to Selene, ran errands for Delilah. Domestic toils punctuated by mayhem and murder in a glittering cage."

"Yeah, so she was there for the golden years of the Bloody Byrnes when the fanged four was in their groove. Where does Novak come in?" Vic asked.

"Lucas turned Kristoff," Quinn said quietly.

Her teeth snapped shut as the words died on her tongue. She glanced at Vic, happy to see that he looked as stunned as she did. It was hard to imagine the vampire who looked like he was ready for a mosh pit had sired a guy who acted like *The Wolf of Wall Street* was about him.

"How come no one told me this story?" He groused.

"I thought the sire bond... well, bonded you more?" She asked. "That fight wasn't family roughhousing. It was just rough."

Quinn shrugged. "It's complicated. Lucas was never an attentive sire. He wanted a servant, not a true childe."

"Let me get this family tree straight." She crossed her arms over her chest like a referee calling for a time out. "Delilah turned you, you turned Selene, she turned Lucas, and Lucas turned Kristoff. So, Kristoff is like your great-grandson?"

"Don't put it like that..." Quinn shaded his eyes with his hand as if blocking the implication then nodded. "But, essentially yes. Bored in Prague, Lucas turned him. I played my own part in that too. I considered myself a master of discord, but even I couldn't have predicted what was to come. Kristoff was obsessed with Juniper. It doesn't matter that you aren't her, that you're a genetic coincidence. Nostalgia isn't just for humans."

"How do I get unclaimed? Kill him, right? That's what I did to the King of the Prairie Dead." Red looked at Vic, but Kristoff Novak's face rose in her mind. Her neck throbbed in remembrance even as her stomach clenched at the memory of the strange pleasure in his bite. She wasn't falling for that new vampire trick.

Vic gestured to his neck. "Killing him would break the claim. Another vampire challenging him and defeating him in formal combat would do it too. All else fails, we run and get the marks lasered off you later."

"What does he have up his sleeve? Any Gifts?" She asked, letting the part about the seductive bite go unsaid. All vampires had super speed, strength, and fangs that could induce a thrall with the perks of immortality as a tradeoff for having to drink blood and avoid direct sunlight. A few had gifts like crawling on ceilings, turning into mist, entering homes without permission, and others. "He's rich, but that isn't a superpower."

"It is for Batman." Vic wagged a finger at Red. "We can take him down."

Quinn shook his head, brow furrowing. "You can't kill him without getting on Cora's bad side. Kristoff is campaigning for her policies among the Bloodliners. His club is hosting half the events of the summit. He's stronger than he should be at a hundred and eighteen and has his own crew of minions."

She stepped away and rubbed her arms. "You're making it sound like I'm already vampire chow."

"Hey, Goonies never say die." Vic said, lightly punching her shoulder.

"Kristoff can only buck the rules so much. Vampires don't have diplomatic immunity." Quinn tilted his head, a slight wince to his mouth as his brown eyes narrowed. "Theoretically."

"The Brotherhood made sure we were sanctioned by Cora," Red insisted. "That must count for something. Then the fight got broken up by the French pirate-looking guy, so he's already had his warning, right?"

"Michel?" Quinn's expression darkened at the name. "Did he see you?"

"No, I don't think so. I tried to stay out of the action, blend in with the crowd. He was more focused on stopping the fight."

"I was upstairs. I don't even know how Lucas got down there so fast. Or how he knew. Did he hear?" Vic snapped his fingers. "That explains something. When I asked him what his favorite TV show was, he said Juniper and disappeared. I was thinking it was a new Netflix show."

Goosebumps rose on her arms as she remembered Lucas's gray eyes, dark history in his gaze, honed over lifetimes, directed straight at his progeny. "He looked so intense when Kristoff grabbed me."

Quinn shook his head. "The soul has tempered him, but that instinct to defend is still there. Juniper was his claimed human once upon a time."

Red turned away from him to stiffen her wobbling chin. It all felt like too much. She felt her life hanging in the delicate balance of vampire politics. "I'm not her. I might not know who I am, but I know what I'm not."

"Damn it, Quinn, you should have fucking told me all this. I would have sent her to Colorado to hide out with my buddy Stan." Vic banged his fist against his palm. "This whole case is tied up in your twisted undead family, and you can't drop a clue, so I don't take her into it? We have a vampire going all serial killer on some models. One of the suspects wants to make my intern his undead bride, and the other is your ex-wife."

"I know." Quinn's shoulders slumped.

Vic laid out his demands. "I'm taking that badass California king in your room. Red's taking the guest room, and you're putting that hulk body on the sofa."

Eyes downcast, Quinn gestured to the closed door to his private office. "I'll give you the tour."

"I'll get the bags," Vic said, flashing Red a grin.

Red couldn't share his joy, too full of dread. She followed Quinn into his small private office then through the unmarked entrance into his basement apartment. Wooden boards creaked under her feet as they stepped down the rail-less stairs. Exposed brick walls gave the place a cave-like ambiance. The open floorplan put the small quilt-covered leather sofa and leather chair next to a tiny butcher block island counter separating the space from the kitchenette countertops.

"There is only so much apartment to show you." Quinn pointed to the three doors off the main living area. "My room, bathroom, second room."

"Is it okay to have me here?" She asked, toeing the ground with her sneakered foot.

"I need to prepare the beds." He turned to his room, leaving her to fidget in the kitchen.

Vic had ordered delivery when he'd gone to get their backpacks. Soon after, the pizza man brought them cheesy pepperoni good-ness. Quinn slipped away after leaving the food. The humans devoured the pizza in silence, huddled over the island counter in the kitchen, more like hyenas hovering over an antelope. The weight of the evening pressed on her shoulders. She might have wondered if she were possibly bisexual, but she hadn't spent this long thinking about a woman in months. Juniper St. James was the reason Red was in this mess. She scowled.

"This is fucking weird," Vic said around a mouthful of pizza. His eyes widened as he swallowed.

"Ugh, I can see your food." She laughed and shook her head. "And yeah, this is Twilight Zone meets Vampire Diaries right now."

"Are you going to be okay? This trigger...um, anything?" He asked, gripping his empty beer bottle tighter as he shifted on his feet. He was the guy in the chatroom who mocked trigger warnings, but he had seen her panic attacks.

Red smiled through her fatigue. "I'm fine. We've been through worse with fewer allies."

Vic stretched and yawned. "Good. I am claiming the shower first."

"Shoo then!" She shook her head, waving him on. He had been going on about the shower since before they left Reno.

After putting the empty pizza box by the trash can, she heated herself a mug of water in Quinn's microwave. The vampire didn't seem to have much beyond glass jars and bags of blood in the fridge and loose tea in the cupboard, so she made do with some chamomile.

She pulled out the small black traveler's journal that Vic had given her after their first hunt. He'd made it clear that it was a journal and not a diary. He said that every Bard kept field notes. She knew that he still treasured his adopted father's journals. At first, she hadn't done more than put short bullet point notes of the monsters they had encountered, but she had started to write more. Each entry seemed to get longer than the last. She was almost running out of space in this one. Tonight's entry would be a doozy.

She had been searching for her real life for months; she had found someone else's instead.

Writing, she didn't hear the door open. She looked up at Quinn. "Oh, hey, you probably want to sleep."

"I'm a night owl." His eyes were as wide as one. He hunched over, trying to take up less space, futile for a man over six feet tall and broad-shouldered to boot.

"Of course. I can get out of your hair anyway." Red had been suspicious of him before but she kinda got it now. He was as wigged out as she had been. She noticed him looking at the fridge. "Hey, it's your kitchen, you can drink in front of me. You only have mugs, so it's not going to look that different from mine." She raised her lukewarm tea.

He nodded and went to the fridge, using his back to block her view of him grabbing two jars of blood to mix and pour into a mug he put in the microwave. "Animal blood," He said nervously over his shoulder.

"Do you mix them for flavor?" She closed her notebook and tilted her head. "Like three parts cow, one part chicken?"

"Modern chickens don't taste good." Quinn frowned as he crossed and uncrossed his arms before holding them to the side.

"Is free range goat where it's at?" Red smiled, trying to make a joke. She could almost hear it crash and burn as his expression grew more remote.

The microwave dinged and he turned to pull out the mug. He sipped it, looking away from her.

"Is it uncomfortable to have me here?" She bowed her head. "You can be honest."

"You're a reminder of what I have to atone for." Quinn gazed at her as if forcing himself to not look away.

She bit the inside of her cheek as she struggled for the right words to say in the face of such deep guilt. "Vic said you were a vampire on a mission for redemption."

"Redemption..." He shook his head. "Vic talks a lot."

"He does. He made it sound like Lucas did too, but I can't get much out of him. You're more talkative." She sipped her tea, trying to seem calm. Her curiosity tugged at her like an unruly monkey.

"I've never heard that before."

"Please, tell me something. I need to know. I could've died tonight." She hated the pleading note in her tone. "Whoever Juniper was, she still has enough pull to make two vampires defy a supreme master."

"If seeing you brought up memories of old sins and dark nights for me, I can't imagine what Lucas sees." Quinn's reserved expression grew more contemplative. "He doted on her. I used to mock him for it when he would bring her books and chocolates. Without a soul, I was incapable of such caring, so I saw it as weakness. He could love, even before, but love becomes twisted without a conscience. He would kill for her—and did. When she was nearly burned at the stake by witch hunters in Prague, Lucas ripped through them. Seeing your face... If I have guilt, he has that and more."

Her mouth gaping open, Red didn't know what question to ask first. Juniper was a witch? Could she have been a part of the mysterious line of witches that Red's mother had supposedly been a part of? What was her real name? How long was she an item with Lucas? What the hell had happened in Prague that had brought her to London in 1900 to die when the Byrnes were cursed with souls?

She sputtered out, "Tell me more about her."

Vic opened the bathroom door, releasing a cloud of steam, and stuck his head out. His black mullet was toweled off and sticking up every which way. "I'll miss that water pressure when we leave."

Red scowled. He had the worst timing.

Quinn nodded to her before he disappeared up the stairs, brooding gaze lingering on the blood in his mug. He walked like Atlas with the weight of the world resting on his shoulders.

"What's his deal?" Vic stepped out, gripping the wide black towel wrapped around his waist.

She groaned in annoyance. "I can already tell there isn't going to be much hot water left."

"What's your deal?"

"You can run the dishes when I'm done." She put her empty mug in the small dishwasher then headed into shower and tried to wash the lingering blood residue off. Shielding the scabbed-over fang marks on her neck with her hand, she sighed under the hot water as she leaned against the white tiles. Her thoughts raced. Breathing deep, she tried to calm her shallow breathing.

In the action with a case in front of her, Red kept her head. That calm eroded once the quiet set in, and she could let down her guard.

The moment when she wasn't going to die was when she felt like she was. Delayed terror made her shake.

The panic attacks hadn't started until she had been out of the Eugene hospital for a few weeks. She fooled herself into thinking she'd managed to hide them for a few more. Like a smothering wave, the panic pressed down on her once the job was over.

Vic was the one that made her get help. Uninsured and paperless, she found it in a moldy Unitarian church basement in Colorado for a few group sessions until a job took them back on the road. They taught her to focus on the little details when she couldn't control her racing thoughts on everything from her research to-dos, fixing a busted light on the Falcon, and vampires A-Z.

She opened her eyes to spy Quinn's surprisingly upscale and unscented shampoo and conditioner. Breathing now steady, she focused on the bottle until her thoughts slowed.

His face wash had a Korean label and felt like a dream to rub on. This was a vampire that cared about his skincare regimen. Quinn might have a soul and live in a basement apartment, but his inner Libertine still appreciated some of the finer things. She had gone from dodging vampires in the West to borrowing toiletries from one. It didn't end at face wash. Her neck proved that.

Red had been warned in Reno. Then again at the Pump House bar. The vampires in the City of Angels walked quietly in the world of man. Let them have their meetings, everyone agreed, there were other monsters to fight. Coming to Los Angeles right now was asking for trouble. Now, she was claimed by one of them.

Her first mistake was thinking that a vampire would obey his kind's rules. Kristoff owned the club; he could manipulate the lighting and music to cover up any breach of the Dark Veil. He was from Portland; he could flee Cora's jurisdiction. The cards were in his hands. She had met the spider in his web, and this spider had waited a long time for a fly like her.

The pieces were coming together, but everyone, including Vic, seemed to know more about the players in this drama than she did. If someone had asked her what tormented her the most about amnesia, it wasn't the loss of a life lived, it was the unending curiosity. Not knowing burned at her. She closed her eyes and hunched over, arms around herself, wrestling with her own demons until the hot water ran out.

Red tried to imagine her troubles swirling down the drain as she turned off the shower and stepped out. Setting a bandage on her healing bite came first. Kristoff hadn't done more than sip at her. It was the coldest of comforts considering what he might have planned for her.

She blow-dried her hair, then brushed her teeth with her plastic travel toothbrush, trying to pretend that it was what passed for a normal night for her. She stared into the mirror at a shared face. Shivering, she absently wiped down the spotless counter with a tissue. She had wanted to shower then crack open her laptop to research Kristoff. Her legs trembled. Exhaustion made her put her head in her hands.

Sleep, it was.

Red wrapped a plush black towel around herself before leaving the bathroom to find the living room empty. She went to the guest room, turning on the lights to reveal the dark blue, windowless walls.

The king-sized bed took up most of the space with a shelf jammed in the corner and a small closet door beside it. She dressed in her pajamas before she flopped on the bed and rolled over. The vague scent of sandalwood lingered in the air. The walls seemed to lean in on her. Closing her eyes didn't help. She glanced around the room before a yawn broke from her lips.

She looked over at the bookcase and got up to peruse the packed shelves. Bookshelves were always her kryptonite, even when she was bone tired. An eclectic mix of books, records, and old magazines mingled with random things shoved carelessly on the shelves. A collection of Lord Byron's poetry sat next to a battered copy of *On the Road* by Jack Kerouac and an old Doc Martens boot. Red focused on an old VHS tape of SLC Punk and tapped at the lime green case.

Realization struck her. This wasn't a guest room. It was Lucas's room. Or at least he stashed his stuff here.

With the loop of regrets, fears, and obligations playing through her head, Red wanted something else to think about. Pulling out the copy of *On the Road*, she looked back at the freshly changed bed and shrugged. She had worn his jacket tonight. Using his blanket wouldn't be much different. Exhaustion pushed the weirdness aside, leaving only the fact that after this freaky day, any bed looked good.

She switched off the bedroom lights and turned on the small bedside lamp, then curled up in bed. The strange apartment felt too quiet and her mind too loud. After turning on the light again, she opened the book and tried to distract herself with the adventures of Sal and Dean being beatniks across America.

The faint sandalwood scent surrounded her as she yawned and told herself that they would hit the road tomorrow, leaving Lucas, Kristoff, and especially Juniper behind.

October 26th, Noon, Smith and Reaper Bank, Downtown, Los Angeles, California, USA

Sitting in the private cubicle at the Smith and Reaper bank, sweating under the high lace collar of her vintage blue dress, Red clutched the purse in her lap. Her mind raced with doubts once the banker left to go find a supervisor after she had given her information to open an account and get a credit card.

She might have chased after bounties doled out by the Brotherhood of Bards and Heroes, but that money only went so far. Vic's checks for field reports were always late too. Small scams kept the Millennium Falcon running and their mission on the road when the honest money petered out. Usually, they passed through small town banks with fake socials and managed to hustle loans or credit cards before leaving a defeated monster behind in trade on their way out of town.

When she had found the notepad with the Smith and Reaper

Bank logo in that dingy motel off the freeway, she hadn't imagined their office would look like this. This was the biggest place they'd ever tried to con. The bank looked like the definition of corporate class, it even smelled like money. She usually did more research on their marks. Desperate times led to stupid measures. She already regretted taking the role of the applicant.

"That social was bogus," Red whispered to Vic. She glanced at the thumb print scanner on the desk. She had panicked when pressed by the banker and actually given her prints like an idiot.

"I paid good bitcoin for that on the dark web. It's legit," he said out of the corner of his mouth. A vein pulsed in his forehead.

"This is big money we're walking away from," she said, thinking of the bounty that Fat Crispin had put on the head of the vampire who murdered his daughter. It was easier to think about the money and not the victim.

Julia had crossed an ocean to make it as a grad student by day and model by night in the City of Angels. She'd ended up dead in an alley. It hadn't left Red's mind since they decided to take Lucas's advice and skip town. A queasy guilt lingered in her belly.

"This credit card will get the tire fixed, and we can ride on the rest before we ditch it," Vic said, hushed. "There was already the stink of vampire conspiracy on this case and then you..."

"You said we were the only hunters with the balls to come to LA with the Blood Summit happening." She shifted in her chair. The empty hunter bar had been enough to prove him right. Who else would work the case?

"Hey, do you want to become some Eurotrash's pet?"

Red glared at him.

"Sorry. I don't like running from a case either, but this is next level strange."

"Strange doesn't cover it. I didn't even recognize myself when you found me, and now I can't go anywhere in this town without some vampire gawking at me." Red touched the large band-aid through her dress lightly. She might have Juniper's face, but she didn't want her baggage.

"You've been looking for yourself, kid, but I don't think you're going to find it here. Spooky red herrings aside. LA doesn't have anything for you," Vic predicted with the surety of a weatherman on TV.

Red looked up at the smiling white-haired banker as he re-entered the cubicle. He wasn't alone.

"Thank you for your patience. I'd like to introduce Sheila Jones from the Special Accounts Division. She will take care of you." Before disappearing, he gestured to a younger woman in a business skirt suit with a severe bob, highlights artfully streaked through the brown hair. She wore a Bluetooth earpiece and smartwatch blinking with notifications.

Sheila shook hands with firm precision before she sat behind the desk. The matte red lipstick smile didn't reach her eyes. "Mrs. Pfannenstiel, it's a pleasure. When we ran your application and prints, we found that you already had an account with us. A large account, to be specific."

"Pardon?" She blinked, ear cocked because she had to have misheard the stern yet fashionable banker. "Who set it up for me?"

"That is the part where the special comes into Special Accounts. This trust was set up overseas under what I'm certain is a fake name. It's not as uncommon as you might think for families to preserve their assets discreetly."

"What kind of assets are we talking about, lady?" Vic asked, raising his chin, gaze narrowing.

Sheila Jones typed into the desktop computer before she turned the flat screen around to show the client record.

Red leaned forward. The slick interface with all its fields was nearly empty of personal information beyond a name—Hermione Granger—and bright red numbers listing a figure with enough zeros to make her blink. In her head, she cursed from shock, but only said, "Oh, my."

Vic whistled low. "Thank you, Grandma Pfannenstiel."

"Now, the instructions on the trust stipulate that the account belonged to whoever matched the fingerprints. There's one more step before we can hand the account and your new card to you."

Head still stuck on all the zeros, she nodded, wetting her lips. "Sure."

Sheila pulled out a small metallic box from her pocket and placed it on the desk then opened the lid to reveal a small interface. "Put your thumb or index finger on the sensor."

Red put a thumb down. She didn't like giving up her prints again, but a burning curiosity drove her on. Why did they already have her fingerprints on file? Who had left her the trust? A sharp, unexpected poke shot through her thumb. What the hell? She lifted it to see the small drop of blood from the wound. Paranoia stung like pin prick. What kind of bank was this?

Sheila closed the box, and her smartwatch beeped. "Fabulous. It's a match." She pulled out the fake ID and a shiny black metal card along with a small plastic bandage. "These are yours."

Red slapped the band aid on her pricked digit. She tried to keep the urgency out of her tone. After months of chasing dreams and ghosts, this was the first tangible clue to her origins. "What can you tell me about this account?"

Sheila clasped her hands on the desk. "Very little beyond the logistics of transferring the ownership. The process can take ten business days, but you'll have access to fifty thousand liquid cash until then. The physical items will be shipped and should arrive in 4-6 weeks."

"Physical items?"

"The package is held abroad. I'll know more soon." Sheila typed into the keyboard again before clicking the mouse. A printer began to whirl under the desk. She pulled out a folder from the desk drawer. "Let's go over the terms and agreements."

Red left the air-conditioned building onto the busy downtown street, blinking into the bright sun. Cars raced by as the world seemed to move too fast for her to process. She had walked into Smith and Reaper looking to get a credit card; she walked out with a trust fund. She slumped against the wall of the bank. "I'm a millionaire. Multi-millionaire."

"I stand corrected. There was something for you in LA." Vic rubbed his cheeks, eyes wide. "We found a clue to your origins, my mysterious intern. A money clue. Many many money clues. Were there really that many zeroes?"

Swallowing back the lingering shock, Red nodded. "I guess I do have a family. A very rich family."

"Who have offshore accounts and use blood for verification." He pointed out, lips crumpling into a cringe. "Kinda suspicious."

"Yeah, what kind of bank is this?" She shook her head, trying to clear the cloud of newfound mysterious wealth. "We should have asked more questions. I got so distracted the second I saw all those zeros."

Brows knitting together, Vic scratched his jaw. "As a newly rich person, I think you need an entourage, and I should be the first one in it."

She laughed, walking toward the underground parking garage. This situation was growing weirder by the hour but at least he was taking it in stride. "Well, I pulled out two thousand dollars. Let's get the van fixed and do some research."

"Does this make me the intern now?"

She grinned. "Don't worry. Being your intern will just be my eccentric hobby now."

"Seriously, Red, you should get out of here." He paused, staring out over the white and beige buildings and the passing traffic. His gaze distant as his Adam's apple bobbed. "I can work the case. We're not just talking about money here. We're talking about Fuck You Money. Ready to burn. This is your escape hatch."

"Where is Mr. The Truth Is Out There? I can't believe you even want to touch this money."

"I bet there are strings a-plenty on this trust, and yes, I smell conspiracy. But damn, those are liquid assets. You can drain that and run without a trace." He shrugged, his hand flapping up uselessly as if he didn't know what to do with them. "Hide out in Mexico if you want. You already know Spanish."

She shook her head, guiding him into the underground car lot. "This is the first real lead on who I am. It's not about having money. I've been searching for some sign of who I am for the last year. This trust could lead back to my family. Too much is happening here. It can't be a coincidence. Doppelgänger, reincarnation, secret heiress, I don't know what. But it's happening here in LA."

"But Novak... He's going to come for you again," Vic pointed out as they walked past Mercedes and Ferraris to the Millennium Falcon. He hopped into the van and turned the ignition.

"We've killed older vampires. I'm not helpless. My magic might not work all the time, but I've done well as your intern. Besides, I have fifty grand liquid in the bank. We can gear up like Batman." Red waggled her eyebrows.

He squealed like a teen girl. "I wanna get a flamethrower."

8

OCTOBER 26TH, Evening, The Pandora Hotel, Los Angeles, California, USA

Sitting cross-legged on the long leather couch at their hotel suite, Red wrote a clipped, peeved, and censored report to Fat Crispin.

The euphoria of a flashy bank account had faded out as the reality of the case settled in again. She might have been safely enclosed in a pricey hotel now, but she could have died at Club Vltava. He'd learn exactly how fan-freaking-tastic that his agreement with the Supreme Master was. In the report, she doubled up on the 'we almost died' factor and left out the doppelgänger weirdness. Still restless after her pointed email, she surfed through the files on Julia Crispin's laptop.

They'd grabbed it from the victim's apartment when they visited the small two-bedroom apartment in Silverlake and spoke to her grieving girlfriend. Red had been surprised, since Fat Crispin's report had only mentioned a close roommate. She'd asked if Julia was bisexual, but the girlfriend denied it and said their family wasn't supportive. Out of all the questions that she had walked out of the home with, one stood out. What was a lesbian from a Bard family, with a cute professional volleyball player for a girlfriend, doing on dates with a bunch of male vampires at Club Vltava?

Vic flopped on the couch, wearing his clubbing blazer from the night before with his hair slicked back. He put his boots up on the coffee table before putting them down again, nervous energy wafting from him. "When are we going down to the bar? What's the point of being in a fancy place like this if we're not enjoying it? You're not even dressed up yet. I am!"

"I found some interesting files on her laptop. I'm uploading them to a thumb drive now." Red had done a computer-wide search for the words vampire and demon, and a surprising number of files and folders came up, each with boringly innocent names like School Receipts, Book Reports, and Period Tracker. Copying them all onto the thumb drive, she clicked on the period tracker. It opened with the red headline "Hell-A" and a table of contents listing sections like City Summary, Leadership, and Death Rates. "Hmmm, she was researching something. This reads like a dossier of the city's dead. It's a huge document. It's taking forever to load."

A pop-up appeared on the screen, asking for a password before blocking the words on the document.

Red frowned. "It's protected."

"I'll crack the password tomorrow. You don't need to watch the files transfer." He hopped up, gesturing to their hotel suite on the second to the top floor. "Come on, we have money to burn, and we're in the safest place in LA."

Decorated in a luxe Southwestern style, the suite boasted three balconies, two bedrooms, two bathrooms, and a sitting room with an attached kitchen. Then there was the magical security system. Unlike most hotels, which didn't have that special essence of home, the rooms here could repel uninvited vampires. Every city boasted of one neutral ground with a sanctuary spell where diverse supernatural beings could mingle in peace. LA was big enough to have a few. The Pandora Hotel was the most luxurious and fortified.

"Let's party like we're the beautiful people tonight!" He lifted a raised fist like he was ready to take a lesson from the Clash and rock the casbah.

She laughed and closed the document, adding it to the queue of transferring files before she put the laptop on the coffee table. He was right. They both needed to blow off some steam. "Okay, okay, you head down to the bar, and I'll meet you after I get dressed."

"Cool."

"Hey, I still owe you $200 from Reno. Here you go with some interest." Fishing out her wallet, she handed him three hundred. He had taken her in without a cent—or even a name to, well, her name. It felt good to begin to pay him back.

"This is the good karma coming in. Hell yeah." Vic pumped his arm and took the cash, leaving with a skip.

Looking down at the laptop's progress on the files, she walked into her room with the king-sized bed and balcony overlooking the darkened Hollywood Hills. This hotel suite cost more per week than all the hotels they'd stayed in for the last few months combined. The opulence was uncomfortable, like new leather boots, but it felt like she had released a breath that she hadn't known she was holding.

After months of rubbing pennies together to keep afloat on the road, it was nice to finally get what they needed, like new tires or wooden bullets. Worrying about monsters was easier when you weren't also worrying about how to keep gas in the tank. Of course, all this newfound money could be from blood diamonds or used to track her for a nefarious end. It also could lead straight to the person she had been. Who knew?

Red didn't.

They had tried to find her identity before, running searches on missing redheads in 2010, showing her picture to hunters around Eugene, even visiting an overpriced shaman in Nevada. Nothing had shaken out. This trust fund had been the closest connection that she had to anything in this world that wasn't a creepy Victorian love triangle. In the meantime, she was happy to take advantage of the money. Vic had already sent out feelers to his sources to get some more intel. If it turned out it was from Nazi gold, she'd cross that bridge when she came to it.

Her accommodations might have upgraded, but she still had the same old military surplus duffle bag. Olive green and dingy, it rested on the all-white bed. She unzipped it to see copies of the same outfit —black top and jeans. There were scattered peeks of color from her pajamas, random shirts, and scarves, but constant travel in a van, demon-related mishaps, and being broke between bounties or credit card scams didn't lend itself to a diverse wardrobe.

Red looked at herself in the mirror. The fifties-style blue dress had a matching lace panel that covered her from the neck to the short sleeves. It almost hid the bandage. She had worn it to the bank to look like a respectable citizen. Since she'd had to toss the green cocktail dress, she didn't have much in the way of cute things.

Going to the attached bathroom, she freshened up and released her hair from the French twist, letting it fall down her shoulders. Red shook out the gentle waves. She put on a hint of red lipstick to brighten up her face. Kristoff hadn't taken all that much blood, and the wound was healing quickly, but she still felt paler than usual. She didn't look bad, but she did look like she could use a drink.

Habit led her to hide her laptop bag and stash of IDs under a bronze varnished dresser. She pushed them flush against the wall. Grabbing her purse, she checked Julia's laptop and noticed the transfer had stopped because the thumb drive was full. Red frowned, wondering what in the hell Julia had in those folders that was bigger than 16 GB. She found another empty drive at the bottom of her backpack by the couch and swapped them out to resume the transfer.

Curiosity tugged at her, but Vic was right. They had arrived in LA two days ago, and it had been one damn thing after another. She could take a break for a glass of wine and process how she'd once been a hunter without a past. Now she was caught up in a supernatural soap opera of doppelgängers and secret heiresses.

Palming the full thumb drive, she felt too lazy to hide it with the rest of her hidden stash. Instead, she scooped up the suite's keycard and dropped both in her purse beside the stake and silver cross before heading out of the room, double checking that the door was locked on the way to the elevator.

The vague tickle of magic made her nose twitch as she entered the elevator. Maybe if she'd had a witchcraft mentor, she could home in on it, but she only knew what she had picked up along the way about her power. She had a third eye that needed contacts, but she could sense the energy in the old hotel. Smudgy vague auras and whisper-thin mists hung over the doorways and drifted to the ceiling.

Red stepped out of the elevator into the high-ceilinged lobby, designed in a 1930s Old Hollywood style with golden wallpaper and cream-colored circular couches in front of the wide angular front desk. The vintage illusion was broken by the pop music drifting from an open hall. She flashed her card key to the pale bouncer by the door to the lounge.

The retro theme continued inside. Packed white booths and tables faced the bandstand, empty but for a DJ, his white suit bright against the red velvet curtain of the stage. Humans and vampires mixed with even more exotic beings. A hooded creature holding a brandy glass in his red reptilian claws chatted with a blue skinned dwarf taking tequila shots at the circular, brass-plated bar.

A few stools down from the dwarf, Red spotted Vic examining an offered box of cigars and walked to him. "This is pretty nice."

"It beats the hell out of a no-tell motel." He pointed at a cigar in the middle of the box. "That one, my good man, and a glass of pinot grigio for the lady. The one you recommended earlier."

The bartender complied with a polished ease found only in upscale establishments where customer service was elevated to client relations. The wine glass appeared with a sip poured in for her to taste.

"Oh, wonderful." She nodded and gave back the glass to be filled. "Thank you."

"Feeling rich is amazing. It's like I have contact wealth," Vic chattered, cheeks pulled up in excitement. He waved the cigar around for emphasis. "I'm already used to this. I refuse to go back to peasant life. I'm taking the blue pill."

She laughed. "Let's not start lighting our cigars with Benjamins just yet. We'll only be here until we figure out the Novak sitch, but I gotta say, my bathroom is like the same size as our last hotel room."

He raised his beer and tapped his pint against her glass. "The water pressure is out of this world. I also suspect that this cigar will be as well..." He grinned and downed the last of his beer before setting it on the bar. "...which I billed to the room."

"I'm happy to play sugar mama for the night. Enjoy your sin stick." Red chuckled as he left with his cigar. She spun on the stool to see him strutting toward the bar door. Her breath caught as Lucas came in. It was strange seeing him after learning the truth, but she couldn't deny that she had wanted to see him. She just didn't expect him to come to her.

In his leather jacket and torn jeans, Lucas stepped into the lounge with the grace of a panther, lazy movements hiding the watchfulness. His gray eyes found hers. His strong jaw tensed even as his gaze softened. That thread of doubt crept onto his face, as if he couldn't decide if he should step back or come closer.

Vic slapped him on the shoulder. "Hey, Greg, great to see you. Watch my intern."

Lucas shook his head and strode to the bar.

Red grinned, snorting into her wine glass. "Of all the gin joints in all the towns in all the world, he walks into mine."

"You've managed to get Vic out of his Canadian tuxedo twice in one week." He smiled, then looked down, a broody cast to his face chasing the smile away.

"It's all him. He's just excited. He chooses to wear a blazer." Red shrugged. She wasn't ready to tell all and sundry about her windfall. The situation was already weird enough without having to give him the even weirder backstory. "We're usually in a van, not a swanky hotel."

"I'm surprised you told Quinn where you were."

"He was honest with me last night. Besides, keeping case secrets didn't exactly help the investigation." She gestured to her neck. It was a walking reminder that this wasn't the average case. "Even safe behind wards, it's good to have someone else watching our backs."

Lucas looked toward the lounge door that Vic left through. "Package set, eh?"

She raised her eyebrows, swallowing the urge to laugh at the vampire's not-so subtle question. She hid her smile. "We're not dating, if that's what you mean. He's like my brother. We've been through a lot."

"How'd you meet?" He leaned against the bar.

"He saved me. Gave me a spot in his van." Red shrugged. She wasn't ready to talk about being amnesia girl either. That led to awkward questions even with people that she didn't have unexpected baggage with. She had learned to stay vague. "Taught me how to be a hunter."

"It's a hard life. What brings you to it?" He sat on the stool next to her, elbow propped on the bar counter. His gaze lasered onto her. It wasn't an uncomfortable stare. He looked like he genuinely wanted to know.

Shifting on her seat, she knew how to handle guys in bars fishing for intel to use to get in her pants. Not a guy who seemed to just want to listen to her. She shrugged, tightening her grip on her wine glass. "Like most hunters, the life found me. What about you? Vic makes it sound like you're on the road as much as we are."

"Something to do." Lucas said lightly as if skimming across the surface of a deeper story. "It's simpler on my bike, running jobs for Quinn occasionally."

Red lifted a skeptical eyebrow. She knew that hunting was more than a hobby for him. It couldn't have just been something to fill the time. "You're like a lone ranger, except instead of Tonto you have a sense of empathy?"

"Something like that." Lucas lowered his head, his face growing reserved. A pause grew between them. Breaking the silence, he looked at the bartender and ordered a draft beer.

"You don't have to shut down," she said once the drink was in front of him, then shook her head. "Sorry, it's just, I know I'm a freaky genetic coincidence, as Quinn put it, but you don't need to act weird around me. I mean—never mind, it's a free country." She frowned and looked down, wishing the ground would swallow her up after her ditzy ramble. Of course, he was going to be weird around her—she looked like a dead woman. "That probably sounded stupid."

"You're trying to be nice. I get it." He shrugged and drank his beer. "You don't need to be."

She heard the hint of self-loathing and resignation underneath the lazy clip of his English accent. He didn't walk with the visible burden of guilt that Quinn did, but she'd seen it through his punk outfit and sarcasm when she first met him. "It's hard, huh? Quinn said it was for him."

"You had a heart to heart over tea?" Lucas's lifted eyebrows disappeared under his tousled bangs.

"Chamomile to be exact."

Rubbing his jaw, he chuckled. "And what did you learn from my brooding grandsire?"

"That chicken blood isn't tasty—I assume because of the hormones, but we didn't get that far." She smiled, leaning in to reassure him. "He didn't spill any of your secrets. I already figured that it was complicated. I can't imagine a vampire-human relationship that wouldn't be. Then enter me, oblivious, thinking that I was unique like a snowflake when I'm more of a carbon copy."

"You have your own flair."

Red brushed her hair off her shoulder and mock fluttered her eyes before rolling them. "Thank you."

The boyishness in his expression faded, replaced by a hardened glint in his gaze. Lucas's eyes narrowed on her neck. "Where'd you get those old bite marks?"

"See those, huh? This dress hides less than I thought. I tried to get them lasered off after a vampire got ahold of me in the Midwest." She rubbed her neck through the lace. The new ones had faded after one treatment. A few of the old were too stubborn to go away. "I was the one who obviously walked away from that fight, so put the worried look away."

His shrug was casual, but his gray eyes were earnest. "You're special even if you didn't look like her."

Red felt the heat rise in her cheeks, cursing her pale skin for betraying her. She got a lot of pickup lines dropped on her in highway honkytonks, but even the smoothest barely earned more than an eye roll from her.

This was different. He meant it.

"You know it doesn't need to be you watching over me. I can understand if having contact with me is too much." She said the words calmly, but something panged at the thought. Call it a weakness, but she always felt protective over the rough types with good hearts. She'd labeled him a cryptic vampire jerk when they first met, but she was warming to him. And not because he was gorgeous. He felt...familiar was the only way to put it. She couldn't imagine how it was for him.

"No, it doesn't hurt. It just brings up the what ifs. That isn't your problem." He sipped his beer before clenching his jaw as his eyes looked past her, calculating his next words. "I know you're a doppelgänger. You're not the first one that I've encountered, but it's different seeing an old girlfriend instead of a Latin teacher."

"You had a Latin teacher?" She tilted her head. "How old are you?"

Lucas put his hand to his chest in mock outrage. "Oi, a lady never tells."

"So coy." She laughed. "Fine. How about we actually just meet each other?" She held out her hand. "Hi, I'm Red. I've been to every state on the West Coast. My favorite color is purple. I'm a terrible singer, but I can't help but sing along to the radio if Tom Petty comes on."

He shook her hand. His touch might have been cold, but it radiated through her skin. "I'm Lucas. My favorite color is black. I was born in 1853."

She shook a finger at him. "What? I don't get another fun fact?"

He grinned and leaned forward on his stool, elbow on the bar. "Er, I don't have a Facebook profile."

"Obviously. You've had a centennial." Red tipped her head forward and bit her lip to stop her smile. She was enjoying this conversation too much. "Do you even have a computer?"

"Hey, I wasn't born in the middle ages. I'm not that old."

"You don't look a day over a hundred." She smirked before taking the last sip of her wine.

He cocked his head. "What's your real name?"

"Red is real enough." She frowned, not at the question, but at the large analog clock on the wall. The black hands of the clock ticked at the top of the hour.

"What is it?"

"Vic's been gone too long." She put her glass on the counter. It wasn't just danger from their case making her wary. He could make more than enough trouble being drunk and cocky, waving a cigar around, acting like a big shot. "He should've come back by now. I'm going to go look for him."

"I'll come with you." Lucas fell easily into stride with her.

Red passed through the lobby and out to the front of the hotel. She scanned the sidewalk of the small drive up to the Pandora. To the left was the smoking area under three palm trees just before the entrance to the underground hotel parking garage.

A yelled curse echoed on the wind.

"Do you hear that?" She looked over at Lucas in time to see him sprint into the mouth of the garage. She jogged after him, feeling impossibly sluggish compared to his speed. Slowing on the garage ramp, she pulled the blessed silver cross out of her purse.

The back doors of the Falcon lay open. A bean bag chair and a half-smoked cigar laid beside the van.

Lucas stopped his blurring speed in front of the shadow of a concrete stairwell. "What's so confusing to you wankers about neutral ground?"

A Black vampire rubbed his bald head as he stepped out of the gloom. Blood splatters darkened the white pinstripes on his suit lapels. It was the same vampire that had broken into Quinn's office. "Mind your own business."

The skinny white vampire, glasses dipping low on his nose and wearing a *Star Trek* T-shirt, pulled Vic forward. He glanced between his partner and Lucas. "He's older than us, TJ."

"No names," TJ said through gritted teeth.

Red trotted forward along the ramp wall, stopping to pick the van's keys up off the ground. Adrenaline bubbled up. All the while, she kept her eyes on Vic. He struggled in the vampire's grip, his nose bleeding and left arm hanging limp at his side.

"I don't recognize you, mate, Or him. Looks like we have some rogue minions." Lucas put his hands in his pockets and grinned. "Killing you two will be fun."

The pasty male widened his eyes and pushed Vic away before hiding behind his partner. "Let's go!"

"No, stay," Lucas said to the squirrely one. "After I stake your big friend here, we can have a little chat."

Vic hobbled over to Red. She handed him the cross, then stepped over to block him from the view of the two vampires. Usually, she was the one with the injuries. It felt weird to protect her mentor.

TJ glanced at her, clever brown eyes filing her appearance away like a banker putting a stack of bills in a safe.

Lucas stepped forward. "Let's start with who turned you two prats and then move on to why the fuck you were breaking into Quinn Investigations."

Shaking his head, TJ chuckled and elbowed his cowering partner. "That'd be scary if I didn't see that weak ass soul in your eyes."

She side-stepped over to the van while Lucas distracted the vampires. Heart racing in her ears, she tried to spot their demon hunting kits. Vic kept the collection of salt, sulfur, blessed silver, cold iron, and stakes in a tackle box strapped the wall behind the driver's seat. The back of the van looked like it had been set on a spin circle in the wash.

TJ ordered, "Take out the hunters."

Dropping the stake, Red dove for the crossbow half hidden under an overturned plastic milk crate. She spun around with it in her hands.

The smaller vampire ran to Vic, but stopped and cringed before the blessed silver cross. Crosses didn't always work for her unless they were blessed silver, but Vic had the power of a true believer behind him.

She fired the crossbow. The arrow hit the nerdy vampire in the side, impaling the *Star Trek* character printed on the side of his shirt. He fell back. She quipped, rushing over to Vic. "Right in the Spock!"

Growling, TJ charged Lucas.

Lucas caught him with a punch to the gut, then a right hook to the face. His arms were a blur.

TJ jumped back, shaking his head before he readjusted his broken nose. The crunch echoed off the concrete walls.

"How's that for my weak ass?" Lucas spun and back-kicked TJ in the chest, sending the vampire in the business suit flying back.

Smiling, she lifted the crossbow with the remaining arrow in it at the undead Trekkie. "Alright, Comic Con, you might want to start answering my friend's questions now."

"Run, TJ!" The nerdy vampire pushed up his glasses and rocketed up the ramp, his blurring pace marred by a slight hobble.

She lowered her weapon to check out Vic's arm and the chalky, sweaty cast of pain over his features. "Your arm is bending wrong, Vic."

"Watch out!" He pointed with his cross, but he was too far away.

Swiveling around, Red raised the crossbow, but she was too late. The cold hand gripped her throat. She gasped, staring at the vampire fangs dripping venom onto TJ's starched collar and tie.

He barked out his demands. "You're letting me walk out of here, or I'm killing this human bitch—"

Lucas moved so fast, he seemed to teleport. He grabbed TJ by the neck and snapped it quickly before slamming the vampire to the floor. Amber shone out through his gray eyes. "Are you okay?"

She nodded and stepped back. It still was hard to see yellowed irises and remember that an ally was behind them.

Lucas pulled a stake out of his pocket, twirling the wood between his fingers, and looked down. "By the law of the bloody supreme, Cora herself, you're dust."

The parking garage spun as Red croaked out, "Stop!"

She was too late. Lucas had already knelt and staked the other vampire. He leaned back on his heels. "Look at me, acting like a good citizen."

TJ decayed to a dry skeleton, leaving only a scrap of tie around his neck bones.

"Shit, we could have questioned him." Red sighed.

"Ah, fuck! My arm." Vic groaned as he walked over to the pile of bones and kicked at it. "This dick broke it."

"Those were the minions who broke into Quinn's place," She said once she regained her voice, mind still focused on the predatory territorial gleam to Lucas's eyes when he'd twisted the minion's neck. She set the crossbow down in the van before closing it up then trotted to Vic.

"They knew I was investigating the murders," Vic said, grimacing. "They wanted to know what I knew."

Lucas looked around. "Come on, let's get you back into your rooms."

"Oh, yeah, the hotel is paying for a private doctor to come here." Vic complained as he walked with them out of the garage. "Unbelievable. We were promised a sanctuary spell on neutral ground. Don't they know who we are?"

"I think that's the problem," she said then looked at Lucas, remembering her manners. "Thanks for the rescue back there."

"Anytime, Red." Lucas said. "Anytime."

She smiled, flushing at the twinkle in his eyes, then hurried to help Vic who began to stumble by the hotel front door.

Lucas beat her to him and put Vic's uninjured arm around his shoulders. "I got him. Let the hotel know their rutting protection spell doesn't work in their garage."

She held the door for them before alerting the front desk, then joined Vic and Lucas up in the hotel suite. The walk to the room had cleared her head. The fight had been brutal, but it was a clue. Those minions had hit both Quinn Investigations and their van. These weren't random robberies. Entering the hotel living room, she looked at the coffee table and frowned. "Where is Julia's laptop?"

"Someone broke the door lock," Vic said from his seat on the couch, clutching his arm. He cursed, pained glare casting over the fancy suite.

Lucas paced behind the couch, sniffing like a hound on the scent.

Shit, if they were going for the tech... Red went into her room and checked the stash under the dresser to find her laptop bag and her wallet full of fake IDs still hidden. She sighed in relief, then moved on to Vic's room in the suite. She preferred to hide low, but Vic was a high hider. She looked around the room before noticing a vent above the slick black desk. Climbing on the desk, she stood on her tiptoes and flipped the knob on the vent to open the slats to reveal a sturdy laptop, built like a brick and running on Linux.

"Looking to break your arm too?" Lucas asked, leaning against the open doorframe.

"Seems fun, but not today." She hopped down from the desk. "Looks like our stashes are safe."

"They didn't do the same smash and grab like at Quinn's." He scanned the room, stepping inside.

"Does Quinn know what they took?" She crossed her arms. Knowing what else their bumbling burglars wanted could reveal their motivations.

He shook his head. "Hasn't found anything missing yet."

"I think they knew what they were looking for this time." Red walked past Lucas to the doorway, inhaling his sandalwood scent as she passed. She looked away from his gaze, feeling the heat rise in her cheeks for no reason, to check on Vic, who groaned on the couch.

A Middle Eastern doctor and a vampire handyman came soon after with a fervently apologetic hotel representative who presented flowers and a complimentary upgrade to their wards. The door lock was repaired before Vic's arm was cast. The hotel representative practically begged them to not tell anyone that their ward malfunctioned in the parking garage or that their rooms had been burglarized. Reputation was what justified the Pandora Hotel's steep room rates. He promised to examine the hotel footage for the burglars.

Vic groaned on the couch as he turned on the TV. An injected painkiller was already causing his eyelashes to flutter closed before an old sitcom theme came on.

Red gestured to Lucas and brought him through her room and out onto the balcony. "When I searched the files on Julia's laptop, I discovered that she was doing research on the vampires in this town. I was able to grab some of the files. Vic will need to decrypt them tomorrow. With him out of commission, I'll have to work double time on the case."

"Bloody hell, Red." Lucas gripped the rail, shaking his head. "You need to lay low until the Summit's over. Hide out here and catch up on the telly."

"Excuse me? I don't need to do anything." She put her hand on her hip. He wasn't her boss. That honor went to the drooling man on the living room sofa. "There've been two bodies in three days. Do you really think it's going to stop? This isn't some vampire breaking the rules. This is bigger."

"You sound like Vic." He crossed his arms over his chest. "Is there a conspiracy, Mulder?"

Stinging at the implication, she matched his stance. With Vic out of the physical fight, she needed someone to trust on the case. Things had started off rocky with this partnership with Quinn Investigations, but they had to put it past them. She had matched wits with harder heads than his. She tried a different tactic. "You're a vampire. You know that nothing is simple when this many get together. I was going to ask for your help, but if you're going to be like that, never mind."

He jammed his hands in his pockets and studied her. "What do you need?"

"A man on the inside." Red lifted an eyebrow and pulled out her phone. She told herself that she needed his number for the case. "Now, you don't have a Facebook. I won't hold that against you, because neither do I. But I'm guessing you have a phone. Give me your number."

Lucas recited it.

She typed it into her phone and sent him a quick message, so he'd have hers, too. Now, neither crew working the case had an excuse to not keep the other updated. "Alright. So, can I trust you to have my back?"

"That and then some." Lucas's grin was cheeky, but his eyes were serious.

"Good to know." Red dipped her head and walked into the living room to wake Vic. She flipped through her phone's contacts before she landed on Quinn Investigations and hit the dial and speaker buttons. It was time for a group powwow on the Greene-Crispin case. She had an idea for the next lead to chase.

The guys were going to hate it.

9

OCTOBER 27TH, Sunset, DB Models, Fashion District, Downtown, Los Angeles, California, USA

Reading the scanned PDF on her computer screen, Red double checked the personnel file of a model named Georgia Erickson. Everything looked normal. Only the physical folder had a sticky note on the inside that read: DEAD.

She saved a copy of the file and transferred it to her thumb drive then filed the paper version in the rolling metal cabinet behind her. The light dimmed from wide, west-facing windows as twilight chased the last hint of sunset away.

She stretched and pushed her fake heavy-framed black glasses down. It had been a long day of digging. The original two victims had been joined by a possible third who was found dead weeks ago. All three models were trying to leave their contracts. Georgia had already been signed by Elite Models when she died. The hours flew by as Red tackled scanning and organizing the files from the last few years.

When she arrived this morning in low kitten heels and a cardigan with a packed lunch in hand, she didn't know what to expect from the house that Delilah Byrnes built. She didn't even know if she could get in. Quinn's ex-wife and sire had been mentioned, but unseen beyond a few pictures of a blonde in designer clothes giving off alpha woman vibes. Last night, she had brainstormed with the guys on how to get into the agency. Quinn hadn't liked the idea. Vic wanted her to hook him up with a model. It took some arguing before they finally agreed that coming in as a temp would give her the best access. Lucas stayed quiet until he said would take care of it. Just show up, he said.

Linda Li, the general manager, had been curt when she arrived. Until she explained herself, then the other woman nearly cried from joy. Ms. Li had been crying out for help digitizing their files for years. DB Models was the oldest modeling agency in LA, and the filing system reflected it. The bustling office was soon filled with aspiring models, photographers, and agents, leaving Red alone with the file keys.

It was like instead of robbing the bank, the clerk just put the robber on the payroll.

Red might have infiltrated their system, but she left it more orga-nized than she found it. She had spent most of the day searching files and trying to eavesdrop on office gossip, but beyond one model saying Delilah's boyfriend looked like a sexy pirate, she hadn't gotten much of anything. Nothing on Julia Crispin or Olivia Greene, specifically. Discreet questions hadn't dug up more than confessions about which three models were dating the same rapper. Lucas warned that her cover would be blown at sunset once Delilah came to work at DB Models. Red still couldn't leave yet. There could be more here.

In red pumps and a matching designer suit, the petite office manager approached the cubicle. "Stephanie, time to clock out. It's past six."

"Hi, Ms. Li!" Red tried to sound as perky as she imagined a Stephanie would be on her first day on the job. She patted the short pile of records stacked next to the scanner. "I'm nearly done with last two years of records."

"I'm glad you decided to start with the new ones. I already

needed to search the digital files today. So much quicker than walking back and forth to the cabinets!" Linda Li chuckled. "Is this what it's like working in the computer age?"

"You're welcome. It's my pleasure." Red had oddly enjoyed the brief experience in a normal 9-5 job. Nothing had tried to kill her once. She told herself to not get cocky. She hadn't even clocked out yet.

Linda nodded. "Keep this up, and you won't stay a temp!"

"That's what I like to hear." Red smiled. "Um, before I go, can you tell me if you have any specific orders on how you want me to organize the files of deceased personnel and models?"

"Oh, those poor girls—two murders and a suicide."

"Did they ever find the killers?" She asked, leaning forward, trying to find the appropriate blend of sympathy and natural morbid curiosity.

"This is a hard town." Linda shook her head and put a hand on her chest. "Keep them off the hard drive so Ms. Byrnes doesn't see. She was so upset. You can actually just pile the folders on this desk, and I'll take care of them later."

"Are you sure?" She asked, casually shifting papers, not meeting Linda's eyes. "If there are more, I can dig those up before I go."

"God willing, those are our only tragedies. I'm already impressed. You don't have to volunteer for more work." Linda put her hand on her hip. "Now, I'm salaried, so I have to stay late. You go and enjoy yourself. Celebrate your new job. I'll see you in the morning."

Red smiled and nodded, logging off the computer and bending over to grab her purse and the thumb drive. After saying goodbye to Linda, who retreated into her own cubicle, she headed for the glass door. She gulped when she saw what was behind it. She glanced around for a sanctuary amongst the open desks and low-walled cubicles. There was no time to hide.

Delilah Byrnes had the classic beauty of Old Hollywood with her oval face, pillowy red lips, smoky blue eyes, and Veronica Lake curls. A thick wave of blonde hair covered the familiar woman's face as she stared down at her phone. She opened the door leading to the sixth-floor office, tucking her phone in her pocket. A precisely shaped eyebrow arched when she spotted Red. "What do we have here?"

"A temp." Red smiled, feeling a bizarre urge to curtsy. She kept her heartbeat steady by breathing through her nose.

"I didn't order one of those." Delilah's eyes narrowed under her fake lashes.

Red furrowed her brow, trying to look perplexed, before laying on her best valley girl voice. "I was told to report to the general manager. I was referred by All Star Staffing. OMG, what if I just worked all day at the wrong place? Do you think they will still pay me?"

"You're good." Delilah smirked coldly. "I almost believe you. Now, who are you, really?"

"Stephanie Connor from the agency." She had the sinking feeling that Delilah was another vampire who remembered her doppel-gänger all too well. She calculated how quickly she could run when Lucas open the door. The tightness in her chest eased.

"Hey, Stephanie, ready to go?" He strode inside, nodding to the other vampire. "Delilah, nice dress."

Delilah crossed her arms over her chest. "Don't tell me you're responsible for this piece of déjà vu."

"Yeah, I met him at a nightclub, and he told me I should apply for this temp job." Red shrugged, tossing out lies like confetti. "I always wanted to be a model."

The vampiress rolled her eyes. "Michel didn't tell me what the girl at the nightclub looked like."

"She's not the same girl." Lucas reached for Red's hand. His fingers entwined with hers, causing little sparks under her skin.

Delilah laughed. "I have eyes, Lucas. Now I know why you paid me a visit last night."

"So, I guess I don't get the job?" Red asked, shrugging, voice pitched higher. She inched closer to the door.

The other woman put her hands on her hips with the poise of a model at the end of a runaway. Her tone coiled like a mellow snake, the venom under the surface. "Leave before I change my mind."

Red let Lucas hold her hand and lead her out into the hall-way. Her pulse thumped in her neck. She released her held breath.

Delilah called after them. "She's just going to break your heart again, Lucas!"

Leaving the high-rise building together, Lucas waited until they were out in the dry heat of the concrete jungle of downtown. Night had fallen on LA, but the rush hour traffic was at its peak. Honks drifted on the winds as bumper pressed bumper on the busy street. He squeezed her hand before letting her go. "And now, you've met the devil who wore Prada."

"That's Quinn's ex-wife?" Red pulled her hair loose from her low chignon then tugged off her fake glasses. Jitters still racing up her spine, she set the glasses in her purse. "I wasn't expecting... Just sayin', she's an intense person."

"You were supposed to leave before sunset." Lucas directed her down the street, cabs and cars rushing past them. "I came once you didn't text the group at five."

"I know. It was stupid of me. I just got lost in the work. I actually did a great job on those files. It's really going to streamline their work-flow." Red pumped her fist before realizing her inappropriate enthu-siasm. She dipped her head as they approached his bike. "I also found clues too."

He reached out to brush his thumb against the apple of her cheek. "Had some ink on you."

"Thanks." She looked down, skin tingling at his touch. "How'd you get me in there?"

He looked down before he glanced up at her, head tilted with the mischief of a little boy. "Managed to snatch Delilah's cellphone last night to send a text to her manager."

"Sneaky, sneaky." She laughed. "So, now what?"

"Ever ride a motorcycle?" Lucas patted the seat of his parked bike.

"Not on the back." She smiled. Her heart jumped and she felt a blush move up her neck to her cheeks. Was this how Juniper felt with Lucas—like anything could happen at any second?

He opened the pannier to pull out a small helmet to hand to her. "First time for everything."

Red took the helmet and passed him her purse to store in the bike's storage compartment. She hopped on the back of the bike, adjusting the skirt of the new green sundress. She bit her lip as she wrapped her arms around his middle. Her white cardigan sleeves looked so bright against his dark leather jacket. "Keep in mind that I'm precious cargo."

"That you are, Red." Lucas put on his own helmet and started the bike, turning them into LA traffic. He drove like the immortal he was, weaving in and out of traffic, only slowing down when he spotted a lurking cop car.

She didn't plan on clinging to him, but she couldn't help but hold on tight. The bike vibrated between her thighs as they sped through the smoggy highways toward the Pandora Hotel. The Hollywood Hills rose higher in front of them. She braced herself as he took the last turn hard, clinging to his waist, leaning her head against his shoulder.

"You can let go, if you want," Lucas said over his shoulder after they'd stopped.

"Oh." Red swung her leg off the bike, brushing the back of her skirt down. She hadn't ridden in months, and her legs felt like jelly. Pulling off her helmet, she handed it over. "How bad is my hair right now?"

"Looks beautiful." Lucas set the helmet down on the bike. He turned around quickly and pulled her purse out, handing it to her without a glance.

"Thanks for the extraction." Red smiled and settled the purse strap on her shoulder. His driving made her life flash before her eyes, but she still had fun riding through the nighttime streets with him. He had really backed up her plan today, too. She had found some information that even the LAPD had missed. This intel hadn't broken the case, but they had a better idea of what connected their victims. She tilted her head, a random question popping up in her mind. "Do you ever go by Luke?"

His shoulders tensed, and he shook his head tightly before walking to the elevator from the underground parking garage to the hotel lobby.

Hurrying after him, her kitten heels clicking on the concrete, she caught up with him at the elevator. The up button blazed red. She noticed his lack of reflection in the steel elevator doors. That myth about vampires was true, but with exceptions. Minions with weak blood cast a translucent reflection. Lucas was strong enough to be completely invisible. She had forgotten what he was as they sped down the freeway, even holding onto him and not feeling him breathe.

He stepped into the elevator, his eyes darting to her as he put his hands in his pocket. "Luke is what she called me sometimes. Only her."

Red nodded. She knew who "her" was. Juniper. She pushed the button for the 8th floor and pulled the hotel keycard from her purse, inserting it into the slot. "Thanks for trusting me with that. I can tell it's not easy to talk about her."

Looking down, Lucas shook his head. "It's easier with you."

The elevator doors opened at the lobby, and a crowd entered.

Red tried to keep from looking at Lucas over the other hotel guests. She was still trying to figure him out. One moment he looked at her like she was the only one in the room and the next, he was stalking away with a dark cloud over his head. When they finally reached their floor, she followed him out of the elevator and opened the door to the hotel suite.

Vic lay sprawled on the couch, head tipped back, arm in a white cast, his laptop on his belly. His black mullet fanned over the pillow. The flat screen TV blared a news program.

Lucas following her, she walked to the coffee table and grabbed the remote, turning off the TV. Pulling the laptop off him, she set it on the table. "Hey, sleeping beauty."

Vic snorted and coughed as he woke up. "Back from bringing home the bacon?"

"Yeah, make some space and I can tell you all about it," she said, sitting on the couch beside him while Lucas sat in the nearby chair. She delved into the story of her day, leaving out the parts about organizing their files and focusing on the facts of the new possible victim, Georgia Erickson, and that the three models were all trying to leave their contracts. The motive for the murders was looking less supernatural conspiracy than business turned deadly.

Red didn't want to connect the dots out loud with Lucas there since Delilah was like his great-grandma, but the female vampire was looking more and more suspicious. She hadn't connected the two burglars with DB Models yet, but she wouldn't be surprised if the modeling agency had decided to branch out. She shared her last big clue. "Kristoff Novak did a photoshoot with each of them in the month before they died."

Red had been surprised to learn that Kristoff was a photographer, but he appeared to do many of the ad campaigns for Novak and Novak Company, which included an impressive portfolio of nightclubs, restaurants, and even a casino on the West Coast. His brother Arno claimed that he had a thing for redheads, did Kristoff also have a taste for models? And had he gotten sloppy enough to leave a body trail?

"Not surprised at all." Lucas screwed up his mouth as if holding back a stream of commentary. He brushed his messy black hair out of his vision before turning away to pull out his phone. Gritting his jaw, he tapped out a text message.

She quirked her eyebrow at Lucas before she turned to Vic. "And that is the hot gossip around the office. How was the work from home life?"

"Well, your day was more productive than mine. Julia's passwords were harder to crack than I expected," he said, a yawn bursting through. "She's definitely done a lot of research on the vampires in town. I just can't access the full documents on the thumb drive. She even has audio and video in there. I sent copies to Fat Crispin, but it was late in the day in London. I haven't heard back. It kills me to say it, but I hope the London guys have more luck than I did."

"Hey, you're tired and on painkillers. It's alright. You can try again in the morning." She patted his shoulder. "You can take a break."

Lucas stepped over, putting his phone in his pocket. "It can't be comfortable on this couch, mate. Not with that arm."

"No, I think I have a crick in my neck," Vic said, stretching. "I'm going to bag my arm and hop in the shower."

She bobbed her head, eyeing his five o'clock shadow and the sweat stains on his shirt. Sitting on the couch next to him had given her a good whiff of him. He had somehow turned the classy hotel suite into a man cave complete with man funk. "Good. You have a lot of Dorito dust on you."

"It's the fuel for the madness." Vic laughed and walked into his room, closing the door.

"I guess it's a type of madness," Lucas commented sardonically.

"Debrief Quinn on all of this, will ya?" She started to say before her feet reminded her how long that they had been encased in these pumps. She was ready to talk shop, but she had to get out of these shoes first. She bent over and slipped out of her heels with a sigh and leaned back against the plush couch. "What's the deal with Delilah? Quinn brought us here because he was too close to the case. Ex-wife, sire, I get that, but I think I saw her at Club Vltava, walking in with Michel and Cora."

"Michel must fancy her because he has no love for me. Not that long ago, he would have used the pretense of challenging Kristoff's claim to crucify me." Lucas shook his head and sat down next to her on the couch. His voice turned confidential. "Don't say anything to Quinn. The poor bastard already knows the frog is her boyfriend. Delilah always loved being in a power couple with a powerful man. It doesn't matter if he has a soul or not. Maybe it makes it easier for her."

"Oh..." Red pursed her lips. When she had imagined souled and unsouled vampires in social situations, she assumed they would have a dodgeball game style split with the remorseful on one side and the gleefully demonic on the other. Not dating each other. "Bad breakup between them, then?"

"It's never good, but they always make up. This has been the longest they've gone without getting back together." He shrugged, but his expression showed more concern than his casual words. In vampire terms, they were his family.

She didn't know what that word meant for her, let alone for him, but she knew it meant something. "Why do they even live in the same city?"

He looked away. "Some people just can't stay apart."

Red glanced down, swallowing thickly, then turned back to business. She repressed the urge to put her hand on his arm to comfort him. "She's our best suspect. She had motive and connection to the victims. What will he do if it turns out to be her?"

"It won't," he said fervently, his brow knotting. "If Delilah wants someone dead, soul or not, she's not going to get caught like this."

Red debated that angle, but the evidence was piling up on the doorstep of the modeling agency. "You sure about that? You think it's Kristoff?"

"Think a lot of things about Novak." Black hair covering his eyes, Lucas leaned over in his seat, looking at Vic's laptop on the coffee table. "The Bard's daughter had more information here than just about Delilah, right?"

"What happened to laughing at the conspiracy idea?" Red stood to grab a small bottle of pinot noir from the fridge. She unscrewed it and took a sip before stepping out on the balcony. It was a theory that she had felt like she had nearly debunked, but there were still too many loose threads in this case.

"That's when I thought it was some out-of-towner getting sloppy." He followed her out on the balcony and leaned against the railing. His gray eyes sought out hers.

"Enjoy the red pill." She sipped the wine before handing the bottle to Lucas.

He took a drink and gave it back. "You thought pretty quickly on your feet with the ice queen glaring down at you. That's impressive."

"She didn't have shoulder pads on that dress, but I could feel their aura. She had a power stance." Red gestured to her shoulders before setting the small bottle on the patio table. It had nothing to do with their conversation, but she couldn't hold back on an observation any longer. "Hey, I have to tell you... You drive like you're in a car chase."

He grinned, biting his lip clearly unrepentant. Guess his soul didn't mind the occasional traffic violation. "You held on just fine."

She huffed, poking his bicep. "I managed to keep on my heels, but next time I'm on the back of that thing, you'd better obey the speed limit."

"Next time?" He glanced up at her through his eyelashes, surprise softening his impish smile.

She leaned toward him, laughing. "You wouldn't pick me up again?"

Lucas brushed his fingers across her cheek. His pale gray eyes focused on her face as if there were no one else in the City of Angels. He leaned forward; his lips whisper-soft against hers. His voice pitched low. "I'd always pick you...up."

Placing her hand on his, Red let her mouth part. She kissed him back.

His voice echoed in her ears, sounding so much like the mystery man in her dreams. Was it a doppelgänger transference? His touch felt the same as the mystery man's as he put his arm around her waist and pulled her closer. The hint of sandalwood rose from his leather jacket. He deepened the kiss, and his fingers trembled as he ran them over her hair.

Goosebumps rose on her arms as she wrapped them around his neck. There was none of the awkwardness of a first kiss, banging arms or noses. Feeling him against her felt so familiar. She bit her lip, pulling away for breath, and stared into his eyes. Gray bored into green. She dipped her head. "What are we doing?"

"I don't know." He grinned before kissing her quickly and murmuring against her lips. "You seem to like it."

"Oh my god, I'm going to hurl." Vic mock gagged, wearing a bathrobe and a towel wrapped around his head as he stared at them through the open balcony glass door from the living room. "Can we keep the PDA to a minimum?"

Red glared at Vic, blushing, as she pulled away from Lucas. She stepped from the balcony toward Vic. "Can you say that louder? I don't think the people in the penthouse heard." She rubbed her neck and ducked her head. "Lucas, it's time to go."

He grinned. "I'll show myself out."

Vic watched him go, holding his tongue until the door closed behind Lucas. "Bad news bears, kid. What are you thinking?"

"He kissed me first!" She blushed, glancing away even as a smile tugged at her cheeks.

"I don't know if you have a big brother, but I'm filling those shoes right now. Watch out. He might be a reformed lady killer, but he can still break a heart." Vic shook his head and went into his room.

Barely noticing her friend leave, she touched her lips. She knew when she was kissing Lucas, she was thinking of him. Who was he thinking of?

Red or Juniper?

10

OCTOBER 28TH, Past Midnight, The Pandora Hotel, Los Angeles, California, USA

Hours later, sipping a glass of wine, Red sat cross-legged on the floor of her hotel room's balcony. Two dozen open tabs lay cramped in her computer browser. She felt like she had been dancing around the same set of clues hoping for something new to shift out.

She had been reviewing the Olivia Greene file, even though she wished she could get her hands on the hotel footage. The camera in their hallway had been on the fritz at the time of the break-in. The hotel's failure got them a few complementary days at the Pandora Hotel, but it meant a dead end on that lead. She had checked out the Greene murder scene days ago, pacing the secluded beach where joggers had found the body, washed up on the sand, lying prone in a long sleeve dress. She looked over the autopsy photos. The coroner had documented the snake eating its tail carved into the model's flesh.

The photos were grim, but it was easier to think about the case than kissing Lucas or joking with him or fighting beside him or how her eyes couldn't help but be drawn to him whenever he walked through a room. Yeah, she would rather read more about murder than think about the warm fuzzies that she was developing for a vampire.

Red never claimed to be normal.

She opened another browser tab to enter the long cryptic URL for a dated database portal that looked like it was built on GeoCities in 2003. Bard Net housed the digital collections of the Brotherhood of Bards and Heroes. The blank webpage looked broken, but she refreshed halfheartedly anyway. Her heart leapt as it loaded. Registered hunters and Bards like Vic—or whoever had their passwords—could get access. It had been down for maintenance for the last week.

She typed Delilah Byrnes into the Bard Net before scrolling through the dropdown menu to select vampire for the species. A picture of Delilah taken at the height of 80s power businesswoman fashion appeared on the page. Scrolling through the entry, she picked up the main points in the biography: turned into a vampire by Alaric in 1672, left her sire to travel with Quinn, and mayhem followed.

Red's finger started to ache as she scrolled through the massacres that the vampiress had either caused, participated in, or finished. She paused as she noticed a painting of Delilah dressed as if ready for a ball at the court of Versailles. A golden ouroboros pendant necklace hung between her cleavage.

A sentence in a nearby paragraph caught her eye. "The local priest reported seeing the ouroboros carved onto their skin..." She read through the paragraph about a massacre outside Madrid in 1738. Quinn and Delilah had left only the local priest alive in the village. She scanned through the rest of the biography to get to the part where the Byrnes were cursed by the soulmancer. She expected an epic blow-by-blow account, yet only one line spoke of the curse that tipped the vampire world into chaos.

On August 1st, 1900, Delilah Byrnes fell to a soulmancer's curse upon attacking the Brotherhood of Bards and Heroes alongside Quinn Byrnes, Selene Byrnes, and Lucas Crawford. See entry on the Defense of Stonetree Monastery.

Red tried to click the link, but the database denied her clearance.

Frowning, she surfed to all the Byrnes' entries, ignoring a pang of jealousy at how beautiful Selene was, and found the same line. The entries on each of the four vampires skipped over their cursing to focus on their lives after the August Harvest.

She furrowed her brow before scrolling up on Lucas's entry to look for a mention of Juniper St. James. She found a quick mention of a redheaded human companion in Brighton and reports that she had died in either Lisbon or Madrid. The entry writer noted that the records are confusing, and the later reports of other redheaded women with the Byrnes in Prague could have been the same woman. The last reference to a mysterious human companion is to her death in Dresden, which set Lucas off on a vendetta against the famed Witch hunter, Peter Svoboda. In an editor's note, the biographer mused on the likelihood of a single human surviving eight years with an evil vampire and theorized that Lucas must have had multiple claimed humans. Not even the Bards seemed to know about Juniper.

Red returned to scan the other biographies and failed to find a snippet about her doppelgänger.

She gulped down the last of her wine before she finished reading the scant details on Lucas post-souling. There was a note about him moving to America and beginning to hunt other demons. It ended with a paragraph about him helping to destroy the founder of the Alaric Order, nearly a decade ago alongside a young Hero in the Brotherhood. Dry and informative, the entry only left her wanting the real dirt.

She closed her laptop. This was the reason other hunters were laying low during the Blood Summit. Vampires were never simple, even if they had souls. They lived too long for that.

Gathering up her mess on the balcony, Red yawned and told herself no more research. She brushed her teeth and hair before she got into pajamas and laid down. Turning and wrapping her blankets around herself, she tried to sleep but only managed to toss and turn like a fish dropped in the desert. She sighed and re-dressed. If she was going to be awake, she might as well be useful. The hotel suite was immaculate, and she needed something to do with her hands.

Leaving the hotel completely, she searched for something to do before she found herself in the parking garage under the building. Kneeling inside the Millennium Falcon, she rummaged through the back of the van, tossing blankets into a plastic bag.

Vic had been attacked in the van, and it still looked like it. Half the van looked like a stoner den with bean bag chairs and solar powered Christmas lights hanging, while the other side was pure storage with tied down plastic and metal crates filled with weapons, dry goods, and supplies. She made notes in her phone of what they were running low on and what could be replaced. They could even stock up on expensive wolfsbane. She still hadn't gotten used to the idea of having money. She felt like she had to spend it quickly before it was taken away. Cleaning usually soothed her. She was waiting for the soothing part to kick in.

A scrape of a pebble on concrete ripped through the quiet underground parking lot of the Pandora Hotel.

Red grabbed the shotgun loaded with wooden tipped bullets from the open gun box beside her. She turned around in a crouch to the open back door of the van.

Kristoff Novak stared at her, hands behind his back, open dark suit jacket revealing a white shirt. The bright lights of the parking garage reflected the golden strands in his dark blond hair. His lips quirked into a small wistful smile. "Red."

She cocked the shotgun, wondering how the hotel's no violence sanctuary spell dealt with self-defense. She should have fired and tested the theory. "You finally learned my name."

"I keep trying to learn more, but you're a tricky woman to research." He grinned, blue eyes twinkling, and the dimple deepened on his chin. His chest only moved with breath when he spoke.

"That's the intention." She lifted the shotgun higher. He didn't have a soul, she told herself. The bastard hadn't just bitten her, he had claimed her. She knew where that road led: being a 24/7 blood bank.

Juniper St. James might have lasted eight years as Lucas's paramour back in his bad boy days, but Red didn't like her odds with

Kristoff. She tried to call on that well of magic within, but ever since she'd thrown TJ the vampire through the window of Quinn Investigations, her energy had been tapped.

"This isn't what I imagined you driving." Kristoff studied the van, rocking back on his heels like a critic examining a new painting.

She pressed her eyebrows together at the mundane topic change. Pride in the black-painted van, ramshackle and smelling of Mountain Dew as it did, rose in her. "Hey, this is the Millennium Falcon. It made the Kessel Run in less than twelve parsecs."

He chuckled. "You never were the pretentious type. I'm not surprised that in your next life you'd be a sci-fi fan traveling with a hunter."

She frowned. Lucas had kissed her tonight, and all she could think about was if he had been kissing her or imagining a dead woman. Now, Kristoff was making small talk as if she were his blast from the past. Her life was on the line, and it was still about someone else. "How would you know? You just met me and then claimed me like two seconds later. I'm not Juniper St. James."

"Then who are you?" He tilted his head. "You may not be her, but you seem to be just as mysterious."

"I'm a hunter, so you'd best give me some space." Red gestured with the shotgun for him to move back. She slid forward to hop out of the van, legs already stiffening from her awkward couching position. The vampire bite throbbed as if sensing the fangs that had made it close by. She wasn't letting him catch her by surprise this time.

"I like that in a woman." He gestured to her weapon. "Wooden bullets?"

"How did you know?"

"What lady leaves home without them?" Kristoff smiled, but then his expression cooled to a stoic mask. "You shouldn't fear me. You could've been claimed by worse."

"Don't think that these marks make me yours. This body is all mine, mister." Her hands were steady on the shotgun, but memories of Oklahoma City made her breath catch. She wasn't going to let a compelling vampire play on her trust again. When they helped you, it was for their agenda. She knew the difference between souled and unsouled vampires. He might have been doing the vampire version of shooting the shit, but she wasn't fooled into thinking he was like Lucas or Quinn. Kristoff had no shackles on his inner demon.

Red had staked how many vampires? LA was shaking her focus. She wanted to know who she was, not more about some historical lady she randomly looked like. A thread of anger grew in her at Juniper St. James. She had to shovel the fallout from that debutante's love life. "I'm not scared of you."

"Your heart's racing. I can hear it."

She scowled. "You snuck up on me like a creepy vampire."

Kristoff smoothed his hair back as he studied her, his eyes dismissing her weapon to focus on her face. His gaze fell on her with the familiarity of a long relationship, curiosity in his expression. "Who is that girl to you? Julia. She's English. A Bard, I heard?"

"Why don't you tell me? You're my number one suspect. What did she see? Health violation in the kitchen?" She asked, deflecting the Bard question. That string led to Vic and the dozen hunters she could name as friends.

"Trust me, I don't kill Bards or leave bodies behind my own club." He scoffed at the idea. "I didn't live this long by being stupid."

"Why should I trust you?" Red inched away from him, even if his words sounded true. His logic was solid. There weren't many hundred-year-old vampires around. The August Harvest, the chaos after the soul spell went viral in 1900, cleaned out a lost generation of young vampires, and many far older. He had to be smart to have survived it.

"Juniper did."

She narrowed her eyes. "Lucas told me you left her to die."

Kristoff leaned forward, shaking his head, his irises flashing amber. "That's a lie. I tried to rescue her from him."

"What happened, then?" Maybe it was dumb, but she challenged him anyway. If she had to take the dramatic walking tour of Juniper St. James' life, she was going to have some answers. The online sources gave her dates and a list of events in Lucas and Kristoff's lives, but nothing about the woman they loved.

"She saved me." His voice sounded like a sad whisper on the wind, too small for his tall frame.

"What?"

"Lucas had beat me to a pulp, and I blacked out. In the most beautiful act of karmic revenge, he got his soul. I wish I had seen that." He looked away, the snark dissolved into surprising amount of pain in his tone for a vampire without a soul. "I never left her. Juniper ordered a friend to drag my unconscious body out before the hunters came. I was willing to die for her that day, when Lucas tried to turn her into a vampire. She wouldn't let me."

"He tried to turn her?" She noticed the shotgun lowering and raised it up again. Lucas had left that part out of the story.

"She was his courtesan, but she wanted more." Shoulders raising, Kristoff looked down on his clenched fists. "She didn't want his gilded cage."

"You think she wanted you?" Red didn't know if all she was getting was some 'he said, she said' but while his claim was hanging over her head, she would have to understand him. Bucking a vampire's claim wasn't as easy as going down to the police station and filing a report. Even other supernatural creatures respected the prerogative. Since she couldn't kill Kristoff yet, she had to find another way to deal with him.

"I know she did." He met her gaze with flashing eyes. "I may not have a soul, but I loved her. I saw him claim a flower, watch it wither, and let it die. You may not be her. You may never love me like she did, but I wasn't going to let him claim you too."

Red tightened her grip on the shotgun. "Yes, I bet it was all altruism, Novak. Not a bit was about getting back at your sire."

"Oh no, that was in there. I thoroughly enjoyed seeing his face when I claimed you. Then punching it." He shrugged. "I'm not a saint, but I won't lie to you."

"No, you'll claim me like a piece of meat, then stalk me in a parking garage. I've dealt with unsouled vampires before." She shook her head, thankful that the hotel had a sanctuary spell. Even at close range, the shotgun wasn't as good a defense against a determined vampire. "I don't have any illusions about what you would do to me if there wasn't a protection ward on this hotel."

Lip curling up, Kristoff crossed his arms. "My sire might have a soul, but I doubt his toys fare any better than before."

"I'm not a toy." Red sneered. "I'm a person. That might not mean much without a soul, but it does to me, and I'll fight to stay my own person. That bite was your last."

"You'll ask for the next one." A promise lingered in his grin. "You enjoyed it. Better than those other marks on your neck. Oklahoma, right? You staked a master there."

She grinned back, baring her teeth. He'd had more luck researching her than she had him. She'd found some business intel and a dry entry in Bard Net about being a beast in the boardroom. If he wanted her to cower, she wasn't giving him the satisfaction. "A supreme master, and it was with a wooden spoon."

Vampires reacted to the news that she had killed a supreme master of a city in a lot of ways. They didn't usually smile in delight.

"I can do it again." Red glowered. "I'm not a house pet to put a collar on."

"No, you're not a *kitten*," Kristoff said, his voice harsh with fervor.

She took another step back at the intensity in his tone. What the hell had cats done to him? She gritted her teeth. "Get that through that thick handsome skull, and keep your mitts off me."

"You think I'm handsome." He put his hands in his pockets, dimple in his chin and cheek deepening, as he grinned.

"And now I think you're arrogant." She rolled her eyes. "Who do you think you are?"

He spun around to hiss.

A vampire built like Hercules, in biker denim with a long blond ponytail, froze in the middle of the parking garage. Shaking off his alarm, he reached in his pocket and whipped out a stake. He tossed it with the precision of a ninja with a throwing star. "Fuck. This was supposed to be a break in."

Kristoff caught the stake a foot away from his chest. "And this was supposed to be a private conversation."

Blinding light flashed.

Invisible hands pulled the muscled biker swiftly back to the mouth of the underground parking garage, gripping the patched shoulders of his denim. His heels dragged on the cement floor as he struggled. "What the burning hell?"

"Sanctuary spell. You broke it." Red smiled cheerfully, grateful the hotel had done something right.

Kristoff raised the stake, waiting, blue eyes focused on the intruder being forced out by the ward. He threw it the length of a football field as the undead biker's foot hit the sidewalk at the opening of the parking garage. The stake hit the other vampire in the chest, and the biker fell back, transforming into a pile of bones.

"Kristoff Novak. That's who I am." Eye twinkling, he nodded to her. His gaze caressed her face as he smirked then disappeared in a blurred sprint.

Red sighed and rubbed her forehead. Now that was unexpected. She was too exposed to freak out here. Putting away the shotgun and locking up the van, she scurried from the garage. She sent a text message to the hotel representative, asking for an anti-theft ward for their van. At least she knew the sanctuary spell worked. She went to the elevator, feeling eyes on her until she was inside the darkened hotel suite.

Red walked into her room and curled up under the blankets. Vic would kill her for not waking him to reveal whoever sent the first guys to break into their van had sent more. She didn't know what to tell him. She was still mulling over her nighttime visitors. Why hadn't she taken out Kristoff? Even with the sanctuary spell, she could have tried to lure him outside of the ward. She had made chit chat with him instead, more interested in Juniper St. James than her own survival.

Kristoff had protected her. Vampires defended their claimed humans as a territory thing, but he held no punches with that burglar.

She pressed her hands to her temples, trying to gain control of her rushing thoughts. Counting her breaths like Vic taught her, she tried to focus on the air filling her lungs. Her heart still raced. She didn't expect to fall asleep, but soon her breathing evened out, and she sunk into dreams as if falling overboard into a dark winter sea.

The room smelled like infection, closed-in and dark with stagnant air.

A familiar English voice whispered in her ear, pleading with her to live. Names and places escaped her in the dream. She only knew a deep emotional pain that felt worse than the wounds on her body.

Rolled on her belly, she felt the mattress lift and angry voices grow louder before a slam and a thud echoed in the hallway outside the room.

A different door opened.

She looked over her shoulder at the tall masculine figure that stepped over to her, carrying a tin of salve. His face was obscured, but his blue eyes stared down at her with devotion.

The dream disappeared into her subconscious when she woke in the morning.

11

OCTOBER 28TH, **Near Midnight, Gianni Construction, San Fernando Valley, Los Angeles County, California, USA**

Sitting in the front seat of Quinn's vintage convertible, Red leaned forward to squint at the aluminum-sided warehouse. A row of parked Harley Davidson bikes stood by the large cargo door in front. Whispers from the supernatural gossip mill led them to Gianni Construction.

She looked over at Lucas climbing off his motorcycle, feeling her cheeks warm before telling herself to focus on the job at hand, not the vampire she'd kissed the night before. Despite the flirty banter they had exchanged last night, he hadn't wanted her to come along. This morning, she had filled in Vic on the details of Kristoff's late-night visit but skirted over her conversation. She hadn't been surprised that he forced her to recount the story to the others or by Lucas' vehemence that she lay low. Mentioning his progeny set him off.

Quinn had been the one to surprise her when he said she'd brought them a clue and made the connection between the biker-looking minion and Gianni Construction. He insisted they could use her.

Red spoke to the private detective in the driver's seat. "It doesn't look like much. Are you sure there's a bar in there?"

"The Valley is the one place in LA County where an unlisted minion could hide."

"Why?"

"Cora's grip eases up north of Balboa Park." His heavy brow and stoic expression concealed his thoughts. A pile of wood could emote more.

Lucas leaned against her door. "No one is willing to drive through the traffic on Ventura to check."

"What's up with this list?" She asked, remembering the warning from the old hunter at the Pump House. Vampires liked to act like they ran the world, but they didn't. Plenty of cities were dominated by shifters, mages, and more. LA was a vampire town for sure, but not like any Red had ever been to. Cora might have looked like a hippie, yet she was as data driven as the FBI.

"It's like a census," Quinn explained. "Cora likes to know her subjects."

"It goes beyond forcing us to all go to her Halloween Ball." Lucas shook his head. "As if that wasn't bad enough."

"She has at least pictures of all of us." Quinn added, his head high and shoulders straight as he scanned the area. Purpose infused his bearing. His tone grew thoughtful, like a mentor parsing which insights to give. "She even has a registry of fang molds of every LA vampire made in the last few decades."

"When you said tight ship, you meant it," Red said, leaning forward, curiosity piqued by the idea of the vegan social worker operating more like the KGB. "How can she make them all fall in line? I know supreme masters have the power of veto over who is turned, but she must have a lot of power to take fang molds."

"Just because she has a soul doesn't mean she is to be fucked with," Lucas warned.

"What about these guys?" She gestured to the warehouse.

"They aren't as scary but keep close to us." Lucas glared at Quinn.

Ignoring the death glower, Quinn nodded. "Keep your eyes open too, Red."

Lucas narrowed his eyes, high cheekbones sharpening as he steeled his jaw. He pushed away from the car. "We shouldn't have brought her."

She scowled. "Hey, I can hear you."

"We're looking to get information and stay under the radar." Quinn crossed his arms. "It's simple reconnaissance."

"I can't believe I'm telling you to be cautious, old man." Lucas shook his head as if saying it to himself. "Adding her into the mix calls attention."

"What do you mean? Look at this outfit." Red pulled off the bandage under the studded strap of her cropped black tank top before gesturing to her jean mini skirt, fishnet tights, and steel toed boots. Her dark leather jacket completed the outfit. She had chosen her least attention-getting wig: a center parted black mane. He was lucky she didn't wear the purple one. Pulling the sunglasses down from the top of her head, she wiggled the frames of her aviators before resting them on her nose. "Someone put an arm around me, and I look like an undead biker's old lady. I'll fit in."

Lucas glanced at the mark before opening her door. "Let's go."

She stepped out of the car and adjusted the small leather pouch hanging off the side of her belt with her ID, cash, and phone. With a stake taped between her shoulder blades, she was ready to party. "So, whose dame am I?"

Quinn closed the driver's side door. "I am going to be asking the questions. You two are eavesdropping."

"You're the one who wanted to bring her." Lucas tossed an annoyed hand up as the elder vampire who ignored him to walk across the gravel parking lot to the warehouse.

Red held back a sassy retort. Lucas was being protective out of good intentions, but she had been a hunter for over a year. That she remembered. She wasn't some casual brought in off the street.

Fighting monsters was what she did. It wasn't the first time someone had underestimated her on a hunt. She forced herself to smile. "You're my gentleman escort then."

He put an arm over her shoulders. "I've never been a gentleman, Red."

Walking to the warehouse door, they caught up with their leader. A panel opened on the door. The guys flashed fangs and the entry opened.

Instinct pushed Red to step closer to Lucas as she walked into the warehouse. A fleet of vans, pallets of lumber, bricks, and other construction supplies looked normal until they followed the heavy pounding of rock music to a rolling garage door open to reveal a dingy illegal bar decorated with hubcaps and old dusty pictures of Frank Sinatra and the Rat Pack.

The place smelled like spilled beer and tobacco smoke, but there was an underlying scent like curled up serpents that rattled the primitive parts of her brain. It was dimly lit, better than fluorescents for immortal eyes, but she could make out nearly two dozen vampires spread over mismatched tables and chairs. She could tell the other two humans immediately. They were the only ones breathing.

The first was with a large male ginger vampire, suit jacket thrown over his chair, playing cards. The human, a blond man wearing too much eyeliner with scabbed bite marks on his neck, cooed over his vamp's shoulder. The next was in the corner with a petite black vampiress in a silver catsuit, laughing on her cellphone. She held a leash attached to the shirtless white man in jeans at her feet.

Red tried not to make eye contact, even under her sunglasses, with anyone.

Lucas played with her hair idly. His fingers stopped as he looked over, as if realizing his absent-minded gesture, but his tense arm remained on her shoulders. "Let's get you a drink."

"Whatever you say, baby," She joked as she had with Vic the countless times that they had pretended to be a couple on a job. The joke didn't land right. She looked down. It felt different when you had kissed the guy. She wanted Lucas to take her seriously as her own person, as a hunter. Stupid jokes weren't going to cut it. Good job, she told herself sarcastically.

Guiding her to the small bar, Lucas ordered two bottles of beer before taking her over to a waist-high floating shelf on the wall. A Pabst sign blinked above them. He took a sip, scanning the room. "New faces in the old."

With this many supernatural ears in the room, he couldn't say much openly, but she understood his meaning. Three unlisted minions were bad enough...dozens were an army. Could they all be from the same clan?

Red hid her peeping eyes behind her sunglasses. "What's on the agenda, then?"

"The night's still young," he said. The worry in his gray eyes didn't stop the small grin tugging at his lips. "There's a poker game that I heard brought in real power players. I'll buy into the next round. Might have to wait for the action to start."

His arm still rested on her shoulders. The touch radiated even through her leather jacket. She didn't know if she should cuddle to keep their cover or if she wanted to do it. She compromised and tilted her head back on his arm. A sudden curiosity struck her at the sight of the neon sign. She didn't know what accounted for small talk with vampires, but historical beer trivia had to be a safe topic. Unless he'd had some dramatic moment with Juniper at the World's Fair. "Were you there when Pabst got its one ribbon in 1893?"

Amused by the randomness, Lucas was confused until he noticed the sign. "No, I wasn't in America then. London, or maybe Dublin? I spent a lot of '93 drunk and causing a ruckus. Both '93s. Cora certainly hasn't forgotten."

"Bad boy from the start?" Red tipped her sunglasses down.

"What can I say, I've always been a rebel. What about you?"

"I'm..." She didn't know what she had always been, only what she had been for the last year. Everything else was a game to jog her memory. "...an explorer. It's probably why I've been traveling in that van so long. There's something about the start of a journey, that next horizon. You never know what you'll find, for better or worse."

"What do you think of what you found in LA?"

"I'm still deciding." She smiled and sipped her beer. Sometimes being a woman of mystery was fun.

His head snapped away from her. "For fuck's sake."

She followed his stare to the center of the bar where Quinn stared down two men in leather and denim. Her stomach twisted at the sight. This didn't look like some acquaintances saying hello.

A grimy barrel-chested vampire with a serious case of cauliflower ear elbowed his friend. "How do I know this fucker?"

In a stained jean jacket patched with a faded Hells Angels logo, his buddy only replied by cracking his knuckles and glowering at Quinn.

The ginger-haired vampire at the poker table chuckled and shuffled his cards. "That's Bloody Quinn Byrnes himself, boyos."

The Hells Angel crossed his arms. "Now, what is the defender of downtown doing in the Valley?"

Watching the drama unfold from across the bar, Red snorted. "And I was the one who was going to attract too much attention?"

"Rub it in my face later." Lucas took her hand and pulled her forward in a wide circle around the bar to stand behind the jeering onlookers. "Go to the car."

She wished she could disagree, but she only had the stake taped to her back. Two master vampires couldn't take on a dozen each even with a hunter's help. She wasn't the only one leaving.

A vampire in an *Iron Man* shirt snuck through a cluster of biker chicks toward the door. It was the vampire who had been smart enough to run from both Quinn's office and the Pandora Hotel. He didn't have his friend TJ to hide behind anymore.

She nodded to Lucas before she stalked the nerdy vampire to the main warehouse floor.

In the bright lights of the warehouse, a fleur-de-lys pin shined on his backpack along with the other fanboy pins. He must have been a Francophile who loved the show *Wynonna Earp*—a well-rounded geek. He looked at her and ran, an action more prey than predator. She kept her pace casual as she took off her sunglasses and tucked them into her shirt.

Noticing the *Iron Man* fan fleeing, the only vampire bouncer at the front door lumbered away from his post as he cracked his knuckles.

Quinn and Lucas were circled by six minions holding pool cues and broken bottles. The two souled vampires stepped back deeper into the bar.

Lucas grabbed a pool cue swung by a snarling vampire in fringed leather before he slammed the handle against the vampire's forehead.

Quinn blocked a knife from a lanky vampire in bell bottoms before punching his attacker in the gut.

The four others rushed them, to the hoots and cheers of the stomping crowd.

Outside the bar, Red tried to focus and summon up her magic, but the energy didn't answer her call. A shaman told her once that she had a capacity of an ocean of power in her, but she barely felt a puddle. She shook her hand before sighing. Fuck sticks. She was still regenerating her energy levels. Looking around, she wished for her revolver loaded with wooden bullets. If wishes were weapons...

Red noticed a pegboard lined with hanging keys on the wall over a low desk. Checking the tags, they matched the licenses plates of the vans. She grabbed a fistful of keys and ran to the vans to unlock one.

This was a crazy idea. She might have been rolling with immortals, but she wasn't one. She looked around, trying to think of something less dangerous than hopping behind the wheel and ramming a van into a crowd of vampires. She saw a stack of bricks and rushed to grab two.

Going back to the van, she stuck the key in the ignition and angled the wheel towards the open garage door that made up the entrance to the bar. She pulled two thick hairpins from the back of her wig, hoping they would be strong enough. She put the hairpins upright on the carpet of the van, propping up the gas pedal before she put the brick on the pedal. The hair pins wobbled and started to bend as she set the van into drive. She didn't have long.

Running around the back of the van to the next one, she unlocked it and turned it on. She pulled out another hairpin from her wig and placed it under the pedal. Angling the steering wheel, she dropped the brick on the gas pedal and jumped back.

The vehicle zoomed forward.

Red ran to the front warehouse door before looking behind her shoulder at the loud impact. The first van slammed into the wall of the warehouse. The other careened into the bar, mowing through the vampires circled around Lucas and Quinn. She hoped it was enough of a distraction.

She sprinted to the closed-top convertible, but when she got there, she realized she didn't have the keys. Quinn had them in his pocket. She rushed over to Lucas's bike to see if he had left his keys. Of course not. She had just kicked over the wasp's nest. Vampires were about to spill out of the warehouse, stronger and faster than she was. She needed more of a head start.

Lucas and Quinn sprinted from the warehouse.

She hopped on the back of the bike and grabbed a helmet from the unlocked back pannier and put it on. "Let's roll!"

Lucas was on the seat in front of her before she could blink.

Without opening the door, Quinn leaped into his convertible. "Split up."

Red wrapped her arms around Lucas before the motorcycle spun out, sending gravel flying behind them, and raced out of the parking lot onto the street. She clasped her arms tighter. The bike drove by cars on the shoulder at 80 miles per hour, turning south down Coldwater Canyon Avenue. Her sunglasses fell off in a sharp turn to be crushed under the wheel.

The rev of motorcycles echoed behind them.

Lucas sped up, passing a semi-truck before darting through an intersection on a yellow light. He weaved through traffic to take a wide left at the next street, following a sign for the 170.

"Don't take the freeway! Not with a vampire gang on our tail." Red shouted to be heard through the helmet and over the wind. The second they got onto the highway, the risk for being spotted by cops or hurting bystanders rose a hundredfold. Her thumping pulse seemed to echo in the helmet.

Taking a sharp right, Lucas began a twisting route past strip malls and neighborhoods in North Hollywood.

"They found us again." She looked over her shoulder at the motorcycle behind them then to the side. Her eyes widened as her lungs hitched.

A second vampire biker sped across the two-lane traffic towards them. Jumping free before impact, he slammed into their back tire.

She didn't have time to scream.

Her magic rushed to her in a panic, and she opened herself up to channel the energy. The moment was too fast to form words. A cushion of air wrapped around her as she flew off the motorcycle and bounced onto the sidewalk. The second bounce broke her magic bubble. She gasped as her helmet slammed against the concrete, knocking the wind from her. Her ankle scraped on the ground. She looked up in a daze to see Lucas regain control of his vehicle and spin it to a stop beside her.

He jumped up, letting the bike fall, to kneel beside her. "You okay?"

Red nodded and pulled the helmet off. It took the wig with it. Panting, she stared at the ground, realizing how close she had come to a broken neck. She only had a few scrapes on her uncovered legs. Maybe that specter in Oklahoma had been right about her mother being a great witch. The rev of an engine made her gasp and look up.

Lucas charged the motorcycle rushing toward them. Stopping the wheel with two hands, he reached out and yanked the bigger vampire off the bike and over the handlebars.

Pulling the stake from her back, she rose to her feet. She saw a vampire in bell-bottom jeans out of the corner of her eye. He rushed her, denim flaring around his legs. She pivoted, catching him in his run with a stake to the chest, letting his own momentum power the blow.

The vampire dissolved into bones.

She bent over to quickly pull the stake from the bare rib cage and tossed it to Lucas.

"Just in time." He caught it over his head without looking, holding the undead biker by the hair with his other hand. He slammed the stake into the vampire biker's heart. Running to her side, he brushed the loose locks of hair escaping her bun back to examine her face and neck. "How are you okay? You flew off the bike."

She smiled, survival adrenaline making it feel goofy on her cheeks. "Magic. Sometimes it comes through in a pinch. Let's get out of here before the others catch up."

He nodded before picking up his bike.

Red took a deep breath and put on the scraped helmet, tossing the wig back into his bike's pannier, before she got onto the back. She set her hands on his waist and held on tightly.

"You up for round two?"

"I'm cool," she said even as her legs shook. She tried not to look at how the impact had scuffed up her leather jacket. Magic and the angle of her fall had kept her bare legs from being covered in road rash. She tugged down her skirt before gripping his waist again.

Lucas sped into the night, back onto Coldwater Canyon Avenue. The road grew hillier as the houses got bigger and more private, with old growth trees and high fences. They whipped through winding roads over onto Mulholland Drive as LA spread before them. The city lights glimmered brighter than any star on the edge of the vast dark ocean.

Her heart pounded in her ears even as the danger passed. Red kept looking behind her, but she didn't see a single biker as they drove to Sunset Strip and turned onto a side street toward the Pandora Hotel. Hopping off when Lucas parked in the garage, she pulled off the helmet, her hair falling loose from the bun, and set it on the bike with trembling hands.

Her mind still raced from the brush with vehicular homicide, but she sent texts to Quinn and Vic that they had arrived safely at the hotel. She looked up to see Lucas staring at her. "What?"

"You could have died." Lips twisting into a grimace, he shook his head, guilt in his gray eyes. "I shouldn't have brought you along."

She put her hand on her hips, annoyance powering through the fear. "What are you talking about? I'm the reason you two got out of that bar alive. It was my vans that mowed down those bikers. You're lucky I was there." Shaking her head, she turned to walk to the elevator. She wrapped her arms around herself, feeling suddenly cold as the adrenaline settled in her body.

"Didn't mean it like that." He appeared at her side. "You did a cracking job. I was the wheelman that let you get bumped off my bike. You should have gone with Quinn."

Softening her girl power indignation, she shrugged. "I don't want to get on a bike for a while, but I'm fine. My magic doesn't always listen to me, but it pops out when I need it." She smiled wanly and pushed the elevator button. "Put away the guilt. I've done this before."

"You're a witch?"

"Sometimes," Red said, blushing. She knew after using so much magic she wouldn't be much of one for a while. Only her near-death experience had wrenched the magic out.

The elevator door dinged opened.

"You have to stay here while I find Quinn and pull him out of whatever fight he is in," Lucas said, putting his hands in his pockets.

"Fine." She stepped inside and pushed the button for the 8th floor. "I guess this is good night?"

"It should be, but not yet." He stopped the door from closing and stepped through, bringing his hand to her face, and pulling her in for a kiss.

Red tugged him closer. The rush of escaping death fell upon in her the security of the elevator; the buzz in her ears and the thump in her chest told her she was alive. Her breath grew heavy. She stared into his gray eyes, then kissed him again.

Their hands roamed over each other's back with frantic energy. Lucas pressed her against the wall of the elevator. His tongue brushed against her lip. His hands circled her waist.

Breaking from the kiss, she nibbled along his jaw to his neck, her hands running through his hair. The black strands were so soft. His skin warmed under her lips. Her body's demands to celebrate survival drowned out every other thought. She leaned her forehead against his neck, catching her breath.

He lifted her, palms under her ass to wrap her legs around his waist before he kissed her again.

The elevator door dinged open and a panicked voice squeaked, "Oh my god, I'll take the next one!"

Red looked over Lucas's shoulder and blushed, then buried her face in his shoulder as the door closed on the 4th floor. She bit her lip and put her legs down. Face hot, she cringed. What was she doing? Had it really been that long? She did the math quickly. Actually, it had been.

"Okay, time for a cold shower," she said, with a small, embarrassed giggle.

"You're remarkable, Red." Lucas tipped her chin up with his finger. He kissed her again, this time slow and soft. Her phone vibrated in her hip pouch. He smiled against her lips. "You're buzzing too."

Blushing, she pulled away and answered the phone to Vic's abrupt barrage of questions as the elevator opened on the 8th floor. "Hang on, I'm right outside."

She stepped into the hallway and went to open the hotel suite. Vic was exactly where she had left him in the living room. She ignored the phantom kiss lingering on her lips to survey the scene. When she retold the story for her mentor, she was leaving that part out.

"Are you okay?" Vic asked from the couch, hand in a bag of chips. "Quinn called twenty minutes ago. He said he saw one of Kristoff's buddies with a mess of minions at that bar. The bastard blew his cover, apparently. He was still trying to shake off the Valley minions."

Lucas gritted his teeth. "I thought I recognized that ginger wanker—Donal Robertson. Fucking Novak has eyes everywhere now."

Red set her purse down. She had told the gang that Kristoff had found her cleaning out the Millennium Falcon last night, but she didn't tell them that he had told her his side of the Juniper saga. Had Kristoff sent his buddy to watch her? No, it didn't make sense, because no one besides Vic knew where they were going. The ginger vampire had been settled in that bar when they had arrived. He hadn't noticed her or Lucas either at first—only Quinn. She had certainly surprised those minions, especially with the careening vans. Only one seemed to recognize her.

"I saw the nerdy vamp that roughed you up. He ran before the action started."

"He wasn't the only rogue minion," Lucas said, rocking on his heels as if ready to fight some more. "Two dozen in that bar, and I recognized a third of the lot."

"I was afraid of that." Neck tensing from pain, Vic rolled up the chip bag one handed and sat up on the couch. "I managed to get into Julia Crispin's files, and she was into some heavy shit. She was investigating the rising vampire population in LA, trying to figure out which vampire went rogue. The Brotherhood has a truce with the Supreme Master here, but she went deep undercover, using DB Models as her entry point. Kept it a secret from everyone."

Red sat next to Vic. "Did she identify our murderer?"

"I only have her early notes with write-ups on players like Delilah and Cora. I think the later stuff was on her stolen computer. Had to be something big." He tossed the chip bag on the coffee table and crossed his arms. "Hired goons is one thing, robbing a hotel like this is another."

"Whoever killed her must have wanted her secrets buried too," she speculated. "Why else go after the laptop?"

Vic nodded before he looked at Lucas as if noticing him for the first time. "Hey! Why aren't you out there finding Quinn?"

"No need." Lucas opened the hotel suite door.

Quinn stepped inside, shoulders hunched, bruises on his face. His features didn't move but frustration hung around him. "Lost them after Ventura Boulevard."

"Thank God for LA traffic then. Never thought I would say that." Vic shook his head. "How did you guys escape that bar?"

Head bowed; Red shifted on the couch. She didn't want to gloat.

Lucas furrowed his brow and looked down. The cloud of guilt was palpable around him, but then he smirked at her. His words came out husky. "Don't be modest."

Quinn folded his arms, but a tiny smile ghosted his lips. "Lucas and I were backed against the wall with two dozen minions at our throat."

The younger vampire put his hands in his pockets. "Then I see this van mow through the crowd. Had enough time to jump to the side and run."

"I might have put bricks to good use." She shrugged, looking away from Lucas, flush climbing up her neck. He might not have wanted her to come initially, but he was happy to share the glory. She bit at her lip trying not to think of how heated it had gotten in the elevator.

"It got us out," Quinn said, a note of cheer threading through his deadpanned voice. "Now, lay low. Our stunt is going to attract attention." He gestured to the other vampire. "We have explaining to do."

Lucas grinned as he walked up to Red. "Don't let the old grump fool you. You did good." He ran a hand down her arm, fingertips making her want to shiver and step closer. "I should have known that you'd handle yourself."

"Yeah, yeah, Greg, 'atta girls all around." Chin lifted, Vic waved him with his working arm. "Get to stepping and use that charm on the supreme."

"And the role of my big brother will be played by Vic this evening." Repressing a sigh, she cocked her head. "But he's right. We're not flying under the radar anymore."

"Wouldn't be the first time." Lucas chuckled and turned on his heel to join Quinn, striding for the hotel suite door. He closed it behind him.

Red held her breath, eyes darting to where the magnetic vampire had exited as if he would pop back in suddenly. She brushed off the odd thought, ruefully wondering when she had become a silly teenager daydreaming about boys.

Vic shook his head. "Oh, to have the confidence of a mediocre white male vampire. I admire your ability to get those chuckleheads out of a sticky situation, but did there have to be an explosion?"

"The tables have turned on the pyromania, I see." She chuckled, refocusing on her mentor. His arm had been broken, but he seemed to have taken it in stride. Being out in the field without him wasn't the same, but maybe it might make him see that she was ready to be more than an intern. He had said she wasn't ready for the Hunter's Challenge when she had last asked. Busting up a barroom of minions had to count for something. "You're not the only one that can make things go boom."

"Was it cool?" He grinned.

She pouted. "The vans didn't explode as much as they could have."

"Wiped that smug look off Greg's face, didn't it?"

She laughed as she shook out her hair. Draping to her chest, it had been twisted into strange clumps by the wind. Or maybe that had been Lucas's fingers? She tried to detangle the rowdy locks. "His name is Lucas Crawford."

"Oh, no. Can we not joke about him anymore? Has it gotten there?" Vic put his head in his hand with a dramatic sigh. "When I told you to play nice with the souled vampires, I didn't mean to go and get a crush on one. This doppelgänger stuff is going to your head."

"Hey, don't go analyzing me. Your love life isn't any more normal. I remember a certain pastor's shapeshifting daughter." She shrugged and forced herself to yawn. "Oh, look at that, time to go to bed."

"Fine, fine, we don't need to paint our nails and talk about boys. You just look like you came from a first date, not near death from a vampire mob." He settled back on the couch. "Be careful."

"You've gone from big brother to Mom," Red said, smiling as she walked over to her bedroom. She had kicked ass tonight and even kissed a hottie. The life of a hunter's intern led to more lonely nights and pummeling than otherwise. She wasn't going to allow his grumpi-ness to spoil her mood.

"I feel like a single mother," Vic grumbled playfully as he turned the TV back on.

Letting herself fall into her nighttime routine of brushing her teeth and taking a shower, she went out onto the balcony off her bedroom when she finished. The lights and sounds of the city bounced off the concrete jungle. Wind blew the hem of her white robe back. She braided her towel-dried hair as she zoned out, staring over the rail.

Even four stories down on another building, she recognized Kristoff. She didn't know why she looked down but he was there. Hands behind his back, wearing another stylish dark suit, he nodded to her before he turned and walked away on the rooftop.

She backed into her room and closed the balcony door, then pressed her forehead against the glass. "Oh God, this is getting complicated."

12

Standing by the filing cabinet, Red looked inside the messy top drawer. She had gone from cabinet to cabinet in the row, but each was crammed with files, loose papers, and faded receipts. The routine organizing calmed her, but she couldn't help but be aware of Lucas reading the computer screen over Quinn's shoulder.

The vampires had assured her that the burglars hadn't touched them. It didn't say much about their filing system. If there was an order to them, she hadn't found it.

Vic had insisted that they come to Quinn Investigations to show Julia Crispin's research and work from the office. They hadn't a chance last night. After regrouping at the hotel from the explosive mission to the illegal bar in Gianni Construction, Quinn and Lucas had left to go tell Cora Moon about the mystery vampires in the Valley. She knew they could have emailed the research, but Vic was getting cabin fever.

Red felt eyes on her—Lucas. She shook her head and smiled

back. "Aren't you supposed to be helping me dig up the files on vampire attacks?"

"Can't help but be curious to see what the Bard chit wrote about me." The British vampire waggled his eyebrows.

Quinn's reserved expression flickered as amusement twisted his lips. "Impulsive, rude, and occasionally heroic. She has your number, boy."

"We already know about you, Lucas." Red smirked. She had gotten to know Julia Crispin through the dead woman's notes. The wry observations never seemed to disappoint. A disconnected grief stabbed at her. She had never met Julia, but she wished she had the chance.

The mystery had deepened around the murders. Like a hydra, wild conjectures kept popping up in her mind even as her logic overruled them. The numbers of rogue minions at the Gianni Construction had blown a hole in her tidy theory around Delilah taking out some uppity models leaving their contracts. They weren't back at square one, but Red didn't know what to make of the separate emerging patterns. Three threads were becoming clear: the two dead women signed to DB Models, the rogue minions multiplying like rabbits in the shadows, and the specter of the Blood Alliance's summit in the background. She strained to connect the dots. "It's other vampires that we need to learn about. With Quinn's sources at the LAPD keeping quiet, we're relying on your record keeping."

"Bloody hell." Lucas looked away, features contorting in the international expression for 'yikes.'

"Vic wanted us to make some progress when he stubbornly went on the food run alone." She grumbled. He was going to get himself killed with his bullheadedness. "He's even hitting up the butchers for you, too." She shook her head, letting the mysterious overcompensating ways of her mentor go to refocus on the files. "I'm really trying to find an order, but your logic escapes me."

"Simple. I stuffed them in a folder once we finished the case." Lucas pointed at the second drawer of one file cabinet. "I started stuffing them in around '93."

"Weren't you drunk for all of '93?" Red asked, skeptically.

"Sounds about right."

"He was a charity hire," Quinn mumbled, hiding his face behind the laptop.

"The really interesting ones, I put here." Lucas walked over to the file cabinet next to her. He opened the top and flipped through at vampire speed, his eyes moving quickly as he scanned the messily written labels. He pulled one out. "This is a weird one. Lots of tentacles in places you wouldn't expect."

"Unless that ends with a vampire attack, I don't think it's what we are looking for." Red leaned next to him to investigate the drawer. She reached out when she spied a label reading *"Vamps in Venice."* Her hand brushed his. Biting the inside of her cheek, she looked down. "This one looks more promising."

"Yeah." Lucas studied her, voice lowering. "Maybe we're onto something."

"Or maybe you're just pissing the wrong people off," Delilah Byrnes said from the open doorway.

She looked like a femme fatale from a noir film coming to see a down-on-their-luck private dick. Long, loosely curled blonde hair framed wary blue eyes. Her classical features were poised except for a trace of annoyance tightening her crimson lips. Tapping the door closed with a red-bottomed heel, she sauntered into the office in a blue Chanel dress that fit like a second skin. She was a nearly 400-year-old vampire and radiated the confidence of one.

"Sire." Quinn stood from his desk, his chin lifting as he looked the vampiress up and down. A trench deepened between his brows. His Adam's apple bobbed as he swallowed. He closed the laptop. "To what do I owe this pleasure?"

Delilah crossed her arms. "You might look like a male model, but you're smarter than that. I asked you to find the culprit killing my best girls, not to have a car chase on the freeway!"

"The case has gotten more complicated, as I told Cora last night," he said, his voice silky and conciliatory.

"Very complicated." Red matched the other woman's stance. "Some vampire is growing an army of minions in the Valley."

Delilah dismissed her with a quick eye roll. She focused on Quinn, leaning against his desk. The vampiress had been the old matriarch of the bloody foursome; she still held her rank on his turf. Their glance exchanged a silent communication honed over centuries. She then studied the human as if observing a zoo animal. "I can't decide if this is like the good old days or an utter perversion. I find it unsettling either way."

Red tightened her arms around herself. She could already tell that Delilah wasn't nearly as impressed with her as her general manager had been.

"It takes me back anyway." She smiled, an act devoid of amusement. "Is she writing your letters now too, Quinn? Or should I say again?"

Lucas stepped forward, his body partially shielding Red. "Bugger off with that. If you're here to scold us, do it. Don't dredge up the past."

"The girl is a rake. She is dredging it up with her very face." Delilah stared hard at Lucas as she jabbed a crimson-tipped nail at him.

Red felt her face and frowned before shrugging her shoulders under her tank top straps. She wasn't a rake...Shifting on her feet from the social awkwardness in the room, she felt lost from all the hidden history swirling in the room.

"I can see Kristoff got ahold of her," Delilah said. "Fabulous. Are you going to destroy his bar like you did Fabio Gianni's? Because Gianni is trying to bill the supreme for the damage."

"I'll have you know that I was following the law. Unregistered minions and all. I did Cora a favor." Lucas gestured, flapping one hand and putting the other in his pocket.

"A favor? Even the LAPD was able to follow your trail, especially the daredevil in the convertible." Delilah glared at Quinn at the last sentence, but her lips puckered up into a repressed smile.

"Guilty as charged." Quinn commented dryly, a challenge in his brown eyes. "Now, when I told the supreme that I found over a dozen rogue vampires in the Valley, she was pleased with me. What changed?"

"You're lucky that Kristoff sent his own to turn back the highway rabble. That three-car pile-up might have been cleaned up. Except every human has a cellphone these days." Delilah shook her head. "We tried to repress the news before the Blood Alliance found it. Then a short video went viral locally. Hashtag trending, boys."

"Bollocks." Lucas said, turning to Quinn. "You didn't say Kristoff helped you."

Red wrinkled her nose, not knowing how to digest that new fact. Novak's role in this saga had been hard to pin down. He might have had a connection to each facet of this mystery, but his actions were all over the map.

Delilah snapped her fingers for attention. "This eternal dick measuring contest with your progeny isn't the point, Lucas. The video of Quinn racing down the freeway was scrubbed off Twitter already, but it's enough to have tongues wagging. The Halloween Ball is in two nights. Cora didn't even want to look at me when I caught her at Hot Yoga."

"What else?" Quinn asked, his tone hardened.

"Then she was..." Delilah looked away from Quinn. "...reminded of Lucas challenging Kristoff's claim in public. She might appreciate the intel, but the collateral damage is a fucking mess." She pivoted to Lucas. "You know you're not exactly Cora's favorite either after everything in '93. The Supreme of Portland is her most visible ally among the unsouled and the Bloodliners, and you sucker punched his ambassador!"

"That pirate told her, didn't he?" Lucas asked, jerking his hands out of his pockets to mime choking a neck. He ran tense fingers through his hair. "That bastard will never forget Paris, will he?"

Red tried to remember what in her research in the bard database that they could be referring too, but their entries had too many demonic dealings to know which one might have pissed off Michel de Grammont.

"Why would he?" Delilah shook her head. "Let's not quarrel. He has been patient with you at my insistence. He's not the one you need to worry about yet, unless you keep pissing him off."

"You can say his name. I know full well Grammont is your lover." Quinn sat back down at his desk. "The warning is received, sire."

"Oh, don't be cold, darling. I came here because I cared. You like to stay aloof now, leaving me in the thick of it," Delilah cajoled, fluttering her eyelashes at him. "I'm off to another PR event tonight, trying to drum up support for Cora and keep our family on her good side."

"You always liked center stage."

Delilah straightened as if burned by his cold tone. "You don't know what it's like. Vampires have been coming in for the Blood Summit since August. Bloodliners and Doves, all agitating in every planning committee. It's pulling pragmatists like me to the extremes." She lowered her voice. "Be careful. Cora now knows someone has gone rogue, and she won't forget that you brought the message, but neither will whoever is turning those minions."

Red felt the tension rocket up. Their recon at Gianni Construction might as well have been a flare gun to their unknown enemy. The scandal was off Twitter, but the vampires at the summit would be discussing tonight in their seminars and cocktail mixers.

"I hear you, Delilah." Quinn crossed his arms.

"Let's see if you listen." She pushed her blonde hair over her shoulder before standing, strutting toward the door without a glance back.

"Do you still wear the necklace that Alaric gave you? The ouroboros?" Quinn asked softly from his desk.

Delilah paused. Cool and polished like marble, she had a smooth retort for the pointed question. "A lady always keeps the jewelry. It's much more faithful than the giver."

He studied his sire. "Two of the victims had a snake eating its own tail carved on them."

Delilah didn't react. Her smooth pale features held their aloof composure. Red tried to find a chink in the other woman's armor, but her expression was inscrutable.

"Strike you as familiar?" Lucas crossed his arms.

"You'll want to keep Juniper 2.0 out of sight, Lucas. The Blood Alliance is what concerns the supreme, not the Brotherhood. Right now, she has precious few allies for her peacenik agenda. Cora will grant sire rights if it suits her." Delilah paused like an actress waiting for her cue before she exited the stage.

Red released the breath she was holding. Silence grew as the three of them found themselves lost in thought as if alone. The phrase sire rights rang in her ears echoing like a death bell. LA County, land of the fluffy reformed vampires, wasn't a sanctuary. Not anymore...if it ever had been.

The door slammed open minutes later.

"Din-din, motherfuckers. I have lo mein and cow blood." Vic hobbled, bent over his arm draped with cloth shopping bags, before straightening as he kicked the door closed. "What? Not hungry?"

Forcing herself not to jump, Red put her hand on her chest then rushed to take some of the bags off his working arm. "You're a real mule. How did you even get this out of the car?"

"Only the weak take two trips from the car," Vic declared, even as his arm trembled.

Red filled him in on Delilah's visit while the others retreated to a corner of the office, speaking quietly. Vic rolled his eyes at the warning, but he held his tongue until the end.

"Well, we knew the case might blow open or, more accurately, up. Didn't think it was going to be some vans," Vic said as he opened the cartons of takeout and plastic pints of blood on the desk. "Maybe it might spook the rogue master into doing something stupid. Now that Cora is on guard, her people might end up catching him."

"You're assuming they're the same person. If I were a vampire creating a secret army, why would I drop bodies where someone would get curious? Leaving a dead girl at the official nightclub of the Blood Summit isn't very sneaky," she said, feeling like they had a version of the same conversation over and over. "Why wouldn't this rogue master keep her in a dungeon for a while, learn her secrets? It doesn't make sense."

"Point. Unless he wanted to break the truce between the vampires and the Brotherhood." He sighed, then picked up his takeout and fork before moving to a couch along the wall. "Hey, boys, secrets don't make friends."

Quinn held up a finger. "In a minute."

Too hungry to care what the vampires were whispering about, she joined Vic with her portion of greasy Chinese food.

"The drive made me think," Vic said, settling back on the sofa. "The last few entries in Julia's files were around Club Vltava. She had a photoshoot there with Kristoff and noted some weird tension between Delilah and him." He glanced between her and Quinn as if wishing he could say more. Did he have more love life gossip on the vampiress? "Julia wrote about a whole group of vamps having a powwow in the club, including Michel and what seems like all the vampires from Portland. No word on if they looked like hipsters or not. Is it just me or do we have too many suspects?"

"A city full, in fact."

A poking thorn of suspicion poked at Red. Just as her boss was nervous to speak plainly around his friend, she felt the same way about spilling her doubts about Quinn. He seemed nice enough, considering his past, but he wasn't over his ex-wife. Delilah was playing hostess at the summit and the bodies kept piling around her. If half of the vampires in Los Angeles could be suspects, then the other half would protect their friends...or sires.

"The motive could be anything," Vic said after chewing his noodles. "There are other former members of the Alaric Order in town, dissidents looking to rile up the authority before their big shindig, and what vampire wouldn't want to eat a model?"

She began to launch into an idea she had been picking at since she had changed bandages on her neck this morning. "I know. I have an idea on how to narrow it down. There is a fang mold database. We could—"

"You need to get back to the hotel," Lucas said, returning from his vamp huddle. Hands in his jacket pockets, he squared his shoulders. "Stay there until my damn progeny leaves town."

"Lucas will flank the van en route," Quinn ordered.

"Delilah says close the case and run, so we're supposed to listen to her?" Red set the food carton next to her and crossed her arms. She struck a determined hunter stance, then realized she had a piece of noodle on her face. Wiping the bit of Chinese food off her lip, she looked away from Lucas. "I'm a hunter... intern. Unlicensed, but that's not the point! This isn't my first rodeo with vampires. I signed on to this job, and I intend to finish it."

"We keep talking about the summit, but you're not getting it, kitten. This isn't just a fucking conference." The lean dark-haired vampire glowered; arms folded over his leather jacket. "Every city in North America has sent at least one master vampire. New York sent over a dozen. Then there's international crowd. Souled and unsouled, squabbling over bullshit and serving up cold intrigues to each other. You took on a few long-dead farmers and pig fuckers in Oklahoma City. This is LA, Red!" Lucas looked away. grumbling. "Don't be bullheaded."

Red crossed her arms and lowered her lashes. She opened her mouth, ready to rip him a new one for his condescension but gritted her teeth instead. She wasn't stupid. They had a mystery killer, a rogue master making minions, and now a pissed off Supreme Master of the City. Kristoff was dangerous, but who wasn't in this town?

All four of them had managed to attract attention. She was far from the only one in danger. Vic had a broken arm, so putting her in hiding would bench half the team.

Vic looked between Red and Lucas. "Come on. We still have options. Cora is pissed at the situation, but she'll do some yoga and get over it. She needs someone looking into this. We might even get a double bounty when we catch this bastard—from her and the Brotherhood."

Lucas gestured to the arm cast. "You're already down a limb. Want to add an intern to the list?"

"Bounties aren't worth it if your partner ends up turned." Quinn shook his head.

Vic shared a long look with him before nodding. "Fine. We'll talk about it tomorrow."

"This case has legs. It won't stop just because we do," Red warned them, letting her frustration sharpen her tone. Julia Crispin wasn't a wrong-place-wrong-time situation. She was on the trail of something big. More than half the encrypted research had been stolen from her hotel suite, but the leftovers were enough to validate her suspicions. She didn't care what macho silent agreement had just occurred. This case wasn't over.

The Blood Alliance's summit would wrap up after the Halloween Ball, and there were voting, committees, and speeches in between. The big finale would be Cora debuting the results of her Catch and Release policy on the last day. There were two—possibly three or more if you counted the new minions—victims, and with days to go until the summit was officially over, there was plenty of time for more to join the death count. Arguing only ate up the clock.

"You're off this job," Lucas said.

Eyes narrowed, Red nodded, biting her tongue. She wasn't an intern for Quinn Investigations. She was Vic's intern, so she saved her arguments for him. "Let's wrap it up then."

Silently, she helped Vic pack away the Chinese food and the laptop in a backpack before leaving the office. She stomped to the van, jostling the noodles with each step. The breeze wafting over the parking lot didn't cool her temper.

"Hey, I'm sorry for calling you bullheaded," Lucas said, popping out in that eerie-ass vampire way. He touched her wrist as she reached for the van.

Shying away from him, she shook her head. "You meant what you said. Be honest. I'd rather hear the truth, the whole truth."

"What is that supposed to mean?"

"All of this history is clouding you. That affects the investigation. And you're holding out on me. You were going to turn Juniper St. James, but you were stopped by the soulmancer just in time."

"How did you know...?" Lucas looked down, clenching his teeth. "Novak."

Red opened the door and climbed into the driver's seat, twisting to set the bag in the back. "If you're so worried about me, be honest with me."

Vic coughed from the passenger's seat. "This is awesome for me as a bystander. If you two are done angsting, I have some chilling Chinese food to eat."

"Goodbye, Lucas." She closed the van door.

Glancing over his shoulder, the vampire stalked away.

Red resisted huffing and rolling her eyes like a teenager at the rev of Lucas's motorcycle behind the Millennium Falcon as it rumbled back to the Pandora Hotel. Gripping the steering wheel tighter, she waited through agonizingly long moments of Vic fiddling with the radio before she asked, "What do you think?"

"I think this is an official Brotherhood investigation." Vic leaned back, drumming his fingers on the wooden chest between the front seats. "Delilah, man, she's always been able to get into Quinn's head. I don't think she's working alone. These are orders from above. Conspiracy, man."

"There's something very personal about these crimes. You don't just carve something into a person for no reason." She took their exit toward the Hollywood Hills and their hotel. The traffic shuttled along quicker than usual. "I'm split, Vic. Why was Olivia Greene killed? Is Georgia Erickson even one of our victims? There's too much going on and too many suspects on the list. Julia managed to get dirt on nearly every vampire who counted in LA, down to the addresses of their lairs. They all have agendas. Any of them might have wanted her dead."

He glowered out the windshield. "She did something real here in LA. Julia wasn't just studying werewolf periods like they do in London, sniffing their own farts about how clever they are to be Bards. This is serious recon on how to take down a rogue master vampire. She saw the pattern first—these minions are coming from the same source. Her father would be proud of the research. Walking away...it feels wrong."

The two fell silent, letting the classic rock on the radio fill the space, as the Millennium Falcon navigated through the light dappled streets. Red didn't say anything as she parked in their usual underground spot at the Pandora Hotel. Lucas's bike was already waiting for them.

"I'm doing an Irish goodbye," Vic informed her quickly before bailing out of the passenger side into the parking garage.

"Chicken." She muttered. Pulling the backpack on her shoulders, she stepped out of the van to face the vampire alone.

"Brassed off at me still?" Lucas asked, hands in his pockets, head lowered.

"Annoyed, but I have more important things to worry about than your old-fashioned protectiveness. It doesn't go with the punk aesthetic, by the way." She closed the van door and stepped away.

Red wasn't stupid even if she had been hopeful before about the Bard's deal with the LA vamps. Cora's laws wouldn't protect her. In terms of supernatural realpolitik, she was an easy trade off. The Brotherhood might fuss, but she hadn't even taken the Hunter's Challenge yet. They wouldn't break a truce for someone who hadn't even joined their order. She couldn't let it stop her. If she ran from every big baddie, she never would have started hunting.

"You need to lay low, even if you're mad at me about it," Lucas warned. "Let me protect you."

"You're not my bodyguard. Even if you were, you still wouldn't be able to tell me what to do," she said over her shoulder. "Good night."

Vic looked down and awkwardly rubbed his neck as he held the elevator for her.

"Nope, don't say anything, dude." Red jerked her head in a tense shake as she stepped in. She did not want to hear any version of 'I told you not to catch feelings' from him right now. "Let's just check and see if the hotel recovered the hallway footage and then eat."

The elevator reopened to the lobby. Waving them over, the front desk clerk smiled and placed a green envelope on the desk along with a rose and old book of folklore. "Aren't you lucky? What a thoughtful gift."

"Yeah, thoughtful." She took the flower and put the book under her arm before snagging the envelope. "Thanks."

Vic took over the conversation with the clerk.

She stepped away from the desk, barely hearing that the footage was still lost. Her eyes were locked on the red rose. Collecting herself, she put it in her pocket before stomping to the elevator with Vic in tow. She already knew who sent the letter before she opened it.

Dear Red,

The book and the rose are an apology for our first meeting. I hope you accept these tokens as the well-intended symbols they are. If you do, I'd like to discuss the book with you at the Halloween Ball as my guest.

Allow me to show you another side of myself. I am not asking for your secrets, only giving you an invitation to learn some of mine.

Kristoff Novak

"You could be our honey trap." Vic stroked his chin as they left the elevator and walked to their hotel suite.

"You mean vamp bait." Red unlocked their door with the keycard. She strode to the coffee table and pulled the takeout bags from the backpack then flopped on the couch.

"No!" Vic huffed. Sitting down, he pulled his cold takeout towards him on the coffee table. "He's a suspect with both the access and a thing for models. I read about him. He was accepted into the Alaric Order, but he left them back in the day during the August Harvest. For an evil vampire, Novak keeps a low profile. He seems to keep the bloodshed to business dealings. You'll be fine. Just pump him for information."

"In front of all the vampires at their own party?" She asked, deadpanned expression and side-eye locked on her friend.

"Not when you put it like that." He started slurping his noodles.

Red dug into her own and had more to chew on than lo mein.

Telling Vic about the night had helped her process, but she still couldn't shake off the weird glimpse into the Byrnes family dynamics. It was tense, but the three interacted with the fluid comfort of age. If Quinn and Lucas listened to Delilah and did leave the case, they needed a new vampire insider. Kristoff wouldn't be her first idea for an ally. "Sending me into the belly of the beast makes me easier to eat."

"I'm just saying if he wants to play gentleman vampire, we could use it. I'm not saying how." Pushing his empty takeout away, he pulled his laptop out of the backpack and fired it up. He pulled out his phone, set it on the coffee table and put it on speaker. "Let's get the big man on the line."

Quinn listened to the idea without interruption, but Lucas made dry commentary in the background. She imagined the two, standing at their kitchen counter, huddled over the phone. A ding of a microwave confirmed her theory.

Vic glanced at her. "The word's already out that Kristoff claimed a human. Might as well let them get a look so they can avoid you."

She grazed her neck, avoiding the scabbed-over fang marks. Suddenly, she wasn't hungry. She pushed her meal away on the coffee table and slumped back on the couch. "Even if I trusted Novak, I could get pulled into some other kind of drama."

Kristoff had bitten her. Then he had protected her in the parking garage. He had even helped Quinn escape the vampires on the highway. She might be able to trust he'd be content with courting her until he grew bored with being a gentleman, but the field was thick with plots at the Blood Alliance's summit.

"This is a conspiracy that's going to the top. I bet someone was trying to silence a mole when they killed Julia." Vic snapped his fingers. "The other girls were pretty and blonde. They were probably killed on accident. Mistaken identity, maybe? This isn't a simple murder case. This is politics, and so is that Halloween Ball. All the vampires will be there that night."

"Dead men love to tell tales. Bloody gossips, the lot of them." Lucas's voice boomed through the cellphone speakers. "They'll want to see the girl that I kicked Kristoff's ass for, and some will want to use Red against us."

She looked at Vic, furrowing her brow at his devilish smile. "He's hoping for it, aren't you?"

"Your idea was solid. The Brotherhood has gotten back with a 3D scan of the victims' bite prints. If I can crack into Cora's registry, I can try to match fangs with the molds she has on file." He grinned into the cell phone as he leaned closer to the table. "If everyone's watching you three at the Ball, then they aren't watching me. Or their computers."

"That would give the Brotherhood a backdoor into all her records." She was impressed by the audacity. Vic never shied away from a risky offensive. "Fat Crispin will love it."

"It would clear through our suspect list," Quinn said thoughtfully on the other side of the line.

"Red, I'll swear to a judge that you're a badass, but you don't have to prove it," Lucas said, annoyance clear even in the small phone speaker. "And Vic, ditch the hacker fantasy, we can just send Cora a bloody copy."

"What?" Vic slumped back on the couch, deflated.

"She has enough geeks on the payroll to do the leg work," Lucas said. "Send Quinn the files tonight, and he can pass them on."

"I'm going to ignore that dig on my hacker realities, Greg." Vic scoffed, but then grew serious. He tapped the touchpad on his laptop and brought a web browser onto the screen. Typing one handed, he frowned. "Can we trust Cora to act on the intel?"

Quinn's voice crackled from the phone. "She wants the murders to stop as much as us."

"We're all still on the same team, right?" Red asked, sharing a glance with Vic. She knew that it was his friendship with Quinn that had brought them here. She wanted to respect that but even he had to admit that this case was going cockeyed. "Working this case together?"

"Of course," Quinn replied softly.

The speaker phone broadcasted Lucas's triumph. "Now, you don't need to bore yourself at the Halloween Ball, Red."

"Only the new vampires are in this registry. We might not get a hit on these marks. Everyone who's anyone will be at the Halloween Ball," Vic argued. "This is our last chance to scope out the suspects before everyone goes home with their souvenir T-shirts for the baby fangers."

She shot a peeved glance at Vic. "It's been a long day. Before I fill my dance card for that evening, I'm going to sleep on it."

"Good," Lucas said, his smile coming through his voice. "You'll wake up knowing Vic's idea is bonkers."

"I'm ignoring you, Greg." Vic grumbled. "Whatever, she's right. This arm is killing me, anyway. Q, you're in the loop. Let me know when Delilah shows up again." He ended the call, then reached into his pocket and popped a pill. One handed, he tapped at his keyboard, awkwardly compensating for his busted left arm. He looked over at her. "It's not a fantasy. I could hack their system, if I wanted too."

"Totally, bro." She mumbled before gulping down her last bite. "Sent the files?"

He nodded and raised an eyebrow at her. "You're not going to sleep?"

"No, I'm going to do some research before I agree to become Kristoff Novak's plus one," Red said. She complained about being pulled into drama, but she was already in it and didn't know where the minefields were until she stepped on them. "Lucas isn't wrong. I don't like the idea of walking into a ballroom full of vampires with just a purse for protection either."

"Quinn could be like your Spanish *duenna*. Cora will be there too so you got another chaperone. It's like prom." Vic lifted his hand out, smiling as if that was a tempting feature.

Waving him away, Red closed the white box with leftovers. She stood up to put it in the fridge in the attached kitchen. "I think there are ways to get intel on Kristoff without me going to a dance with him."

"It's a new millennium. Women can choose their own dates." Vic stumbled to his feet. "I already have the research on Kristoff open on my computer. Don't turn it off when you're done. Quinn's file is still uploading."

Red watched him go to his room before looking at his laptop. She had already read the short summary of the vampire entrepreneur with a flair with photography. That didn't tell her anything beyond the fact that he was wealthy, well-connected, and rising in the vampire world.

She could already tell that by looking at Kristoff Novak. He had been the essence of a cocky vampire, lording over his nightclub empire with a supermodel on his arm. She knew he wanted more than her blood. He had extended the olive branch by saving Quinn the night before. That didn't change the fact that he was a person of interest that she hadn't finished questioning. She opened his gift to see engravings of fantastical creatures. A note fell out of the book with a single phone number.

Walking out onto the balcony, she pulled her phone out of her pocket and called the number. She didn't need to go to a ball to question some vaguely European vampire. Waiting for an aloof hello of a bored bartender or receptionist, she practiced what she would say in her head. *Hi, I need to talk to Kristoff Novak. Yeah, I'll wait but he'll want to take this one.*

The phone picked up and she blurted out. "Hi." She forgot the rest she had planned.

"Red." Kristoff rolled the R gently. "How did you like your gift?"

She swallowed, not expecting him to answer her directly. Vampires were as secretive about their phone numbers as they were about their lairs. Then again, his had an Instagram account. "Hi. Um, yes, that is why I called."

Silence deepened on the other end before Kristoff asked, "And, what is going on in that clever mind?"

Red blushed, then launched into her questions. "I want to know what the deal is. Are you trying to lure me out of the hotel so you can grab me? You've shown that you're more interested in chatting than torturing me, but what do you want? I really have no idea. That's what is going on in my clever mind."

"The deal is, I want you to get to know me. Maybe then you'll want me to get to know you." Kristoff's smirk was practically audible. "You can still investigate me at the Ball."

"I don't have to go on a date with you to question you."

He chuckled. "Have you ever seen a real dark room? Or developed a picture on your own?"

"What?" Red pouted as she scrambled to keep up with the topic change. "No. I've used Polaroids though."

"Come to the club. My gallery is in the same building. You have questions about my motives. I fully accept that I'm a person of interest and I'm happy to give you full access."

She snorted. "Happy, I bet."

"I have a new exhibit about muses through history. You'll want to see one of the portraits. You'll see what we all keep going on about."

"So, you can capture me and keep me in your dungeon?" Nonetheless, Red wondered exactly what he would show her. Her heart already knew. Her stomach twisted in knots.

"Bring stakes, crosses, and wrap yourself in blessed silver. Tell everyone on Instagram that you're coming. Actually, please do, and use the Club Vltava LA hashtag. We're trying to make it go viral." He paused. "I want you to see that I'm not someone you should fear."

"Even if you hadn't bitten me, vampires always have more than one angle." She bit her lip, the words 'genetic coincidence' looping in her mind.

"I do have a proposal, but it is business. I promise to shoot straight with you."

Red fell silent before she nodded her head. This case was too hot to back down now. Every second cooled their leads. Halloween was too long to wait to get more answers. "This is a bad idea, but I'm on my way. If I'm not back in an hour, you'll have hunters at your door."

"I expect nothing less." Kristoff sounded amused at the threat.

"Text me alibis for the nights of the 24th and 25th. I want to check them out. Your brother doesn't count as an alibi." She hung up the phone.

Lifting a hand to her mouth, Red closed her eyes. She was running headlong into the lair of the unsouled vampire who had claimed her. He was at the top of their list of vampires with access to all the victims before their deaths. Person of interest...That was an understatement. Second to Lucas, she hadn't thought of any vampire more.

Her phone vibrated. It was his prompt text message with times and dates of people and places to vouch for him. Red shook her head at the star-studded name-dropping then forwarded the messages to Vic with an explanation.

Red grabbed a black hoodie and strapped on her small demon hunting kit to her waist and upper thigh. She hung a hand-sized blessed silver cross on her belt before jamming the stake into her hoodie pocket. Passing by Vic's room, she didn't wake him up. He would be bummed to miss out on some action, but he wasn't in fighting shape if it came to it. Kristoff would clam up around the Bard anyway. She could use the vampire's nostalgia to make him slip up. Vic would understand. He had taught her to do what it took when it came to a case.

Red tried to tell herself that she was going to dig deeper into Kristoff, even as all her bubbling questions came back to Juniper St. James.

13

October 29th, Night, Club Vltava, Los Angeles, California, USA

Pulling down the hood on her black zip-up sweater, Red questioned her sanity and walked up to Club Vltava.

The queue of fashionable clubbers stretched down the sidewalk, even at the early time of half past ten. In old sneakers, faded jeans, and a black tank top, she looked more like a girl about to do laundry than hit the hottest new club on Sunset Strip.

She was still trying to convince herself that meeting Kristoff Novak alone for an interrogation wasn't a crazy idea. Being alone with one vampire to get intel was better than being alone with over a hundred at the ball, right? The rationalization was still a work in progress. She had come prepared at least with a blessed silver cross and a snub-nosed revolver filled with wooden bullets. The leather demon hunting kit strapped to the top of her thigh and belt bounced with her quick steps.

Hiding her nervousness, Red lifted her chin to walk past the aspiring glamazons and part-time actors. She pushed her loose hair over her shoulder, brushing the clean bandage over the scabbed bite. The last time she was in this club, she had ended up with holes in her neck.

What was she doing?

She was supposed to be investigating Julia Crispin, not Juniper St. James. Questions dug at her, pricking at her curiosity like thorns. All she had found in LA were questions. Out of all the players in this game, only one wanted to tell her anything: Kristoff Novak. At every turn, she walked into the fight blind, because she didn't know what her enemy saw—Red or Juniper?

Kristoff stood at the head of the line beside the large bouncer. Dark blond hair slicked back and wearing a fitted suit without a tie, he held his hands behind his back. His twinkling blue eyes studied her approach without a glance at the other women waiting in their mini dresses and heels. He grinned, deepening a dimple in his cheek. "I'd offer my arm, but I don't suppose you would take it."

She stopped in front of him. "And I thought you didn't know me. You said you had something to show me."

"Do you want something to drink first?"

"I'm not up to the dress code." Red looked down at her outfit, taking her hand off the silver cross on her belt to reveal it. She kept the revolver in her kit. He didn't need to see all her cards.

"Business it is." Kristoff nodded and led her into the entrance of his building but instead of taking the elevator up to Club Vltava, he guided her through the glass double doors on the ground floor. The low lights in the open lobby of the gallery were compensated by the ceiling fixtures highlighting the framed photography on the walls.

Glancing around for henchmen and finding none, Red reminded herself that she was under the protection of the Supreme Master of the City. Not that it had helped that much last time. Hiding her disquiet, she met his gaze. "Everything is on the record and I expect you to be honest."

"I will tell you the truth as I know it. That is why you are here, isn't it? The truth?" Kristoff tilted his head, considering her answer. His high forehead furrowed above his piercing blue eyes.

Red didn't like the X-Ray vision in his glance. She looked away. "Why did you mention a dark room?"

"A person's passion is where you see them in their truth. Or at least one of them." He led her past the white walls filled with photography both hyper realistic and surreal, of people from around the globe. Not a single print was of a building or landscape, only humans living out a second of mortal life, captured for eternity.

Red let the silence grow as her mind rattled with what she found on the Bard Net, but it was dates and named events like the Sack of Paris and the Last Bloodline War. She knew he had been dubbed the Butcher of Cologne after a vampire clan battle. Only Julia noted his gift with photography. "Did the Byrnes chose you because you were a photographer? I read that Delilah demanded each member of her clan to be skilled in an art."

"She didn't demand that of her minions." Kristoff laughed. "I was chosen to shine boots. Much like in business, I am a self-made man in my creativity."

Red knew conversation bait when she heard it. This wasn't a date. It was an investigation. She pulled the topic back to the case. "You said that you had a proposal for me? Enough with the gallery tour, let's get to business."

"My business model is to mix business with pleasure."

"You can explain and flirt at the same time." She crossed her arms, marching past the framed photography and barely seeing the subjects.

"I need your help." Kristoff looked down, glibness disappearing. "Julia Crispin's untimely demise behind my club is raising questions from more than flame-haired hunters. I think it's a frame up. When the surveillance footage was returned, it was edited, and half my outdoor cameras were broken around the time of her death. I saw the recording of her walking out of the club, going across the street then toward the alley. She didn't come back the same, much like my tape. I'm guilty of many things but not her."

"You want me to clear your good name?" Red planted her hand

on her hip, pausing her step. She had speculated on what he was going to ask her, but that certainly hadn't been on the list.

Kristoff lifted his dark eyebrows; a hard edge entered his blue gaze. "I want to know who thinks that they can sully it. I would pay. I know hunters love their bounties."

"I can be paid off, but if this is a goose hunt so you can make time with me, I'm out." Startled, she stepped ahead to avoid his eyes. Then she remembered her newly acquired trust fund. Having Fuck You Money still hadn't sunk in. She bit her tongue as he began to speak.

"I am an ambassador with the Supreme of Portland, Prince Marek, himself. This summit isn't just a meet-and-greet for folks to take back to their districts. Real players are in town. I'm already in hot water since I claimed you so audaciously." A small smile bloomed on his face.

"You could have the grace to be ashamed." She sneered, walking faster.

"Shame is hard when you don't have a soul. I would have preferred more of a courtship. But I won't lie to you. I will never regret choosing you, especially if it keeps you alive. You see my bite as a chain. I see it as a tool for you to use." He took her over to a makeshift white portrait backdrop in the center of a small exhibit hall and picked up a camera on a stool. "Interactive exhibit. There will be two pictures left on the reel."

"You're not taking my picture." She held her palm up, readying herself to block a shot of her face.

"You're taking mine. It should be worth a thousand words, give or take." Kristoff handed her the camera and strode to the backdrop before turning around. "Now, for the record, I don't prefer studio setups. I like taking my pictures where the action is."

Red studied the thick lens and the dials on top of the camera. Part of her wanted to play with the buttons, but she figured it had been adjusted for the gallery lighting. "Why did you come to Los Angeles early for the Blood Summit? Couldn't an underling open a club?" She lifted the camera up to study the subtle play of surprise on his handsome face through the viewfinder. "What? I'm putting some action in this studio."

"Action, is it?" He licked his bottom lip.

"An interrogation is an action." She bit her cheek to restrain her curving smirk. Her picture-taking finger grew itchy.

"That isn't a digital camera. You have to choose your shots carefully." He dipped his head, rubbing the back of his neck shyly.

"I am." Red smirked, watching the distraction on his face through the viewfinder as she put him off balance. She liked seeing the tables turn on a vampire. "Answer my question."

Kristoff regained his composure and straightened his shoulders. "I came early because my master wanted eyes on the ground."

She kept the camera to her eye as she waited for the perfect shot. It felt easier to talk to him from behind the device. She had too many questions for him to chicken out now. "Like a red-haired vampire who frequents bars in the Valley?"

He nodded. "You've seen Donal then."

"Did you send him to watch me?" Red asked.

"No. Independent orders. He didn't even recognize you. He did a video call so I could see the brawl. An early birthday present, to see my sire staked." Kristoff perked up at the thought before his brow furrowed. "He was sadly wrong, but I spotted you in the background, rushing out the door. It gave me enough warning to gather my men to help. When I only found Quinn, I went to see if you made it home. I assume the explosions at Gianni Construction were your work."

"Someone had to deal with all those minions," she said absently, concentrating on the viewfinder as she primed her finger over the shutter button.

"You're brave," he said, chin lowered, and his blue gaze met the lens. His face had seemed so arrogant earlier, yet for a moment, it lay open and vulnerable.

Perfect. She snapped the picture and lowered the camera. "Or bullheaded. I'm still working that one out."

Kristoff narrowed his eyes as a name formed on his lips before he swallowed it and straightened his shoulders. He said instead, "Courage can be mistaken for stubbornness."

She looked down at the camera to avoid his real stare. "It's harder to decide when I find myself playing America's Next Top Model with a vampire."

"I might have been called a butcher, but I won't harm you, Red."

That might have been the truth as he knew it, but it wasn't a promise that she could rely on. "Harm means different things to humans and vampires," she said.

"You're right," he said without being flippant. His expression grew more earnest—if conflicted—as he searched for his next word.

Red didn't know if he was reaching for a lie or a truth. Maybe he didn't either. She took another picture to capture the moment. She had the feeling that it wasn't often that he was at a loss for words. "I think that is all of them." Lowering the camera, she tilted her head trying to guess his next move. He looked different in the viewfinder.

"Then let me show you how the magic happens." Kristoff smiled, oddly innocuous like a shy child showing off his best toy. Restraining himself, his reserved cool returned as he gestured to an unlabeled door.

"Before I let the dastardly vampire lead me off to a secret room, I want to know why I'm really here. It wasn't to take your picture, and you could've asked for help in your letter. You had something else to show me." Red lifted her chin, having to raise her face to meet his over six-foot height. "Let's keep to business."

"So professional." Kristoff dipped his head and put his hands behind his back.

"We've played enough." She echoed old advice that Vic had given her. She wasn't certain who the statement was really for—him or herself. "Being focused on the job is how a hunter stays alive."

"You have someone else watching your back now. I won't let anything happen to you."

"You say you're protecting me, but I know it's to protect your territory. There is a difference." She'd had a long night and a longer week, wading through vampire shenanigans, and had the bags under her eyes to prove it. She gestured to herself in slouchy jeans, leather kit on her thigh, and a zip-up hoodie. "If I'm so precious, why show me off at the Ball?"

"I claimed you. I want them all to know," Kristoff said it with all the emotion of a human declaring they were running to the store to get milk.

"Ugh. Be less gross." She made a face. "I'm doing my job and questioning you, but I haven't forgiven you for biting me."

"I told you I'd be honest." He shrugged.

"And paternalistic." Red shook her head. "Nothing you've said tonight makes me think that you'll be content to see me walk out of your life. You're playing nice so I put down my guard. It doesn't matter that you're happy to take it slow. You're immortal. Any second, you could get bored, and this gentleman act falls away."

"I'd rather be a knight." He held out his hand to take the camera.

Red handed it over. "You didn't address my concerns, Sir Vampire."

Kristoff looked down at the camera before he set it aside on the stool by the interactive art exhibit. "I might have claimed you, but I don't own you. People can't be owned. She told me that."

"How progressive." Red laughed dryly, crossing her arms, fighting the urge to squirm with curiosity at the reference of Juniper. "Now, I'll sleep easy."

"I'm growing fond of you, but I've only just swiped right. It's a bit early to chain you up and have you as my concubine, don't you think? Buy me dinner first." He mirrored her posture, an amused challenge in his smirk. The handsome arrogance, remote yet inviting, returned to his expression.

Rolling her eyes, Red jerked her thumb toward the lobby. She had played enough games. Just like in the nightclub, she was letting herself get close to the charming spider because she was curious about the intricacies of the web. The part of her that said that she was being a dumbass for being alone with him grew louder. "Time's a-wasting, and if this is a preview of what you have to tell me, I'm ready to bounce."

"Before you call the cavalry, you'll want to see this." He guided her around a white detached wall.

She followed him through another section of the gallery. They passed an eclectic collection of photography like Alice B. Toklas in black and white, Eartha Kitt radiating power, and a vibrant life-sized Angelyne in the Muses Exhibit. Jaw dropping, she stared at the sepia portrait on the wall. It pulled her to it like a magnet.

It was her. Or rather, it looked like her. Exactly like her.

A foot wide, the antique gilded frame of carved rosettes wrapped around the oval photo. In a dark Medieval bodice, flowing white skirt, and her loose curls tumbling down the cape on her back, the young woman looked like a Victorian dream of Camelot.

Red knew she was the new kid in doppelgänger land, but she didn't expect it to feel like this to finally face her. It wasn't like looking at a mirror; it was like looking at another world.

Juniper St. James sat on a high-backed chair, knees facing forward, but turned at the waist to lean her elbow on the armrest. Chin under her knuckles, she stared at the camera. She had been posed before, but this was a candid shot. The photographer had caught a small wistful smile in a secret moment. Her eyes locked on the photographer and not the camera.

Kristoff's voice was low when he began. "I thought I was dreaming when I saw you. I had them so often after she died. Dreams where I would call out, but she would always disappear."

Red couldn't look away from the face that could be hers. There was a sadness in the eyes that the dreamy smile couldn't reach. Kristoff had captured...Was it bittersweet longing? "When was this taken?"

"Prague in 1899 before a masquerade ball. I took all the women's pictures. This was one I snuck of her."

She did the math quickly. "She died a year later in August."

Kristoff nodded. "It was the beginning of the end for her. It was the end of the beginning for me."

"You were both so young." Red's voice sounded far away to her own ears as she studied Juniper. This was the woman that they all saw.

"I was made only months before."

"Did she know that Lucas was going to turn her?"

"Maybe she knew what was to come, but she didn't accept it. She had a plan." Keeping his focus on Juniper, his voice grew hoarse. "I didn't know that things were going to change. When I took that picture, all I knew was that I would follow her into hell. If I had my way then, I would have."

She looked away from the raw emotion showing through the cracks in his control. "What was she like?"

"Clever. Her hands were always moving. Fixing clocks, flipping through a book, always stained with ink. I noticed that first about her. It was later I realized her courage. A spirit that not even a golden cage could extinguish." Kristoff grinned and shook his head. "Women weren't supposed to be interested in science or adventure. She defied convention even as she made use of it."

"How did she end up with vampires?" She squinted at Juniper St. James peeking from the frame. The portrait showed a young woman with hard experience in her eyes. Quinn and Kristoff described a capable woman. Where had it gone wrong?

"Juniper kept her secrets well, collecting them like books. I knew she was from America. She had been on the run from a warlock when Lucas found her in England. Maybe that was why she stayed so long with him." He stared up at the portrait. "I knew her favorite book, her favorite tea, but I don't even know if that was her real name."

She had been told that Kristoff had a thing for Juniper, but it wasn't infatuation in his voice; it was devotion. "What was she to you?"

"She was the making of me." He met her gaze with intense certainty.

Red felt her heartbeat pick up. Her palms started to sweat. She blurted out. "Was this taken when you started your affair with her?"

"Before. You'd be surprised to know that it was Quinn that opened that door."

"He said he was a villain in the story." She avoided his look. "I didn't know he played matchmaker too."

"Quinn Byrnes is a vampire whose brutality and cunning was legendary. You wouldn't know it from how he slouches around now." Kristoff pursed his lips, then shook his head as if the peculiarities of souled vampires were beyond his pay grade. "A master of mayhem, he liked to set up schemes and pull the strings—especially when he was bored. One day, he decided he wanted to sketch Juniper. The short of it was that I saw more than I should have of my sire's courtesan."

"What happened?" Red had held the torn sketch in her hands at Quinn's office. Staring at Juniper filled in the blanks on cream-colored paper in her mind's eye. This portrait was why she had come, but the Mona Lisa smile revealed nothing even as it seemed to be the key to everything.

"You need to buy me dinner to get the full story." Kristoff smirked and bounced on his heels. "Afterward, I was cocky, as vampires are wont to be. She put me in my place. We were friends again after that."

"Friends?"

"Surprisingly, I am capable of having female friends. Stick around, and you'll meet a few." He grinned, but his smile fell. "I think we honestly thought we could be friends. Time changed all that." He shook his head. "Is this unsettling for you? Learning about a stranger with your face?"

"You finally figured out we're different."

"I know you are. I hope your fate is different too." Kristoff raised his hand, his fingers ghosting over her cheek without touching her. He pulled away. "After she died, they lied about her. She was full of light like you. I don't want to see that snuffed out."

"Don't mistake me coming here." Red shivered, telling herself it was nerves. She stepped back. "You might have claimed me, but that doesn't make me your girlfriend."

"I won't bite or undress you until you ask. I know the rules." He looked over at the portrait, his flirtatious demeanor fading. "I couldn't help her at the end, but you might still find me useful. She would want me to help you. It's trite, but the truth can be."

"I can accept help, but not with strings attached," she said. "Unsouled vampires do terrible things to girls like me. Death and nihilism are the family friendly part of it. I can believe that there is some lingering bond between you two that makes you want to help me or even that your better angels might win out. What about your friends?"

Red had more questions she wanted to ask, yet they all crowded her throat, choking her. She took a last look at Juniper. The woman might be reaching out through history to her, but the present beckoned. She needed real intel, not backstory. "Who else at this Ball might recognize my face?"

"The supreme wouldn't, but her second-in-command might. Delilah for sure. A few of my people have seen this portrait, but they'll be on their best behavior around you." Kristoff left out the implied *or else.* "Juniper traveled around Europe with the Byrnes for years. Who knows who she might have met? The August Harvest would have claimed many of them, so we have that on our side."

"Will you be on your best behavior at this Ball? Not that I am going." She coughed to cover her slip.

"Have high expectations for me. I'll exceed them."

"I'll keep you to that." Red raised her chin and tried her best determined face.

Lips twitching in a repressed smile, he put his hands behind his back. "Let's see how that photo turned out."

"Changing the topic doesn't mean the interrogation is over. What are the Bloodliners saying about the murders? That's what you call the unsouled faction, right?" She followed him, leaving the woman with her face behind.

"Murders? What should I expect to be charged with?"

"Fewer than you've earned, but at least two." She glanced at him as they walked through the winding gallery of detached walls and framed faces. "What does a snake eating its tail mean to you, Mr. Novak?"

"The ouroboros. Infinity to some, wholeness to others. It means the Alaric Order to me."

Red hoped for more shock, but he seemed unfazed. "You were inducted into that Order and left. What does it even mean to be inducted? Did you get a sash or something?"

"It was more like the mafia than the Elks Club. You could say that I became a made-man in Paris."

"So, how do you go from working for Lucas to the order?"

"Even vampires have higher authorities. Not long after that picture was taken, I fought in Alaric's horde as it stormed across Europe. Lucas drank and bitched the whole war." Kristoff's tone grew icy. "You want to know why the Byrnes were the worst of the worst? They came from it. Unsouled vampires are bastards, I'll give us that. Yet even among the bloodline elders—and I am talking the old and cold—they chilled at the abominations that passed for entertainment in Alaric's court."

"Gotcha, they were monsters to monsters." Red rubbed her upper arm, suddenly feeling cold even in her hoodie.

"You won't have to dig deep to find the bodies they left behind. Delilah kept her little clan out of his court, but not forever, not when her master called. I left once I had nothing to keep me."

They reached the unlabeled door by the white backdrop in silence. Red glanced around the interactive exhibit, wondering how they had gotten back here so fast. She had been lost in her musings about the tangling lives of immortals.

He took the camera before opening the door. The scent of chemicals and a red light drifted out of the dark room.

She reached for her silver cross on her hip to flash it at him as she walked through the door. "Don't get any ideas."

"I'm full of ideas, but I know what you did to those minions in the Valley." He put the camera on a worktable inside.

"Keep that in mind when you start sharing your passion." Eyes adjusting to the gloom, she kept on a deadpan expression even as goosebumps rose on her arms. Her gut told her that he had been honest with her before, but she knew he could choose his words with the best of them when he was concentrating. What would she shake loose when he was distracted by another project?

"I know how to keep it professional." He gestured at the trays of chemicals on the table and the hanging photos in different stages of development. "I work mainly in digital now, but there's still something about a dark room."

"How does it work?" She asked, letting the cross pinned to her hip go slack to take in his setup of pristine white surfaces and mysterious devices.

Kristoff led her through unrolling the film to choose the last picture of him. Explaining as he went along, he put the negative carrier into the enlarger to project the photo onto a flat easel.

After a string of questions about the equipment, Red remembered to get back to the case. "Lucas knows you asked me to the vampire prom." She tried to imagine what the Halloween Ball would look like—the Met Ball or a gothic Anne Rice fever dream?

"How did my sire take the news?" He asked dryly, staring at the film strip under the magnifying lens of the enlarger.

"Sarcastically and with threats of violence." Red studied Kristoff as he created the print.

"Sounds like my sire." He shrugged a shoulder, concentrating on transferring the blank-looking print to the trays of chemical washes. The dynamic of their maker-progeny relationship was clearly established then. "I've been in town a month. I'm surprised we've only had one fist fight."

"You two pissed off Michel and Cora by fighting over me." Red told herself to focus on the play of emotions on his face, but she was distracted. His photography development setup might as well have been alchemy to her.

"Cora owes me for keeping her peace, and she knows it. Michel on the other hand..." Kristoff shrugged. "I'm surprised we haven't had a fist fight yet."

"You're good at making friends, I can tell. Why would he recognize my face?"

"If there was one thing that Juniper had in spades, it was secrets and names. She disappeared after Prague and made a new life. Instead of serving vampires, she staked them. You can see why I'm fond of you."

"Yeah yeah." Red looked down, biting her bottom lip. She didn't need him buttering her up. "What happened?"

"I only know that he saw her, but I have my suspicions that they met before. It was a clan battle in a railway station. We weren't on the same side. Michel attacked Lucas to let her escape. I don't know why. Who knows if he will remember that rainy day that he saved a damsel in London? For a vampire like him, it might be quite novel." Kristoff smiled. "For the record, that took place after the affair began."

She put her hand on her hip. The interrogation was slipping from her control. "For the record, what was your affiliation with Julia Crispin, Olivia Greene, and Georgia Erickson?"

"I photographed them all. They were in the marketing campaign for the club opening. Are you saying the other two are dead too?"

"Yes, shortly after their shoots with you. Hence why you're a person of interest."

"I slept with Olivia. But I didn't see her again after she started dating a guy from a Netflix show." He shrugged, looking embarrassed. "Honesty was the policy."

"You have a way with the ladies, Kristoff. I heard a rumor about some weirdness with Delilah. What's up with that?"

He laughed. "That's an older, longer story. There's a reason why both Quinn and Lucas don't like me very much."

"We have a Casanova on our hands." Rolling her eyes, she put her palms up in mockery before asking him more about his relationship with Olivia Greene.

Kristoff answered her dogged questions but sighed as she started to repeat herself. "Yes, the relationship was over in a week. No, I wasn't sore about it. It had been a decade since I had been dumped, but technically, I didn't know we were dating. Check her Instagram. You can see the change in boytoys. Olivia took a selfie every ten minutes."

Looking up the woman's Instagram account, she noticed photos at Club Vltava, but the rest were with a buff bearded hottie. Red clicked on the Club Vltava hashtag and scrolled through a week's worth of content to see a video posted on the night that the first victim died.

She clicked on it to see an old livestream to the club, showcasing the bartenders mixing drinks for the fashionable. She fast-forwarded through the video to see Kristoff sitting at the bar with a tall woman. Red looked up. "I thought you were fucking with me when you put Khloe Kardashian as an alibi."

Kristoff grinned. "She has surprisingly good taste in wine."

"I bet," she said absently, more interested in the time stamp on the video than his celebrity pals.

It was the same time that the coroner listed for Olivia Greene's death. As far as Red knew, bilocation wasn't a vampire superpower. He could have hired an underling to kill Olivia, she reminded herself. The connection felt weak. Kristoff was here on business, trying to gain favor with Cora Moon. By every account, from Julia's notes to word on the street, he had been toeing the line. If he wanted to really get rid of his ex, he could have just had Olivia taken up north to Portland. Fewer questions in his home territory.

She frowned, realizing that she didn't think he had anything to do with the murder. Playing politics and opening businesses in LA meant blending into the human world. By all accounts, Kristoff had been operating under the radar. Social media aside. Killing an ex-girlfriend with fifty thousand internet followers and letting her be found on the beach was sloppy. It sure wasn't blending in.

Red took a screencap of the livestream and texted it to Vic. She lifted her eyebrows and put her phone in her pocket. "So, you and Olivia were done-zo. Now, what about your photoshoot with Julia Crispin?"

Directing the interrogation and leaving out the dead woman's investigation, Red peppered him with questions about who was there and why, to match up against Julia's notes later. Filtering through were ones about the technique of making the tester print and bathing it in the chemical washes.

She bit her cheek as she realized she was leaning over the photo, staring at the developing print, more interested in the dark room than the murder case. She pulled back. "This was very fascinating, Kristoff, but this print will take time, and I have a curfew. We need to get back to the case."

"I'm an open book." He leaned closer. The dimple in his left cheek and chin emerged as he grinned.

She held her breath, ready to remind him about personal bubbles when her hoodie pocket vibrated. She answered her phone out with a raised finger at Kristoff and stepped out of the dark room into the brighter gallery, blinking to adjust.

"Red," Quinn said, wind and static breezing through his phone as if he were cruising down the freeway with his convertible top down. "Another girl was found. She was dumped outside my office, but I found her in time to call an ambulance."

"Shit, where is she?"

He rattled off the name and address of a hospital. "I tried Vic, but he didn't pick up."

"He popped a painkiller. Out like a light." Red cursed. This night was going to be a long one. She thought quick. "Another model?"

"I think so. This girl needs guards."

"I'm there." Red ended the call and tapped to find her rideshare app, typing in the address, ignoring Kristoff's eyes on her. She'd had an unsettling—but not exactly unpleasant—interrogation, but more duty called.

"You don't need to call a ride," he said. "I know the hospital. They are happy to sell blood bags under the table."

"Ew." She eyed the surge pricing and thirty-minute wait for a ride. "Fine. We need to hurry." She quickly texted Vic where she was going and with who, then sent a follow-up: *DON'T TELL LUCAS.*

Smirking, Kristoff walked her over to an elevator, blending in with the white gallery walls. "Your secret is safe with me."

She blushed and looked away, following him. "He's not my keeper."

"I like an independent woman."

The elevator took them underground to a parking garage. Kristoff placed a light hand on the small of her back to guide her around a corner to a Mercedes Benz. He lifted his hand to push the remote key control, then opened the passenger side. "Your chariot, my lady."

"I'm a hunter," Red said as she slid into the passenger side of the luxury car. She shook her head ruefully. Quinn had asked for guards. He didn't specify how back up should get there. "You're dropping me off then heading off, Kristoff."

"It will be the best Uber of your life. Five stars." He slid into the driver's seat and started the car, engine roaring to life with a purr. "You didn't say yes to my business proposal, but you'll see that you'll want me as a client."

"Keep your money. I don't want you as a client." She closed the door. "How about I just find whoever killed Julia Crispin and this poor girl? Since you swear it's not you, your name will be clear. Everyone wins."

"You don't have to trust me to make use of me." He pulled out of the space. The underground parking garage door opened, and he turned onto the street.

Red stared at the car window, where only her own reflection faced her. She focused on the spot where his should be. "I can believe in your better angels, Kristoff, but I'm not betting on them yet."

14

Kristoff looked over at her, hands on the wheel as the Mercedes Benz rolled to a stop outside the Culver City Hospital. The glow of the hospital's lights filtered through the car's windshield, leaving his face in partial shadow. "We're here."

Even looking out the window, Red was surprised to see the automatic doors of the hospital. He had been content to play chauffeur and let her zone out. She had been lost in her thoughts once they hit the freeway. Her evening at his gallery answered plenty of questions about the case, but it only added more mystery to her doppelgänger. She knew that Quinn's call for help only put a pause on unraveling Juniper St. James' secrets.

"I told you. Your best Uber ride. I didn't talk, and you controlled the radio."

"It's a change of pace." Red chuckled, checking her phone for a text with the room number. She looked over at Kristoff in the driver's seat as she undid her seat belt and opened the door. After all he had shared with her, she didn't know what to say. "You shared some painful history with me tonight. It couldn't have been easy, not with this face staring back at you."

"It's a good face." He nodded. "You're more than a doppelgänger. You're a decent shot."

She bit the inside of her cheek to suppress a smile. "Thanks for your cooperation, Mr. Novak."

He leaned his head on the head rest and smiled at her. "You can interrogate me anytime."

"I just might have to." She stood up and out of the car before closing the door.

The window rolled down, and Kristoff called out, "What about the Halloween Ball?"

"I'll let you know if I'm busy that night." Red waved. She might not have had to shoot him tonight, but she wasn't ready to slap on formal wear and join him at a gala.

Kristoff grinned and shook his head before putting the car into drive and speeding out of the hospital parking lot.

Red turned around to see Lucas step through the automatic doors. Her heart started racing. She didn't know why. She didn't owe him anything, but she still felt awkward. "That was him. Novak."

Lucas put his hands in his pockets as his gray eyes followed the car. His brow furrowed and his shoulders slumped. Instead of angry jealousy, he radiated worry. "Find what you were looking for?"

"I saw her." Red walked to him. She didn't know how to make him understand. After a year of not even finding a single picture from her past, wondering who she really was, even seeing a doppelgänger's portrait was something she couldn't miss. "Kristoff has a picture in his gallery."

"I'd like to see that." A sad earnestness crept into his voice. He turned and started walking to the door. "Quinn wants all eyes on this girl. I left him upstairs."

"What? No lecture?" She asked when she caught up, the sterile hospital air already making her skin crawl. He'd been growling for her to stay out of the action since she arrived in LA.

"You said you can handle yourself." He took her past a nurse's station to an elevator. "Didn't expect you to be hopping out of his car, but a man has to assume you have reasons."

"I hadn't finished questioning him. I wasn't satisfied with sitting on the case."

Lucas lifted his eyebrow. "Are you satisfied now?"

"He didn't kill Olivia Greene, since he was with a tabloid queen at the same time." She held out her phone to show the screencap of the timestamped livestream in the club where Kristoff was in full view at Olivia's time of death. "Now, I know he didn't attack whoever Quinn found outside his office. Beyond her body being found at his club, there isn't any evidence that he had anything to do with Julia Crispin either. Those are facts." She put her phone away in her back pocket. "I'm not so naïve to think he's an ally. I can hear the worry, even if you aren't saying it."

His jaw twitched as he looked down, before taking an unneeded deep breath. "You gave me the business, Red—trust you or don't. I'm going to trust you. Not him."

"I'm not asking for that. I learned enough to know that ship has sailed." She opened her mouth to continue, but the lights went out, and the elevator car shuddered to a stop. "A blackout? Not now."

The emergency lights flickered on.

"No such thing as coincidence." Lucas glanced around at the elevator car. "Quinn is alone up there."

Red hit the emergency call button. "Fuck, no one's answering." She looked up at the small door in the ceiling, thanking her lucky stars for outdated elevators. "Boost me up." Stepping onto his cupped hands, she opened it before jumping back down. "Okay. Do a vampire thing and get help."

"We're between floors. Give me a mo' to pry open the door." He jumped straight out of the elevator, landing on the top with a thud. His voice echoed in the empty elevator shaft. The mechanisms jerked to a start. He jumped back down, landing in a crouch, black hair covering his face. Head cocked to listen, his nostrils flared as he sniffed the air.

"Maybe it was a rolling blackout," Red said, but the sentence caught in her throat. She knew she was wrong.

The elevator opened to chaos. Alarms rang as flashing lights strobed on beige linoleum and a deserted nursing station. A doctor in blue scrubs ran after two cops around the corner. They ran after them. Lucas shot ahead. Leaning on the threshold, she peeped into the hospital room.

In a pool of blood, a blonde woman twitched in a hospital bed surrounded by nurses and doctors. She was the model that giggled about Delilah's love life before a meeting at DB Models.

Lucas turned Red away from the terrible sight. "Don't watch."

She gasped, recognizing the woman from the modeling agency. Her name was Carrie Baldwin, and she'd been so excited about a marketing campaign that she'd just landed that she'd decided to stay with the agency. S

Red shook her head and covered her mouth. Carrie should have quit. She should have told her to.

Quinn appeared behind her in the hallway. "I lost them." His brown eyes were haunted with the same failure that she felt.

The heart monitor beeps went flatline.

"11:48 p.m. She's gone," a doctor called out, wiping his arm across his forehead, leaving a smear of blood.

Pulling away from Lucas, Red turned away and clenched her fists. She had come to LA to stop these murders, not see the bodies pile up around her. Blinking away tears, she watched Quinn speak to the officers without seeing.

"Let's get out of here," Lucas said quietly and led her out of the hospital into the darkened parking lot. He didn't speak, but his steady touch on her wrist soothed her.

Quinn soon joined them, his steps silent on the asphalt as he hung his head.

Red stopped processing, numb from the carnage. She didn't speak until she was bundled into the back seat of the convertible while the men took the front. "What the hell happened up there, Quinn?"

"I stepped out to speak to an officer then the blackout hit." Quinn said as he got into the driver's seat and started the car. He pulled out of the lot. "When I came back, I found the nurse screaming. The woman was going to wake up. Until they cut her throat."

"Why your place? Why would they dump her there?" Red inspected the rearview mirror, it reflected only her in the backseat. She wished she could see more than the vampire's profiles. They avoided her stare. "Vic keeps talking conspiracy, but this pattern feels personal. Two of the bodies were left at the lairs of former members of the Order of Alaric. Why would someone want to leave you a drained woman like a cat with a bird?"

"I don't know. It's a message, but I don't know who it's from." Quinn looked back at her. His brown eyes met hers before refocusing on the road.

"Three girls in a week. That's a hell of a message." Lucas cracked his knuckles. He perched in the front seat, hunched over the dashboard. "I got one of my own for the sender."

Red felt the same, but they still didn't know who to blame for these terrible murders. The sight of Carrie Baldwin dying seemed seared on her eyelids. She tried all the meditative breathing that they tried to teach her in that PTSD support group. Falling apart over Carrie wouldn't bring her killer to justice any faster.

The car ride from the hospital was too short to fully calm her nerves, but her stomach had settled at least. The tension jerked back into the place as the convertible parked in the lot behind the office strip mall where Quinn Investigations made its home. Blue and red lights from cop cars painted the white building.

She stepped out onto the asphalt with her eyes on the cops and crime scene techs scurrying around the lot. A breeze carried the scent of curry from the Indian restaurant next door. She unzipped her hoodie to let it drape down over the leather kit on her thigh. The outline of her snubby revolver didn't show through the bulky leather, but habit moved her hand. She followed behind Quinn and Lucas toward the office door.

A dark-skinned detective, badge on the lapel of her navy pantsuit, met them on the sidewalk. Young for her position, she surveyed the crime scene with her arms folded like a commander. The flyaways in her shoulder-length relaxed hair, wrinkled suit, and pressed lips spoke of a long night without words.

Red pulled back to stand beside Lucas, trying to blend in with the scenery. Her standard operating procedure with cops was to avoid them. Hunters looked a lot like violent drifters if you didn't know what was behind the Dark Veil.

Quinn nodded. "Detective Callaway."

"This is the part where you spill what I need to know about this vampire shit." The detective spit out the word vampire with a shudder. She raised her hand. "And if you just say Blood Summit and disappear again like I'm supposed to know what it means, I'm not answering the phone when you need information again."

Red relaxed her guard. She had worked with cops who had known about the supernatural before. It certainly made hunting easier to have an ally on the force. She knew that Quinn moonlighted as a sketch artist for the LAPD, but she hadn't met any of his contacts yet. It was almost comforting to know that Quinn did his laconic, cryptic guy act with everyone and not just her.

"If I knew who was doing this, they would have been staked by now," he said.

"This vic isn't the only one. I'm finding more drained people than ever. Brass is keeping it quiet." The cop rolled her eyes and huffed. "As usual."

"It ends after Halloween," Quinn said softly.

"That's not good enough." Callaway raised her palm to stop him from interrupting. "I'm speaking. I staked a vampire biting a dishwasher on Cienega last week. Souled. Thought you people were the good guys."

"You shouldn't have been hun—" he said.

"You know what he told me? He said it was time to choose sides."

Red snapped her gaze to Quinn at the detective's words. She cursed his lack of emoting. Delilah had mentioned that the factions were rallying in the city. What did he know? The Blood Alliance was a centralized authority, but the supreme masters still ruled their cities with complex networks of vassal masters and minions with local treaties and truces.

Callaway curled her lip, dropping her clenched fists to the side. "I don't care about bullshit vampire politics. These murders need to end."

He nodded, broad shoulders seeming small, wrapped in an aura of guilt.

"You're giving me nothing, Quinn. You're not the one who has to lie to this poor murdered girl's family." Callaway looked down and hugged herself for a moment before her expression grew remote, and she straightened her arms. "Choose a side."

Red watched Quinn's shoulders slump, but when she looked back Detective Callaway was already walking away to her car.

Lucas commented drolly, "The Bloodliners are working hard to get the voters out."

"I didn't notice any lawn signs or get any vampire robocalls," Red quipped involuntarily to break the tension.

"It's no democracy, but the management likes to take the pulse of public opinion," Lucas said.

"Or influence it. Cora is taking the stage at the Blood Summit after the Halloween Ball to promote her catch and release policy," Quinn said.

"Let me guess, she still isn't gaining friends with it." She looked over at the yellow crime scene tape wrapped around the five parking spaces, then to the entrance to the suite of offices where Quinn Investigations rubbed elbows with a massage therapist and an accountant. "Were you able to search a bit before the cops came?"

Quinn shrugged. "I did a look over the parking lot, but I was too focused on stopping the bleeding and calling the ambulance to pick anything up."

Flipping through her tidy mental dossier on the case, she thought back to Julia Crispin's murder scene. "Did you see anything that looked like an antique?"

"What are you thinking?" Lucas grinned.

Red pulled out her phone to scroll to a picture in her gallery of the broken locket. It had been stolen along with the laptop. "Did you see anything like this? Remember, I found it in the alley at Club Vltava."

Quinn stared down at the small portrait in the locket and furrowed his brow. "No, but that woman... Lucas, does she look familiar to you?"

He shrugged. "Not ringing any bells."

"You never remember anyone." Quinn sighed as if they had bickered about this longer than Red had been alive. They probably had.

She looked around at the officers getting a witness statement from a waitress by the Indian restaurant and forensic technicians taking pictures of the blood splatters marked with yellow cards. "They'll pick the scene clean."

"You should leave. You can't do anything here." Quinn nodded to Lucas. "I have business."

Red blinked and he was gone. Only the rev of the convertible engine from the street hinted where he had gone. "The detective is right. That disappearing stuff is annoying."

Lucas held up his motorcycle keys. "Let me get you back to Sleeping Beauty at the hotel."

It might have been Vic's bedtime, but it wasn't hers. "You weren't long after Quinn in finding her. Did you see if she had a mark carved into her?" she asked.

He gestured to his left arm. "Just like the rest."

"Consistent." Red focused on the patterns in the case even if her head spun from the questions. The three disjointed threads in the investigation were weaving together. How soon before the threads were tightening around their necks? She realized she had gone silent and coughed to cover it. "You're going to come back here and case the scene, aren't you?"

Lucas tensed as if preparing for an argument. "From the roof."

She nodded, the trains of thought multiplying as she started walking toward the door to Quinn Investigations. "We'll need to text Vic whatever we learn."

"Where are you going?" Lucas asked, lips quirked in amusement.

"Um, the roof?"

He tensed as if to argue before he nodded toward the other side of the parking lot. "Ladder is this way."

Ducking her head, she smiled and shook her head at herself for assuming he'd stop her before following him.

Two days before Halloween, four murdered women, and more vampires than she could shake a stake at—Red felt beyond back at zero. Her gut told her that Kristoff might be a danger to her, but he wasn't their murderer. The evidence validated it, even as more questions bubbled up. After a week, she had successfully confirmed at least one vampire had not killed at least one of their victims.

That left the rest of the vampires in Los Angeles as suspects.

15

October 30th, Midnight, Quinn Investigations in Culver City, Los Angeles, California, USA

Feeling only stray burnt kernels at the buttery bottom of the bag, Red pouted before wiping her hands on the napkin. "All gone."

The rooftop breeze whipped her hair back. Her dinner of a greasy noodle bowl felt so long ago after Delilah's warning, questioning Kristoff, and then another victim left behind in the parking lot of Quinn Investigations. She had nearly inhaled the popcorn and would do it again.

"Call Guinness, it's a record." Lucas tilted his head, an easy smile on his face. "I think it took less time for you to eat it than it did to make it."

"Reconnaissance is a hungry business," she said primly before glancing back at the crime scene in the parking lot. Perched on the edge of the roof, she could see the crime scene technicians bent over evidence tags and blood splatters. The crew was packing up the last of the evidence. She smiled at Lucas. "Thanks for making it."

"I burnt it." He shook his head, but a small grin lingered on his lips.

Red couldn't help but match his expression. There were times that it was hard to remember he wasn't human. "Is it a vampire thing because you're not a solids man, or is it you?"

"Personal failing. I'm told I over-spice too."

"Huh." She had read about vampires, met her share, even knew one who made a mean plate of chicken and waffles, but she had never gotten close enough to observe the less lethal vampire quirks. "That's weird. You'd think with your sense of smell your taste would be enhanced."

"Food doesn't taste the same. Can't eat much of it." He raised his beer can. "Thank the bloody lord, drinking is another story." He took a sip before he looked at her and laughed. "I can see the question, and no, I don't pee. Whatever magic keeps me walking, that takes care of it."

Red blushed from him being able to read the juvenile question on her face. It didn't stop her from asking another. "Can you throw up? I'm imagining something cat-like."

"Everything with a mouth can ralph. That's science." Lucas smirked self-deprecatingly. "I paid more attention in literature class than in biology."

"I noticed your bookshelf." Red could believe it. He struck her as a dreamer underneath all the layers of rebellion. It was nice to meet another reader. Vic was great for talking about TV shows, but he didn't crack open a book unless it was about demonology. Reading was how she passed the time while Vic was driving on long haul hunts across state lines. She didn't have a backstory yet, so she read about characters who did. "You had some good books in there mixed with the random crap like your boots and a few old joints in a teacup. You need a real ashtray, by the way."

"If I'd known Quinn was turning the place into an Airbnb, I would've tidied up." Lucas smiled shly. "You left *On the Road* by the nightstand."

"I've read it before, but sometimes I like to visit my old friends." She bit her lip. Was it weird that she had looked him up in the Brotherhood's database instead of just asking him about his life? Social etiquette was confusing as a hunter. "You were a writer before the Byrneses found you?"

"I was a glorified clerk at my father's shipping business, but yes, I did fancy myself a writer. I scribbled more on my overwrought stories than worked." He shrugged. "Nepotism got me the position. My father's death kept me in it."

She realized that she had no idea what he did when he wasn't hunting. Eternity was a long time without any hobbies outside work. "Do you still write?"

Lucas lowered his head, black hair falling into his eyes. The messy locks hung over his ears as if he were just a few weeks late to the barber. "I've picked up the pen a time or two, but to Delilah's chagrin, that literary flair died with me. I was too busy drinking deep from the cup of life in the early days to write about it."

"What about now? At the very least, you have a memoir in you. A long one."

He lifted his head, a ghost of a bemused smile on his lips. "The truth was that I wrote stories about the lives I wanted to live but didn't have the stones to. I was a bored romantic. Then Selene swept into my world in a whirlwind of moonlight and mystery. Of course, I said yes to wherever she would take me."

Red remembered the small picture of Selene Byrnes from Bard Net, the vampire with the angelic face and raven hair who had sired Lucas and brought him into the harsh glittering supernatural world. The entry made note of their passionate affair. Why had Selene taken Quinn's name instead of Lucas's? Vic had said that she was mad as a hatter even if her visions were true. Red understood how such a creature could have swept a young poet off his feet.

"I didn't live until I died." Lucas raised his beer can to her in a toast. "That isn't a problem you have as a hunter. You've seen more adventure in the last week than I saw in my entire human life."

"The people you meet on the road do liven things up." This was the part in the conversation where a normal girl would talk about herself, share something about her family, or talk about college. Red didn't have normal conversations. There wasn't enough in her memory for one. She talked about demons, murders, and the occasional sci-fi show. Lucas had shared so much about himself, but she still couldn't lay down her cards.

"I have time for a story."

"It looks like they're leaving. Let's do a quick sweep." She stood, grabbing the popcorn bag with her.

Red climbed down first. The ladder was hidden between a fence and the small one-floor office strip. She dropped to the gravel and crept around the side of the building with Lucas on her heels. After throwing away the popcorn bag, she walked over to where a strip of yellow police tape draped on the ground.

He circled around the five spaces in the parking lot where the murdered woman, Carrie Baldwin, had been dumped.

Red had taken notes with her phone on the areas where the CSI had marked blood splatters and lingered taking samples and tire prints. She went over the areas, finding only signs of the cops, before crouching down to check under a car.

"Red," Lucas said with a nod to the opening back door of the Indian restaurant. A stream of waiters, cooks, and dishwashers left the restaurant, chattering with varying degrees of excitement, worry, and annoyance as they pointed at the crime scene.

She stood. If there were any clues left, the rush of cars and people leaving the lot would destroy any leftover evidence.

"That was useless. All the real clues are wherever she was drained, not where she was dropped." He opened the office door for her.

"Dropping her here was a clue." Red walked into the darkened hallway shared with other offices and stopped by the door to Quinn Investigations. "Come on. Until Quinn gets back with more than the name of the victim, we don't have much to do besides look over the old files. Whoever is building that little army in the Valley must have been at it for a while. Those minions might be new, but not that new."

"Don't you think you should get some shut-eye?"

"I'd just toss and turn. Might as well get on with it. You two need another set of hands around here." She needed to keep moving. It was the silence that made her thoughts race too loudly in her ears. This case had gotten to her. She wasn't ready to psychoanalyze why she saw herself in Julia Crispin, mourned Olivia Greene, or felt guilt over gossipy Carrie Baldwin.

Red stepped into Quinn Investigations as he turned on the lights. It looked cleaner than before, but she knew the file cabinets hid chaos. And maybe even a clue to the power player behind the scenes in this city.

"Then let me at least make you coffee," Lucas offered.

"I'd love one, but I gotta ask. Are we on the same page about where I stand on this team? I get that Delilah freaked you both out earlier, but you and Quinn can't buddy cop your way out of this alone."

His protectiveness didn't come from a bad place. Red could forgive it, but she couldn't forget it when she had a job to do. Playing hot and cold, holding back intel, they couldn't solve this case unless they worked together. "I'm still a hunter. Well, like an apprentice, but still. Did you try to keep Vic out of the hunt when he was Quinn's intern? I highly doubt you play rugged defender for all of your hunter buddies." She bit her lip, realizing she was rambling. "I get that I look like her, but I'm still me."

Lucas pulled his hand out of his pocket and ran his fingers through his dark hair as he shook his head tightly. His gray eyes filled with guilt. "I try not to see her when I look at you, but I do."

"There's a lot of baggage that comes with this face, but we have a case. You have to focus on what's good for the job. It's not about me."

"It is for me." He sighed and cocked his head at her. "With Kristoff in the picture, I can't think. I hadn't wanted to turn her. I kept kicking that can down the road for years. Then it all changed the night she died. I was given a choice: turn her and take her away or...

well, it wasn't much of a choice. It wasn't me she'd been running from all those years. It was her past. Kept it close to the chest, but it was bad. In my own twisted way, I thought I could keep her safe, so I did what I did. I failed. Now you know the rest of the story." Lucas gritted his teeth and looked away. "The fallout is my rutting problem. It's not you. I know what you can do."

"Lucas..."

"How about that coffee?" He put his hands in his pockets and shifted back on his heels. His voice rougher from emotion. "Sugar or no?"

"Sugar." Watching him disappear into Quinn's private office to go into the apartment below, she knew that it couldn't have been easy. He had been raw and real with her tonight. "Thanks for being honest," she whispered to the empty room, wondering if he could hear.

Red found file boxes peeking out from behind the front desk. Had Quinn been going through these? She sat down in the chair and reached into the box, pulling up files to discover CD-ROMs and floppy disks. The modern computer at the desk didn't have a floppy drive, naturally, but she popped the first disc into the drive. Her phone vibrated, and she pulled it out to see a text message from Kristoff. She opened it open to see a short video. She unmuted it and turned the volume down low.

"Consider this another alibi for tonight." Kristoff grinned and panned the camera to show a part of Club Vltava she hadn't seen before, revealing a stage where Michel and Delilah stood with smiles and waves.

The video ended, and Red put the phone back in her pocket. She shook her head. This is what she got for giving a vampire her number. Vampires couldn't appear in a mirror, but videos and photos were fair game. She'd heard a rumor that it was a vampire who took the first selfie.

She put away her thoughts to keep sifting through the disks and CDs in the box. Most were empty, but a few had files on them.

Sipping at the coffee Lucas brought her, she put another CD in the computer when the door opened.

"You blew up my phone, but you couldn't wake me?" Vic called out as he stepped into the office. His black mullet lay tufted and tousled on his shoulders. Partially obscured by his arm sling, his denim vest lay inside out on his shoulders.

Lucas chuckled. "You needed your beauty rest, Constantine."

"Shove it, Greg." He stepped over to the desk and sat down on the edge to glance at the computer. "Is it just me, or has it been a long night?"

"You slept through most of it, but yeah." Red filled him in on what he'd missed. "There wasn't much in the parking lot to begin with, but the tech swept it clean, so I figured we might as well look for signs of a rogue master in their old files. You're at the portion of the evening where I've found more of Lucas's old playlists than evidence."

"Is that what you have in there?" Vic leaned over to click on a folder. "I wonder if we'll just find a bunch of Billy Idol and the Sex Pistols, or if he'll have some real punk like Bad Brains."

"Just a video." She clicked a file. "The last one was of Quinn blinking and dropping the camera."

The video opened on a familiar curb in the Fashion District. Olivia Greene lay sprawled on the sidewalk. A blonde in a cocktail dress stepped into view. She looked around, showing her classic profile. Stepping over to the body, she picked up the dead weight easily before she disappeared with vampire speed. The video ended.

"What the hell?" Vic's face went through the stages of grief, stopping at confusion. "That was Delilah moving one of our victims. Why does Quinn have this?"

Red looked over at Lucas. "Did you know about this?"

"I don't even know what you're seeing." Lucas appeared behind them and leaned over her shoulder to play the video again. "Bugger."

Vic hopped off the corner of the desk, confused horror turning to anger on his face. "Q didn't offer me his couch... This is why! Goddamn that ex-wife of his!"

She twirled around in the office chair. "Easy, Vic."

The office door opened, and Quinn stepped in. He raised his hands. "Vic, I can explain."

"Do tell. I'd like to hear how you've been using me to help cover up for Delilah. Add some legitimacy by bringing a Bard in, huh? Throw us at some rogue minions and have something to distract Cora with." Vic paced in front of the desk. "I'm seeing it all clear now. Fucking crystal."

Lucas stepped between the men. "Come on, lads."

Quinn sighed, and his shoulders slumped. "Delilah didn't do it. The body was planted on her building's doorstep. She brought me in to find out who was targeting her. There have been murders of old members of the Alaric Order for years. She was scared, didn't want anyone to know, but I knew you might see something I couldn't."

Red crossed her arms and looked away. Right now, Vic's aura radiated with enough betrayal that even her busted third eye could see it. She didn't want to add fuel to the fire by sharing a skeptical glance.

She had given him the cliff notes version of her interrogation with Kristoff Novak in a text message. She wondered if Vic was thinking of it too. When Kristoff found Julia Crispin dead behind his club, he informed his Prince in Portland, the Supreme Master of Los Angeles, and the LAPD, in that order. Why didn't Delilah call Cora, if they were yoga buddies? Red shot Lucas a peeved side-eye, but the vampire was too busy walking to stand beside Quinn.

"Don't flatter me or lie to me." Vic shook his head and folded his arms. "I came when you called, and this is what I get? A fuck it bucket of lies. You're hiding evidence! How much of this case have you been manipulating? You didn't tell us about the Alaric symbols on the victims, and now you're hiding surveillance footage."

Quinn's usual stoic demeanor cracked. "I didn't hide any tapes. I didn't even know there was a tape!"

"A tape? What is this 1995?" Vic barked out a dry laugh. "I can't believe anything you say. Not when it comes to Delilah."

Lucas put a hand on Quinn's shoulder. "Take it easy, Vic."

"You don't know her," the elder vampire said.

"Never wanted to, Q." Vic gestured around. "I don't need to know her to guess what she's up to. She's playing both sides, building up her street cred with her new boyfriend and the other Bloodliners with a killing spree. Dealing with uppity models trying to leave their contracts was a bonus. She never could go too long without twisting your head up, so why not bring you into the game? Delilah is playing you."

"Maybe she thinks she's protecting them." Red furrowed her brow, trying to keep her voice light to balance out Vic's booming indignation. The evidence was there. If Vic wanted to walk out with it, then he needed to play it cool despite the bromance broken heart. She ejected the CD and secured it in a case before putting it under her shirt and standing. "Quinn is her progeny, and Lucas and Kristoff are part of her line. By leaving bodies at each of your lairs, maybe she's trying to show that you guys are on their side too."

Vic snapped his fingers. "Exactly. She is showing that the Alaric Order is still around. You're dancing to her tune."

"You're talking about things you don't know anything about," Quinn said, clenching his fists before catching himself and crossing his arms.

Vic's eyes bored into his friend, his voice rising. "I've read what the Brotherhood has on you two. Spain, 1700s, you two liked to carve up villagers leaving an ouroboros behind like fucked up graffiti. Delilah's at it again!"

She stood up to step between the men. "Everyone relax. Shouting at each other isn't helping."

"We won't find any help here, Red." Vic shook his head. "Let's go."

She looked at Lucas. "Can you swear to me that you didn't suspect it was Delilah or that Quinn might cover for her?"

Lucas looked away, hands in his pockets. "I—" He licked his lips and stilled. "I didn't know."

"But you're not surprised." Red shook her head, following Vic to the door. She had thought he was telling her the full story tonight. She felt so stupid letting her crush infect her good sense.

"You were my Batman, Quinn." Vic hunched his shoulders and stomped out of the office.

The night hadn't just been long, it had turned the case upside down. If someone had told her that Kristoff would be the only vampire to be honest with her tonight, she would have laughed. She kept thinking that the soulmancer's spell, to give a vampire back its empathy, conscience, and all those elements that made up a human soul, made them completely good. It didn't. It just gave them the choice to be good.

Humans had souls and could still be tempted into evil by money, greed, revenge, and love. Vampires were no different.

Quinn had been pulled in by love. What about Delilah?

16

OCTOBER 30TH, Afternoon, Le Retro Diner, Hollywood, Los Angeles, California, USA

Red poured maple syrup in the shape of a smiley face on the pancakes, then set down the syrup and turned the plate around to face Vic Constantine. "Look, I'm a brunch zombie, I'm going to eat this face." She turned the plate pretending to speak for the pancakes in a squeaky voice. "Save me!" She took a bite dramatically.

Staring into the distance, forehead wrinkled in forlorn contemplation, he was dead to the world.

"There is a life on the line, Vic."

Stirred from zoning out the window, Vic glanced at the ravaged pancakes. "Welcome to the real world, kid."

She waved at him. "Good morning, sunshine. Thanks for joining me at brunch."

Loud chatter filtered in around them from the other booths at the diner as quiet pop hits played in the background. He had been quiet after they left Quinn's office and catatonic when he woke up. It had taken all her charm to get him out. He had been rocked to the core after seeing the video of Delilah with Olivia Greene's body. She understood being disappointed. It had been a kick to the throat to know that Lucas had been holding back his own suspicions to protect the other vampires.

She tried to smile. "Your pancakes are going to get cold."

Vic shoveled a forkful into his mouth. "Should have gotten waffles."

"Ugh, say it again with less food in your mouth."

"I'm just questioning all my decisions. I should have gotten waffles. I should have gotten an Impala instead of a van. What if I had decided to take more comp sci classes instead of ditching to play sidekick to Quinn? I could've invented Snapchat."

"That's a leap."

"Yeah, you're right. It would have been a shady cryptocurrency startup." He chewed on his dry pancake sadly.

"At least put some more syrup on it. This is how I know you're not okay." She picked up the syrup and flooded the plate like he usually took his pancakes. "Alright. It's not good, I know. You've got serious trust issues with your shadowy mentor. We're on our own with this case now, but the good news is that I think he is doing this out of love. Not malice. I don't think he's turned bad."

"He is a professional Captain Save-A-Ho, and she is the original Ho."

"We have proof she had direct contact with the body, that she felt like it was targeted at her, and that she wanted to keep it quiet. Maybe she didn't kill Olivia." Red said it with a straight face, pushing her own doubts away for objectivity. Technically, they had only seen Delilah move the body which already looked dead on the video.

Vic swallowed his mouthful of pancake in a pained gulp. "Or she got some chump to do it."

"Obviously, she knows something. We can't get the wrong vampire. The Brotherhood has a truce with Cora, so her souled vampires are off limits. Delilah is still one of those." She shrugged, acting more casual than she felt. Vic wasn't thinking straight, and he was injured. Even if he wasn't, they were in over their heads. He couldn't blunder into a brawl with an aged demon because he had a bromance breakup. "If this is deep state stuff, then Cora will want first crack at it."

"That Jezebel still has Quinn's balls in a jar."

"Ew. Let's not fixate on Quinn's balls." Red looked down at her breakfast sausage and grimaced with distaste, pushing it away with her fork before looking at Vic again. "You're really hurting over this."

"Don't go pop psychologist on me and ask me about my Dad or Henry."

Red looked away at the mention of Vic's adopted father. Freud would have had a field day with the daddy issues in play, but it wasn't her place to point out the obvious. "I didn't mean—"

"I know. The facts are that I blindly trusted Quinn, then I got my arm broken and had my intern claimed by a vampire for my troubles. All while he knows more about the fucking case than I do."

"Fat Crispin wants to kill the vampire who murdered his daughter. Himself, preferably, but he'll settle for us. You have a lot of good reasons to be mad at Quinn, but are you mad enough to stake the love of his unlife without being one hundred percent certain?" She lifted her eyebrows, hoping that he wasn't.

"She's not the love of his unlife, Nora Roberts." Vic mumbled around a mouthful of pancakes. "This isn't Twilight."

Red rolled her eyes. "I'm going to ignore the fact that you think Nora Roberts wrote Twilight. I'm just saying, Delilah's been the love of most of his unlife. We need to be careful."

"We need to bring her in."

"We need to see what's on the rest of the video. Or find out what happened that night. Fat Crispin sent us because we're the best that he could do. The smart hunters left town. Our only real ally here is Cora, and we won't win any favors from her by ruining her big party or killing her bestie." She pointed her fork at him. "Delilah is not exactly easy pickings."

"She is probably the rogue master. We could call in Cora and have a vampire SWAT team to help us collect the bounty."

"Come on. Stop acting like you're Paul McCartney and she's

Yoko. You're eating pancakes. You can't talk about offing your buddy's ex-wife over pancakes."

"Still a free country." He pouted. It looked ridiculous on a man who hunted werewolves and other monsters for a living.

"Not for that. The Halloween Ball is tomorrow. We know Delilah might want to hide out, but Cora is making it mandatory for the LA vampires. I can pull her aside and question her, try to get something out of her. Put a camera on me or something, I don't know, but give it a day."

"You're willing to go to the vampire prom with Kristoff now?" He leaned forward. "You hung out with him, and now he's cool?"

Eye twitching, Red wasn't cool with it, but Kristoff seemed to be the only one willing to be honest with her. All his intel had checked out. After last night at Quinn Investigations, honesty counted for a lot with her. This case would have gone differently if Quinn had been upfront about Delilah and everything else from the beginning. "It's not about him. We need real intelligence. We can't count on the other for that."

Vic glowered at his broken arm. "You'll be on your own in a fight. I don't like it."

"I know the risks." She poked her pancakes. The syrup smile had dripped into a grimace. She tried to perk it up with her fork. "We have evidence that he didn't kill any of our victims. The other alibis checked out. I'm also pretty sure that part of my appeal is that it pisses off Lucas."

He looked worried. "It might be a no-no for vampires to kill each other now, but they still obey some of the old rules. Sires can reclaim the blood. That's undead fancy talk for stake his ass. We still need Novak."

"Lucas is protective, but I think he'll try to mend fences with me instead of start fights," she said. Not that she was ready to play nice with her shifty collaborators. After last night, she was more likely to slap the vampire than kiss him when she saw him next. "He'll need to grovel."

"Ugh." Vic lifted his hand. "I can see that you have a weird thing a-brewing with Greg."

"Lucas." Red sipped her coffee, primly.

"Whatever. Okay, so, you get to the prom with Eurofangs, then what? You can only snoop so much by yourself, even if you get Delilah to admit anything to you. You can bet they'll sweep the place for bugs and confiscate phones from human guests at the door, so putting a camera on you is a stretch."

"I don't need to be by myself. You said you have hacker realities. What about their security system? You can peek on all the cameras, be the guy in the cloud. I noticed Club Vltava has beefed up their surveillance and security systems. They won't confiscate their own equipment, even if they turn the cameras off."

"I could turn them back on again."

She grinned, liking any plan that had him safe behind a computer and not running after Delilah on some bros-before-hos vendetta. "The Novak Boys are hip with tech. Everything is digital, but I can't imagine their Wi-Fi system is that secure."

"I don't even have to hack in if you can get me into their system." Vic pursed his lips before he took a bite of pancake.

"What about sound? It's a Ball." Red twirled her finger in the air. "It will be loud."

"They'll sweep for bugs, but they aren't going to do that all day. They have furniture to move, blood to pour, and do whatever vampire caterers do. You have an in with the host. Ask for a tour."

Her forehead creased as she thought out the logistics. The club was two floors and a rooftop in an even larger building. That was a lot of ground to cover. "I can't sprinkle mics around like confetti."

"I'm betting if anyone can get us a bunch of spy equipment on short notice, it's Smith and Reaper. Maybe they have more in their bank vaults than your inheritance." Vic leaned over. "We still have to deal with Delilah."

"I don't need more than one. Let me handle her. We'll have a chat, just us girls."

"Like she'll tell you anything."

"No, but she might tell someone else right afterward." Red paused when the waitress came back to freshen up their coffees. She used the time to try and make her vague ideas into a plan. "We put a mic on her."

Vic grinned. "Okay, I'm following you. I like where this is going."

"This way, we can be sure to hear it from the horse's mouth." She cocked her head. "Or at least have more of an idea of who's involved."

"What do you think happens after we find out?" He gazed out the window at the In-N-Out Burger across the street like a man after a breakup hearing their couple song. "You know we'll have to question her ourselves. Centuries old vamp...that's a lot of blessed silver."

"Let's just find something out first." Red said delicately before she pulled out her phone and called Kristoff's number. She still hadn't put it in her contacts. The phone went straight to voicemail without a message. "Hey, it's Red. I'm in for vampire prom."

"Alright. We're rolling the dice then." Vic chewed on a bite of pancake, giving her a searching look as she hung up. "You've been doing a lot of solo fieldwork this time around. Pun fully intended, these are high stakes. You've done good. You put the case before your feelings and got us new leads. I know you could've found a way to kill Novak last night, get rid of the claim, but you did your fucking job. Objectively."

Her smile froze as his words sunk in.

He continued, "Maybe I had this all wrong. This is some pop psychology for you. Maybe Quinn wasn't Batman. Maybe I was my own Batman all along. And you're my Robin. That's kind of deep. Maybe I should put that on a shirt. Like, a men's empowerment thing —*Be Your Own Batman*."

Red stopped listening. She hadn't understood at first what he'd meant when Vic said she could have killed Kristoff last night. In an open fight, he would win. Then she thought about it. She'd had a stake, a cross, a revolver full of wooden bullets, and a vampire distracted all evening.

The thought of killing Kristoff hadn't crossed her mind at all last night.

17

October 31st, 10pm, Club Vltava, Sunset Strip, Los Angeles, California, USA

A Halloween moon peeked through the smog above Sunset Strip. The humans might have been dressed as ghouls and spooks, but the night had a hush. It was as if the whole underworld held its breath as the vampires gathered in Los Angeles.

There was no line stretching from Club Vltava tonight. Red was a little disappointed. She could have used the wait to still her beating heart.

A plan scribbled on diner napkins had turned into a reality complete with borrowed high-tech spy equipment. The real challenge had started the moment that she had left Vic in the parked Millennium Falcon to go undercover solo at the Halloween Ball. Solo, she strode up to the two tuxedoed undead bouncers, both bald muscle heads in sunglasses and earpieces.

Standing at attention at the open doorway, the guards turned away a gaggle of Halloween clubbers dressed like the Avengers. Thor flipped them off before moving on.

"Hi, I'm Red. I should be listed as Kristoff Novak's plus one."

The guards shared a look like twins exchanging a mental message. "Your purse."

Handing over her gold clutch for inspection, Red watched the other guard wave a metal-detecting wand over the A-line skirt of her green gown. She kept her focus on his face and not on the spy toys hidden in plain sight. Vic had been right, Sheila Jones at Smith and Reaper had been able to loan them disguised mics.

The wand beeped over the gold charm bracelet on her wrist and the golden brooch attached to the center of her sweetheart cut neckline, but the guard wielding it didn't pause. His eyes flicked over her jewelry, assessing them for danger. "Clear."

"No phone?" The other one handed the bag back.

"I was told they'd be confiscated, so I left it in my car," she said, trying to strike a balance between cowed by vampires but experienced in their presence, as expected from a claimed human.

The guard jerked his head to the entrance in dismissal. "Go."

With even, casual steps, Red entered the atrium to the open elevator. She glanced at the glass door to the gallery where her doppelgänger's portrait was on display...much like she would be at the Halloween Ball. She gripped her stiff-backed purse, fingers curled protectively around it, sensing but not feeling the thin phone secreted in the inner lining of the purse. Her feet moved on autopilot. She had already visualized the first steps to the plot. Finding a way to get Vic's program onto one of their computers was the easy part to plan. She'd have to improv the rest especially getting the mic onto Delilah.

The elevator door closed, leaving her alone in the muted light reflecting off the stainless-steel walls.

Red squared her shoulders, heart beating like a war drum, before pulling the compact mirror out of her clutch. She reapplied her crimson lipstick with military precision. The gold leaf comb in her hair glimmered in the low light, tucked over her right temple. Her loosely curled locks cascaded over her left shoulder. The hairstyle was engineered to show off Kristoff's mark by the stylist he had sent.

She checked her shoulder out in the mirror, looking to see if the foundation on her tattoo had smeared. Catching a glance of her own green eyes accented with winged liner, she closed the mirror and shoved it back into the purse with the lady's silk handkerchief.

Kristoff had spared no expense or detail from the stylist to the shoes. The dress had probably cost the same as a week at the Pandora Hotel.

Red breathed deep. Her hands smoothed her chiffon A-line skirt compulsively, feeling the thin stake tied against her thigh, before pulling up the front of the fitted bodice. Fluttering fingers patted the four thin chains of her choker necklace and the low neck of the strapless hunter green dress. The formal wear wasn't a Halloween costume, but it felt like one.

Red jumped as the soft elevator bell rang to announce her floor. The reflection of her form in the steel doors, split to reveal the spider's web. She let her arms fall to her sides and lifted her chin. There was no backing out now. It was time to go to work.

The ball would officially begin in twenty minutes. It had to be enough time to find a computer on their secure Wi-Fi. She stepped around the edges of the nightclub. The white lounges and chairs were gone, leaving the floor empty beyond the long bars along two walls. She squinted at the black screens on the counter of the nearest one. Club Vltava had state-of-the-art point of sale systems. The Brothers Novak might have been born in the 1800s, but they did their business in the new millennium.

A shiver ran down her bare arms. She glanced over, feeling and not hearing him enter the room.

Kristoff appeared at the foot of the stairs. He stopped to stare at her, shy yet delighted like a poor orphan handed a toy, until his expression closed. He walked over to her. His pleased tone belied his stoicism. "You wore my gifts."

"The stylist you sent saved me the trouble of shopping." She said, then shrugged and let down her tough girl facade long enough to concede. "It's a lovely dress."

"You look like a dream." He held out his arm. "I assume you'll want to get the lay of the land."

Red studied his offered arm as she tossed her hair over shoulder. She let herself fall into double undercover mode. There was a thumb drive in her bra that needed to find a computer. Not that Kristoff knew that. Taking his arm felt strange, but she could feel her window of time to get Vic into the computer network slipping away. "I didn't get a chance to snoop upstairs."

His eyes focused on her neck before meeting her gaze. "I recall."

She gulped. "Remember, I'm undercover. It doesn't matter if you're cooperating. You're still a person of interest."

"Or am I just someone you find interesting?" He asked, resting a gentle hand on her lower back to guide her towards the stairs to the second level of the nightclub.

She had told herself to prepare for flirting. It was easier to be aloof when she practiced witty deflections in her hotel room than when he touched her. "You're different than I would've expected. I'll give you that. I haven't met an unsouled vampire quite like you."

He smirked. "That's because there aren't any."

"Okay, I have met vampires as arrogant as you." Red walked with him up the stairs. She pushed the conversation back to her real target —his computer network. His cash registers should be connected to it. "Now, aren't you going to offer a girl a drink?"

Kristoff grinned. "I thought this was another interrogation."

Her swell of bravado ebbed as she noticed the vampires setting tablecloths on the dozens of round tables in blurred flutters of cloth. "Even if I weren't about to face a room of vampires, I'd want a drink before a ball. Be honest. How much small talk am I in for? Please tell me I can just hold on to your arm and look pretty."

"You will certainly look beautiful, but you might be surprised. The vampires in this town are real bleeding hearts. Some might want to make a political point to address a human politely." Kristoff led her to the bar along the wall.

"Oh, joy. I get to be the token human."

"You'll see a few others. Donal is bringing his boyfriend, Trey. I'll introduce you two. You might find out that it's not that bad to be claimed by the right vampire."

She snorted. Her eyes focused on the flat screen cash registers.

Shaking his head, lips curving up, Kristoff brought her behind the counter and waved away the bartender who tried to assist him. "Stay with me. This is going to be a snooze of a party, but cunning vampires can make weapons out of words."

"Any enemies I should know about?" Red scoped out the cash register, spotting a small USB port on the bottom. She waited until he turned away to pull the thin, compact thumb drive from the center of her cleavage. She palmed it and stepped closer to him, leaning back against the register.

He pulled out a top shelf bottle of white wine. "You made some mischief in the valley with those souled stooges." His voice was low, growing serious as he poured a taste of the wine. "As far as I know, I'm the only other vampire who knows exactly how much."

Hand hidden behind her skirts, she felt for the USB port and plugged in the thumb drive loaded with Vic's spyware. "From your mouth to the Gods' ears."

Kristoff cocked his head and handed her the glass.

"Just some weird saying I picked up somewhere. You wouldn't guess it but Vic is into going to church." Red shook her head, sipping the wine and handing the glass back. When she had been hyping this plan at the diner, she'd imagined herself being more suave. Hopefully Vic wasn't listening. "More of that, bartender."

A dialogue box popped up on the cash register interface. She mentally cursed Vic. The program was supposed to just run.

Pouring the drink, Kristoff opened his mouth to speak, but his suit pocket vibrated. He looked at his phone and handed her a glass to reply to a message.

Red discreetly tapped the screen to load the spyware. If the rest of the program did what it should, Vic would get a bird's eye view of the action from every camera in the nightclub. She posed with her glass, hoping it was a long text. Waiting for the vampire to put his phone in his pocket, she remembered to pull out the thumb drive.

"Usually my kind are fashionably late, but not tonight." Kristoff shrugged, then guided her from behind the bar. "We should head down to the reception."

She followed him down the stairs. "I understand now. That's why you really invited me, so you didn't have to stand alone shaking hands."

"What can I say, I'm evil." He stepped off the stairs to the transformed lower level of the club. A set of crimson fangs was projected onto the middle of the dance floor. Tall round tables covered in champagne glasses dotted the area. The white lights under the bar had been replaced with scarlet ones.

Red inched closer to him at the ding of the elevator.

Kristoff put his hand on the small of her back, fingers light on her bodice.

Five black-suited guards strode into the room in triangle formation before breaking off to scout the chamber, revealing the Supreme Master of Los Angeles. Cora Moon pulled white, heart-shaped sunglasses off and tossed them over her shoulder. "Far out."

A bodyguard nimbly caught the sunglasses before they fell.

She twirled to take in the nightclub, causing her white kaftan to flare around her legs. Her afro framed the smoky quartz crystals shining on her leather headband. She walked over to Kristoff and kissed him on both cheeks. "My fucking lord, you have outdone yourself. I keep asking, but really, when can you move to LA? I need a vamp like you on my team."

"Cora, you make the sunny days bearable."

"Flattery...But listen to that intuition, handsome. You know which way is up." She looked over his shoulder. "Kristoff..." She glanced at him, a spark of suspicion blazing in her airy expression before she stepped closer to Red. "You are most welcome, hunter chick. Tell the Bards how groovy this party is, okay?"

Red nodded, wondering if she should curtsy or offer the Supreme Master a fist bump.

The spacey glaze to Cora's soulful eyes grew focused. "You're happy to come to my ball, correct? I believe in consent culture, little sister."

"I wouldn't have missed it. The Brotherhood values our agreement." Red smiled and put her arm through his. "Plus, he owed me a new dress."

Cora smiled and turned back to Kristoff. "Now that I see her in designer wear, I see you were restrained in defending your claim." The serious cast to her face dropped as she turned to study the room. She walked away in a samba shuffle, her bodyguards trailing her like ducklings. "We need music!"

Red gulped the last of her wine and looked at Kristoff. "Political statement."

"We're vampires. Everything is." He glanced toward the elevator. "Go grab yourself a glass of champagne."

She nodded even though she already had a glass of wine, already guessing who would arrive next.

Kristoff might have owned the club, but the real hosts were Cora and her team. The summit brought LA under the magnifying glass of vampire society from more than just North America as the signature event of the Blood Alliance. This wasn't a party. It was politics.

Red turned and ducked behind one of the towers of champagne glasses. Spying through the flute stems, she waited for the elevator to open on the vampire pulling the strings with the media—the stick to Cora's carrot in the land of the fluffy bunny demons. Souled vampires might have ruled here, but they still had unsouled ones around to do the dirty work.

The opening notes to "California Love" by Tupac and Dr. Dre filled the air.

Striding forward in a black tailored suit and white eyepatch, Michel studied the room. His withering disdain for the decor was clear. He wrapped an arm around Delilah, hand resting on her hip.

Blond hair in a French twist, she glimmered in a long-sleeved, high-necked, skintight gold gown. A burgundy shawl hung off her elbows. Golden studs glittered on her ears. Her red lips were pulled in an aloof half smile, but her blue eyes darted around. She glanced straight at the champagne glass tower before her troubled gaze moved on.

Red didn't let go of the breath she was holding.

"Novak." Michel paused his stride, pulling his companion closer and sparing a unimpressed glance for the host. He didn't shake hands. "You cleaned up the Soviet discothèque. It will suffice."

Glass in hand, she stepped back beside Kristoff when the others made a beeline to Cora in the DJ booth. "What's the deal with them?"

"Let's wait until the room fills up before you begin the interrogation." He tilted his head. "Until then, I want to hear about you. You're the only one I actually want to make small talk with."

Red tried not to make a face. She'd rather talk monsters. She had hoped he'd be distracted by the event, but he seemed to have cleared off his schedule to devote his full attention to her. Goodie, she mentally snarked, it was her favorite activity—answering questions about herself. "You don't need to keep flattering me. I'm already here."

"This is friendly conversation. Unlike certain hunters, I'm not going to ask about any lost loves and old feuds."

She laughed at the ribbing statement even bracing herself as if facing a firing squad. "Fine. Shoot."

"Easy question." Kristoff smiled. "Where are you from?"

"Just outside Eugene." Red technically was telling the truth. As far as she knew, she had popped out of the earth on the banks of Coyote Creek. Her real origins were still TBD. That kind of honestly required a lot of backstory to explain. She hadn't even told Lucas about her amnesia yet; she certainly wasn't going to tell Kristoff. That information could be used against her.

He perked up at learning she was from his state. "You're always welcome in Portland whenever you want to return to Oregon."

"I never stay anywhere long." She tried to smile but felt it grow crooked. The truth slipped from her. She bit back a wince as it escaped. "Eugene was never home."

"Where is home?" He posed the Coca-Cola of questions so commonplace you didn't even notice it anymore as a traveler.

Red had a rote answer memorized, but the words dissolved on her tongue,

Wearing a curious expression, head cocked, Kristoff wasn't just asking her to make small talk. He really wanted to know.

"I haven't found it yet." The words came out, and she realized that it was the truth as she knew it. She was spared more questions by the trickle of vampires coming into the nightclub.

The next vampires who came up to Kristoff seemed content to not make the political statement of addressing the human. Especially not the one that, rumor had it, Lucas Crawford had gotten a bloody nose for speaking to.

Keeping a polite smile on her face, Red studied each vampire, ignoring Kristoff's light touch on her lower back between handshakes. She carefully counted her breaths to keep her heartbeat steady as the predators strode into the ballroom.

The mandatory Halloween Ball brought out all the vampires in the city. Formalwear had been widely interpreted from gowns worthy of the Met Gala to a dusty vampire in buckskin who squinted at the low lights. While the mood in the room seemed light, not everyone came with their party hats. Many leaned up against the walls or perched by the drink tables, looking down at their watches and phones with an aura of killing time.

She looked to her left, stopping herself just short of jumping in shock to see Quinn standing beside her.

In a tuxedo and an expression that begged to be anywhere else, he turned to face her. "I'm sorry about how things ended last time."

"Me too."

"Tell Vic." Quinn glanced at her escort, speculation in his brown eyes, before disappearing into the growing crowd.

"He used to be more fun at parties," Kristoff commented idly. A smirk twitched at his lips as his eyes scanned the crowd.

Red looked down at her half-filled wine glass and knew she would need it. "You can send me away when he comes in."

They both knew who she was talking about.

"I'm fine with him seeing you."

"With you, you mean," she snarked, but the bite to her tone trailed off when she met Lucas's gaze in the mingling crowd as he came closer. Her eyes darted between the two vampires. Heat crept up the back of her neck. She had been ignoring him after the rift erupted between their two crews. It still felt tacky that their first meeting after the fight had to be while she was on what looked like a date with his progeny. He could probably guess that Vic had sent her undercover, but it had to have stung at first sight.

Kristoff glanced down at her, lips pressed tight, before his focus flicked to his sire. The repressed smirk bloomed on his face.

Lucas flouted the formal dress code by wearing black jeans, white shirt, and a leather trench coat. His tousled black hair set off the chiseled pallor of his handsome features. While hatred stretched across his features as his gray eyes met Kristoff's, it softened on her.

Red couldn't look away from him. She mouthed the word, hey, as her fingers made a quick wave.

Kristoff put his hand on her lower back as he stepped closer.

Lucas tightened his jaw, putting his hands in his pockets. "I fucking hate parties, but it's worth it to see you all dolled up." His grin turned sweet as he looked at Red. "You look beautiful."

She had so much she wanted to say to him, including "fuck you for not telling me that Quinn was covering up for Delilah," but also high up on the list was the need to tell him that she wasn't on a date with Kristoff. It was silly. She had kissed Lucas a couple of times. They weren't dating. She couldn't say anything with so many supernatural ears around so instead, she said, "Thank you."

"She does look beautiful in my... gifts." Kristoff brushed a stray lock of hair off her shoulder.

She bit her lip, knowing that he revealed his mark. The two neatly scabbed-over fang wounds in her neck had been covered with liquid bandage and then foundation, but any vampire would notice. "Come on. Play nice."

"Parties end, Novak." Lucas turned and walked away toward the back tables.

She looked up at Kristoff's smirking face. "That was petty."

"I enjoyed every second."

"You say that now, but wait until he runs you over in the parking lot." Red crossed her arms and broke from her cover as his obedient claimed human to step away. She rubbed her forearms, wishing for her leather jacket, before dropping her hands.

"You're optimistic," he said, entirely too cheerful and pleased with the awkward encounter. "My brother is betting that Lucas jumps on me during the speeches."

"I said you'd be jumped on the way to hear the speeches. It looks like I almost won the wager too," Arno said as he stepped up to them in an expensive-looking black suit. His hair, darker than his brother's, was slicked back in a similar style. Tall, he was still a few inches shorter even at six feet. Up close, she could see he'd been turned earlier in life than his brother. He gawked at her before covering his curiosity.

"Well, keep on like this, and I'll join the betting pool on you not getting through the reception," she quipped, trying to ignore Arno's stare.

"I'm on my best behavior." Kristoff straightened his lapels.

"I sat Crawford in the back corner to ease the temptation. Try not to piss off your sire before you get to your table." Arno shook his head. He looked at Red, turning confidential. "I'm running the show so he can act like a bigwig to impress you." He didn't give her a chance to respond before gesturing for them to go up the stairs.

Kristoff offered Red his arm, and they went with the rest up to the next level where the tables were set up. She followed him to one near the front. They passed Donal, the redheaded vampire, sitting beside a nervous-looking young blond man—the only other human so far. That must have been Trey. She recognized them both from the bar in Gianni Construction even in formal wear.

Donal raised a glass and winked at her.

Letting Kristoff pull out a chair for her, she sat, expecting him to do a creepy vampire thing like sniff her hair, but he merely pushed the chair in and sat down next to her. She glanced around and shrugged. "So, this is vampire prom." She pointed to the table arrangement of reddish succulents. "Swanky."

Kristoff's chuckle rolled over her. "Are you enjoying it?"

"It has promise." Red looked over his shoulder with a small smile. She had a bird's-eye view of Delilah's golden back.

18

OCTOBER 31ST, Night, Club Vltava, Sunset Strip, Los Angeles, California, USA

Operation Vampire Prom was going off without a hitch.

Leaning against the closed bathroom stall door, Red slipped the phone back into its hiding place in her clutch purse after sending a status update to Vic. Being Kristoff's date wasn't as awful as she thought it would be and she was in sight of Delilah. It was blue skies on Vic's end too. The spyware had worked. He was in the system. The security footage could be sent to the Brotherhood for facial analysis of known vampires.

Now, they were ready for phase two. This was the hard part.

Stepping out, she took off the golden charm bracelet and washed her hands. She removed two charms before replacing the bracelet back on her wrist. She twisted them open, revealing hidden microphones then tucked one inside her bodice over the valley of her cleavage. Jagged metal teeth around the edges of the tiny microphone clung to the fabric. The other, she palmed and walked out of the bathroom. A silent female minion followed behind to guard her.

When Red left the table during a speech, Delilah and Michel had gone to go wait by the stage. Now, he strutted on stage while his partner watched from the stairs. Her eyes were fixed on him with the fervent focus of a beauty pageant mom. She mouthed the words as he said them.

Michel spoke into the microphone. "We are building a dream in Los Angeles. We invite you to dream it with us."

Red waded through the tables to pass by Delilah's table. She brushed her hand against the dark burgundy shawl, feeling the palmed mic catch securely on the cloth

Her steps quickened when she met Kristoff's eyes. She slipped into the chair beside him. The Portland vampires still gaped at her when they thought their master wasn't looking. She smiled, covering the jolt of paranoia that his team had caught on to the mole in their network. "What'd I miss?"

"A blood toast, polite clapping, and now Grammont is going over his time slot. How many speeches must he make in one night? My brother must be seething with a clipboard somewhere." Kristoff replied drolly. "The dance was supposed to have started already."

"Oh god, we're going to have to dance. Together," She said to herself, cringing. She hadn't really thought of this when she had come up with this idea.

"I won't step on your feet."

"I might step on yours," she said glumly, cursing his super hearing. The type of dancing she did was shaking her booty while doing karaoke with Vic. It's just a job, she told herself.

The final applause died away, and the stage cleared. Red took Kristoff's arm automatically. Walking with the crowd, she stumbled over her dress, catching it with her heel, falling into him. She saved her bodice from slipping down and flashing the ball goers as she staggered.

Kristoff caught her and wrapped her up in his arms until she was stable. He brushed a wild lock of hair off her cheek. "It's not that bad in my arms, see?"

"Yeah, flirt later," Red said, biting her lip before pulling back to retake his arm properly. Lucas stared at her across the room. "Let's get this dance stuff over so I can do some real eavesdropping."

"Back to business." Kristoff led her with the crowd down the stairs to the open dance floor on the lower floor.

"Just because I look like a snack doesn't mean I'm yours." She scanned the diverse faces at the ball. The champagne tables had disappeared, leaving only the slow spiraling outline of crimson fangs on the dance floor.

The LA undead brought their own sense of style, coming from every walk of life, yet all had the unnaturally white jaws of bloodsucker. The traditional five senses were sight, smell, taste, sound, and touch. Red would argue that there was another: danger. Right now, the sense that guided her primate ancestors as they left the safety of the canopy screamed at her to run. Her free hand fell to hover over the stake strapped to her thigh under the layers of green skirts. She wished she had a flamethrower.

"I'm letting you paw at me for tonight only, pal."

"You technically pawed me back there."

"Falling isn't pawing," she huffed. "Is Cora going to have the first dance or something?"

"She is too much of a hipster for that kind of ceremony. I think she's preferring to DJ tonight," Kristoff said, gesturing to the raised booth. "Clever. The view is better from there."

Arno strode out of the shadows, red light casting shadows over his face. Jaw tight, he put a hand on Kristoff's arm. "We need privacy."

"Excuse me." Kristoff nodded to her, letting his brother pull him aside.

She watched them go, wishing she had a mic to spare to bug him. Crossing her arms, she tapped her foot to the old Motown song playing.

"Delilah did it..." The whisper drifted from a passing pair of women in black suits.

Red stepped away from the Novak brothers to eavesdrop, walking toward the edge of the dancers. She tried to find the whispering women again, but they had disappeared into the throng.

"I spy an Amazon in our midst."

Startled, she spun around. "Excuse me?"

Michel de Grammont looked down at her. The club's lights turned his white eye patch red. "If I were to speculate, I would say you were a fighting woman, but we both know that I am a man who doesn't need to speculate. Can you claim I am wrong, Amazon?"

She thought fast as she squared her shoulders and struck a confident pose, lifting her chin. Kristoff had warned her that Michel might recognize her. Was this another case of mistaken identity? She wished she had a glass of champagne to use as a prop. Something to make her fit in and look less like a claimed human waiting for her keeper. "You say that because you've forgotten my name."

"You see through me so quickly. I'll admit when I saw you from the stage your name escaped me. It bedeviled me through my own speech until recognition overcame me. You're the hunter Kristoff claimed. The one they call Red."

"Word travels fast," she said curtly.

"When I want it to. You know who I am."

She knew more about him, particularly his love life, than he might have expected. It didn't mean that she felt at all comfortable talking to vampire that functioned as the strong arm of the supreme. "Who doesn't, here? Cora Moon is lucky to have you at her side."

"Flattery suits you, dear girl. I can already tell that you're too good for Kristoff." Michel tilted his head, studying her. "You've stayed obligingly quiet to your Brotherhood about his bad behavior. Even if I wouldn't have blamed you in the least, it does serve our cause. We have a cornucopia of problems. I'm glad the Bards aren't one."

Nodding, she stayed quiet. How did he guess that she hadn't told the Brotherhood the whole story. Or did he know? A PR man to the core, she figured that he would fill the silence if she let him.

"Can I repay your silence with candor?"

"Sure." Red said, wondering when Kristoff would come rescue her from this small talk. Maybe he'd know what kind of political statement that Cora's right hand was making.

"You've been claimed by a monster. I say it as someone who is monstrous. The Butcher has crossed lines that even vampires respect. Betrayal is the nature of that man." Michel said 'man' as if he meant to say bastard. "Novak isn't your only concern. Lucas Crawford may charge in on his metal steed like a hero, but his armor is stained with old blood."

"He has a soul," she said, even as a chill went down her spine.

"The worst murderers in history had souls, child." Michel shook his head. "It's the mind that fuels a vampire's actions, no matter if there's an angel or a demon on his shoulder. They left chaos in their wake when they were friends. As enemies, they are even more dangerous. Between them, even an Amazon should know fear."

"Fear is a sign you're not a moron. I know the score." Red tried not to look away.

"If you did, you wouldn't have made yourself look so bewitching and graced us with your presence. You would have run." The white eyepatch didn't obscure the pity in his gaze. His vibe shifted to thoughtfulness. "Unless this is part of your plan?"

The silence grew as she fought her instinct to take his advice and run, but she couldn't look like prey among the predators, even if it was the truth.

"Cora has been trying to reach you," Delilah said as she emerged from the dance floor. She leaned against Michel, shining in her gold dress against the black of his suit, and played with his dark ponytail. Her burgundy shawl was missing. "She told me to send you along for a private chat in the DJ booth. Just you."

He kissed her cheek. "The faithful servant is commanded."

Delilah crossed her arms and waited for Michel to blend into the crowd before speaking. "This was a stupid move."

Red tensed her shoulders, biting back a scathing reply. They were in this mess because Delilah hadn't gone to her yoga buddy about finding Olivia's body.

"I keep expecting you to be smart because Juniper was, but I'm as much of a fool as they are. You're not her. You're a knockoff."

Red's cheeks heated. The words didn't sting as much as the realization that the shawl wasn't in sight. Had the vampiress discovered the mic and ditched the burgundy wrap? Or had she left it upstairs on accident? Either way, it was one mic down. She cursed at herself for wasting one of the two.

Delilah continued, satisfaction in her voice. "My mistake. No, you're not Juniper St. James. She knew enough about us to pick her battles and get the last laugh."

"What do you mean?" Red looked up, cocking her head. She'd had her fill of cryptic banter from vampires for one night. Michel had given her enough for a lifetime. "How'd she get the last laugh?"

Sighing, Delilah looked away. "Let me get you back to Kristoff."

"I'm not a pet dog to return." Red tried to keep her voice hushed, but the annoyance pitched her volume up. The agenda for the evening had not included spooky warnings, but she was going to get it back on track. She knew that her version of the plan would be easier on Delilah than Vic's, but the vampiress was already getting on her nerves.

"No, dogs are loyal. I like dogs." Delilah snapped her fingers over her shoulder and started walking toward the edge of the room. "You're more like a stubborn cat who keeps scratching at the wrong doors."

"Eventually I find the right one."

"Right for whom?" The vampire sneered. "Because it won't be you. I'm not the one for this girl-on-girl empowerment yoni egg bullshit, but here's a hot tip from a bitch who's been around: you're in the deep end, honey, and there's no lifeguard on duty."

Red looked away, already feeling the water up to her neck. She didn't have a smart retort for that as they approached Kristoff.

"You were supposed to stay with me." Hands behind his back, he looked between the women. His expression was as composed as his carefully parted and slicked-back blond hair. Only the blue eyes revealed his worry.

"You were technically the one who stepped away." Red smiled tightly before looking away with a wince. "I was left to mingle with Michel and Delilah."

His jaw tensed, but he said nothing.

"I thought she was stupid, but you take the prize tonight, Kristoff." Delilah put her hands on her hips.

He smirked. "Are you the only one who's allowed to move on?"

"Like this is moving on." Delilah waved them on, eyes rolling up in disdain. "I can't yell at you like I want here."

Stepping in front of Red, Kristoff looked to her as if waiting.

She covered her surprise at a vampire looking to a human for permission. Hidden by his bulk, she pulled the mic out of her cleavage before she stepped forward and put her hand on Delilah's shoulder to place the mic among the golden studs. She smiled cheekily as she felt the tiny mic latch firmly onto the fabric. "What's on your mind?"

"I might not want you dead, but that doesn't make us girlfriends." Delilah rolled her shoulders, sneering but seemingly unaware that anyone would be listening in now.

Red backed away with her hands up, trying not to smile. "You have your office swept for bugs, Kristoff?"

"Tonight? Every thirty minutes," he said.

Delilah led them to a door marked private next to the bar and opened it to reveal a gray hallway of bronze sconces and artful mood lighting. She went to the third door on the left, twisting the knob off and dropping it before she jerked her thumb inside.

Red lifted her eyebrows at Kristoff. The vampiress certainly knew her way around Club Vltava.

Shrugging in reply, he walked into his spacious office. He strode over to a metallic globe and ran lazy fingers over the surface before turning to Delilah. "Should I make us all a drink, or do you want to start with the lecture?"

Red stepped into the low-lit office behind him. She glanced at the bookshelf on the wall, expecting business books but instead noted Sun Tzu and Karl Marx alongside an old copy of *The Great Gatsby* by F. Scott Fitzgerald. On the far wall, a couch lay next to an unmarked interior door. A bronze-plated desk anchored a corner of the office with a small sitting area of plump leather chairs opposite it.

Delilah perched on the desk and crossed her legs, her voice surly like a dockworker contrasting with her gold dress and fashionista polish. "What the fuck, Kristoff? You don't have a soul making you act stupid. Your master sent you here to support Cora. You're a liability right now if any Bloodliner decides to use Little Miss Déjà Vu as leverage against you. You need to get her out of here. Out of the city. Send her up to Portland and act out *Fifty Shades of Gray* for all I care. She seems silly enough to be won over by a fancy condo and helicopter ride."

"I'm still here." Red pointed to herself.

"And that's the issue. Keep up, sweetie." Delilah bobbed her head, the condescension clear. "This is actually me being nice, so appreciate it."

"It's true." Kristoff shrugged. "Red's safer if they know she's mine."

"She's safer if no one ever saw her, but that ship has sailed. So, get her on a ship, and set sail." Delilah put a hand on his chest, her snark fading into concern. She straightened his already immaculate lapels. "You can love, and you always could. Death never took that away. But you also kept your sense. Use it. You know you have enemies."

He leaned his face closer to hers, his even tone coming out a near whisper. "Keep this up, and I'll mistake you for a woman who cares."

"Don't tell anyone." Delilah rolled her eyes, then sighed and put her hand on his cheek. "From the beginning, I saw what you could be —so much promise to fulfill. You're barely past a hundred. Much is ahead for you. Don't waste it."

He nodded as he laid his hand on hers. Eyes widening, his cool composure slipped, a small genuine smile appearing in the cracks.

Red felt like an accidental voyeur, looking away. She almost felt guilty now.

Kristoff knew that she was going undercover at his club, but he didn't know that she had an even deeper purpose. One that could kill his old friend. He thought Red was just here to look around. He didn't know that if it came to it that she would take Delilah in for Brotherhood justice. Would his nostalgia for Juniper stop him from protecting a vampire that he had known for lifetimes? In that moment, Red wasn't sure.

The vibrating in his coat pocket broke the moment. He pulled away from Delilah and stepped back toward Red as he pulled his phone out.

She looked over his shoulder and saw the first part of the text message from Arno: *Cora's coming to arrest Delilah.* Her heart skipped a beat.

Delilah pulled her phone from her chain purse and put it to her ear, turning away. "Hello darling."

Kristoff furrowed his brow. "We have to go. All of us."

"We don't want to be there when it happens." Red only heard whispers from the phone conversation as the vampiress retreated farther into the corner of the office, but she knew Delilah could still hear everything that they said clearly. Vampire hearing was a bitch. "I can continue the investigation and maybe get some answers afterward."

"There's no trial. You can't get answers if she's..." Kristoff looked over and straightened. That honed cool melted as he gazed upon the other vampire. His high forehead creased. Lucas might have turned Kristoff, but Delilah's blood ran through them both. He wasn't going to give her up to Cora without trying to help.

Putting away her phone, Delilah raised her fingers to her lips and wrapped her other arm around her waist. Suspicion drew her brows together, even as her blue eyes grew distant.

Red tried not to think about what Lucas might think of this. Vic's Plan B was better than whatever Cora had waiting for Delilah. She opened her purse to paw for her phone. "Fine. I have a driver waiting. You'd better be able to get something from her."

"What do you think you'll get from me?" Delilah asked, coy with a hint of poison in her tone.

"An honest answer." She looked up from her text to Vic, warning him that they were coming in hot. "Why does Cora want to arrest you?"

Jaw dropping, Delilah recovered her composure, but it was brittle as new ice. "She wouldn't, but..."

"Tell us on the way to the parking lot." Kristoff shook his head and gestured at the door. "Let's get you out. Maybe you can find a ship."

Red nodded before walking out of the office, avoiding his gaze. He thought he was saving Delilah from the Blood Alliance and Cora. Her stomach churned from guilt. He was only leading them to where Vic waited with a blessed silver net.

19

October 31st, Halloween Ball at Night, Club Vltava, Sunset Strip, Los Angeles, California, USA

Red hiked up her green dress, jogging to keep up with the vampires escaping down the employee hallway of Club Vltava. The night was going to shit, but at least she'd worn flats. Kristoff had guessed correctly when he had sent the stylist.

The Halloween Ball had dissolved from a recon mission to an active extraction. She didn't know what Vic had caught on the mics on Delilah, but she hoped he was checking his phone. Their scheme was unraveling.

She'd planned for minimal small talk and enough evidence to keep Vic from slaying his buddy's ex-wife on circumstantial evidence. Now, she was fleeing with Kristoff and Delilah down to the parking garage to get a head start from Cora's justice.

At least they thought she was.

Red was actually bringing the vampiress to Vic and asking him to what, help Delilah? Stake her? Hand her over to Cora? He wanted to ship her off to England to be executed by the Brotherhood.

Red was a realist— Delilah probably killed those women. The burglary on Quinn Investigations and the Millennium Falcon could have been shoddy henchman work to cover up her crimes. The three threads of this mystery had seemed so disjointed in the beginning, yet every string led to the aged vampire. Delilah had motive to kill the models and with the Blood Alliance's summit coming to a head, it made sense that she might score some points with the evil faction. Or maybe she wanted control of the city herself and was rebelling against Cora with her own legion of minions. Whatever her motives were, the facts said that Delilah deserved what was coming to her and then some.

Something still wasn't adding up. Why leave the bodies so conspicuously? Why the ouroboros? Was it just to fit in with the Bloodliners? Or was it a bigger conspiracy like Vic suspected?

The case should have been open and shut, yet Red could hear the rusty hinges creaking. If Delilah went into Cora's custody, she wasn't coming out. Any answers died with her.

Kristoff raced ahead to an unmarked exit and tapped a code into a keypad above the knob. He pulled it open. "Let's get my old friend into something sporty."

Red trotted to him, ready to argue.

Lucas stopped short from a blurred sprint, leather trench coat flaring around him. "Now, where's the afterparty, kids?"

Kristoff smirked from the doorway. "It's a private affair."

Delilah spun around, resting bitch face on point. "Lucas, you've managed to not annoy me all night, do keep up the streak."

"We don't have time for this," Red said, while fishing a tie from her purse and smoothing her hair back into low ponytail. The loose waves were cute but kept getting in her eyes. "Let's go."

Lucas put his hand on Red's arm and tilted her chin up. "Oi, tell me, love."

She relaxed into his touch before stiffening. How could she tell him that he might lose family tonight? "Cora is coming to arrest Delilah for murder. Probably more."

"Alleged murder," Delilah pointed out.

"Bloody hell." Lucas glanced over at Kristoff. "Is that why that brother of yours is looking for you? All the Portland vamps are in a tizzy."

"Fuck." Kristoff pulled his phone from his jacket. "The Prince has already called twice." He gave Red a sideways glance and nodded to the door he held. "Just get her out of here."

"You can't." Lucas said the words to Red, but his eyes were on his progeny.

"Already gone." Red turned around, pulling away from Lucas to go to the exit. Head tipping up, she tried not to react at how Kristoff looked at her with a wistful smile. Her heartbeat picked up.

"Tell me where you take Delilah." Kristoff leaned in and brushed a fallen lock of hair off her shoulder. "You looked beautiful tonight, Red."

He didn't touch her skin, yet Red felt the goosebumps raise where his fingertips hovered. She opened her lips, but she had no idea what to say.

Delilah walked around them, glowering as she went through the door. "She's putting my ass in an Uber to LAX."

"Yup!" Jerking her head in a nod, Red ignored the dryness in her mouth, decidedly not looking at Kristoff. "I'm not playing hero."

"Good." The two male vampires said at the same time before glaring at the other.

Red swallowed, preparing herself to lie to them. Before Cora got her answers, Vic and the Brotherhood would try to get theirs. "I'm getting out of this city. So, should you guys. If they're going after Delilah, you two are probably next."

"I'll stall them as long as I can," Kristoff promised.

Lucas rolled his eyes. "And I'll actually do something."

"Do what you can do." There was never time for goodbyes on a job. Red had more to say, mostly orders not to kill each other, but she only nodded and closed the door.

Once they were out of sight, she ceased to think of the two vampires she had left. There was only one vampire in her line of sight. This one more dangerous than those she left behind.

Red followed Delilah down the steps to the parking area under Club Vltava. Shiny Mercedes Benzes and Ferraris lined up along the walls. The Millennium Falcon, the rusty black van she called home, stuck out like a goth at a Texas beauty pageant at the end.

Vic and a mess of blessed silver hid inside.

"They care about you," Red said to the vampire as they power-walked through the garage. "Didn't even ask why the Supreme Master of Los Angeles would want you. I'm certainly curious. Aren't you and Cora supposed to be besties?"

"So, you know about me. Big deal. None of my boys will tell me anything about you."

"I'm just a hunter."

Delilah crossed her arms. "I'm not a fool with a nostalgia boner, gaping at the freak of DNA. You're working with Cora and the Brotherhood, playing each side from the beginning. Is that how you ended up with that corner suite at the Pandora instead the usual fleabag motels that hunters drift through? Must have been a damn good payday."

Red walked ahead. "You might actually survive if I know a little bit more—" she faltered—"so I can get you out."

Delilah appeared abruptly in front of her. "Hand over your keys and be grateful I'm only taking your car."

"It's a stick shift." Red tried to stall, wondering how to warn Vic without tipping off the vampire.

"Honey, I fucked Henry Ford in the first Model T. Give over the keys."

"Don't have them." Red opened her purse to illustrate. "Like I said, I have a driver."

Delilah cocked her head. "How many hunters did you invite to the party?"

"Enough." Instinct made Red run for the Falcon. "Vic!"

Delilah rushed forward, and jerked the hunter painfully back by the hair, tugging the ponytail loose. She twirled Red around and dug fake nails, filed like claws, into Red's very mortal neck. "Maybe there's a bit of Juniper in you after all."

Red squeaked, bleeding under the vampire's sharp grip. She tried to summon some energy, channel any element, but she only managed to blow a lock free from Delilah's French twist. So much for her theory that her magic responded to mortal danger. She tried another theory. "You have a soul!"

"This is a mercy, darling. You won't feel a thing." Delilah reared back, fangs out to strike. A red dot appeared on her forehead before two more targeted her chest. She looked down at the laser lights dotting her like chicken pox.

Cora sprinted up in a blur. Heart-shaped white sunglasses perched above her quartz headband and forehead like a crown. She put her hands on her white kaftan-covered hips. "Drop that girl." She snapped her fingers before barking the order again in French.

Relief filtered through the throb of Red's pained scalp and bleeding neck. The night's plan had been fucked on every level, but she might just get out alive.

Five vampire security guards in suits stepped out from between the cars in the parking garage

Delilah pushed Red away and flicked the blood on her nails off onto the cement. "I was going to release her after I caught her, Cora."

"My intuition says bullshit. We ain't getting into the fact that she's a claimed human and a fucking hunter in the Brotherhood of Bards and Heroes. The ones I so painstakingly negotiated a very groovy truce to save undead lives. No, that would be bad vibes for any day." Cora balled her fists. The spaced-out hippie vibe curdled. "How long do we go back?"

Pressing a handkerchief to her aching neck, Red stumbled away from the vampires, but Cora's accusation made her look back.

"You helped me get on this throne, Delilah. How long have you been trying to push me off it?"

Delilah lifted her eyes as the red sniper dots traveled up her face to cluster on her forehead. "When did I get on the purge list? I hosted your census rally not two nights ago!"

"And I thought I had a friend until two nights ago. It wasn't until Michel brought the molds out on stage... You helped me set up the registry and never gave one. In decades!" Cora cocked her head. "That's enough time to raise a fine crop of minions, isn't it? I was impressed with you before. Badass, centuries old, and running the best modeling agency in LA, all while balancing a soul. Now, I know you did all that while raising dozens as a single mother too."

"Wait a minute." Delilah raised her hands. "I haven't been turning anyone. I have enough progeny problems without adding some shitty millennials."

"Girl, you must be operating under the mistaken assumption that I'm stupid." Cora shook her head. "I have the LAPD around my fucking finger. If fangs are involved, I have a man on the inside giving me the skinny in 3D. We ran your bite mold after the rally. The hunters gave us the idea."

Red stiffened at Delilah's glare. She knew that only the threat of snipers kept the vampire from attacking her again.

"Now, that's bullshit, girlfriend," Delilah said. "Check them again."

"You can't pull that 'I want to talk to your manager' act with me. I'm the manager!" Cora's fangs jutted out caught in mid-fury before she shook her head, flaring her nostrils in a deep breath for composure. She looked to her guards as if she couldn't stand the sight of Delilah anymore. "Take her, and make sure she talks. I want to know where all her little bastards are."

Michel sped up to the scene. He held his hands out. "Mademoiselles. Let's speak like civilized creatures. Whatever Delilah may be accused of—"

"Pick a side. I've been betrayed and you're already looking like an accomplice to a rogue master." Cora said something more in French, too quick for Red to follow.

"Mon dieu."

A vampire bodyguard slipped a noose of thickly braided silver around Delilah's neck. She hissed, eyes rolling up in pain, and balled her fists. "I didn't betray you, Cora!"

Red backed up against a pillar and scanned the garage, searching for the most discreet route to the van. Her train of thought was derailed when Quinn appeared beside her, stepping from behind an SUV. Where had he come from? Had Lucas sent him?

He shook his head for silence and handed her a piece of plastic.

Red looked down to see a gray top set of realistic teeth and fangs. What the hell?

"A copy." Quinn stepped forward, pulling a rounded tray the size of a small hockey puck out of his jacket. "Take care of Vic. Tell him..." He shook his head. "Just get him out."

Red put the plastic fangs in her purse. He was trusting the wrong woman. She had been ready to take his sire straight to a furious hunter. There was something about his faith in Delilah that panged at her.

Quinn stepped out from between the cars. "Cora, I have evidence of Delilah's marks that will exonerate her. She's innocent."

"Innocent?" Cora huffed a bitter laugh without a trace of humor. "None of us are. I know you wouldn't help her kill so many people. Don't fall for that big-eyed blonde act." She ordered her guards. "Lock him up until he sees sense."

Red fought her instincts to help him and backed away to find Vic and get the hell out of here.

"Don't go anywhere, hunter," Cora said. "We caught the murderer, but we need to get you somewhere safe."

Red gulped. Why didn't that feel comforting?

Quinn didn't resist the guard who dropped a blessed silver noose over his head. His flesh sizzled on contact. "Reminds me of Prague."

Delilah rolled her eyes, chuckling darkly. "You hated Prague."

"I don't think I'll like this either," Quinn quipped.

Weary, Cora rubbed the tension lines in her forehead. "I need to find my center. Just take them upstairs." She glanced to Michel, her doe eyes turning feral. "Have something to say?"

The Frenchman bowed without a look to his captive girlfriend. "I await your orders, Supreme."

Red held back a derisive snort. So much for undead loyalty but that was a unsouled vampire for you.

"Get the hunter to her car safely, then report back." Cora turned on her heel, calling over her shoulder. "You have work to do."

Gaze lowered and expression blank, Michel held out his arm to Red.

Red let the vampire escort her as Delilah and Quinn were led away by security. She should have been happy that the killer was caught, and that the detective would get out of this alive. Hadn't the case been solved?

She had a sinking feeling in her stomach that the night wasn't over.

20

NOVEMBER 1ST, After Midnight, Club Vltava, Sunset Strip, Los Angeles, California, USA

Red shook her head, trying to clear out the fog, until Michel's words made sense to her. He asked about her ride home, hadn't he? She pointed out the Millennium Falcon at the mouth of the parking garage.

The walk to the van felt long with the contemplative vampire by her side. Body still aching from her lost catfight, she kept flashing back to Delilah and Quinn being led away by Cora's security force. The murderess had been caught but the job still felt half done. Especially since Vic would want to bust his buddy out of lockdown next. The party might have raged on the top floors of the building, but the underground lot felt deadly quiet.

She waited until they were in hearing distance of Vic in the van before she said loudly, "Michel, this is mine. I'll just be going now."

"There's a human in there." He frowned. "Something's wrong. The heartbeat is too slow. There's blood."

Heart skipping, she sped up even as time seemed to slow down. All her own aches and pains "Vic!"

Michel rushed forward, getting there first, and threw open van's back doors.

Vic lay sprawled out amongst the bean bags, twisted in an unnatural position. The colorful fabric framed the mottled bruises on his face. His blackened eyes lay closed. Fang marks bled onto his collar.

Before Red could fully comprehend the sight, Michel was barking into his phone. "We need an ambulance at Club Vltava. Parking garage."

Fear tightened her ribs as Red ran forward, cursing her human slowness. Her boss only looked worse with each step. She climbed into the van and grabbed a blanket to press against Vic's neck. "Hold on!"

Vic had his waist holster on under his hoodie but hadn't even gotten a chance to pull out his gun. Blood gushed from the messy marks marring his too-pale throat. His arm sling lay askew. Gore slicked his mullet up at his temple as if someone had pushed his head back to bite harder. He coughed, his eyelids fluttering.

"That's it. Clear those smoker's lungs." Red said roughly, visually examining his wounds, being careful to not move his head or back as she tried to slow the bleeding. They had been in rough spots, but he pulled them out. She didn't know what to do when the tables turned.

A security guard dressed in sniper gear sprinted out of the gloom. "Sir?"

"Tell Cora that she might have problems with the Brotherhood." Michel waved the guard off. "This had to have been Delilah."

She jerked her gaze from Vic's bloody face, staring at the vampire with wide eyes. "What are you talking about?"

"She told me she'd been bugged at the Ball then left me to my own devices after my speech." Michel gestured to the spare laptop showing footage of Club Vltava inside the van. "I suppose she found the source."

Red had left Vic wide open by leaving the mic so carelessly on Delilah's shawl. Tears slid down her face. Wanting to kick her own ass, she instead pressed the blood-soaked blanket tighter against his wound. "Come on, boss!"

Sirens echoed in the distance. Vic still didn't open his eyes.

"Little Amazon, until we meet again." Michel stepped away as an ambulance turned into the parking garage, its flashing lights strobing against the concrete.

Red moved aside as two medics jumped out of the ambulance. One ran over to the van while the other pulled a stretcher out of the back. The ridiculous image of a corsage on her wrist popped into her mind. Vampire prom had ended the only way a vampire prom could —in blood and mayhem.

Pulling herself out of the daze, she hiked up her skirts and followed the stretcher. She barely noticed the back doors closing, too focused on the EMT bandaging Vic's neck before slipping a neck brace on him. The other one went up front to sit beside the driver.

The ambulance raced out of the parking garage, flashing its lights, and turning sharply onto the street. Charging through traffic, the vehicle rumbled over the road.

Satisfied that Vic was prepared, the medic turned his back to pull out an IV bag.

Red opened her purse to pull out her phone. She sent a quick text to Lucas, hoping he hadn't been caught. Then she noticed the plastic fangs in her purse. She took Vic's hand. He had a bite mark on his wrist. It was clearer than the messy one on his neck. Almost as if it was carefully placed. The fangs were widespread. She glanced into her open purse again. The marks on his wrist were far larger than the daintier plastic copy. She glanced into the front of the ambulance.

The nervous driver focused on the road, face turned from her. She knew the pimpled nerd from the rogue minions even if she couldn't see him in the rearview mirror. His backpack was under a seat with pins covering it, including the fleur-de-lys that she'd seen at Gianni Construction.

Red studied the EMT in the back with her, finally noticing his pallor and eerily white teeth, and discreetly pulled Vic's gun from his holster.

At such close range, it was hard to miss. Blood and brain matter splattered against the side of the ambulance.

Her hand didn't pause between rounds. Ears ringing, she aimed and pulled the trigger on the vampire already spinning around to leap from the passenger seat. She missed the heart with the first bullet, but the second was true.

His chest exploded in a wave of red before his bones dropped.

The ambulance swerved, and she steadied Vic on the stretcher. Her eardrums throbbed from the reverberation of the gun blast in an enclosed space. She pressed her weapon against the side of the driver's head. "I keep running into you. I should know your name."

"Oh shit, oh shit!"

"Name." She dug the metal deeper into his temple. Her heart thumped in her chest, beating against her rib cage.

"Francis! Please don't kill me."

"Were you going to kill me, Francis?" She asked the question quiet and slow.

"I don't know. I'm just a delivery boy," he whined.

"What about my friend?" She demanded, baring her teeth. This whole ambulance was a death trap for them. Who had the clout to set this up?

"Oh, him?" Francis gulped. "Yeah. We weren't going to take you to a real doctor, so I guess he was probably toast."

"You're taking me to the nearest hospital. Now." Red cocked the gun. She wasn't going to let Vic be another victim. "Drive safely."

"Seriously though, please don't kill me."

"You'll be lucky if I do it and not your sire. You failed big time, Francis. What's this, like, the third time? You're like the kiss of death to diabolical plans."

"Hey, he knows I did my job." Francis tried to sound tough, but his eyes darted like a cornered rabbit's. "And you're right, you're a lot less scary."

Red pressed the gun harder against his temple. "So, Delilah's a patsy. Fabulous. But he can't keep it up. He's gotten sloppy." She went through the list of important male vampires in her head as she tried to stay in control of this shitstorm in an ambulance hurtling down the nighttime streets of LA. Her tightening throat reminded her that every second could be one too late for Vic.

"They have the video and the bite marks."

"The break in—you were dropping something off in Quinn Investigations, not stealing. What about the bite molds? You tampered with them?" Red pressed the barrel to his head. "Well, now, they don't need them once they pull her actual fangs out and check."

"Too late. Michel already has everything he needs to take over the city. You'll want to be on his good side!"

She leaned closer to Francis. The name pounded in her ears. Of course, there was always something too showy about these crimes. They were made to be seen, they were selling a narrative. And everyone had bought it.

Michel already had the media under his thumb, now with the Blood Summit, he must have been able to play politics to find Bloodliners eager to take a souled vampire master off her throne. He had lost a city, now he was taking one.

Red thought fast. "You know that Cora will stop him. If you flip now, she might use that soul of hers and take pity on you."

"Do you think so?" Francis wheezed.

"Turn right," she said when she saw a sign for the Hollywood Hospital. "You say you only know what he tells you, that you don't know the next step of the plan?"

"I swear. He turned me, but it's not like he tells me stuff. I swear!" He stopped the vehicle crookedly in the hospital's parking lot.

Red flicked the safety on and de-cocked the gun. She couldn't shoot him here. "I believe you."

"You do?"

That wasn't a good thing for him. She slammed the butt of her gun against his temple, feeling the bones crush.

Francis slumped forward over the wheel, dazed.

Red pulled the stake from the band around her thigh and staked him. She wiped her hands on his shirt before leaving his bones to climb into the back again. Gazing down at Vic, she knew she had to get out of there. Three skeletons and one unconscious man with a woman in bloody formal wear? That raised the wrong kind of questions. She grabbed her purse and settled its strap on her bare shoulder.

The back doors of the ambulance swung open.

21

Two women dressed in scrubs climbed into the back of the ambulance and barked questions.

"Where are the EMTs?"

"Why wasn't this phoned in?"

Red trembled as she stared at Vic. She had to focus, but the ringing in her ears overshadowed the voices. The ambulance ride from the Halloween Ball had changed everything. This whole time she had wondered what the dead models, the rogue minions, and the Blood Alliance's summit had in common— Michel. Dating Delilah got him access to the agency and knowledge of which models were on the outs with their boss. He killed Julia Crispin and the other women, leaving them at places connected to Delilah to cast suspicion on his girlfriend before switching the bite molds to make sure that he couldn't be traced to the bodies. All of this was happening when Cora was the most distracted. It wasn't a coincidence. This was a long con.

The city was almost in his grasp. Red had just killed three vampires, but if Michel won, she'd have a wave of the undead coming for them. They would have been uber fucked even if Vic had two working arms and consciousness.

The Millennium Falcon and all their weapons were out of reach. The Pandora Hotel would be watched once Michel's minions didn't report in. If it hadn't been already. They were probably responsible for all the burglaries. The only vampires in Red's corner were either captured or probably fighting for their lives.

One of the medics, a tall pock-marked Black woman tiptoed around the broken skeleton on the other side of the stretcher. "What on God's green earth?"

Red looked up. "It wasn't God." She didn't have it in her to think up a lie. "They had fangs, and their eyes turned amber when they attacked us."

"Honey, breathe deep. What's your name?"

Red shook her head, trying to clear it. They were fucked. She tried to tell herself that they'd been in tight spots before. But they'd had each other then. Now, she was on her own. Maybe not... "Get Detective Callaway. She'll know what to do."

"We know her." The older, bleached-blonde medic glanced knowingly at her coworker, then put a hand on Red's shoulder. "Come on, honey. Let's get you out of here. We need room to maneuver." She led Red to a waiting orderly who wore a freaked-out expression. "Juan, get her inside, call security, and come back. We have three skeletons and an unconscious man with severe neck trauma. Unknown bites."

"Another one?" Juan crossed himself before holding out a hand to Red.

Curiosity broke through the swirling fog of panic. Furrowing her brow, she hopped down from the ambulance with Juan's help. Her blood-streaked green gown fluttered around her legs. She matched his quick pace, walking into the hospital entrance to the lobby. "How many others?"

"Let's just say I don't take home enough." He took her to the front desk and called for security. "It didn't used to be like this."

Moments later, the medics came charging through with Vic prone on the rolling stretcher. The older blonde stopped to whisper to the blue-uniformed security guard before she went back to her patient.

Eyes on Vic, Red followed, hands clutching her skirt.

The security guard stepped forward. His name tag, reading *Earl*, was at eye level. He had a plain, olive-skinned face, craggy from the sun and age.

She peered around the unusually tall man in time to see Vic disappear behind double doors leading deeper into the hospital. "That's my friend. I need to make sure he's alright."

"I understand, ma'am, but we need to get you checked out and ready for when the police come."

"What? I'm fine." Red rubbed at her ears which were still ringing from the gunshot blast. She tried to wipe the freaked-out expression from her face.

"You need your neck bandaged." Earl put his hand on her shoulder.

Red put her hand to her neck. Somewhere along the way, she'd lost her necklace and golden hair comb. Dried blood caked her skin from the wounds caused by Delilah's sharp nails. Her skin was tender to the touch, and she could imagine the bruising. He was right. She let him guide her out of the lobby.

He led her to an examination room down a different hallway off the front desk and left her alone.

Sitting on the examination table, Red let her head hang down and fished her phone out of her purse to call Lucas. The phone rang once, then went to a full voicemail message. She tried Kristoff's and found it disconnected. She sent off a quick text message to Lucas to beware of Michel. Then she scrolled through her phone contacts, but she didn't have Fat Crispin's direct line. The icing on the cake? Her data had run out again. "Fuck."

In the whole rush of investigating dead models and a rogue vampire building a minion army, she hadn't hit up the store to upgrade from her rinky-dink burner phone. She couldn't even email the one human who might be able to get the Brotherhood to warn Cora and release Delilah or Quinn. She scrolled through her phone some more, finding the numbers of hunters who might float her message through the grapevine, but it wouldn't reach England until it was old news. She tried to connect to the hospital's Wi-Fi only to find it on the fritz.

"Fucking hell." She shivered in bloody formal wear under the fluorescent lights in the cold sterile hospital room. Her brain bounced between plans and freak-outs.

A nurse came in to bandage her up and bring her a change of clothes—leopard print leggings a size too small and a baggy knock off pink Nike jersey with three swooshes on the front. It wasn't Red's first brush with charity bin clothes, so she didn't react to the poor fit. She didn't speak beyond a thank you and to decline a hospital bed. The nurse left, avoiding eye contact in a way that made Red nervous.

Red changed her clothes, plotting as she did. Each fantasy of grabbing Vic and escaping LA seemed crazier than the last.

When the security guard came in to take her purse, she roused herself. "Come on, Earl. I need my phone."

"I have orders from above." He frowned, confused. "It's not what I want to do."

Red looked away as he left the room. She bit her tongue. It's not like he would know more than her. News traveled fast in this town... straight to Michel. She glanced around the hospital room, feeling the walls close in. His tentacles squeezed LA tighter as she waited in borrowed pants. She didn't even know if Vic was alive or dead.

That was the thought that broke her.

She leaned forward, putting her head between her knees as she struggled for breath. Her vision blurred, and she put her hand over her heart, trying to calm herself. Her chest felt like it was seizing. She sucked in a harsh breath. Her thoughts spiraled in a loop. She tried to pull herself together, tell herself that she couldn't freak out now, but all she could do was rock back and forth fighting off panic.

What would she do without Vic?

The door swung open. "I'm Detective Aisha Callaway."

Red looked up, wiping her eyes, and swallowed to try and clear the lump in her throat.

The detective strode inside in a dark pantsuit with a holster on her hip and a bump under her suit jacket. Her dark eyes were wary as she glanced behind her and closed the door. Circles from lack of sleep lingered under her brown eyes. Her black hair was swept back in a careless ponytail. "Didn't I see you with Quinn? Where is he? I've called both his cell and office phone."

"You won't get ahold of Quinn." Red tried to not think about the curls of smoke that had risen from the silver noose around his neck. "He was captured. I don't even know if he's still alive."

Callaway tipped her head up and rubbed her eyes. "The fuck? By who?"

Red's words came out in a panicked spurt. "I know which vampire is responsible for all these murders. The problem is, he's already taking over." She couldn't stop her rambling rush as her voice pitched higher. "Michel manipulated Cora... if she's still the Supreme Master of the city... I don't know. It's all happening so fast. Quinn is locked up. Lucas is probably next." She put her head in her hands. "I tried to call him, but they took my phone. And my partner... Vic was bitten, and now I don't know what's going on."

"Slow down. I'm not following." Aisha Callaway held up her hand. "What do you mean master of the city?"

Red took a deep, hiccupping breath before launching into a fast, panicked ramble. "Every city has a vampire who controls it all. The big head honcho. LA is run by a souled vampire named Cora Moon. Or at least it was. I'm not sure now. It could be controlled by a guy named Michel who has a serious grudge against Quinn and Lucas for some reason. I don't know how deep it goes, but he must have clout because he was able to get a fake ambulance and managed to make a lot of new minions. Cora was the one who tried to make this a more 'care, share, and grow' kind of city. Only she's losing control. You might have even seen her—beautiful, Black, teaches a yoga class in Inglewood?"

"Oh shit. She's the hippie who runs a drop-in space, right?"

"Yup, and now we have a mutiny on our hands." Red dropped her head back into her hands.

"Is that how you got the marks on your neck?"

Peeking up from her hand, Red sighed and shook her head. "No, that was another vampire. The one that all those murders were pinned on."

The detective cursed, hands on her hips. "I knew shit was going down. I'm getting orders that don't make sense."

"Michel runs media relations for the vamps. I wouldn't be surprised if he has connections in the LAPD. Cora bragged that she has men on the inside. Who knows how many have turned coat?"

"Fuck it. They might take my badge for this but..." Aisha Callaway's dark eyes narrowed, and she shook her head.

Red stood, not sure if she believed the words.

The officer pulled a gold purse out of her jacket. "I got the rundown from the nurse. Your friend's in a coma. They think he has spinal damage, but they aren't sure how much."

"He's paralyzed." Red said the bald truth just to stop Callaway from dancing around it. She looked down and stared at the blood still in her nail beds.

Vic's blood. The guy who loved IPAs, Lynyrd Skynyrd, and baby Jesus. He played the roughneck, but he got up every day to save lives and still tried to get to church on Sundays. He pushed away the comfort of being a Bard in their ivory tower to get his hands dirty with the hunters. He never forgot the mission. He had given her a name and a home when she had nothing. Now, he was in a coma with a busted spine.

And that was if he recovered, and Michel didn't kill him first...

Red leaned her forehead against the wall, hunching forward. Her breath caught in her throat. Mascara dripped into her eyes. She slapped her hand against the wall.

"Hey." Callaway turned her around and handed her a tissue. "I know what you're going through. It's some fucked up shit, but I have orders to detain you."

"Fucking fabulous. I'm glad I called the cops. This is why people like firemen more!" Red grabbed the tissue and blotted her eyes. Anger took the edge off her grief.

"But I'm not." The detective held out the purse. "Take this."

She blinked at Callaway. All her mind could do was reverberate with the understanding that Vic was in a coma. She barely recognized her own purse. "What're you doing?"

"I'm letting you go. Find Quinn and get him out. If they have men in my department, I'm going to need a dead man of my own. He's the only one I trust."

Red dug out Kristoff's gift of a fancy silk handkerchief. It was stained with dried blood now. She blew her nose and then tossed her hands up. Raw and ragged, her voice cut like a knife even to her own ears. "What can I do?"

"I don't know. Aren't you like a goblin or a fairy or something mystical like that?"

"If I was, do you think my partner would be lying in a hospital bed right now?"

"You're freaking out now, but this is the real shit going down. I have to hold it down here and try to catch the fallout. I need someone ready to take them on and get our guy out."

Red glanced away, failure dragging her neck down, her eyes hot from frustrated tears. "It's hopeless."

"What part of this night says quitting is an option?" Aisha Callaway put her hand on her hip. "They already have you. They have your partner. Are you going to just wait for this Michel guy to kill you? For him to eat up this city?"

Red lowered her head. "No."

Callaway studied her, then softened her voice. "Listen, I'm not risking my badge because this is going to be easy. I'm doing this because it needs to be done. I already know we have vampires tugging the strings, and I'm ready for it." She walked closer to Red. "Not because there's hope but because we have a city full of people who have no idea, and they are gonna be bled dry. We've had murders, we've had drainings, but it's been kicked up for the last few months. If that's because this guy is making his move, then we need to stop him. I can't do it alone."

"I've only been hunting them a year. I'm an intern. I can't do it alone. Vic could be dying up there."

Callaway squeezed Red's shoulder. "Hey, I've had a partner die on me. Antonio Diaz was the one who taught me what this freaky shit was. I found him drained in his own apartment, and the sole witness was a crackhead who only could say that a fucking pirate did it. I had nothing and no one, but I kept going. Quinn did me some favors, and now I'm doing him one. If your partner were awake, what would he do? What would he say?"

"He'd tell me to suck it up, buttercup and tell me to keep fighting because there were people on the line."

"Well, buttercup, what are you going to do?"

Red took her purse and opened it. A stake lay next to her phone and the gray plastic fang. She pulled out the stake and put it in her legging's tight waistband. "Keep fighting."

"That's it, girl. One foot in front of the other. It's the only way."

Taking the fangs out the purse, Red handed it to over. "Take this. It's Delilah's. Michel must have switched up her file. For a guy with one working eye, he's seen to everything."

"One eye?" Callaway furrowed her brow.

"Yeah, he has an eyepatch..." Red trailed off and looked up. "Your partner."

"Michel is the bastard's name?" A hard gleam flashed in the cop's eyes. "Get your phone out."

Red nodded, wanting to take a step back from the growing anger radiating from the detective, but she only took out her phone.

Callaway rattled off her phone number for Red to type into her phone. "Tell me when you have Quinn out. I'll try to protect your friend before going after Michel."

"I can send someone to get Vic." Red scrolled through her phone's contact list. "I know what you want to do, but if Michel is going to take over the city, he'll need more troops. You're the only one with morgue clearance. We need people ready to take them out. I'll warn Cora Moon."

Callaway turned away. The determination turned her young and pretty features old and grim.

Red held the warning lingering on her tongue. She couldn't say she wouldn't have the same look if Vic died. The cop wanted revenge. It wasn't smart, but Red would take the allies that she could get. This mission looked hopeless, but maybe the good guys could pull off a Hail Mary. Putting the phone to her ear, she waited for it to ring.

"Sheila Jones, Reaper and Smith."

Head down, Red kept her orders brief. She didn't have time to talk about the weather. "I don't know if this is in your wheelhouse, but I have my partner at the Hollywood Hospital. He's listed under Vic Constantine. He needs to be moved somewhere secure, private, and guarded."

"I can have him moved in ten minutes. The code is pineapple."

"That'll do." Red hung up. "There should be people from Reaper and Smith coming to get him."

Callaway raised her eyebrows. "Maybe you don't have powers, but you must have deep pockets."

"It's a recent thing." Red shrugged self-consciously. She still wasn't sure how she felt about the spooky bank being in her corner.

"Get out of here before I change my mind. Your friend is in 2208." Detective Callaway frowned at her and pulled a ponytail holder from her pocket and tossed it at Red. "Do something with your hair and look less shady."

Red followed her out of the room, putting her hair up, and turned down the hallway while Callaway distracted the nurses at the desk. She slunk past them through the double doors Vic had been wheeled through earlier.

Trotting down the hallway, she took an elevator up. There was no way she could leave without seeing Vic. She needed to know if the medics would come. Again, she couldn't believe that the freaky bank could do this, but Sheila had bragged that they put the special in special accounts. Vic said they specialized in the paranormal, but she could only hope they were neutral when it came to vampire conflicts.

Red got out of the elevator. The hallway buzzed with activity. Another stretcher with a man bleeding from the neck passed by, nurses and doctors shouted orders with the same pensive look. She slipped into room 2208 and found it dark. The glow of the heart monitor illuminated Vic's face.

Walking to the bed, she put her hand on his and squeezed. "I don't know if I'll see you again, but you'll get out of here. If I can, I'll try to save your Batman, Vic."

Tears in her eyes, she sniffed, feeling the weight of her uselessness. She tried to summon up that well of energy inside of her. That warmth of energy and magic that sparked within her and died like a neon sign blowing a fuse. She felt nothing but fear. The shaman in Nevada had said that she had power. She felt powerlessness.

There was a knock on the door, and Aisha Callaway popped her head in. "Those medics are here. You're rolling in deep, girl, let's hope you can get yourself out."

Red smiled tightly. "I'll try my best."

"Your best is getting the fuck out of here." The detective's words were harsh, but her tone held the compassion of one who had known loss.

Red nodded and left the room. She passed by two medics in matching blue windbreakers stamped with the logo for St. Brigid's Hospital. "Reaper and Smith?"

One nodded. "Pineapple."

"2208. Get him." She looked over the nurses' station at two pale men in police uniforms. They were too handsome to be regular cops and too serious to be strippers. She'd seen them before outside Moon Enterprises. Neither were breathing, but the East Asian one had a tinge of worry in his brown eyes when he looked over at his blond partner.

Red felt her earlier panic drain away as the mission took over her focus. She had come to LA to bring a killer to justice. Either way, she wasn't leaving this city so she might as well do what she came here for. She warned the medics from Smith and Reaper. "Don't trust any cops."

"Never do," the dark-skinned medic chuckled, quietly. "Coming with? We're at the back entrance."

"Go. I'll clear the way then meet you there." Red stopped walking and leaned against the wall, trying to find a way to get past the vampires in police clothing that seemed ready to block off the hallway. Once the medics passed her, she stepped forward to meet the eye of the undead blond.

He checked her over, thin lips disappearing into a line. The merciless eyes of a demon stared back at her. He nodded to his partner.

Red ducked into a stairwell and started trotting down the steps, her purse bouncing against her side. She felt the eyes on her back. Steps rang out behind her. She ran down the stairs, pulling the stake out of her waistband.

"Stop! Police." The words echoed in the stairwell. It was the blond cop. His tone was lazy with a gleeful note in it, hopeful that she would run. He obviously joined the force to bust heads.

She felt the motion behind her and turned with her stake raised.

"A hunter. It's been a while since I've tangled with one of you." The blond vampire smiled as he tipped his hat up. He wasn't afraid of her or her stake. There was no soul behind his eyes. "Let's dance then before Chang spoils my fun."

Red saw his green eyes on the stake. "How long have you been working against Cora?"

Shock took the arrogance off his face.

She smiled before head-butting him. Her head rang, but her hand rocketed to his chest, impaling him on the stake. She pushed him over the rail.

The vampire dropped over the edge, shouting.

Fuck, she was off her game, missing the heart and probably only hit a lung. She rubbed her aching forehead. That was going to bruise. She ran back up the stairs to a door into a quiet hallway and ducked into an elevator to go to the ground floor. Rushing from the opening doors, she slowed to a normal pace before asking a passing orderly where the exit was. She crept out of the hospital and around the back.

An unmarked ambulance waited, the back open with Vic laying inside, still and silent. The medics looked up before the dark-skinned one hopped out and jogged to the driver's side. His Caucasian partner closed the other door and yelled to her, "come on!"

Vampires sprinted toward Red from the other side. Time slowed. This was the end, but it didn't need to be the end for both of them. Vic had saved her life more than once. Gave her one. It was time for her to return the favor.

"Go now!" She hit the back of the ambulance, and it sped away.

The vampires in uniform raised their guns.

Red lifted her hands over her head, heart trembling in her chest. She swallowed back the fear in her throat. "Aren't you going to read me my rights, officer?"

"You have the right to die when the supreme says you do," The blond said as he came toward her, gun pointed at her face.

Chang sprinted to pull her hands behind her back. His hands were gentle even as he handcuffed her. "We'll get this sorted out. Just cooperate and you'll be fine."

Complying with the fake officer, Red licked her lips, fear had turned her mouth into a desert. None of this was fine. Her shoulders sagged. Detective Callaway should have found another hunter to rely on.

Chang led her to the waiting unmarked white sedan parked illegally on the red-painted curb next to the hospital back entrance.

Red tilted her head to show off her bite scar. Hopefully, the bandages and the bruising hadn't obscured it too much. Human laws didn't apply, but she could hope that vampire laws still did. "So, when do I get my phone call? I got to check in with Kristoff Novak. Claimed human and all that."

"Shut up." The blond vampire said as he pushed her head down to force her into the back seat. "You have no rights for me to read."

Chang sent an inscrutable side eyed glance at his partner as he broke the chain of her purse delicately and took it, then closed the door. He climbed into the passenger's side.

Red watched the two vampires, noticing that that neither had a reflection in the darkened rearview mirror. They weren't weak even if they were minions.

"Let's get her back to headquarters in Inglewood quick," Chang said as he pulled out his phone to send a quick text. "Cora will want to make sure the Bards know their hunter is secure."

"The little bitch nearly staked me. I say we—"

"Walk it off, man. We have a job to do." Chang fiddled with the radio until he landed on a techno song.

"Put on something good. Let's get some AC/DC."

"Get with the now, Fuchs. Listen to something from this century."

"This century sucks."

Red could feel Fuchs' gaze on her, even if she couldn't see his stare in the rearview mirror. The two vampires worked together with the ease of old colleagues, but the silence was sour like old milk. Looking straight ahead, she focused on studying the vampires in the front. Unseen, two masters pulled the strings in the car. Whose power would win out?

She tested the handcuffs uselessly as she stared out the window. Would the streets of Los Angeles would be the last thing she saw? She knew Vic was out there somewhere, and Lucas too. Would they ever know what happened to her?

Callaway had said quitting wasn't an option. From where Red was sitting, defeat certainly was. Ever since Vic had found her unconscious on the banks of Coyote Creek, she knew she had been running on borrowed time. It was up.

22

Fall had finally come to Southern California. Red felt it through her
borrowed leopard-print leggings. Or maybe it was just the chill of
death whispering in her ear.

She had gotten Vic to safety, fingers crossed that she could pull
the same for herself. The evening started in formal wear and ended in
handcuffs. She might have had some new fancy connections, but no
one liked her enough to cross a supreme master in a vampire-domi-
nated city like Los Angeles. No one besides Kristoff Novak.

Red shivered at the idea that he was her last hope.

Fuchs opened the police car and yanked her out into the parking
lot catty-corner to Moon Enterprises. It was empty of human life.
The tall building loomed over her like a gravestone. No one would
see her enter. Would anyone see her leave?

She hoped, for Vic's sake, that she wouldn't see him in whatever
dungeon that Cora threw her into. Praying to the God that Vic
believed in, she asked for her boss to get out of LA as soon as possible.

"I'll get her into a cell." Chang took her arm from his partner and led her into the side utility door of the vampire headquarters, past the main entrance where the needy could get free vegan breakfast and sunrise yoga.

When they were inside the sterile linoleum-floored hallway, she scrutinized her captor. The golden tint to his pale skin was clearer in the dimmed fluorescent light, but that hint of worry she thought she saw in the hospital had disappeared. Maybe it was hopeful delusion that made her think he might have a soul.

Red had one last card to play and she had already played it. She fought the cringe at her own desperation. Taking herself out of Chang's hands only put into another's. "Can you let Kristoff Novak know I'm here? He'll want to know."

"I'd keep quiet until Cora summons you," he said, voice hushed and neutral. "She'll hand you over to him soon enough."

Hope deflating, Red felt stupid.

Kristoff would've packed up his brother and his minions by now. He had certainly already ditched his phone. His claiming mark could be a tool, he'd told her. It wasn't a very useful one now, not to her anyway. Had he left her to die just as Lucas said he did to Juniper? She thought the only thing she had in common with her doppelgänger was a face, but now she was going to share the fate of dying young.

She tried to concentrate on Chang, pulling at the magic that was supposed to be in her, but she couldn't even mess his hair up with a breeze, let alone light it on fire. Only her steps echoed in the hallway. His were supernaturally light, and if not for the pressure of his hand on her elbow, she could have sworn she was alone. In the truest sense, she was.

The building seemed more like a maze than a skyscraper as the vamp cop guided her through empty hallways and up stairwells before taking her to a service elevator. It had been scary to see the place full of vamps, but it was eerier to see it empty. Where was everyone?

The elevator opened. A mounted camera was in a ceiling corner.

Who was spying on the other side of the lens? The doors closed behind them.

Chang put his thumb against a scanner then pushed an unmarked button, eight up from the bottom. They rose with the quiet of a funeral. Looking around as if something was missing, he raised his dark eyebrows under his police cap.

"What?" Red asked, she didn't like that look of suspicion.

"There isn't any music. Cora insists that an elevator isn't one without a tune." He glared at her as if he'd said too much, and it was her fault.

She shivered and wondered who was controlling the playlist now. Concentrating hard to look out of her third eye, she couldn't see even a misty sign of an aura. It felt more like something was suppressing her senses. Cora had put forethought into defending her headquarters from magic use.

Red hoped she had a backup plan for a renegade second-in-command.

Chang took his hand off her arm and stepped out of the elevator first, looking around. Unlike the sparse utility of the previous hallways, this hall was decked out to impress with discreet low lights built into the ceiling, shining down on gray granite tiles.

"What's this hallway supposed to sound like?"

"Ha," he said dryly and gestured her forward. He brought her to a black door and opened it. Inside was a small toilet, the porcelain lid missing from the tank, and a dusty sink with a soap dispenser hanging next to it. "I'm going to uncuff you, and you'd better not make me regret it."

Red turned around to let him free her hands. "Thank God."

"God isn't the one letting you take a whiz. It's Joe Chang." He left the door cracked open, his benevolent deed only going so far.

She peed quickly and washed her hands and arms up to the elbow, trying to get the funk of the hospital off, scrubbing as hard as she could at the traces of blood still in her nail beds. When she finished, she pushed the door open and held her wrists out.

Chang twirled his finger to have her turn around and cuffed her again.

She followed him to another room. It would have looked like it was for meetings in a fancy bank if not for the cells. Instead of a long conference table, four empty cells rose along the opposite wall. Small, embedded LED lights along the ceiling molding reflected off the silver-plated bars to cast thin shadows on the polished dark cement floor.

He opened the cell in the middle, which had a long metal bench against the wall, and nodded inside. "Get in."

Red sat on the bench, trying to imagine how to find a comfortable position with her arms cuffed behind her back. Her left hand had already fallen asleep. She leaned back against the wall and shifted position, looking up at Joe Chang and the closing cell bars.

He shifted his gaze away and left in a blur, door shutting behind him.

Closing her eyes, she tried to quiet her mind and breathe deep. She needed to keep a cool head on the unlikely chance that Cora did summon her and on the very likely chance that Michel would. The door opened after what couldn't have been more than five minutes and Chang came back in.

A peeved expression on his face, he had an energy drink tucked in the crook of his arm and a banana in his hand. "It's the best I can do." He opened the cell door and put the can and fruit on the bench next to her, then put his hands on his hips and stared down. Muttering to himself, he reached for her before saying louder. "I'll break this arm if you try anything funny."

"No funny business from me." Red twisted around to give him better access to unlock the cuffs.

"If anyone asks, this was on Cora's orders."

She bobbed her head. "That's the story and I'm sticking to it."

"Ration the liquids." He shook his head. "I can't promise that Cora will be quick about seeing you."

"Thank you, Joe Chang." She rubbed her right wrist with her left hand. She tried to make a connection with him. He clearly wasn't as terrible as his partner. Maybe he was one of the good guys. "I'm Red, by the way. We didn't get an introduction."

"I know who you are." He called over his shoulder, slamming the cell door and left the room. "Pipe down."

Exhaling harshly, she shook her head at her own naivety. He might not be as bad as Fuchs, but he still was a jailor. Her stomach rumbled, and she devoured the banana before setting the peel and the can out of view under the bench to hide the break in Chang's stern demeanor. Curling up, she closed her eyes and rested her head on her arm.

The dream of woodsmoke and burning flesh evaporated as soon as she opened her eyes at the turn of the doorknob. She rubbed her eyes, mouth dry, and shook her head to clear the fuzzy fatigue.

In the windowless room, she couldn't tell if she had been asleep for hours or minutes. Her neck creaked as she looked over at the opening door. Instinct pleaded for her to hide in the corner, but grim logic told her that vampires could sniff her out even in the shadows of the dark room. Red tilted her knees toward the door and put her hands behind her back, trying to appear as docile a prisoner as possible in case it wasn't Chang.

The door slammed open and long shadows appeared across the threshold.

Red barely recognized Quinn's bruised face as Fuchs pushed him into the room. Smoke curled off the silver noose on his neck and the silver cuffs on his wrists. His tuxedo jacket was missing, and the shirt was streaked with blood. He stumbled, but a proud bearing still hung on his broad shoulders.

Fuchs tugged the silver leash and shoved him into the open cell next to Red's. "Get in there, Byrnes."

Chang followed behind with Delilah thrown over his shoulder. He tossed her against the wall in the cell on the other side of Quinn's like a sack of potatoes. She grunted on impact.

After locking them in, the two vampires in police uniforms left as suddenly as they came.

Bloody lip and bruised eyes illuminated by the small ceiling lights, Delilah glanced over at Red. "Christ, can't get rid of you, can we?"

"Like a bad penny." Red stood and put her hands on the bars to look at Quinn. The immortal imported his hair gel while his minimalist wardrobe of black on black was always pristine down to his flaring trench coat. In a roughed-up tuxedo with silver burns on his face and neck, he barely looked like the PI that she knew. She asked, "how're you holding up?"

"Just peachy," Delilah said waspishly. "It's like we got back from a day spa. The facial was fine, but the seaweed wrap was too tight." Her head fell forward, and her loose golden hair, streaked with blood, covered her face. She had gotten more attention from the torturers. Blood soaked through her torn, golden skin-tight dress. The studs on the shoulders survived. Did the mic? She moaned before falling into a daze.

"Rest, darling. The sun will be up soon." Quinn murmured, crouching down to reach for her through the bars, silver sizzling on him. Delilah was too weak to meet his fingertips. Pain crinkling his forehead, he looked over at Red. "How did Joe and Fuchs catch you? Is Vic here?"

Red shook her head, stomach twisted at the thought of her mentor.

"Good." Quinn stood and stepped back from the bar, refocusing on his unconscious sire in the other cell.

"God, you don't know." Red bit her lip, tears coming to her eyes in an instant. "He's in rough shape, a coma. I don't know if it was Michel or one of his minions." She whispered the story of the ambulance ride from hell and how she had only just managed to get Vic out of the hospital. "I couldn't get ahold of Lucas, but Callaway knows what's up—for all the good it does us."

Quinn didn't speak a word during her story. He clenched his fists, knuckles cracking in the still room as he looked away. The fury on his face ignited before he composed his features. The fire still flashed in his eyes. In that moment, she finally saw the demon under the surface that had given rise to all the stories about Bloody Quinn Byrnes, the Black Libertine.

Noticing her shock, he composed himself. He straightened his ripped formal shirt with his cuffed hands and sat on the bench.

Red followed suit, perching on her own. Only the silver bars separated them.

Quinn leaned his head against the wall. Closing his eyes for a moment, he took an unnecessary breath. "Cora still rules."

"Not everyone. Fuchs is one of Michel's."

"Grammont should win an Oscar for the performance pleading for her life." He looked over at Delilah. Even through the bruises, his concern shone in his brown eyes. "It's going to break her heart."

"He's been planning this a long time."

"Since 1899."

"That was the year he lost Paris." Red remembered from Julia Crispin's notes. "Michel's been looking for a city for a while, then. Now that I know, he's not going to let me walk out of here."

"No, it suits his purposes to have Delilah be the villainess."

"I'm trying to wrap my head around this. I can see why getting two of Cora's most powerful allies out of the way helps him. Plant some bodies, fake a mutiny, distract the Supreme Master, gain a city. It makes sense. But why aren't you two dead yet?"

"He asked Cora to spare us until a full investigation could be done. Walking the line between lover and loyal servant." Quinn chuckled. "A part of me can't help but be impressed. What a tangled web he's woven. Back in the day, I would've applauded such subtle treachery—if I wasn't on the wrong end of it."

She hugged herself. It wasn't exactly comforting to know that the Black Libertine was giving Michel the villain's seal of approval. "If he were smart, he'd kill us now. Then the city would be his."

"The city isn't the point."

Red took a deep breath and gritted her teeth. She'd had enough with the one sentence answers. "Okay, old, wise, cryptic master, what is the point?"

"Revenge."

"Then he's having it served up cold like froyo. Still, why not kill you two? It was Alaric that took his city, and that guy is like ten years dead. You two are the next best thing."

"The Alaric Order only took Paris because my family helped. Revenge wouldn't be as sweet for Michel de Grammont without me watching her suffer." Quinn tried to rub his knuckles against his shirt, an old habit prevented by his handcuffs.

"He hates you that much?" She didn't get it. Michel could win right now.

"Oh, I'm high up the list, but I don't flatter myself. Neither of us is the entrée. There is one he hates even more," Quinn said. "I don't even know if displacing Cora is the coup de grâce."

"How can Los Angeles just be the cherry on top?"

"That locket you found. I have a photographic memory for faces, but I had only seen her from afar. Even if I engineered her downfall. I didn't recognize her when you showed it to me."

"Who was she?" Red asked.

"Penelope. His childe, his lost love. I should have guessed when I saw the locket." Quinn's voice had gained a gentle Irish lilt long suppressed, brought forth in the rhythm of telling an old story. "Callaway said her evidence from the Crispin murder scene was stolen. My sources said that Michel himself had taken an interest in the case. He even sent minions to waste management to check the dumpster that had been in the alley. He must have been looking for the locket. It was probably the last memento that he had of her. Nostalgia is as much of a vice for us as drinking blood."

She tried to remember more from her research. "She was murdered, wasn't she?"

"On her initiation day. Back in the bloodline days, that meant more than it does now."

"Fucking hell. So, the Bloody Byrneses killed his lover, and none of you considered that, gee, maybe the mysterious bodies might be from the guy you all screwed over?"

Quinn lifted his eyebrows as he shrugged. "I've made more enemies in my time than I can keep track of. All of us have. I crossed him off the list when he started dating my ex-wife. Figured it was revenge enough."

"Fucking vampires and their secrets." Red punched the silver bar between them. Jumping up and shaking her now-aching hand, she paced the length of the cell. "Vic could be dying or may have died, for all I know, and I'll be next. You brought us into this shitstorm. How many people have died because of this centuries-old blowback? Do you know how much Vic idolizes you? He thinks you're his Batman! You nearly got your Robin killed. They think he's paralyzed. Even if he lives, he can't walk, can't hunt, can't provide for himself. You did this to the chump that thought of you as his hero."

Pausing her rant, she rubbed her eyes, feeling the mascara burn her irises. "And I'm the bigger chump, because I could've gotten us out of here when I smelled bullshit. Which I did from the beginning!"

Quinn watched her without a word.

"Well? Aren't you going to say something?"

"You're right."

Her shoulders slumped. She wanted indignation, a refusal, something. Not this stoic acceptance of his failure. "So, this is it then?"

"No. He won't kill any of us until he gets what he really wants."

She rolled her wrist, gesturing him to continue. "And that is?"

Quinn grunted out, "Lucas."

"What? Wasn't he was drunk during that war?" She thought back to her historical chatter with Kristoff at the gallery.

Kristoff and Lucas hadn't just fought together in a minor clan conflict for the Alaric Order, it was what the Bard historians called the Last Bloodline War. Before the August Harvest had swept vampire society into anarchy, the undead had been split between eight bloodlines composed of countless mighty councils, middling clans, and tiny nests battling for power for millennia. The Blood Alliance had done away with the system long before she had been born. Obviously, time hadn't healed all wounds.

"Why him?" she asked.

"Because Lucas was the one who didn't just help capture Penelope. He drank her blood."

"Huh? Vampires don't eat vampires. They're amber-eyed people eaters. That's an—"

"It's an abomination. But the Alaric Order celebrated abomination. Unholy communion most profane to gain power." Quinn stared straight ahead. "Penelope was a step too far considering her rank, so the Order didn't publicize it. Lucas didn't speak of it to me. Didn't tell anyone, but I found out from Selene when she had a vision. Penelope was his initiation. Maybe if she had just been staked, Michel might have mourned and moved on, but that wasn't what happened. Alaric gave her blood to Lucas as a reward for sacking the city."

Red slumped back down on the bench. "Then I guess that's why I haven't heard from him. He's probably already gotten Lucas and is waiting to spring his final revenge."

"The boy is slippery, always been a survivor. He is still out there. Michel won't stop until he has settled all the old scores."

"Then we're even more fucked than I thought." Red put her head in her hands. "The funny thing is, between me and Vic, I'm the optimist. But it's hard to see the sunny side of things when you're in a cage. I should've told Vic that we needed to leave."

Quinn pointed out, "I was the one who asked you two to come."

"You're right. It's your fault." A hysterical giggle bubbled up in her throat. "Oh God, I wish I were the praying type. Vic was. He'd go to church and I'd read in the van." She wiped her eyes, feeling his blood even on her clean hands. "He's like the brother I'll never know if I had. I can't tell him that now."

He looked away while she composed herself. "Why did you stay?"

"Because I had a clue about where I came from. I thought I might find out who my family was, but instead I just damned the only one who felt like family." She lifted her head and sighed, swiping the running makeup under her eyes, staring at the smears of mascara and foundation on her fingertips. "I guess it'll stop hurting once I'm dead, and I dunno, maybe my life will flash before my eyes, and I'll get some answers. At least Vic has a chance." She shrugged. "Unless Michel finds him. Hell, even if Cora wins, she might just kill us all too."

"No. Cora is angry, but despite all the torture, she is better for the city. She won't do anything to Vic."

"The phrase snowball's chance in hell comes to mind."

"We have one, if Cora can hold on long enough to stop the coup."

"Yay, go Team Vampire!" Red raised her fist and sneered. "Y'all are just a bunch of tools."

"Michel hasn't won yet. Cora has allies." Quinn reached through the bars to put his hand on her shoulder. "This isn't the beginning of the end."

His words sunk in. They jolted her memory. Over his shoulder, she noticed something in the corner of the room: a camera. The shadows almost hid it, but her eyes had finally adjusted enough to see it. Red smiled. Cora wasn't the only one with allies.

"It's the end of the beginning," she quoted without explaining the reference to Quinn.

"Chang, I know you can hear me! Get Novak!" She stood and walked to the edge of her cell to look at the other corners of the room. Cameras. Where there were cameras, there were microphones. Cora's playlist might not be playing in the elevators, but she still had some loyal followers. Hopefully.

"What are you doing?" Quinn hissed at her. "Michel has more than enough reason to hate Kristoff. He was beside Lucas every step of the way, taking Paris. He did enough damage that Alaric brought him into the Order. I doubt Michel has forgotten."

"Lucas is probably dodging Michel's men right now, if he hasn't already been captured." Red planted her hands on her hips. "Do you have any other vampires to call on?"

"If Kristoff can get you out, can you get away from him?"

"One problem at a time. Besides, Goonies never say die."

"What the hell does that mean?"

Red waved her arms again to speak to the camera, trying to conjure up an ally. She played her last card again. Hoping the third time was a charm. "I'm a claimed human of the ambassador of Portland. You heard what he did to Lucas Crawford—his own sire. If you want to keep Cora happy, you know you have to keep Novak happy!"

23

November 1st, Daytime, Moon Enterprises, Inglewood near UCLA, Los Angeles, California, USA

Staring at the ceiling of her cell with her arms behind her head, Red counted to ten as she breathed in and held the deep breath before letting it out.

Her captivity at Moon Enterprises had lasted through the night. Joe Chang hadn't shown up to release them. The rant at the camera hadn't done anything besides wake Delilah up. Kristoff's claim wasn't much of a tool after all.

Turned out that playing a bad hand over and over didn't magically make it a good one.

Novak must have been less important than his stock portfolio made him out to be. She had been awake for hours, mulling over her decisions like a montage of bloopers and pratfalls. Quinn had let her know it was daybreak before he fell into a slumber. She tried not to look at either him or Delilah. They had the stillness of corpses. It only made her feel more alone.

Red had let herself cry, rage, and had even fought through a panic attack. Now, there was nothing but silence and stillness. And the uncomfortable press of her bladder. She peeked her head up when the door opened.

Joe Chang walked in with a single look at the vampires before he padded to Red's cell. He pulled out his gun and pointed it at her but didn't meet her eyes. "Get up. Bathroom break."

Standing, Red raised her hands and stepped forward. She waited until the cell door opened and followed him to the bathroom in the hallway. With the door cracked, she used the toilet before splashing water on her face.

Staring at her reflection, she wondered when she would see it again. She wiped the old foundation and blush off her cheeks and forehead then pulled off the dirty bandage. Delilah's nail marks on her neck had darkened even more, giving her a grisly looking necklace of bruises and scabs. Her stomach rumbled. She brought a handful of water to her dry mouth.

Chang opened the bathroom door, gun barrel raised at her face. "You're done. Come."

Even after having guns pulled on her all night, goosebumps rose on her skin. Red nodded, mouth dry again. "What time is it?"

"What part of piping down confused you, hunter?" He took her back into the cell room. He frowned and paused; shoulders slumped.

"Working early then? Or late?"

He grunted, shoving her back in the cell then glanced at the camera.

"You're looking tired. Have you been on guard duty this whole time, listening in?" She held onto hope that something she had said might have reached him. Quinn had dropped enough bombshells last night that it had to have created some doubt in the officer's mind.

"It's a job."

"The part where Cora was supposed to see me. When is that happening?" She watched the subtle play of emotion on the undead cop's face. Chang tried to hide it, but the worry was back. "You floated this up the hierarchy and got radio silence."

He tensed. "She is a busy woman."

Red shrugged, then looked slyly at her captor, fanning the flames of his doubt. She could tell that his old law dog instincts were howling at him. He wouldn't have been so nice if Fuchs were listening in either. "I guess she needs to prepare for the presentation on her catch and release policy, huh?"

Chang frowned, shunning her gaze.

"Is that where your partner is? Guarding the Blood Summit? Or is he watching us?"

"We aren't joined at the hip."

"No, but you're supposed to stick together. One souled and one unsouled, another symbol of that vampire unity. How's that going?" Red asked, lifting her eyebrows, holding back a cheeky smirk.

Chang bared his unnaturally white teeth at her in a rigor mortis grimace. "You're talking about things you don't understand. I don't care what Quinn told you."

"Oh, for Fuchs' sake, no one needs to tell me anything. Your partner is off the reservation. He's working with Michel. You saw what they did to Delilah and Quinn, but their story isn't changing. She's a patsy. Cora has a mutiny on her hands, but it's not from Delilah. I can prove it."

"You have no evidence. Just whispers from her childe. Byrnes would do anything to save her." He raised his voice at the end and turned on his heel. "Just as I would do for my sire."

"Your gut isn't lying to you," Red said. "Neither am I."

"The Byrnes acted against Cora. Face it before they drag you down, hunter." He paused in the doorway, then slammed it as he left.

Sighing, she tipped her head back and rubbed her cheeks. Perfect. She went back to her bench and put her face in her hands. Her breath hitched as she tried to think about what Vic would do. He was a Bard; duty was his second nature. What was hers?

Looking up at the camera, she said, "You're loyal to Cora and you know something isn't right, Chang. Quinn was telling the truth. If you can't believe that then you know for a fact that Cora needs Kristoff and the Portland vampires. Then the deal with the Bards. Do you really think either agreement will survive if I end up moldering in this cell?"

Only silence answered her.

She cursed herself, wondering why she bothered. Chang might not have been on Michel's payroll but how much would he put himself on the line for a supreme master who was going to fall?

Red folded her arms and let her eyes fall closed. She still had most of the energy drink left, but she knew she was a long way from the Pandora Hotel. There was no room service in a cell, and who knew when her next potty break would be.

Hours passed between sips of the energy drink. Nervousness kept hunger at bay, but thirst wasn't so easy to settle. The sticky warm beverage had lost its carbonation, but it wet Red's parched mouth. It didn't sit well on her empty stomach—or maybe it was just nerves making her stomach churn. Finally, the sugar rush forced her to pace in the cell.

"It's past sunset." Quinn sat up, chained cuffs rattling.

She jumped. The transition of dead to awake startled her as much as his words. "Damn. You need a bell."

"I'll work on that." He looked at the door.

Delilah stood up with a hobble, even if her expression was haughty as ever. The bruises had partially healed on her face. "They're coming."

Red straightened her shoulders and took a step back. Her fingers curled, she wished for a stake. Her heart leapt into her throat as the door swung open.

Fuchs and Chang walked in with two other vampires in ripped denim and leather biker jackets behind them. The blond cop bared his fangs at her before he pointed to the others. "Take them."

The bikers raised guns and shot metal darts into Quinn and Delilah's torsos.

"Fucking hell," Delilah rasped and staggered forward. Her body dropped on the floor in time with her ex-husband. The rough-looking vampires unlocked the cell to pull the Byrneses out. One threw her over his shoulder while the other dragged Quinn out by his feet.

Chang nodded to Red and unhooked the keyring from his belt. "Are we handing this one over to Novak?"

"All those Portland vamps fled already." Fuchs stepped closer to the cell, mindful of the blessed silver. "Did you hear that, bitch? Novak left you behind. I guess you're not that special."

She stood her ground. Flinching in front of a vampire only made them want to bite harder. Fuchs was a bully with a badge. She had met his kind before. He might have been undead, but he was mostly just an asshole.

He cracked his knuckles. "You put a stake in me. I can put a few in you."

Shifting her feet, Red clenched her fists matching his stance. The silver-plated bars separated them, but she made sure to stay out of his arm reach.

Chang stepped forward. "Novak wants his human back. We can't keep her here."

"Who the fuck cares what he wants?" Fuchs' hand drifted toward the black police baton on his hip.

"Cora does." Joe Chang glared. "She wanted the hunter safe too."

"Loony Moony doesn't always get what she wants." Fuchs smirked.

Red inched closer to the cell door, watching Chang's face fall. He didn't look surprised, only disappointed. Fuchs had finally made the wrong wisecrack.

"How long?" Chang asked quietly as he raised his police baton and shook it to release a stake from the tip.

"Want to try me, soul boy?" Fuchs rushed forward and pressed his partner against the silver bars to wrestle the baton away.

"Don't make me do this!" Elbowing his attacker with one arm, Chang dropped his key ring into the cell.

Holding her breath, Red picked it up and began jamming keys

into the cell's keyhole, fumbling to find the right one. Outside the bars, the fight only intensified.

"I was hoping you'd resist arrest," Fuchs said. "Finally give me a reason to shut that sanctimonious mouth."

Joe Chang punched the other vampire in the side of his head and pulled a stake from his utility belt. "You prick! Cora is going to have your hide."

Fuchs fell back and shook his head. "Michel will take care of her and her beatnik bullshit soon enough." He slapped the stake away. It clattered noisily to the floor. "Your sire is going to die!"

Chang roared. The two rolled on the ground, cursing and growling at each other, years of grievances over the radio bubbled up.

"I fucking hate House music!"

"Journey sucks!"

Fuchs rolled Chang over to straddle him. "That soul taints you."

Finally finding the right key, Red unlocked the door and pushed it open. She dipped down to pick up the dropped stake. Heart pulsing in her ears, she ran forward and jumped for Fuchs. She buried the stake in his black uniformed back. She didn't miss this time.

He hissed and reared back before his flesh decayed rapidly and his bones tumbled onto the floor, covering Chang in his dusty remains.

"Get Club Vltava on the line." Red panted as she pulled the stake back. She pressed her hand to side, trying to catch her breath. She wrinkled her nose from the vampire dust.

Chang climbed to his feet and brushed himself off. "Already tried. I got a voicemail. We need to get Cora. I lost track of her."

Red cursed.

Fuchs had made it sound like Cora was alive. Alive wasn't the same as being in power. If the supreme had already fallen and Michel had already made his last chess move, they were better off fleeing town. She tried to tell herself that Cora was cunning, and Michel wouldn't strike until he was sure. It felt like a flimsy hope, but making Quinn and Delilah disappear could be hidden, full revolt against the

Supreme Master brought his plan into the open. Cora had to still be here somewhere.

"You need to even the odds," Red said. "Those bikers were Michel's."

"What about you?"

"I can warn Cora."

Joe Chang's head jerked back. "That's suicide."

"Michel won't kill me yet. He has other plans for me. Somehow, I don't think he cares that much about one of Cora's pet cops."

"He wants to hurt Lucas Crawford, huh?"

"You were listening." Red looked up at the camera. "Who else was?"

"The security room is empty." He punched his palm. "Turncoats. I'm sorry I didn't believe you. It wasn't until I saw that it was only unsouled vampires guarding the building that I realized you were onto something. Then to see the presentations on catch and release moved to before sunset and the last committees cancelled...I knew Cora wasn't running the show anymore. I wanted Fuchs to prove me wrong. Give my old partner a chance."

Red understood that the partner bond was tricky. Who knew how long the two had been patrolling the LA beat together? She was past being held captive and ready to move on to the next crisis. "It's okay. When did you last see her?"

"I tried to talk to her before her talk on catch and release, but Fuchs kept calling me back to watch the cell camera feeds." His fangs popped out as he gritted his teeth. "I'll round up the other souled vampires. I can at least warn them before they're turned on."

"Get a hold of Detective Aisha Callaway too, Chang. She already has her feelers out on the morgues, keeping an eye out for new minions. And she has a real replica of Delilah's fangs. That's proof Michel is ready to strike, and he's not going to stop." She nodded to the door. "Where can I find Cora?"

"If Michel is holding her, she'll be in her penthouse on the top floor. You'll see the stairwell on the left to get to her quarters."

Red swirled the stake in her hands. "It's a start."

Chang led her out of the cell room. "You're on your own until I get back. Wherever the Byrneses are... they aren't coming back."

"Every hunter is alone in the end," she said, trying to shrug casually. It was something Vic told her, but it wasn't until now that she felt the truth in her bones.

Chang nodded, then ran down the hallway too fast for her human eyes to track. Only the slamming door of the stairwell showed where he went.

Red steeled herself. This was it. Vic had given her a year and enough training to go out with a bang. They said that everyone in LA had their ten seconds of fame. If she did her job right, she'd give these vampires something to talk about for a century.

24

NOVEMBER 1ST, Past Sunset, Moon Enterprises, Ingle-wood near UCLA, Los Angeles, California, USA

Moon Enterprises was as still as a vampire's chest.

The stairwell up to the top floor seemed endless, even though Red knew it was only four stories up. Each step, she wondered where the guards were. There had been a conference in this building, but it felt like she was the last person left on Earth. The telltale red pinpoint light on the ceiling cameras were dark.

The revolution would not be televised.

Red was taking a lot on faith. Faith that Cora would be better for LA, faith that Michel could be stopped, and faith that she could make any kind of impact. It was better than the alternative. She had no doubts about what would happen if Michel won.

Stepping out of the stairwell, she entered a hallway decorated in creamy velvet wallpaper with macramé wall hangings and a white marble floor. Something told her it hadn't been redecorated since the Manson Family roamed the valley.

Cora paced down the hallway with her bodyguards lining the

walls. She barked orders into a cell phone. "The sensors tell me the guest rooms are empty. Get the last of these ingrates out of the lobby for the party at Club Vltava now. The Blood Alliance might want to bump up my agenda, but we can roll with it. Act like everything is normal. Put on my playlist. You have the key to the liquor stocks even if the Novak Boys are gone."

There was no trace of defeat on her proud face. Despite the white caftan dress and crystal necklaces, Cora Moon looked less like a hippie with a scowl worthy of Churchill in the war room on her face. Like Joe Chang, she hadn't gone to bed after the Halloween Ball. Eyebrow arched, she noticed Red immediately and hung up the phone. "Little hunter chick, shouldn't you have run off with Novak, or did he send you to plead for Delilah too?"

"Um, what? I spent the night in a cell. I came to—" Red looked around at the bodyguards, realizing that each one of the five had tensed at the sight of her. "See if you were ok." She finished lamely, trying to find the right words. She shook her head, realizing that being subtle wasn't going to get them anywhere. "Michel didn't tell you that he had held me along with Delilah and Quinn? He had some biker dudes take them away."

"Is it fuck-with-me day?" Cora looked around and her fangs jutted out. "Bring Michel, since he won't pick up his phone."

Her bodyguards reached into their pockets with gloved hands, and pulled out chains of blessed silver. Their stoic expressions didn't change, even though their loyalties had.

Guts twisting, Red backed up, raising her stake. Her throat clenched tight, calculating the odds. It was five against two. Michel had really gotten to everyone.

"Fuck it. I'll get him myself." Cora leapt straight up over their heads. Hands and knees on the high ceiling of the hallway, she hissed and ripped out the chandelier, dropping it on her traitorous guards.

They staggered as the golden chandelier hit but managed to avoid the direct impact.

Cora dropped down on the first guard. Her hands burned as she grabbed at the blessed silver he held. Using both hands, she pulled it up and yanked it through his neck, sending his head tumbling back.

A bare skull joined his bones on the floor.

Red pulled out her stake, stabbing it into the ribs of a second guard and angling it up to pierce his heart. He fell back and decayed into a skeleton.

The other two traitors circled Cora.

Another bodyguard pulled Red into his arms and put a gun to her head. "Cora! I'll spray her brains all over the wall."

Panting through her nose, Red swallowed thickly. The metal jabbed into her temple, pressing on her rapid pulse.

The gunman called out. "Michel says you can leave LA with your life if you don't fight."

"He also lied to me so I would have my best friend tortured. His word is worth as much as his depth perception." Cora jumped up and bounced off the wall, her skirt flaring around her legs as she drop-kicked the vampire. Her foot whooshed by Red's ear as she knocked his head back at an awkward angle.

Red pushed away from the twitching vampire and pressed herself against the wall.

The elevator door opened. Lucas and Kristoff burst out of it and charged the other two bodyguards.

Exhaling sharply, Red grinned at them. Michel hadn't gotten his hands on them after all. Relief spread through her.

Lucas spun and kicked his opponent in the knee before staking the rogue.

Kristoff punched his hand clean through the other guard's chest and pulled out a heart that crumbled to dust in his hand. He looked at Cora and bowed. "My lady, forgive the intrusion."

Lucas rushed to Red and cupped her chin. "Kitten, we have to get you out of here."

Kristoff glared out of the corner of his eye, turning to face them.

Red nodded to Lucas trying to ignore the glower.

Cora held up her last surviving guard, his legs dangling uselessly as he gaped at her. "You have some explaining to do." She gritted her teeth. "What, can't talk? Then you're more than a traitor. You're useless to me."

Lucas tossed a stake to Cora.

She staked the vampire and kicked at the bones that remained. "The back up isn't much, but it'll do."

"Joe Chang's out there trying to round up the souled vampires," Red said.

Who knew how many would answer his call, but he'd get the word out. Michel couldn't have possibly accounted for Fuchs slipping up and betraying the conspiracy. If he was keeping up the pretenses that Cora still ruled, then he wouldn't tip her notice by ordering her childe killed yet. He would speed up his plans once he realized that Cora was onto him. It would be a race to see which master vampire could rally their minions and vassels faster.

Cora nodded. "Good. Joe will hold it down."

"What dungeon are you keeping Quinn and Delilah in?" Lucas gritted his teeth, the amber reflection of a predator in his eyes as he looked around. "They can't be far. I can still sense them."

Relieved, Red said, "Michel had some bikers take them."

"You have a helipad on the roof, right?" Kristoff asked the Supreme as he wiped blood off his hand with a handkerchief. "I can call a helicopter and get us to safer ground."

Cora nodded before making a call. "Joe, there's still some life in the mission. Michel isn't taking my city. The lower floors have been taken over. Bring who you can find—souls only. I'll be leaving from the roof to rally the rest in a second wave. We have a battle to finish." Confident head held high and strutting like a warrior queen, she led the group to the elevator.

Spirits rising despite her fear, Red walked between the men and looked them over. She hadn't ever been so happy to see vampires in her life. She grinned, hand on her hip. "Took you two long enough."

"I wouldn't leave you." They said at the same time. The sire and childe sized each other up.

Cora sighed. "Stop the competition vibes. I know Kristoff is the

275

only reason you got out of Club Vltava, Lucas. There is still some love, boys."

Lucas looked away at Red's curious glance.

"Let's not sing kumbaya yet," Kristoff said.

Cora snapped her fingers. "No. I need you two to kill some rogue minions, then we can have the drum circle."

Red smirked as Kristoff and Lucas stepped in front of her to shield her when the elevator door opened but only managed to jostle each other. Then everything happened too fast for her to even scream. She heard the ping of a silencer, but she didn't see who it hit until it was too late.

Cora dropped to the floor. Lucas and Kristoff fell after her. Thick metal tranquilizer darts dotted their chests. She had three sticking out of her torso, while the male vampires had only one each.

"Sh—!" Red snapped her head up to the horror coming from the open elevator doors.

Michel de Grammont stood under a vine-covered trellis on the rooftop garden. His black hair blew loose in the Santa Ana winds over his suit-jacket-clad shoulders. His white eyepatch was stained orange by the smog-filtered lights of the city. Beyond his smug face, Quinn and Delilah, gagged and bound, struggled against silver chaining them to the cement floor beside a gazebo. Two pairs of chains lay empty across from them. Michel raised his hand and snapped his fingers.

A dozen vampires dressed in black SWAT gear stepped out from behind him, like modern demons invading the Garden of Eden. Cora had lost the arms race. Michel's troops were already waiting.

"Thank you, Little Amazon. I knew you would prove essential in bringing both Crawford and Novak out of hiding." Michel spared a glance at Cora with his good eye. "Pity she decided to resist. It would have been smarter to flee and fight again another day like I did. Chain the men and get the Supreme secure for the next step. She's already so helpfully evacuated the building."

Red backed up in the elevator, but there was nowhere to go. She could only watch.

Two of the vampires in tactical gear wrapped Cora up in a blessed silver net and lifted her up. Lucas and Kristoff were dragged out next and chained on the opposite side of the gazebo from Quinn and Delilah.

Red knew she was next, but she swore she'd fight even without a stake.

Michel glanced at his chained enemies with a quiet satisfaction. He sighed dreamily as if it was all turning out better than he had imagined. Turning his gaze back to Red, he smiled winningly like he had on stage at the Halloween Ball. "I have a modest proposal for you. I think you'll be most interested, since I know you want this above all."

"What is that?" Red lifted her chin, knowing that if she could summon her magic, she would have set the undead Frenchman on fire.

"To know where you came from." he stepped up to the elevator and held his hand out.

Without conscious thought, she put her hand in his. How did he know?

25

Michel took Red's hand and tucked it in the crook of his elbow before leading her from the elevator onto the rooftop. His light step had a bounce in the heel as if he could have broken out into skipping. An unnaturally white grin shone down at her.

His touch made Red sick. It was the touch of death. He had murdered so many, nearly even killing her friends, and now he was on the precipice of victory. She should have found a way to stake him. Yet she only let him guide her towards the gazebo. What did he have to tell her?

The top of Moon Enterprises was an urban oasis. Leafy green grape vines curled around a trellis-covered path lined with raised beds of flowers, tomatoes, and leafy greens. Potted palms, hoes, and a bucket of trowels lay nearby. A wooden crate of yoga mats cast a shadow on the concrete from the lights of the city. Beyond the garden, a helipad lay empty on the other side of the rooftop.

Tranquilizer darts in their chest, Lucas and Kristoff lay unconscious in their restraints. The SWAT team had disappeared with Cora Moon to hold down the building. Quinn struggled against his chains as they passed.

Delilah stood stock still to stare at Michel, blue eyes narrowed, before she turned away to hide the hurt in her gaze. Wisps of smoke wafted off the blessed silver chaining her wrists and ankles. A small glimmer of gold on the ruined dress caught Red's eye. Was it the hidden mic? The recording might still be beaming into the cloud database that Vic had shared with Fat Crispin and the Bards.

Michel gestured to a wicker chair at the table and released his grip on her hand. "It looks unseemly, but if you knew the full story, you would be begging me for their blood. This treatment is too good for the likes of them."

"It looks pretty extreme," she said mildly even as her heart thumped in her chest.

He frowned pityingly. "Little Amnesiac Amazon, I imagine that this has been quite startling for you. I'm here to bring insight to your ignorance."

"I think you're here for more." Red gulped, looking at the captives, her stomach dropped at Lucas's slack pale face. "How are you planning on killing them?"

"That depends on you," Michel said, his voice deepening from anticipation. "I wanted this part to be a petty treat for myself then it became so much more. Whims can be like that."

"Why? I don't get it. You used me to get Lucas and Kristoff here. You have everything you want. The city is yours. Vengeance is yours. I'm surprised I'm even alive unless you're trying to keep the Bards off your back."

"I have a longer history with them than you realize. I'm the only reason Cora was able to make her truce. I hold them in no ill will, even if few had the vision that my old friend Jack Constantine had."

Red puckered her lips, trying to make sense of the idea of Michel having anything to do with the Brotherhood. It had to be a lie. "Are you talking about Vic's adopted father? His name was Henry."

"Iron Jack is an older apple from that tree." Michel sighed. "Alas, all truces must end. The natural order will be restored, but they'll be given a boon. I have exactly what the Crispin clan wants: blood for poor Julia."

She glowered at the false sympathy in his tone. He murdered a woman who was on her way to becoming a great Bard. He had no right to say her name. "That was you, wasn't it?"

Michel waved his hand. "Semantics. Jake Crispin will be more than satisfied with taking Delilah's head. I'll throw in Quinn for revenge for that old massacre of Bards in Scotland. They'll see it as the bargain it is."

"You killed those innocent women—Georgina, Olivia, Julia, Carrie." Bile rose in her throat as she recited the names. She had to. They needed to be remembered.

"Not Georgina. But Delilah didn't kill her either. She was simply happy to see the ungrateful wench had suicided after leaving the agency. I had to listen to her harping about it for ages." Michel mock yawned before smirking at the chained woman. "Tedious, but it did give me a spark of inspiration."

Red nodded, knowing that she had to keep him talking. The straits were dire, but Joe Chang could come rolling up with soul vampires ready to rumble soon. She just had to keep everyone alive until then. "That was quite the plan, turn the Bards and the Blood Alliance against Cora while setting Delilah up for the fall. Why are you waiting? You have everything."

"What do you give the man who has everything? The thing that is impossible to give." Sadness infused Michel's expression. "I thought I did have everything, you see, but then you made me realize what could be."

She leaned away from him. Her hands chilled as his intense stare pierced her. She didn't like where his villainous gloating was going. "I'm just a hunter."

"Oh, my Little Amazon, you are far more. It's written on your pretty face."

Hugging herself, she looked away from him. His stare might have cut through her, but the sight of Quinn and Delilah gagged and smoking from silver burns wasn't any better. Neither was Lucas and Kristoff unconscious and bound. She was with five vampires who couldn't separate her from a doppelgänger.

Red knew that she could yell at them until she was gasping, but it wouldn't shake their certainty. She wasn't who they thought she was. "My face might be a rerun, but beyond being a creepy reminder of Lucas' ex-girlfriend, I really have nothing else to offer. You already have them."

"No. I don't have her—Penelope." Michel pulled out a broken golden locket from his pocket and looked down as his thumb ran over the picture. "I had to break into your hotel room to find it, but my gift has always been to enter uninvited."

Red looked down at the beautiful feminine face captured in the small sepia daguerreotype. Her breath caught. "Quinn told me what Lucas did."

"Then you know they're monsters among monsters. Don't let the souls fool you." Michel glared at Kristoff and Lucas's prone bodies. "You can right that wrong."

"How? I don't understand what this has to do with me."

"You have everything to do with it, Red. I need to know how you did it!"

"Did what?" She cried out, confused. What the hell did he want from her?

"How you managed to come back!" Michel stood in a bolt of frantic energy, his hands lifting. "Tell me how the witch Juniper St. James managed to be reborn into the modern age, and I will tell you where you come from. That is the deal. Not only that, I'll tell you exactly where you can find Juniper's greatest enemy—the warlock Maxwell Baldacci."

Red waved her hands like a ref calling time out. When you had amnesia, it was hard to tell when people were fucking with you about the past. Was Michel just pulling cryptic names out of his ass to freak her out? "Whoa, whoa, I have no idea who this Michael Baldwhat-ever is. Honestly, I didn't know who any of them were before I came here. I'm a bystander in this mess, brought in on a job."

"Don't play coy, little Amazon." Michel raised an eyebrow before his face softened into thoughtfulness. "What do you know about the witch who shared your face?"

Red shrugged, not expecting a pop quiz. "She was Lucas's kept woman at the turn of the last century."

"Is that what they want you to believe? She was a mere lady of leisure? Now, that is an insult to her memory." Michel scoffed. "Juniper St. James was one of the most powerful dark witches of her age, until the warlock brought her low. She infiltrated the Brotherhood of Bards and Heroes. Even regaining only a fraction of her magic, she was able to rip a swath through London. She destroyed the most dangerous vampires in the White Lady's cadre. I saw the shell of a burnt mansion in Essex where she massacred dozens with a zombie horde, turning them against their masters. She was no kept woman!"

The sounds of the city seemed to slow as the breeze shifted through the grape vines in the rooftop garden.

Red tried to fixate on the little details to calm the heart beating loudly in her ears. Murder, necromancy, and betraying the Brotherhood—Kristoff and Lucas had left out those points when they had waxed poetically about Juniper St. James. Was that why the Brotherhood had sealed up their records of what had happened at the Stonetree Monastery?

Juniper was killed by hunters. Now, Red knew why.

"She was e-evil," she stuttered the words out.

"Vengeful, to be precise. No more than would be expected after dealing with these brutish Byrneses." Michel smiled and sat down to pat her hand in a quick burst of stiff comfort. "I saw you, and I knew she'd brought herself back to find her magic. I need to know how she did it!"

"I don't know." Red shook her head. He'd figure out the truth once she tried to do anything magical. "I can barely float a stake. I'm not the witch you think I am. Maybe a creepy doppelgänger, but..." She gulped, putting her hand on her face, wanting to pull it off. She wore the face of a dark witch. After a year fighting dark beings, it made her skin crawl to look like one. They had said that Juniper was a survivor. They never said what she had done to survive. Red gritted her teeth. She couldn't be the second coming of the Wicked Witch of the West. "If I was a badass dark witch, I would've figured it out by now."

"You sought the truth in Nevada and Oklahoma, didn't you? You unseated one of the most powerful supreme masters in the Midwest to find it." He chuckled at her surprise. "My tentacles stretch farther than LA county, dear witch."

"There are gaps in my memory, but I know who I am."

"Oh, you don't lie as well as she did."

Red didn't take the bait. She chewed on the inside of her cheek, wondering what other revelations that he would drop on her. He wasn't showing her who she really was so much as what she didn't want to be.

"I can help you! You don't know where you came from, but I know. You can regain what's yours, destroy your old enemy, and restore your magic, but I need your word that you'll help me get my Penelope back."

Red bit her lip. Her eyes darted to the four chained vampires. How much had they heard? She pushed away yet another existential crisis again caused by Juniper St. James. She tilted her head, trying to keep him talking. "You still love her so much."

Michel laughed. "Why the shock?"

"I just didn't think that an unsouled vampire would care so much. She was more than just progeny to you."

"Penelope was my everything."

She had met vampires in her time and read even more about them. Unsouled vampires were supposed to be incapable of love. Quinn had convinced her that Lucas had felt it for Juniper, but she had trouble imagining that it was a common trait. "Even without a soul, you could love her?"

"Love doesn't come from the soul. It's in the blood." Michel sighed. "I had been so cold, so empty, even after a century of ruling

Paris. I longed for the open seas of my human years when I roamed between Jamaica, New Orleans, and Martinique."

"So, you were a pirate!" Inappropriate vindication surging through her, she wagged a finger at him.

He laughed. "Penelope said much the same thing. She had been a simple country girl when I found her by the cold shore in Brittany, but she had eyes like warm Caribbean waters. An innkeeper's daughter, she had a face worth preserving for eternity and the quick wit to make the time pass quickly. I proposed marriage in a fortnight, and like Eros with Psyche, I kept her safe in my estate outside the city. She wanted to join me in my court, but I couldn't bear to expose her to the politics of an urban clan."

"You kept her alive and away from other vampires?"

Michel glared at Lucas's still unconscious body in chains. "Unlike this barbarian, I didn't force my delicate human companions to suffer vampire society, but mon dieu, my court was never the savage nest of brutality that Alaric's Order reveled in. Eventually, cholera pushed my hand. I turned her on Christmas Day in 1899. She thought it was a gift, but she was the gift."

Red put her hand to her mouth as she calculated. "She was barely months in death when..."

"Oui." Michel curled his gloved fist closed, fangs appearing over his pale lips. His glower at Lucas and Kristoff could have frozen wine. "The horde of Alaric ran over my borders. I had them closed up in the catacombs. The siege was ready to crumble when Lucas and his butcher boy broke all the rules of vampire war. Yes, little Amazon, vampires have rules even if the Alaric Order could make Satan hang his head in shame. The fiends stormed my mansion during the initiation ceremony, and they took her. Then they..." His voiced choked up. "...fed on her."

Red gawked at him. She hadn't expected the reddish tears in his eye. Her sympathy was genuine even if her words trembled from shaky nerves. "That must have been terrible."

"Vengeance kept me going after my city was lost, then it was honed like a blade in the August Harvest after these dogs brought the great curse upon us!" Michel's English dissolved into a rapid outburst of angry French before he adjusted his suit shirt collar and composed himself.

She waited, noticing Lucas and Kristoff rousing from the tranquilizer darts. Quinn and Delilah tensed as if readying themselves. Formidable together, the four were still bound in silver without Joe Chang's back up in sight.

Red asked another question to draw out Michel's vilain monologue. "Lucas kept Penelope a secret. How did you find out?"

"A minion, souled and wretched, confessed during torture what had happened to her. But it was only half-truth. I thought Alaric had drunk her blood, so for years I tried to destroy him. I worked with the Blood Alliance to crush the bloodline system and rout out relics like him, but he was too established. It was only after he perished that I discovered he had offered her blood to his best hounds." Michel pointed at Lucas and then Kristoff.

Her mouth dropped open. When Lucas implied that his progeny had once been close, he didn't mention that it was a friendship bonded in shared blood—they had killed Penelope together. "You fed on her too, Novak?"

"Guess it never came up." Kristoff brushed the dust off his suit jacket as he stood. The casual motion was betrayed by the angry shake to his fingers. He shared a glance with Lucas who had also risen next to him.

Michel hissed. "This one was a minion with the stink of the grave around him, and still that monster offered a jewel to him. My jewel!"

Red tried to get his amber glare off the chained captives. "What does it mean for a vampire to drink another?"

"My ancient blood flowed through her veins. And it pains me like a thousand suns to know that it flowed through them." Michel shook his head and grimaced from the taste of his own words. "Having to touch Delilah was torture, but every day in her bed, I told myself I was getting closer to my goal. Alaric met his end at the hands of another, but I could still know that he would be rolling in hell at the idea of his precious daughter killed, her bastards destroyed, and the last of his line snuffed out." His fangs popped out in his fervor. He snapped them back in with a twitch of his lip.

Red couldn't look away from his wide stare. Chills tickled at the back of her neck. "Mission accomplished then."

He leaned forward, cracks forming under his fingertips as he gripped the glass table. "No, it changed when I saw you, I knew that Penelope might yet still have the taste of immortality she deserved. I only need your word that you'll share your secret."

Red held her breath before exhaling a shaky sigh. She had tried telling him that he had found the wrong woman, but now she was ready to play along. "How do I know you won't turn on me like you did Cora? Obviously, you're an experienced mutineer."

"It's how I landed my first ship." Michel smiled at the chained vamps. "Running circles around these fools has been child's play."

"You mangy prick." Lucas raised his chained hand to flip off Michel.

Kristoff shrugged, as if conceding the point.

Red nodded, ignoring them all as she tried to process. Fury grew inside her. She felt it boil, but underneath it something else stirred—magic. "You framed Delilah, then killed Julia Crispin. It sounds like you've been picking off members of the order of Alaric for years, turning minions behind Cora's back. Tell me why I should trust you."

"Because I can get you the memories you seek. In my quest to destroy Alaric, I know exactly where you come from and how that damnable warlock—"

"I have no idea who that guy is. He's probably long dead too. Why should I care?" Red crossed her arms. It sounded like he was reaching for anything mysterious and shiny, so she'd deflect to his side. "How do you even know about Juniper St. James and her supposed enemy, anyway?"

"Because I was working with the head Bard, Constantine, when she was his bodyguard," Michel said.

Red furrowed her brow. Vic mentioned that his adopted father, Henry, had come from a long line of Bards. Iron Jack had been the one that he had idolized the most. Juniper must have deceived him on her vendetta for revenge. Just the idea of betraying the Brotherhood made her feel queasy. "She was a double agent. Probably lied all the time."

"She was a survivor." Michel gestured absently, as if it was no matter. "She was also curious like you. You can feel that coiling up like a viper within, even if you don't like the truths I tell." He leaned forward. "I'll help you get all you desire, because then I will get my most fervent dream. The true question is, how do I trust you? You have but a simple task before I can. This is one you may even enjoy. You must show me you have no allegiance to the Byrneses."

"How?" Red stared at the chained vampires, already chilled by the implications in his voice.

"Delilah and Quinn have been claimed by the Bards for execution, but the others...." He held out a stake. "Choose which one will know the mercy of the stake—Lucas or Kristoff. Understand that it is a mercy, for the one who survives will suffer torment that even Alaric will feel in hell."

Stomach dropping, she looked between Lucas and Kristoff. "Is this a trick?"

"No, it's a choice. Something I doubt either of them will give you." Michel stood, twirling a roughly hewn stake in his hand.

Lucas growled at him. "You bleeding bastard."

"You could choose the one with a soul who did more to torment your past self than nearly any other." Michel gestured like a used car salesman presenting a Honda. "The one who is still selfish enough to want to claim you again and incompetent enough to fail."

"Oi!"

Michel gave Lucas a dismissive glance. "Or you could choose Novak, the one who wants to do everything Crawford did—and then some—with all the imagination and frustrated purpose of an unchained demon with a century to dream up nightmares."

Kristoff sneered at the accusation.

The Frenchman flapped a hand at him. "Oh, tell me, I'm wrong."

Heart pounding in her ears, Red stood, gaze darting between Lucas and Kristoff. Resistance pulsed through her, making her feet drag as she stepped forward. Her lungs shuddered for breath. The hardest part wasn't choosing, it was knowing that this was all a part of a sick game. Either decision would just delight Michel.

Lucas mouthed the word *run*. His features might have been pulled back in fury, but fear glinted in his eyes.

Hands clasped, head dipped, and eyebrow raised, Kristoff ignored Michel to study her. A contemplation settled into his rage-tinted reserve.

Michel smiled. "To which monster will you show compassion?"

She held her hand out for the stake.

He handed it over, piercing gaze running over her face.

Red made the decision before she thought about it. The Santa Ana winds whipped up as she glanced at Kristoff and Lucas one last time. She gripped the stake and rushed forward.

Michel caught her with ease. He turned her around, pulling her close to his chest, a sigh of disappointment rattling in his dead lungs. "Oh, my little Amazon, that was the wrong choice." His hand tightened on her wrist forcing the stake to drop. "I had so hoped you would be an ally, but I can make do. You showed me the possibility, but you aren't the only way. Perhaps this is best. They will truly understand my loss tonight."

Red struggled in his impossibly strong grip. She was surrounded by four supernatural allies, but bound in silver, they would only be able to watch her die. The friendly neighborhood vamps weren't coming. Failure hung over her, but she still kicked her heel hard against his shin. She sneered. "Whatever secrets that Juniper St. James had, you won't ever find them."

"Neither will you." Michel brushed her hair off her neck before dragging her forward to stand between Kristoff and Lucas.

"The difference is that I couldn't care less. You'll never get Penelope back." Red closed her eyes.

The spark of energy within her, tiny as it may have been, burned bright. The ward against magic ended at the rooftop. She surrendered to her power. Not pushing it or commanding it, she released her desire for her origins or even the hope that Joe Chang or Detective Callaway had had enough time to rally the troops. She reached for that magic inside with a single fevered hope for the soul of the City of Angels.

A rustle of wind blew her hair back. The whizz of the stake tore through the air.

Michel released her wrist to snatch the airborne wood. "Is that all the mighty Juniper St. James has? Barely controlling the air. I thought you had more fire in you!"

Red looked up, the spark tingling her fingers. Finally.

Blue eyes twinkling, Kristoff grinned.

Lucas's mouth dropped open.

She spun, hand raised, ghostly flame growing in her palm, and slapped Michel. "Maybe I do."

He bellowed, jumping back. His eye patch smoldered, and flames caught his black suit jacket. He tossed it down.

Red kicked the jacket, keys rattling in a pocket, toward Lucas before she turned around. She shook her hand, but no more magic fire appeared. "Shit."

She ran.

"I'm glad the warlock stole your magic!" Michel snarled, chasing after her.

Kristoff swung the silver chain connected to his arm out to trip Michel.

Red picked up a garden hoe by a raised garden bed and swung it as Michel fell, hitting him in the head.

He dropped on his side, blood gushing from his dangling ear.

Heart galloping, she lifted the hoe up again and swung it in a brutal arc to catch Michel on the back of the head. The metal blade dug deep into his skull by his spine. He wasn't dead but he wouldn't walking it off. She wiped the blood spray off her cheek before ripping the hoe out and throwing it aside. "I'm not Juniper St. James. My name is Red."

Lucas freed himself from his chains using the keys and sprinted forward. He tossed the keys to Kristoff before picking up the stake on the ground. Raising it, he jumped on Michel's twitching back.

"Save me a bit of the bastard," Kristoff called out as he unlocked himself from the wrist and ankle manacles.

Red grabbed the keys before passing them to Quinn. She might have turned Michel into a vegetable with that head wound, but his troops were alive and well. She needed all four of her vampires ready to party with their fangs out.

The thump of boots sounded from the stairwell. Michel's black clad minions in body armor stormed out with automatic weapons raised. They filled the garden with their numbers, guns pointed over the tomato vines. "Halt!"

Kristoff, unchained and fangs out, stood in front of Red.

Quinn and Delilah dropped their chains to stand behind her. She appreciated the support, but they faced a dozen vampires with guns. Michel had been like a hydra, they had cut him down, but more enemies had taken the fallen traitor's place.

The squad leader of the rebelling minions called out, "We have you surrounded."

Helicopter blades chopped the air as a spotlight shone down. Illuminated in the bright light, headset on her ears, Detective Callaway stuck her head out of the open door of the helicopter. A speaker crackled to life. "LAPD."

Grinning, Red looked up. Her borrowed pink jersey flapped in the wind created by the helicopter. Relief sunk into her muscles. She had stalled long enough. The white hats had finally arrived.

Joe Chang appeared out of a nearby stairwell, face bruised and police hat missing. A silver-burned and pissed Cora Moon marched beside him. They led a dozen vampires in civilian clothes ranging from surfer board shorts to mini dresses. He raised his gun, "I think we have you surrounded, traitors."

The vampires in tactical gear glanced at each other, inching closer together in a circle. Guns wavering, panic rippled through the dozen minions even as they held their line.

"This is still my motherfucking city!" Cora stepped forward and raised her fist, the net pattern on her face and arms was red and grisly in the spotlight. "Stand down before I tell my people in the 'copter to mow you the fuck down."

Lucas lifted an unconscious Michel, using a stake jammed into the bleeding vampire's side as leverage, and smiled, revealing his fangs. "I'll kill him before a single bullet is fired."

Kristoff added, "I'll take an arm as a souvenir."

The leader of the tactical squad lowered his weapon.

Sweat beading on her forehead, Red released the breath that she was holding. It was finally over.

"Fuck it," one of the rebelling vampires said and took aim at her. He pulled the trigger of the semi-automatic weapon.

Her brain hadn't processed the sight before instinct moved her. Like a volcanic eruption, mystical energy gushed up from her spiritual core. Red lifted her hands, hearing the pop of the gun, even if she couldn't see the bullets, and felt the fire sizzling the air. Flames blinded her as she fell back.

The bullets melted in the air, the metal dropping down like rain on the concrete. Michel's rogue vampires were hit with the magical fire. Screaming, they went up like torches before their charred bones fell into a heap, leaving only Kevlar vests behind.

Red laid her head down on her arms, panting and fighting the urge to barf. The smoke made her wheeze. Nose wrinkling, she tried to breathe. The surge of magic left her limbs limp and sweaty. She tried to push herself up, but all she managed to do was roll over. Trembles rushed through her body, rattling her teeth together. A haze hung over her racing disjointed thoughts.

Lucas and Kristoff rushed toward her. Kneeling on the ground beside her, their words were lost in the chopping of the helicopter blades as it landed.

Eyes, gray and blue, blurred in her vision. Through their legs, she saw Cora run to Delilah. Blinking again, Red felt herself being lifted. Shaking from exhaustion, she closed her eyes. Her head dipped back onto the cold firm arms that held her.

She murmured, "We saved the city."

26

November 5th, Sunset, Somewhere in Los Angeles, California, USA

Red coughed as she woke, trying to sit up but only managing to lift her head. Blinking, the fuzzy image of a white room sharpened into focus. A hospital. Great. The thoughts felt as heavy as her head.

"Red!"

She looked to Vic propped up in the bed beside her own. She grinned, the motion lazy and slow as if she were wading through chemical wave of sedatives. "I slayed the dragon."

"You sure did, kid." He chuckled, but his image swam in her vision.

Consciousness left her as soon as it had come. She didn't wake again until three days later. The sun was already setting when she finally bullied the nurses in the private hospital room to let her dress. They couldn't tell her where Vic had gone. He had checked himself out the day before but said he would be back when she woke up.

Red wasn't going to wait for him. Someone had brought her

duffle bag and her collection of black shirts and jeans. The clothes were the same, but she felt different. Her conversation with Michel under the smoggy LA sky had rattled around in her head as soon as consciousness gripped her. She avoided the mirror.

Juniper St. James was one of the most powerful dark witches of her age...

Determined to find her mentor, she was sitting up on the bed tying her shoes when Joe Chang in full uniform walked inside.

He took off his police hat, a bandage on his forehead. "Cora wants to give you her thanks personally. Your friends will be there."

"Then take me away, officer." Red followed him out confidently but was dozing on highway until they arrived in front of Moon Enterprises. The lights of the city dappled the tall building. It almost looked peaceful as if a battle for the soul of the city hadn't raged inside.

Red followed him through the empty lobby to the elevator. It had been cleaned up, but signs of a struggle still showed in the rips in the carpet and the bullet holes in the murals. She guessed it would be a while until the yoga classes and soup kitchen opened again. "You guys did some damage."

"We showed those unsouled bastards that we came to win." He grunted as he put his thumb on the scanner in the elevator.

The ride felt short, as the strains of an instrumental version of California Love pumped through the speakers until they were at the top.

She walked through the garden, her eyes finding the burns and the tiny spots of melted bullets on the cement. Chilled sweat dripped down her back. She still didn't know how she had conjured up that flame even after trying again. The woozy flu feeling of using too much magic was her only answer. Vic would be impressed to know she had finally tapped into two of the elements. Hopefully someone had bragged to him about it.

Three dozen vampires stood at attention in a circle around the helipad half of the rooftop facing the Supreme Master and her betrayer. Cora stood with her hands on her hips, dressed in a black bodysuit, facing them. The lights of the city glinted on her afro and onyx covered headband. She didn't look at the bound vampire at the center of the gathering.

Kristoff stood in the back, wearing an immaculate suit with his blond hair slicked back. He turned his head and spotted Red first. He winked.

Delilah rolled her eyes when she noticed her. She inched closer to Quinn.

Lucas grinned and gestured Red over.

Staring at Michel, Vic looked pale but determined in a wheelchair, black mullet blowing in the breeze above his denim vest.

Red walked to stand beside him and put a hand on his shoulder. When Joe said that he was taking her to meet her friend, she hadn't quite pictured that it would be at an execution. Had she slept through whatever counted for vampire due process? Honestly, she thought that Michel would be dead by now.

Cora stepped forward. Contained rage had sharpened her beautiful features. Her presence was enough to quiet the murmurs from the assembled throng. "You've heard from the Bard, you've listened to the audio recording, and you've seen with your own eyes how Michel de Grammont not only betrayed his supreme master but also put the Dark Veil in jeopardy. His treachery over the course of a century led to countless murders of our fellow vampires. Due to his arrogance and incompetence, over ten unregistered fledglings rose this week in the city's morgues, and even more rogues were staked. His rebellion failed. The final death is his sentence."

Michel stared ahead, black hair loose on his shoulders, his hands and feet bound by blessed silver. He had the dignity of a nobleman before the guillotine. His wounds had healed, but his left ear was gone. Without his eyepatch, his face looked no less haughty, despite the cross-shaped scar on his sewn-shut eyelid.

Joe Chang came forward with a curved sword. Cora took it without ceremony, a chilly blankness on her face. Her beauty and weaponry made her look like an avenging angel.

Michel opened his mouth, scanning the crowd. "I would have shown you who you really are."

Chest tightening, Red knew his last words for her alone. She forced herself to meet his gaze.

Cora swung the sword across her chest. The lights of Inglewood reflected off the blade as it swept up in a steel arc to Michel.

Head tumbling off in a clean blow, his body decayed to dust.

Even the vampires seemed to exhale a nervous breath as the Santa Ana winds blew Michel De Grammont away. Then the chant began. "Cora. Cora. CORA!"

Vic looked up at Red before turning his motorized wheelchair around. "Let them have their rah-rahs." He smiled wanly as they left the vampires to return to the elevator. Waiting until the doors closed behind them, he asked, "What do you think Michel meant by that eerie-ass shout out?"

Red shrugged, even though she knew she would never forget the look on Michel's face as he died. Her curiosity had gotten her into enough trouble lately. "It doesn't matter."

November 9th, Late Afternoon, the California Arms Apartments, Culver City in Los Angeles, California, USA

Red and Vic's new reality settled on them like a smothering pillow to the face.

The last few days had been spent on the couch of their new apartment, watching reruns of sitcoms with only food deliveries and the arrival of Vic's quiet nurse to break the television marathon. Takeout boxes and cans of IPA collected on the coffee table, then a pile gathered on the floor by the large sectional couch. The pop-up question on the Netflix interface seemed more and more desperate as it asked them if they were still watching.

Red didn't say much, and Vic didn't ask. They might have stayed in sight of each other, but they licked their wounds separately. Each glance at him gave her a pang of guilt. He was in that chair because she had a stupid idea to go to a Halloween Ball and bug Delilah.

The apartment had three bedrooms, but she hadn't slept in her own bed yet. At first, it was the fatigue of doing magic that kept her inside, then the looping panic and self-analysis made her stay. One look at the large mirror in her room was enough. Curling up on the couch and passing out to sitcoms felt safer than facing her own reflection. All the laugh tracks in the world couldn't cover up the one thought that circled in her mind.

Juniper St. James was one of the most powerful dark witches of her age...

Red had read over Vic's emailed report to Fat Crispin. She'd had nothing to add. The Brotherhood of Bards and Heroes might have hoarded knowledge, but she didn't need to tell them everything. Who knew what the mic on Delilah had picked up anyway?

She was happy to leave her conversation with Michel behind. Doppelgänger, secret heiress, and possible reincarnation of an evil witch...she had wanted to know who she was. Now, the sinister possibilities crushed her. What if the vampire who had bitten her and left her to die along Coyote Creek had been trying to do the world a favor?

The knock on the door startled her, but she only pulled the blanket higher on her shoulders.

A key scraped in the lock, and a pensive Filipino man in nursing scrubs walked in. His nose wrinkled as he looked around the darkened living room.

Vic sighed in his wheelchair, head hanging low, and rubbed his face.

Red turned over on the couch. If she pretended to be asleep, maybe everyone would ignore her. It had worked so far.

"Hey Hiram, I think I'll take you up on that shower," Vic murmured.

"Can I open the window or the balcony door too?" Hiram's voice was as quiet as his steps on the wooden floor.

The electric wheelchair whizzed behind the couch toward a bedroom. "Whatever blows your skirt up," Vic said. The balcony door whooshed open to let in the sounds of Culver City. Hiram's hesitant steps crept to Vic's room before he closed the door.

A WITCH CALLED RED

Red rolled onto her back, releasing a breath. She looked over at the messy coffee table, seeing it in natural light. She wished she hadn't. Her inner neat freak rebelled, but the self-loathing didn't care.

Juniper St. James was one of the most powerful dark witches of her age...

Only her bladder made her get up. Red passed by her phone, charging for way too long on the kitchen counter. She ignored the red blinking light of notifications.

She went into the bathroom. Flushing, she washed her hands quickly and turned to lean against the counter. How long could she wait in here? There were enough crumbs in her sports bra to live off of for a while. She tried to meditate, but only managed to zone out until she heard the front door close.

"Red, get your ass out here."

"Yeah, boss." Obeying, she ran a hand through her greasy hair and sighed.

"No sass. Get out of your pajamas and into your street clothes." Vic sat in his wheelchair in clean jeans and a Metallica shirt under his arm sling. The takeout boxes were gone, and the apartment lights were on. The TV was off. He lifted his finger. "Actually, shower first and then dress. We need to get out of here."

"But I like here. We're comfortable here, and if we don't order something from Old Shanghai soon, they might worry."

"They're already worried about the creepy stinky hermits who keep ordering lo mein."

She crossed her arms. "Touché."

"Now, hop to, intern."

"Where are we going?" Red whined like a sullen teenager.

Vic just grunted and waved his hand before turning his wheelchair around.

She rubbed her eyes before turning back to the bathroom, shedding her clothes, and walking into the shower with all the enthusiasm of a cat. The water felt nice, but she still shampooed and conditioned like a robot. The couch beckoned her. Brushing her teeth before wrapping herself in a towel, she stepped out into the living room darkened from the setting sun. Dressing in her room, she avoided the mirror and put her wet red hair up into a ponytail before coming out again, hoping her boss had returned to his senses.

"Your purse is packed with your phone already, so get dressed. I even tossed a stake and a tampon in there. You got everything a girl could need." Vic called out, his phone wedged between ear and shoulder then resumed his earlier conversation to whoever was on the other line. "Oh, grow up. Its natural...." He paused, rolling his eyes. "Yeah, whatever. I doubt you'll remember my order. It's fine."

Red sighed and stared longingly at the couch. She didn't know what non-TV watching bee had gotten into his bonnet, but she didn't like it. They still had five more episodes of *Parks and Recreation*.

"Now that we're so fresh and clean." Vic waited for her to finish the line from the *OutKast* song. One that she forced him to listen to until it became his earworm too. She didn't have the heart for the early 2000s superhit. He shook his head. "Okay, I know why I'm depressed—I'm Lieutenant Fucking Dan. You should be fine, Forrest Gump."

It was hard to wallow in self-pity knowing what he had been through. She had managed it but still. "Eh. I can't complain."

"But you want to. You remembered how to dress. Let's see if you remember how to drive." He held up the Millennium Falcon's keys with the familiar alien keychain they'd picked up in Roswell. He tossed them to her.

Red caught them before staring at the new remote dangling off it. Where had this come from? Had he snuck out when she was napping? This mystery could not stand. She followed him out into the hallway and locked the door behind her.

He zoomed to the elevator in the outdoor hall.

She rushed after him, feeling more and more annoyed to be leaving the cozy den of their apartment. Arranged by Reaper and Smith, and paid for by her mysterious trust fund, it might have been funded by human trafficking for all she knew. She only had so much guilt left in the tank.

"I want a burger. I hope it's there when we arrive," Vic said.

"Where are we going?"

"You used to ask fewer questions." He glared at her without malice as the elevator door opened on the parking garage.

Red chuckled for the first time in days despite the marathon of sitcoms. "No, I didn't."

Vic wheeled ahead before stopping by the Millennium Falcon. "Oh, I missed her."

"Did she get a facelift?" She examined the washed black van and the modified side door.

"A gift from Cora. You're not the only rich chick I know now. Use the clicker, will you?"

Red tapped the unlock button before noticing another one. She pressed it. The side door opened, and a wheelchair lift creaked out. The interior of the van still had Tibetan prayer flags, but the bean bags were missing.

Vic sighed and rolled up onto the platform, strapping the wheels in place. "Let's get this show on the road. We have gridlock traffic to suffer through."

Getting into the driver's side, she clicked her seat belt before clicking the remote to close the side door and waiting for the ramp to fold into place.

"So much for quick getaways." He sighed bitterly at his legs.

Heart clenching, Red didn't reply as she pulled out of the small underground parking lot. Classic rock piped through the speakers when she turned on the radio.

"At least the mechanics didn't fiddle with my tunes," he said before giving terse turn by turn directions.

Snails moved quicker than the rush hour traffic in Los Angeles as they made their way past strip malls and billboards advertising new movies. The sky darkened on the autumn evening, casting shadows on the handicapped parking placard in the rearview mirror. Something about being on the road in the Falcon calmed the rotation of shit in her head. She bobbed her head to the first strains of Tom Petty's "I Won't Back Down."

A question appeared in his eyes, but Vic let her get through half the song before he spoke. "What happened on that rooftop, Red? You went all Firestarter, which you should be happy about. Isn't that what you wanted?"

She turned down the song, not wanting to taint Tom Petty. "I found out some shit that I didn't want to."

Vic rolled his hand. "And?"

"Juniper St. James was one of the most powerful dark witches of her age." Red repeated Michel's words. Goosebumps rose on her arms to say it out loud.

He blew a raspberry from the back of the van. "So?"

Clenching her teeth, she huffed. Vic didn't get it. "So? Is that all you have to say about the Victorian hooker who copyrighted my face?" She slammed her hand on the steering wheel. "Damn it, the biggest clue to my mystical amnesia is that I am a carbon copy of an evil chick and all your sorry ass has to say is 'so?'"

"Turn right."

Flicking on the blinker, she turned without even noticing the street name. "I can't believe you just said that! My life, what I have of one, has been turned upside down ever since I found out who she was. She had my face, and I have her fucking baggage. She was a dark witch who was killed by hunters. Ripped through London like a hurricane. Even turned on your great-great-*great*-grandpa Iron Jack Constantine. And all you have to say is 'so?'"

"You ain't her, Red. I don't care what bullshit Frenchie told you."

She deflated in her seat and peeked at him in the rearview mirror. "Quinn told you?"

"No, you just did." Vic crossed his arms.

"Fuck." If she weren't driving, she would have kicked herself.

"That's been the cloud over your head? You're worried you'll be like her?" The rough tone disappeared from his voice, the grumble turned hesitant. "Evil or something?"

"Well, yeah." Her voice sounded too small even in her own ears. She avoided the rearview mirror and brushed the tears from her eyes.

"You're not. We don't know the pub trivia info of your life, but I know you, Red. You've been the best intern a Bard could ask for, and you've done more heroics in a year than most people do in their lives. How many times could you have bailed out and said fuck this hunter shit, I'm going to live like a normie and poop out some babies?"

"Ew, Vic, that's not where babies come out." She giggled and hiccupped.

"Eh, whatever. You get my point. You're good! Sure, you're a doppelgänger with terrible taste in Gregs, but you're a good person." Stifling a pained grunt, he leaned forward to put a hand on her shoulder. "Believe me. I'm full of bullshit, but I know people. What I know is that I'm the Batman and you're my Robin, kid."

"Damn it, Vic, you're making me cry."

"Mop yourself up before I do." He sniffed. "Okay, let's stop this emotion train because we're almost there. Another right."

She turned at the familiar block of offices, nail spas, and an Indian restaurant onto a side street and took a quick left into the parking lot behind it. "Are you ready for this?"

"Eh, at least we can get the best parking spot." Vic shrugged. "I got a new job for us."

Red parked and hit the clicker to open the side door and let out the wheelchair lift. She got out of the van on shaking legs to stare at the window to Quinn Investigations. The first time that Vic had brought her here, he had made a lot of promises about that job too. Look how that had turned out.

He rolled ahead of her and pressed the button on the stand of the building's automatic door opener.

Quinn was already in the doorway of his office before they reached it.

"Out of my way before I run you over, Q." Vic grumped as his chair went to the door.

"Hey." She forced herself to look Quinn in the eyes. He had heard everything Michel had said to her.

"Red. Vic." Quinn nodded and stepped aside.

She felt Lucas there before she met his eyes. The tension in her shoulders drained a bit. She waved at him with one hand and rubbed her upper arm with the other, dipping her head.

"There she is." He hugged her.

Vic coughed. "I'm reporting this as a hostile work environment."

"Oi, it's your first day," Lucas scoffed.

"Leave Greg alone." Laughing, Red put her hand on her hip and gestured around the office. "Is this the job, Vic?"

"You know these losers need our help."

Chuckling, she couldn't argue with that logic. As far as she could tell, Michel probably would have been running LA already if they hadn't come to town.

Lucas grumbled, "Again, I say 'Oi!'"

Quinn leaned against his desk, a small smile on his face. He gestured to the unopened In-N-Out Burger bag on the coffee table. "You're just in time."

"We got a tip from an Ice Dwarf that some primordial boogie-boo is rising off of Santa Monica pier soon," Lucas said, lips curving into an impish smile.

Quinn added, "We need some research done before we hit the streets."

"How much saving does one city need?" Red wondered aloud, scanning Quinn Investigations. It was a supernatural detective agency, but still, it seemed so normal. This was her new office. She didn't know if she had ever had one of those. Would she have talks around the water cooler next?

"It never ends in LA." Vic rolled his wheelchair to the fast-food bag and pulled out a burger. He started chewing before he looked up at Quinn. "You remembered my order."

Brown eyes twinkling, Quinn nodded. "Always."

Red grinned at the male bonding.

Vic coughed before pointing his burger at Lucas. "There's always another baddie looking for their five minutes of fame. It's why I hate this town."

"Everyone hates this town." Lucas flopped down on the couch. His storm-gray eyes shone at her and patted the cushion next to him.

"That's why they need us." Quinn walked around his desk to sit down.

"Then let's get to work. Tell me we have something more than Lucas' filing to go on." She sat down next to Lucas and reached into the bag for some fries.

Red had thought that Los Angeles would just be another job when she drove in from Reno. Julia Crispin had called it Hell-A, and she wasn't wrong. This city had twisted her inside out and made her face more than just murder and mayhem.

They had taken down a rogue master and more hits than she thought possible. The answers she found here brought up more questions. A part of her still wanted to be in her pajamas, but with another case in her hands, Red knew this was home. Not the city itself, but that feeling of doing good. That was where she belonged.

The door opened with a knock.

"Hiya, this is Quinn Investigations, right?" A blue-skinned dwarf in a jogging suit and backpack stepped in with a tourist map in his hand. "There you are. Thank Odin, all these buildings look the same." His white beard shook as he struggled to fold the map. He tucked it under his arm in discreet surrender. "Anyway, I came back because I forgot to tell you something." He stopped to gawk. "You're her!"

Red tensed, bracing herself for doppelgänger weirdness. Hadn't the universe tossed enough her way? She'd had a lifetime's worth of mistaken identity hijinks packed into a week.

Lucas put his hand on her shoulder.

Vic swallowed his bite of burger, sauce on his lips as he glared at the newcomer.

"I can't believe we stayed at the same hotel!" The dwarf grinned as he stepped closer, shaking his finger. "Remember, I sat next to you at the bar? I wasn't in my gym clothes, so you might not recognize me."

She blinked, only vaguely remembering him. Was he going to blindside her with a cryptic clue about her doppelgänger?

The short humanoid was oblivious to the tension in the room as he put his hands on his hips and chuckled. "Who would have thought, my first night in town, I'd rub elbows with you! Word on the street is you're the hunter who took down that big-time vamp. You're that witch! Your name is a color right, like Violet or Amber." He snapped his fingers. "Red, that's it!"

Red smiled and ducked her head, feeling the shadow of Juniper St. James dissipate. "That's me."

EPILOGUE

In a quiet manor house in the English countryside, a brass cage elevator opened onto a floor forbidden to any but the most trusted servants.

Edward Krandel pushed a well-oiled dining cart with a bottle of scotch out into the stately hallway. It was decorated with strange foreign curios like shrunken heads and marble statues. He dusted each one enough to know them in the dark.

Open windows beckoned the growing winter's chill. He had had opened them this morning to take advantage of their first dry windy day in weeks. The sulfur stench of his master's projects still lingered even after hours of ventilation. Unholy foul odors wafted from under doors that were never to be opened—even by him, the chief steward. The cold burrowed deep into his old bones, but he didn't close the windows.

As he had done for decades, he knocked on the last door in the long hall and waited to be allowed in to take whatever remained of his master's dinner.

"Krandel, my boy, tell me you have that new scotch with you," the master boisterously called from inside the office.

The servant smiled and shook his head as he entered the chamber. Of course, he had the aged bottle from the Oban distillery. The routine of the other man's agenda had become his long ago. There were many things Edward knew about the white-haired titan of a man who had dominated the manor for a lifetime. Yet few he could mention in polite company.

With a smooth thick mane and facial hair to match, his employer cut a fine vigorous figure in a dark tweed jacket with corduroy patches on the elbows. Standing at his massive desk by the large windows, the glow of the large double computer screens reflected on his wide smirk. He was by far the elder of the two men yet had aged as well as his alcohol.

"It's uncouth to eat and work, I know." The master gestured to his emptied plate by the keyboard. His grin grew mischievous. "Yet tonight, it was worth the bother. I'm almost done reviewing this report."

"Very good, sir," Edward said, placing the discarded dishes on the cart. The other man was too jubilant and off schedule, it made him feel unbalanced. When not in London or farther afield, his master took evening meals with a side of reading before dismissing his steward for the evening. Then over after-dinner drinks, he called associates to check on what he claimed was an international trading business. Edward strove to remain ignorant of the dealings that paid for this opulent household. He already knew enough.

His master poured himself two-fingers of scotch in a glass and peered with satisfaction at the image of a one-eyed man embedded in an email. Black haired with a white eye-patch, the pale stranger had been photographed at a distance. "Now, I won't have to worry about my interests in California. He's been sniffing around them for too long."

The statement wasn't an invitation for conversation.

After so many years, Edward had become a silent sounding board for contextless utterances, much like an old dog. A response wasn't required. He tried to be discreet as he set the bottle on the desk, but knocked the computer's mouse aside accidentally. His liver-spotted hands, knuckles gnarled from arthritis, were clumsier now. It was dangerous in a house like this that required a light touch and a blind eye.

The screen shifted, and the email scrolled down, revealing half of a red-haired woman's face. The photo was taken as she looked over her shoulder, green eyes wary. She was lovely. He could only assume she was doomed.

Paling, the master set his drink down, his brown eyes fixed on the woman as if he had seen a ghost.

Edward took an instinctive step back. He had seen his master face phantoms with a laugh.

The other man took the computer mouse in hand and moved it down the screen, skimming the text. His unsettling worry dissolved as a small smile like a challenge quirked his lips. "Oh, Krandel, this is a most productive work-dinner indeed. It won't do to dirty my hands now, but thankfully this witch has a lot of enemies. I'll send a whisper to the right ears, shake open the right tomb. This problem might solve itself."

Edward didn't relish the confirmation of his speculation on her fate. It simply was. Much like the smell in the hallway.

"Do you think she is beautiful? This witch they call Red?"

"She has symmetrical features, sir," the servant said diplomatically.

His master smirked and sipped the fine scotch slowly. "She'll be dead before Christmas."

THE RED WITCH CHRONICLES CONTINUES IN *LONG WITCH NIGHT.*

Find it and the entire series reading order at
samivalentine.com/books

SNEAK PEAK AT LONG WITCH NIGHT

The setting sun shone over the Hollywood Hills into the bay windows of the living room. A golden hue was cast over the white piano, cream throw pillows, and a mix of antique and modern furniture. The coziness would make an Instagram influencer sigh.

Latin chanting broke the illusion.

"Hoc non est tibi. Suus tempus abire tibi est. Relinquam in pace. Reliqua," Red recited the exorcism at a specter who had overstayed their welcome. Just another day for a hunter's intern in the Brotherhood of Bards and Heroes.

The furious pinks of the sunset landed on a bowl of holy water and a blessed silver cross on the coffee table. Red held the battered leather journal higher to block the reflected light. It was easier to ignore than the celebrity looking over her shoulder.

Vic Constantine whizzed past behind her in his wheelchair, holding a bundle of sage in one hand and a stick of Palo Santo in the other. The Korean hunter didn't look like your standard New Ager. Watchful brown eyes narrowed as he glanced around the white living room. His shaggy black mullet slicked back, he wore his fancy outfit, and a blazer over his Led Zeppelin T-shirt. Usually, the hunter wore denim on denim and called it a day. He'd been hunting for over a decade but had never done a job for a movie star either.

With the eight-year gap in her memories, Red was clueless about recent popular culture. It was her worst category at pub trivia. Yet even as Amnesia Girl, she had heard about Nevaeh Morgan. It was hard to escape the blonde starlet's face smiling from magazine covers in truck stops and convenience stores. Red would rather focus on the dark, shadowy spirit in the corner. She was used to ghosts. Famous people, not so much.

"Did y'all feel it get colder in here? Or is it just me?" Nevaeh rubbed her neck, pushing her blonde hair off her shoulder. She shifted in her designer dress.

Her husband, introduced as Steve but known to the world as DJ Shake, put an arm around her. Visible goosebumps rose on his dark skin below his rolled-up beige cashmere sleeves. His brown eyes widened. "It's not just you, baby."

"We aren't alone." Red concentrated on the figure in the corner. With her nearsighted third eye, she couldn't see more than that it was tall. On the other hand, she felt the trauma spiking off of it.

Red might have been a witch, but she'd picked up her few magic skills on the streets. Other witches might have been able to clearly see the spirit's form and other traces of paranormal activity in the room because of proper training. She saw elusive smudges in the air of varying colors, unless something wanted her to see it.

Obviously, this ghost was shy.

According to their celebrity clients, it hadn't been last night. DJ Shake had told them with a repressed quaver how the spirit had run screaming into their bedroom. The ghost has been bold enough to show sound and fury then.

Vic joined her in the chant, reciting the words from memory.

"Hey, I thought I said that if it was going to get freaky, they couldn't go all Old Priest and Young Priest in here?" DJ Shake tried to keep his voice gruff as befitting a rising West Coast rapper. The cover-up was more obvious than the temperature drop. It wasn't little blonde Nevaeh who had dialed up some ghost busters. He had been the one to call Quinn Investigations. "They need to take the Amityville Horror outside."

"They can't, handsome. It's a ghost, not a mouse." Nevaeh's Southern accent grew stronger from her fear. "They're trying to send him into the light."

Red felt her attention flicker as her own words slowed.

"Don't stop, Red." Vic warned before he turned to the clients. "Hey, this is a standard cleansing. We need to focus."

The shadowy ghost in the corner began to take human shape. The chains on his wrists appeared first. Long loops of spectral metal drooped to the floor. A middle-aged black man in white Antebellum clothes, rough and poorly made, stepped forward. Deathly weariness cut deep wrinkles into the man's forehead above his darting eyes.

"Vic, are you seeing this too?" Red asked over her shoulder.

Nevaeh screamed.

"Everyone is seeing it." Shoulders squared and jaw clenched, Vic set the already extinguished Palo Santo stick on the coffee table. He rolled forward in his electric wheelchair.

Red swapped the journal for his sage bundle. There was a reason she was still an intern. She took too long for simple cleansings. Vic had way more experience. "Let's get some true faith up in here then."

Even as the air grew colder than Los Angeles had any right to be, the situation didn't feel dangerous. Red could tell after a year of monster hunting that the spirit was one of those souls trapped between this world and the next. He had appeared when the couple bought an antique candlestick set salvaged from an abandoned Tennessee farmhouse.

"Is he—" DJ Shake stumbled over his words. "He's a slave."

The chained man opened his mouth to speak, his jowls trembling. His squinted gaze traveled over them to land first on Nevaeh and then on DJ Shake. He shook his chained hands, yelling harder. His words might have boomed in the spirit plane, but they weren't even a whisper for the living.

Vic chanted; his eyes focused on the ghost. Sweat beaded on his brow. He repeated the Latin banishment.

Red leaned down to hover over his wheelchair. This was taking too long. Vic usually could bless confused spirits into the beyond with the best of them. She whispered so the clients couldn't hear. "He's getting stronger."

"I see that!" Vic snapped. He chanted louder.

The spirit glided toward DJ Shake. His chains scraped against the wood floors. The glow emanating from his face highlighted the whites of his rolling eyes. He tried to raise his hands, but even in death the chains stopped him.

"What are you trying to tell me, brother?" DJ Shake stretched his arms out between Vic and the spirit. "Stop!"

Vic only lowered his voice.

Red looked over Vic's shoulder at the book and started to chant the cleansing spell under her breath along with him. A spirit manifested to this degree could become unpredictable. They could either have a touching scene connecting two men across centuries or have a poltergeist trying to choke them with his chains.

The ghost rumbled a trembling echo as if dragged out of the beyond with all his might, yet his voice skipped like an old CD. The last words came out in a boom. "You...suffer...SELF...FREE!"

"Yes, brother. Freedom. We're all free. Lincoln did it." DJ Shake rested his hand on the spirit's shoulder as if it was flesh and bone instead of spectral matter.

Nevaeh called out from behind her husband. "You can be, too. Go into the light, friend!"

With an unearthly clatter, the chains fell off the spirit's wrists, disappearing as they hit the ground. The long-dead slave looked down at his freed wrists. He stuck out his hand to DJ Shake.

DJ Shake pulled the ghost into a hug. "You're free, brother. Free!"

Red spoke the last line of the cleansing along with Vic. Releasing a deep breath, she wiped sweat off her brow. She lowered her sage, tension fading from her shoulders, smiling at the Haunted Hallmark moment.

A golden glow brighter than the sunset radiated in the living room before dissipating in a flash.

DJ Shake blinked down at his empty arms. He sniffed, biting at his lip.

"Oh Steve, you did it! You put that poor soul to rest!" Nevaeh wrapped around her husband's waist, nuzzling her head into his shoulder.

Vic's lips turned down. His cheeks hollowed and he bit back his natural sarcasm as he sat up on the edge of his wheelchair seat. They had heard that kind of talk before a private client decided to run out on a bill. This was why they preferred bounties from the Brotherhood of Bards and Heroes. The Brotherhood always paid up.

Smiling, Red whispered into Vic's ear. "Don't worry, they paid in advance."

Vic sank back in his wheelchair. "Then let's get this over with before they start taking post-exorcism selfies." He went to speak to the couple to give them the sage and post-haunting directions.

Red was happy to be the intern when it came to clients, even if it meant lugging the supplies. She gathered up the cross and put the journal in her leather hunter's kit. A lingering presence of magic remained, but Red wasn't worried. Vic did the exorcism, after all.

Usually ghosts didn't leave a stain, but she could imagine a tormented slave had more than its fair share of unfinished business. Paranormal activity could leave a residue. It was a lot of money and effort for an antique candlestick set. Red bit her lip as she looked at the brass candelabra on a bookshelf. Cute, but she wouldn't brave a ghost for it. Hopefully, the famous couple had learned their lesson: buy new.

Haunted furniture aside, Red liked how cozy the room looked. The gold records and framed posters of Nevaeh's movies popped in the otherwise light decor. It made her want to do something more with her place, even if her views were of the parking lot. She had been slowly adding personal touches to her landlord-furnished apartment that she shared with Vic, but two months in, there were still stock photographs in the hanging picture frames. After over a year on the road, Red had the urge to nest.

Something fluttered in the corner of her vision. Red squinted at the open archway to a dining room.

The dark mass that made up the head did not have eyes, yet it watched the young couple hugging in the center of the room. It felt different from the other spirit. Only curiosity stemmed from it. Then the faceless shadow turned.

Red felt the unseen probing stare like demanding fingers.

It recognized her.

Find the *Long Witch Night and a list of the rest of the series at samivalentine.com/books*

AUTHOR'S NOTE

I very much appreciate that you read my book and *fingers crossed* have enjoyed my writing. Let me know what you thought and give a review. This is my first published novel. After a brief soul-crushing stint in a university creative writing program, I stopped writing for years. Now, I am making up for the lost time.

Who am I? I am an urban fantasy writer who grew up in the desert, raised on Buffy the Vampire Slayer, Anne Rice, and the Lost Boys. Add some Game of Thrones, Wheel of Time, and a bit of Christopher Pike's crazy 90s teen thrillers then stir vigorously to get my wacky brain.

Thank you for reading my debut novel!

Cheers, Sami

PS. You get free reads, updates on my new books, and the skinny on the latest hot Urban Fantasy/Paranormal titles by subscribing to my newsletter at SamiValentine.com. Get access to a prequel novelette about Red and Vic's adventure in Oklahoma, deleted scenes, epilogues (read about Red and Lucas' first date), and more. Go here to sign up! http://samivalentine.com/mailinglist/